# CHILD OF THE MOON

## The Lycanthrope Protection Agency
## Book 2

CJ Ravenna

# CONTENT WARNINGS

- Off-page murder of a pregnant woman and child and on-page graphic depiction of their corpses

- Descriptions of graphic violence, murder, and injuries

# AUTHOR'S NOTES

I have taken some creative liberties regarding the ancient Roman myth of Romulus and Remus, and the tomb of Romulus. The location of the tomb was discovered beneath the Forum in Rome. In this story, Romulus's tomb is located in Mount Vesuvius. At the time of writing this story, I hadn't realized there was a tomb at all. As for my other liberties, well, that should be pretty obvious as you read on.

# Chapter 1

# HOMECOMING

MAX GALLAGHER SMILED AT the New York City skyline glittering golden in the sunrise. After escaping certain death, he was so glad to be home that tears prickled his eyes. His wolf howled for pack, for his home, and he ached to get off the motorcycle that was roaring in his ears and plant his feet in the earth.

Gabe Reyes shouted something in Spanish that got drowned out by the roar of the bike. Some jerk in the lane next to them had cut in front of them. Gabe's abs tightened beneath Max's arms, his broad shoulders hunching toward his ears.

"Chill out! We're almost home!" he called, hoping Gabe heard him through the helmet's Bluetooth speaker.

Gabe's shoulders loosened. "I don't know," he said, voice carrying easily through the speaker. "I kinda wish it could just be you and me, out on the open road forever. No crazed fanatics aspiring to godhood—no fucking traffic!" he added, growling as he veered around a van that stopped suddenly in front of them.

Max held Gabe tighter and rested his head against Gabe's back. The glittering city skyline looked like a utopia, but at the reminder of the uncertain future awaiting them, he wished he and Gabe could be assured of a lifetime free from fanatical werewolf cults.

1

But John Stone was still out there, and as long as Stone drew breath, he would plot to use Max's lunar powers in his plans for godhood.

And Gabe was bound to pursue him.

*One will rise, the other will fall.*

The prophecy Gabe revealed to him weeks ago made Max's stomach twist into knots. Stone had disappeared into the wilderness, and Max couldn't hope to guess what his plans were next, only that they involved Max and Gabe.

The motorcycle's rumble growled and died when they finally parked on Park Avenue. Max stumbled off Gabe's bike, legs wobbly from the long ride and ass thoroughly numb.

They put their helmets in the bike's storage compartment. Gabe swung his arm around Max's shoulders. Max nestled his nose into Gabe's neck and breathed in deep the scent of his leather jacket and springtime flowers and life. The scent of his mate.

They hadn't claimed one another yet but they would, as soon as the threat of John Stone no longer hung over their heads. It was a promise they'd sworn to one another despite the uncertain future ahead of them, so Max swept all worries and doubts from his head, kissed Gabe's neck, and let their promise warm him.

"Home sweet home," Gabe declared, leading Max past the doorman and to the elevator. Max's heart pounded, his stomach doing flips as they ascended toward the top floor, and Gabe grabbed his shoulder and squeezed. "Excited, Lobito?"

"Yeah..." It wasn't a lie, but he was sweating profusely. "Uh... Was anyone mad at me?"

Gabe grinned. "Hell yeah. I wasn't sure if I wanted to kiss you or throttle you with my tongue down your throat."

"So, my mom's probably pissed, right?" Max wouldn't blame her.

"Of course," Gabe said. The elevator doors opened with a ding, and they approached Gabe's front door, their shoes brushing over the carpet. "I mean, you just ran off on a self-sacrificing mission without telling anyone."

Max sighed, running a hand over day-old stubble. "Telling anyone would have defeated the purpose!" He hoped she and the rest of the pack could forgive him.

Gabe fumbled with his keys. "Don't worry. I'll protect you."

Before Gabe could stick the key in the lock, the door swung open. A smile broke across Max's face as his mother answered the door. She broke down in tears and swept him into her arms. Max held her tight, unable to suppress the joyful sobs that spilled from his lips.

"He's home! Max is home!" she cried.

She didn't have to say another word; the entire pack gathered around Max and greeted him. Ryan Kelly pulled Max into a bear hug and slapped him on the back, grinning ear to ear. Ben Stroud glared at Max, seemingly torn between a reprimand and a relieved greeting. "Dumbass kid," he growled, wrenching Max into his arms and crushing him to his burly chest.

"Oh yeah, that reminds me," Ryan said, adjusting his glasses. He conked Max on the head. "The fuck were you thinking, you idiot?"

"Ow."

Max looked to Gabe for help—and found him laughing. So much for being his protector. He looked to his mother and found her glowering as she wiped tears from her streaming eyes. He wondered if dying at the hands of John Stone might have been quicker and less painful.

Ben snorted. "And you decided to take matters into your own hands and go running off without your pack?" A smile made his mustache twitch. "Fuckin' ballsy, kid. I'll give you that."

Kendra shot him an incredulous look. "Don't you encourage this, Benjamin Stroud!"

Gabe winced. "Last name. And she's not even your mamá."

Kendra stomped toward Max. "You are the most reckless, most foolish—brave, sweet boy." Her voice broke, and she threw up her arms in exasperation. "And as soon as I'm done being so relieved you're alive, I'm grounding you!"

Max pulled her into his arms and held her tight. "I'm twenty, Mom."

"I don't care!" She sobbed.

"Max?" a quiet voice croaked. Izzie Reyes stepped around Gabe. Max's breath caught, his eyes stinging when he remembered Stone's claws slicing through her flesh. There was no sign of a wound. She'd recovered.

"Izzie," he gasped, throwing his arms around her.

Izzie's body shook with sobs, and she held him tight. "I was so…" She cleared her throat, sucking in a shaky gulp of air. She tried to speak again, but her voice was gone. Max's heart sank.

"Your voice… is your throat okay?"

Tears welled in her eyes. She gave a hopeless shrug. *Zach donated his blood,* she said telepathically through their bond. *He healed a lot of the damage, but I'll need to see a speech therapist for a while.*

Max hung his head, wrestling with his emotions. He was relieved Izzie was alive, but at the same time, his heart broke for her. "When I saw what he did to you, I thought…" A fresh wave of anguish washed over him. Izzie just squeezed him, nuzzling her face into his neck.

Gabe sniffed behind them.

*Gabe, don't. I'll be fine.* Izzie wiped her eyes determinedly. *I'll get well. Like this will stop me.*

Gabe's eyes were wet, his mouth a thin line. "Yeah. I know."

Max couldn't even imagine the guilt Gabe must be feeling. Stone had hurt his family for the second time. Hurt Max. Hurt Gabe's friend. Max's stomach churned. "Where's Zach?" He was nearby, the signature scent of his coconut shampoo a dead giveaway. "Zach? I want to see you too."

The guest room door opened. Zach couldn't meet Max's eyes. His eyes were red-rimmed, his face wet. Ryan went to his side and tried to touch his shoulder, but Zach moved out of reach. He closed his eyes and took in a breath. "I just want to say I'm sorry, Max, Izzie." His voice cracked. "I take full responsibility for everything that happened."

Max shook his head. "It wasn't your fault, Zach. Stone tortured you. He was going to kill you unless you lured Izzie and me to him."

"You all are my family. I should have laid down my life for yours without question." Zach shook his head, lips trembling. "Gabe, I want to apologize to you."

"No," Gabe said through gritted teeth, and Max's heart sank when he saw the fury and pain in Gabe's eyes. "I don't accept your apology. Not now. Not ever."

Zach winced but said nothing.

Ryan snapped, "He didn't have a choice! They were gonna kill him!"

"Ryan." Zach touched his friend's shoulder. "It's okay."

"Gabe," Izzie rasped. "Don't."

Gabe gripped her shoulder, walking past her to stare down Zach. His whole body shook with emotion. His scent was hot with fury, but buried beneath it, Max picked up notes of anguish. Gabe spat, "You of all people know what he's done to my family. Because of you, he almost killed my mate! My sister!"

"And you know John Stone!" Ryan yelled, eyes blazing. "You know the way he hurts others."

Gabe's face turned stark white.

"Ryan, stop," Zach snapped. "Gabe... Gabe, I'm so sorry."

Gabe paced away, clutching the counter for support. "I... I can't even look at you right now."

Ben spoke, his low voice a contrast to all the yelling, a calm in the storm. "The Council of Lycanthrope Affairs will want to know everything we know about John Stone's escape from the city, and I'm obligated to keep them informed."

"So what does that mean for Zach?" Max asked, pacing.

Ben rolled his shoulders, shaking his head hopelessly. "I don't know! They could decide any number of things—that he's too high risk to be trusted. They could take him away to observe him. Hell, they might even banish him from living among packs and condemn him to exile."

Max's stomach twisted. Zach had betrayed their trust, but he'd tried to make up for it. Didn't that count for something? He didn't want Zach to suffer at the Council's hands.

Zach squared his jaw. "Ben, let me take the blood oath."

"What's that?" Max asked.

Ben narrowed his eyes. "Zach, are you sure?"

"Positive. It's the only way I can think of to fix what I've done." He addressed Max, saying, "A blood oath is old druid magic. It's a bond that persists for so long as one party owes the other a life debt. It's paid when the debt is fulfilled. Izzie, Max, let me make this right."

Izzie's olive complexion went ashen. She shook her head. *"I don't want a part in this. You saved my life, Zach; for me, that's enough, but you still owe Max an apology. Max, if you want to accept Zach's offer, it's up to you."* She stepped back, one hand rubbing her throat.

Zach said, "Max, let me take the oath. I need to make things right."

Max turned to his mother. "What do you think?"

She shook her head, lips tight in anger. "If he wants to make it up to you, so be it. If you cross us again, so help me, Zach, you won't live long enough to regret it this time."

Max closed his eyes, parsing through his emotions. He was angry at Zach, even if he was sympathetic to the pain Stone must have caused for him to break down and betray them like he had. He didn't want Zach to be indebted to him, though, or to die for him.

But looking in Zach's anguished eyes, Max saw that Zach needed to make things right or else he'd never be at peace. If this was what Zach truly needed, then Max wouldn't deny him his chance to fix things.

"You really want this, Zach?"

Zach nodded without hesitation. "Please, Max. Let me prove my loyalty to you."

Max looked to Ben. "Is this blood oath difficult to do?"

"Depends on how squeamish you are," Ben answered. "It's a ritual, done at night under the moon. Requires some bloodletting, but it's short."

Max looked at Zach and found no hesitation in his gaze. Max said, "Then let's do it tonight."

Ben nodded, and Max hadn't realized how tense he was until he felt his shoulders slumping in relief.

Zach exhaled, chin to his chest. "Thank you, Max." His voice broke on the words.

As the moon rose, Ben drove Max and Zach to Brooklyn and parked outside the Cypress Hills cemetery. Max swallowed. "Do we have to do it in a cemetery?"

Ben grinned at his nerves. "Won't work anywhere else. This spot's one of the oldest ritual sites in the state."

Ritual sites? Those were a thing? A shudder ran through Max, and he hurried to walk between Zach and Ben as they roamed among the gravestones, dry leaves crackling under their feet. Max tried not to imagine he was walking over the bones of the deceased. He failed. "Won't we get in trouble? It's pretty late…"

"Relax, kid," Ben said. "We're here. The Sacred Grove, that's what werewolves call it."

Max shivered, remembering the Sacred Grove Stone had taken him to.

Ben drew a circle in the dirt. He set a knife and a stone bowl in the center.

Max sniffed at the air and wrinkled his nose at the smell of blood dried into the bark of the trees. "Please tell me I'm the only one smelling blood."

"You're not," Zach said unhelpfully, mouth quirking as Max practically squirmed.

"Wait… so this ritual is magic?" Max supposed it was strange to possess the powers of the moon and still be unable to wrap his head around magic rituals.

"Close as it gets," Ben replied, checking the yellowed pages of a tome, the leather cover cracked and peeling. "This is a grimoire of ritual magic crafted by Atticus, King of the Druids. And one hell of an asshole if the stories are true."

Max leaned over his shoulder, breathing in the smell of old leather and paper. Every page bore strange symbols that made his skin crawl. He reached out and Ben held the book out of reach. "Careful. This is the Council's tome. They authorize who gets to use it."

"What do those symbols mean?"

Ben shrugged, leafing through yellowed pages. "Hell if I know, but they're Celtic in origin. The Council's lore masters say druids were the guardians of werewolves in ancient days. They used magic to defend and strengthen the pack, but Atticus decided he wouldn't serve wolves. He revolted against the packs he'd sworn to protect. Wolves and humans teamed up to stop them. We hunted them all down during the Witch Hunts." Ben shrugged. "Maybe it was the best outcome in the end. Humans hate and fear wolves without throwing magic into the mix."

Max thought back to the silver dagger in Stone's grasp, crafted by the druids to get vengeance against wolves who turned on them, and thought he agreed with Ben. The world was better off without magic. "So the druids are completely gone."

"Far as we know, thanks to wolves and humans. Just the odd relic here or there to remind us they existed at all. Kinda funny that after all these years, their old magic is still helping us. Or cursing us. Both of you kneel, face each other across the circle."

Leaves crunched under Max's knees as he knelt. Zach faced him, unblinking and stony-faced.

"The offending party goes first," Ben instructed, handing the knife to Zach. "Repeat after me and once the incantation is done, make a cut across your palm. Max, cut your finger. Zach's wound will heal but I don't want you sustaining any nerve damage."

Zach laid his hand flat across his knee and accepted the dagger.

Ben swallowed hard. "This ritual's a great lie detector. Tons of people have tried to avoid trouble with the Council or trick others into trusting them by taking the blood oath. Just so you know, if you have any malicious intentions, Zach, you'll die the minute the ritual's complete."

Zach nodded, his lips set in a determined line. He clasped the knife in a steady grip. "I'm ready."

"Good. Now, repeat after me. I swear to you, Maxwell Gallagher."

Max shivered as Zach met his gaze. "I swear to you, Maxwell Gallagher."

"Before the eyes of the goddess, I pledge to see this oath to its end. Until you deem this oath fulfilled, I will right all wrongs against you or die trying."

Zach echoed Ben's words, then drew the dagger across his palm. He clenched his teeth but made no sound, closing his fist and dripping blood into the stone bowl.

Ben handed the knife to Max. "If you accept, then cut. You can always walk away if you've changed your mind."

Max looked into Zach's eyes, at the blood oozing from between his clenched fingers. Despite it all, he wanted to trust that Zach meant every word. He drew the blade across his palm, despite Ben's suggestion. It stung and throbbed, but Max exhaled through the pain.

"I accept your oath, Zach." His blood ran into the bowl, mingling with Zach's.

Ben swirled it together and overturned the bowl. The blood ran throughout the channels of the circle.

"And there you have it. The oath is fulfilled when Zach has righted his wrongs against you."

"How will we know when?" Max asked, not quite understanding. "Does he have to do something for me? And what is it?"

"That's for you two to decide and figure out for yourselves. I really don't know." Ben stood, dusting leaves and dirt from his knees. "Max, get that bandaged up." He rummaged in his bag for bandages.

Zach stared at him across the circle. "Thank you, Max. If you're ever in danger again, I'll do everything I can to protect you. I promise."

"Let's hope you won't have to keep your promise anytime soon." He opened his palm and the moonlight above turned the wound to a scar before his eyes. Ben and Zach gawked. Max's face reddened.

"Um, so... about that." Max sighed. "It's a long story."

# CHAPTER 2

# AN EMPTY SEAT

THE SLAUGHTERED LAMB BUSTLED with activity as Gabe sidled in, peering over the crowds. He and Ben were supposed to meet for drinks. It had been too long since they'd just relaxed, wolf to wolf, in a bar without the threat of death sitting on their shoulders. He spotted Ben's familiar profile at the bar.

Another man sat beside him, clean-shaven and bald, his face lined and his expression warm. He wore weird robes. Gabe smirked. Was some weird monk trying to preach in this den of sinners?

Ben waved Gabe over. "Gabe, this is Greg Harris. We go way back."

Gabe and Greg gave each other an introductory sniff. He smelled like incense, pine trees, and lunar flowers. Greg grinned, looking him up and down. "Gabe, as in Gabe Reyes? Manuel's boy?" He laughed, slapping Gabe's shoulder. "My word, you've grown!"

Gabe smiled, pleasantly surprised... and confused as to how this monk knew him. "How'd you know my dad?"

Greg laughed. "Oh, you were too young. You won't remember me. I'm a lore master for the Council. Your father and Ben and I go way back."

Gabe vaguely remembered going on trips with his dad to Montana where the Council had headquarters in the town of Wolf Point.

"Remember me?" Greg asked hopefully, smiling expectantly. "I gave you maple candies!" He pouted when Gabe smiled blankly. "Well, it's wonderful seeing you again. You look so much like your father. My word, Ben! It was good catching up! It was just like old times."

Ben smiled, silver eyes wandering around the bar as if envisioning it from times gone by. "I know, right? Remember when we used to hang here with Manuel? Drink our weight in beer, shoot the shit."

Greg laughed, shaking Ben's shoulder. "Yeah, and you were all panicked 'cause you'd just figured out Isaac was your mate."

A shocked ripple traveled over Ben's body. Greg's smile fell off his face. Gabe coughed and scratched his head. He'd never seen Ben look so stunned, as if the mere mention of his lost love's name had driven a nail into his heart.

Greg cleared his throat. "Anyway, I should get going. Don't want to miss my flight."

Ben smiled, shattering the ice that seemed to have enveloped him. He clasped Greg's hand and shook it. "We gotta do this again."

Gabe smiled, trying to be polite even though he couldn't remember a thing about this man. "Nice meeting you, Councilman."

Greg said goodbye and Gabe dropped into his empty seat.

Ben chuckled. "You don't remember him at all, do you?"

"Not a bit."

"He's one of my oldest friends. He's a historian as well as a councilman. I was telling him about Max and his weird cosmic moon powers." Ben blinked. "Max *has* told you, hasn't he?" Gabe nodded and Ben scoffed. "Hell of a thing, huh? Anyway, Greg was impressed. He said there have been wolves with similar powers, but not for a hell of a long time. He said he'll ask around at the monastery during his next pilgrimage."

Gabe raised his brows. "Pilgrimage to where?"

"The Monastery of the Moon. He just got back from his summer pilgrimage to Italy. Before you ask, I'm not sure about what exactly goes on at the monastery. He's not allowed to talk much. Personally, I'd go nuts if I had to spend a whole summer doing, what? Meditating under the moon? Not for me."

Gabe waved the bartender over for a whiskey.

"So, good news," Ben declared. "Stone's on the run, and we made sure his cultists are dead. The Moonborn cult is officially history."

Gabe took a sip of whiskey and managed a smile. For two decades, the Moonborn cult had terrorized hybrids in New York City, and their reign of terror was over. It was a victory in every sense, even if Stone was still roaming the wilderness somewhere. Moonborn ideology would always live on in the minds of the most depraved werewolves, but without Stone around to give them a voice, bigots would crawl back under their rocks in time.

"I'll drink to that." Gabe raised his glass in a toast.

"Damn straight." Ben clinked their glasses together and they drank.

Gabe checked the time. He was meeting Max at his mamá's apartment in an hour, only a short walk away from the Slaughtered Lamb. "How'd the ritual go?"

Ben took a gulp of his drink. "Zach's serious about making things right with Max. And with you."

Anger heated Gabe's skin. "Am I wrong for being pissed with him?"

Ben shook his head. "You're entitled to your feelings. I love Zach. Kid's like family to me. But I can't say I'd be forgiving if any of you endangered my sons. Just... give him the chance to make things right."

Gabe clenched his glass so hard, he heard it crack. He slammed it down. "I'm pissed at him, but I'm even more pissed at Stone. Izzie might never get her voice back. Max could have been killed. Zach almost died."

The thought of Stone's claws at his sister's throat, of Max helpless at Stone's mercy, turned his blood to ice. Gabe hadn't been there to keep them safe. He blamed and hated himself more than Zach.

"Never again," he snarled, meaning every word. John Stone would never hurt another person he loved.

His skin prickled at the feeling of Ben's eyes on him.

"Gabe, you can't spend the rest of your life holding your breath and waiting for Stone to appear. You gotta decide to live eventually, before you wake up and realize life's passed you by."

Gabe shook his head, the whiskey burning in his belly. "My father should have lived, Ben."

Pinching his lips, Ben nodded into his empty glass. "He should have. But he's gone, Gabe."

Gabe squeezed the glass. "I know that. I'm reminded of it every single day." The words were a growl in his throat.

"I'm aware of that."

Anger nipped at him. "No, you're not. Your father is still alive. You can call him on the phone. You can see him whenever you want. He got to meet your kids, watch them grow up." His throat tightened and Gabe took a quick gulp of whiskey. The burn numbed that rawness in his throat.

Ben's bushy brow furrowed as he gazed into the amber contents of his glass. "Gabe, how much is it gonna take? How much more are you gonna lose, or almost lose, before you realize? It's the ones who are here that fucking matter!"

Gabe squeezed the glass in his hand, blinking hard. "He should be here, Ben."

"I know, kid. But killing Stone won't make any of that hurt less. Stone's gone. Someone matching his description crossed over the state border while you and Max were on your way home."

Gabe's jaw tightened. "Where was he going?"

"West, I think. He could be anywhere by now."

Gabe's fist curled. "Is anyone doing something about it? The police? The Council?"

Ben sighed. "I talked to Alpha Hanson last night. I got a lot of talk, but based on the Council's history of inadequacy, I'm not holding my breath. I'm going to assemble a team to hunt him down before he gets too far and hurts other people."

Gabe's heart lurched. "Now you're fucking talking, Viejo." He had to join the hunt.

Ben sighed. "I know how personal this is to you, so I wanted to give you the chance to join the team. But I also want you to consider if taking off and leaving Max and your family behind is worth it."

Enthusiasm fading, Gabe scrubbed a hand over his face. "I don't have any other choice. Max will understand."

"You sure about that?"

The answer wouldn't come. Gabe had no idea how Max would feel, but he could guess.

"If you have any doubts, then leave it to me and a few agency wolves."

He shook his head. "I can't do that."

"Gabe. This isn't a lecture. It's advice."

Gabe met the silver of Ben's eyes.

"What you've got with Max is something most shifters spend a lifetime looking for. Don't fuck this up. Don't think for one minute that if you leave this city tomorrow, things will be the same when you come back. You can't ask that boy to wait for you to wake up and realize what you two have. He's had a shitty time as it is without following you into danger."

Gabe gritted his teeth, not appreciating the lecture even if the old man was right. "I'd never ask him to follow me anywhere." The words were clipped. He knew that if he left this city, he would be leaving Max, and his heart ached. But how could he just let his father's killer escape his grasp?

Ben gripped Gabe's arm. "Listen to me. Don't you blow this up. You hear me?" His voice was gruff, but Ben was pleading with him. "I've been... left before. It's not easy to come back from."

Gabe's claws left marks on the bar. "I won't be like Isaac. I'll come back to Max, no matter how far I go."

Ben slumped, letting out a sound between a sigh and a growl. "I know that monster hurt you. I know he took from your pack. Gabe, don't let him take Max from you, too."

Gabe hit the bar, rattling dishes and glasses. "That's why I've got to follow him! I'm not going to sit around and hold my breath, waiting for him to come back and take Max away from me!"

The bar had fallen silent. Gabe's fangs prodded his lower lip, and he swallowed the rumbling growl building deep in his chest.

He whispered down at the bar, "He wants Max. You think just because he's out of the state he won't come back? That he won't come after Max?"

How could he just sit around and wait for someone to harm his mate?

He wasn't a helpless boy anymore.

He threw a twenty on the counter and stood. Pushing the barstool away, he marched for the door. He sucked in a lungful of city air sour with bloated garbage bags piled on the curb, making a feast for the rats. He forced himself to breathe, made his claws retract, and closed his eyes tight. Ben was right, damn it. The old man was always right.

Gabe couldn't make Max stay behind while Gabe chased after Stone. He couldn't do that to Max. He also couldn't sit around and lull himself into a false sense of security knowing his mate was the key to Stone's dreams of godhood. How could he enjoy a life with Max while holding his breath and waiting for the monster from his childhood to come back and take Max away from him?

Who else would Stone take from him? His sister? His mother? Ben or the other agency wolves?

But if he left, if he followed the path of vengeance, he feared it would destroy his relationship with Max.

The door opened and closed behind him. A lighter clicked. Ben lit a cigarette and blew out a cloud from his mouth. "Guess I ruined drinks."

Gabe laughed, though he wasn't amused. "No, I did, Viejo. Sorry." He checked the time. "I have to meet Max at my ma's place soon."

Ben's mustache twitched. "Finally meeting the pack, huh?"

Gabe's chest warmed. "Yeah." He'd never thought he'd meet anyone he liked enough to bring home to Mamá Reyes.

Ben held his gaze. "Treasure him, kid."

"I do."

Which was why Gabe could never allow anyone to hurt Maxwell Gallagher again.

Not anyone, and especially not John Stone.

GABE'S MOTHER LIVED IN a quaint brownstone apartment on Greenwich Street. Max buzzed the intercom, and Izzie answered the door.

"Welcome! Come on in!" Izzie cleared her throat.

Max followed her to their front door on the fifth floor, panting. "Your mom must be in peak shape."

"She is, actually." Izzie let him in.

The smell of spices and chicken made Max's stomach rumble. He took off his shoes and followed Izzie into the living room, which was open to the kitchen where a petite older woman stir-fried onions and sweet-smelling peppers. She had olive skin and long glossy dark hair. A grin reminiscent of Izzie's brightened her face, and she hurried away from the stove to greet him.

"You must be Max! It's so nice to finally meet you!" She had a warm Spanish accent.

She drew him into a hug that was so welcoming, it was hard to move away. She smelled of coconut conditioner and vanilla perfume—and she was human. He'd only just met her, yet his wolf wanted to roll over and show his respect to the Reyes pack matriarch. He'd never felt this way around a human before.

She laughed when she heard him sniff. Max's face warmed. "I'm so sorry!" He stumbled out of her arms and smiled, trying to reassure her he wasn't a total creep. "It's a wolf thing. You're Gabe's mom, so you're already someone important to me."

She squeezed his shoulder. "Oh, I'm very much used to you wolves and your ways. I'm Veronica."

"Thanks for having me. I brought this." He handed her a bakery box containing a cheesecake.

"You are too sweet. You're going to have to help us eat this, or else I might eat it all myself." She put the cheesecake in the fridge and returned to the stove. "Make yourself comfortable. Would you like anything to drink?"

Max sat down on the sofa and Izzie brought him his requested glass of water. While Veronica finished cooking, she asked Max a few questions about himself. Max talked so much his throat went dry, and he had to take a gulp of water. He learned a fair bit about Veronica.

"My parents emigrated from Madrid when I was a girl. We lived upstate for years, and I grew up working a farm."

Max smiled. "That sounds lovely."

Veronica laughed, transferring the onions, peppers, and chicken from the pan to a plate. "It was, but it wasn't the life for me. I had dreams of living in the big city. Manuel and I met in college." A girlish smile softened her face, and she looked young and in love all over again.

Izzie shot Max a look and rolled her eyes. *"And she fell madly in love with a werewolf. Such a drama queen, Ma."*

Veronica glanced at her daughter, a worried pucker to her brow.

"How did your parents feel about that?" Max asked, sipping his water.

Worry wiped from her face, Veronica smiled from behind the counter. "Badly. So after college, Manuel and I eloped and moved to Manhattan."

Izzie batted her eyelashes. *"What a rebel!"*

Veronica ignored her daughter's playful teasing. "Meeting Manuel changed my life."

Max could see that. A statue of the She-Wolf nursing the twins was suspended in the archway to the kitchen, yet she also had crosses and a figure of the human god Christ. He found it interesting that Veronica worshipped the She-Wolf and a human god. He supposed Veronica was more religious than Gabe or Izzie.

"I like your statues," he explained when she gazed at him from around the island counter. "It's pretty cool to see a human worshipping a werewolf goddess."

"I get that quite a lot," Veronica said, walking around the counter with some plates, which she set on the table. "I was raised Roman Catholic, and Manuel introduced me to the She-Wolf religion. I wanted my children to grow up believing in whatever deity they liked."

"I love your den," Max said, admiring the high ceilings and the view from the windows. The accented brick wall in the living room, which was painted yellow, gave the home a touch of industrial flair.

"Thank you, dear! We've lived here for years."

Max smiled, marveling at the legacy of memories this home must hold, down to the old claw marks and Crayola on the wall. It made Max miss the apartment he'd grown up in before he and his mom moved into Richard's penthouse.

"It's close to where I work, too."

"Oh? What do you do?"

"I'm a teacher." Veronica called, "Izzie, where are the tortillas?"

Izzie hurried away to help, and Max stood and explored the living room. He ran his hands across the credenza, let his fingers drift over the top of the TV and run along picture frames, introducing his scent to Gabe's pack den.

There was a photo of a much younger Veronica surrounded by what Max assumed were her pupils. He smiled at a teenaged Gabe, a heartthrob even then, posing with an older man who shared his smile and warm eyes.

Max couldn't look away from the older man, realizing it must be Gabe's father, Manuel.

The intercom buzzed. Izzie bounded over and answered the door.

"Is it Gabriel?" Veronica called.

*"Yup. Late as ever."*

Max's heart raced as Gabe shouldered open the door, panting from a jog up the stairs. "Mamá, how do you manage these stairs?" He smiled despite his exhaustion as he met Max's gaze. His mother hurried over for a quick kiss on the cheek.

"You're just in time for dinner." She invited everyone to sit down.

The steaming fajitas made Max's mouth water. Gabe lunged to fill his tortilla, but his mother shot him a look. Gabe pouted and rolled his eyes over at Max but copied his mother when she put her hands together and turned her eyes skyward.

"Holy Mother above, we thank you for the food on our table, our good health, and for bringing Max to us this evening."

Max had a tiny sip of wine. He liked Veronica already.

Izzie said telepathically, *"Wow. These fajitas are great!"*

Veronica frowned. "Izzie, have you been using the bonds to communicate a lot? Your doctor said—"

*"I know!"* Izzie made a face. Clearing her throat, she said out loud, "I know." Her voice cracked, and Max's heart clenched at how broken she sounded.

Beside Max, Gabe hung his head, sadness clouding his eyes.

"It's just—ahem—easier to use the bonds."

"I understand, but you need to practice speaking out loud. What time is your speech therapy tomorrow?" Veronica asked. "Do you want me to come and take notes?"

Izzie smiled, though it didn't reach her eyes. "I'll be fine."

Guilt welled up in Max's chest. He'd been right there, but Izzie had still been hurt.

Gabe said, "Stone left the city, Ma. We're safe." Max heard the unspoken *for now.*

Veronica fixed him with a look. "I've told you, we don't mention that name under this roof."

"I know. I just wanted to reassure you."

Veronica's hands trembled. "Please, let's just eat."

Once dinner was over, Veronica went to cut and serve the cheesecake.

"Mamá, let me help," Gabe insisted, hurrying to the kitchen.

Max wanted to wash his hands of fajita grease. "Where's the bathroom?"

Izzie waved at him. "Right here, Max," she said aloud, her voice hoarse.

He washed his hands and when he stepped out, he stopped to admire the pictures on the wall: Izzie as a little girl in a purple dress, Gabe as a gangly but handsome teen, Veronica looking radiant in a white dress on her wedding day.

Beside her stood Gabe and Izzie's father smiling a familiar megawatt smile, his eyes all soft and crinkled in the corners as he held his wife. The wedding bands on their fingers declared their love for each other.

"It's a nice picture, isn't it?" Izzie wandered up beside him, smiling at the photo.

"Yeah. That's your dad, right?"

"Yes. Has Gabe talked about him much?"

Max shook his head.

Izzie adjusted the picture, sweeping some dust from the edge of the wood frame. "He was a good man. The first hybrid on the Council. He had all these plans to protect hybrids from discrimination. But he... died before he could see them to completion."

"He and Gabe look alike."

Izzie caressed the frame surrounding a portrait of her father, his big arms around Gabe and little Izzie. "Next Friday will be another year without him."

Max winced, his chest tightening. "I'm sorry. That must be hard."

Izzie folded her arms over her chest and stared vacantly into her father's face, frozen in happier times. "Gabe irritates me sometimes. He gets so angry, so dark. He wants Stone dead, as if that will bring our father back and make it all better. What if something happens to him? I'll lose my brother along with my father."

She coughed and winced. "Grief is hard, Max," she continued, voice strained. "But missing someone is a reminder that you loved and were loved. I'd take tears any day over this... He's frozen in time, and I can't do anything to help him."

Max couldn't speak. Words were meaningless. He wished he could help her, help this family who already had a home in his heart.

"Izzie, Max! I just cut the cheesecake," Veronica called.

Izzie forced a smile back onto her face. She took his wrist and Max followed, stealing a glance back at the portrait of the man who haunted this house.

The man whose murderer was still out there, waiting to strike.

# CHAPTER 3
# I'LL WAIT FOR YOU

THE BREEZE WAS PLEASANT against Gabe's skin as he reclined in a lounger on the roof.

The night air was invigorating, carrying the earthy smells of soil and the various herbs, fruits, and vegetables growing in his mother's rooftop garden. He couldn't remember ever feeling so full, but he still felt restless and not even the view of the sleepy neighborhood could soothe him.

He kept seeing his father's empty seat. Izzie's hoarse voice wouldn't leave his mind. His thoughts whirled, trying to piece together what he wanted to say to Max, how to get him to understand.

Behind him, the wind chimes sang, and he turned as Max stepped out onto the roof. Gabe's breath hitched as their eyes met. Max had sought him out—and he wasn't ready. Not for this. Gabe forced himself to breathe as Max came closer, the moonlight shining in his hair as he knelt before Gabe. A freckled hand settled on Gabe's knee and squeezed.

"Hey. I was looking for you. Is something wrong?" Max asked.

Gabe shrugged. "Can we talk, mi amor?"

Max sat by Gabe's feet at the end of the lounger. He ran a hand over Gabe's thigh and squeezed his knee tight. "I... I can't imagine how hard it is for you to see Izzie in pain." Gabe swallowed around the lump in his throat. "To know the man who hurt her is out there roaming free. Waiting to strike again."

Gabe gritted his teeth, trying to fight down what he wanted to say.

"Did you ever understand why Stone targeted your family? You specifically? Was it just a fluke?"

Gabe hummed softly. He'd asked himself that question over and over again. "Stone and my father both served on the Council. When my father became the first hybrid councilman, that was the tipping point in Stone's radicalization. Seeing a hybrid holding a seat of power only pure-blooded wolves had ever held must have been an insult he couldn't let slide. He broke away from the Council, took a few angry assholes with him, and started his damn cult." He wet his dry lips. "He used me to get at my father. He hurt my sister. I can't let this go, Max."

Max looked up and held Gabe's gaze. "You want to go after him, don't you?"

Gabe tried to swallow. "Max, the Council isn't taking any steps to pursue Stone. Ben's getting together some agency wolves to hunt him down. I want to join them."

Max's eyes widened. "You're... you're leaving?" Max tore his gaze away from Gabe's face, blinking fast. "When?"

Gabe raised his shoulders and dropped them. "I don't know. As soon as there's a sighting. We can't waste any time. He evaded the Council for years. If we let him slip away, we might not know where he is, and who knows what he'll do while he's off the radar."

"So you could take off any day now? In a week? A month?" Max's voice was small, thin with anger.

"Max." His voice came out a croak. He tried again. "I don't have a choice. It's what I have to do. For us. So we can have the life we deserve without that monster looming over us."

"You do have a choice!" Max snapped. "You're choosing to leave me here and disappear for who even knows how long. I want to come with you." Even as he said the words, Max knew it was a foolish demand, but he couldn't let Gabe go without a fight.

"You can't. He wants you dead, Max. Fucking more than that, he wants your soul. And if anything happens to you—"

"I'm not scared of him. I kicked his ass. I could do it again!"

"No, Max!" Gabe's voice echoed over the rooftops.

Max blinked fast, hurt bright in his honey orange eyes.

"Zach could have been killed. Izzie lost her voice. You almost—" Gabe sucked in a breath and realized his face was wet. "He hurt my family *again*. And he did it to get to me, I know it." Gabe paced, sneakers slapping over the roof. "I was helpless *again*. My mother could have buried her child next to her husband. I have to do something, Max. John Stone can never harm my family again."

"I... understand that. I do." Max's hand trembled when he touched Gabe's face. "But how do you think I'll feel if I lost you? How do you think I'll feel, waiting up at night, not even knowing if you're still alive? How could you put me through that?"

Gabe swallowed hard. He never wanted to hurt Max or tear his own soul in two by leaving Max's side. "Then tell me to stay." One word from Max, and he would do it. It would kill him inside but he would do it for Max, if Max truly wanted him to.

Tears glimmered in Max's long lashes. He blinked rapidly and a single tear tumbled down his freckled cheek. His throat bobbed when he swallowed.

Gabe squeezed Max's hand, afraid to let go in case this was their last moment together, the moment Max realized he deserved better and left Gabe to roam the wilderness chasing a monster.

"Do you *want* to stay?" Max whispered, the sound carried away by the summer wind.

Gabe gritted his teeth. "I'd feel better knowing I wasn't a sitting duck waiting for him to come for you and my family. But Max, if you need me to stay... If you tell me to, I will."

Max leaned back, regarding him. His chest rose and fell with a long exhale.

"I need you to stay, Gabe. I want you to stay." Max exhaled, squeezing Gabe's hands so tight Gabe thought his bones would crumble. "I know why I can't go with you. I'd just be a liability. Something Stone could use against you."

Gabe exhaled and closed his eyes tight, the tension loosening in his chest just a little. That was that, then. He would stay. He could do that. For Max.

Until Max said, "But you won't be happy, will you?"

Gabe opened his mouth, then shut it. He was at an impasse because he knew what he said next would be the beginning of their goodbye. He blinked hard and looked away from Max. "I love you, Max—but I loved my father, too." His eyes burned, his throat so tight and painful he could hardly speak. "And he died because of me. For so long, I didn't care about what happened to me, just that I lived long enough to hurt Stone the way he'd hurt my family. Then I met you, and I'm happy in a way I never thought I'd be. And every time I think of our future together, it kills me that my father will never get to meet you—"

Gabe slumped back in the lounger, throat aching. He pressed his fingers into his eyes, sucking in one short gasp after another. "I have to do this, Max." He reached out, clasping Max's hands in his. "I know I can't ask you to wait for me because you've been through enough pain. You've made me dream of a future at the end of all this when once my life meant nothing to me. I'll never ask for more than that."

Max was quiet as Gabe smoothed his thumb across his cheek, drifting from freckle to freckle. He expected Max to pull away, and Gabe's heart cracked in two at the thought, but he wouldn't stop him. He was grateful for every minute they'd spent together.

Gabe held his breath as Max's fingertips ghosted over his skin, tracing the shape of his jaw, and then he claimed Max's lips in a kiss that was soft and slow, as if the night would never end.

Max's breath hitched as they pulled away, his eyelashes wet and spiky. "I promised you that if this was what you had to do, then I would stand with you. I meant that. I'll wait for you."

Touching their foreheads together, Gabe was unable to stop the flow of his tears. "I'll come back."

"You'd better," Max whispered.

Gabe touched their lips together, running his fingers through Max's hair. "I promise."

AND SO, IN THE first week of August, Gabe packed his bags. He would be leaving in the morning. Stone had been sighted in Pennsylvania; it had happened so much sooner than Max had thought.

Max had never realized how quickly time passed, not until he was desperate for more. He didn't want to go to sleep, not with knowing that when the sun rose, Gabe would be leaving with Ben. All he wanted was to memorize every detail of Gabe's face and burn him into his memory before they had to part. To keep him here in this bed with him, their legs tangled up, their hands locked together, for just a few hours longer.

"Tired?" Gabe chuckled.

Max jolted, his eyes opening. He didn't laugh. He couldn't. He reached out, dragging his fingertips across Gabe's jawline, his cheekbones, his lips, trying to memorize him down to his very bones. Gabe leaned in close, bringing his forehead to Max's.

It used to make Max nervous when Gabe looked into his eyes; his stomach would get all fluttery, his heart would speed up. Now he never wanted to look away, just appreciate the kaleidoscope of colors in those eyes that at first glance were honey amber.

Up close they were so much more, flecked with greens and yellows and golds all swirling together, and Max loved that he knew these little details. He was unbelievably lucky to be allowed so close to Gabriel Reyes.

His breath hitched at the uptick in Gabe's heartbeat, his heart clenching as gentle fingertips ghosted across his skin.

"Say it?" Max whispered, his throat thick and achy.

Gabe raised his brows in a silent question, eyes wandering across Max's face as if he were losing himself too, trying to memorize Max's face.

"That you'll come back."

Gabe's shoulders rose and fell, and he choked back a strange broken sound, blinking hard. His hand settled at the nape of Max's neck, the pad of his thumb gliding across Max's skin. "I'm coming back, Max."

He squeezed his eyes shut. "Promise me."

Gabe's lips wandered, charting a map of every freckle that dotted Max's jaw to the little one right above his mouth that Gabe loved to kiss. Their lips met and when Max realized he didn't know when they'd kiss like this again, he didn't want to be tender or sad. He wanted to burn Gabe into his senses, etch him like a tattoo into his skin.

Curling over Gabe's chest, Max rained kisses onto his face. Gabe's fingers threaded through his hair, and he bit down on Max's lip as Max arched his pelvis.

"Mate with me," Max whispered. "Before you have to go. I need you."

Gabe swallowed, eyeing Max's neck. His fangs lengthened, his chest rising and falling quickly. He tore his eyes away, his lips trembling. "I can't. Max, I couldn't do that and then leave you."

Max pushed his face into Gabe's neck, nipping at his skin to satiate his longing. "What if we never get the chance to?"

Trembling hands clasped his face. Gabe pressed his forehead to Max's. "If we mate tonight, I don't think I could leave in the morning."

Blinking hard, Max couldn't hide his disappointment. Gabe clutched his elbows, urging him close. Max was hurt, even if he did understand. It would only make leaving harder, but he couldn't bring himself to pull away as Gabe pulled him down, lips melding together in a fusion of desperation.

Squeezing his hair, Gabe's claws pricked against Max's scalp. His fangs nipped at Max's lips as if he wanted to consume him. Max pushed his tongue past Gabe's lips, craving his taste. Gabe held him tight and Max hardly noticed as he rolled them over. He was swift, slicking himself quickly with lube from the dresser and then lining himself up and sinking deep into Max.

Max clung to Gabe as he filled him, driving in deep until they were fused at the pelvis. It burned, but the pain faded quickly as Max lost himself in the pleasure of their union. Gabe's mouth burned against his neck, breath hitting his skin in short, hot gasps punctuated with every pound of Gabe's hips. Clutching Gabe's hair, Max tugged him up to meet his mouth.

Their fangs scraped, tongues smoothing over any cuts or soreness. Their eyes met just before they finished. Gabe's breath warmed Max's neck, and his fangs pinched Max's skin but didn't bite down. He could tell Gabe had just barely resisted going back on his word. Max held him tight, eyes closing as the waves of his release crashed over him. He never wanted to return to reality. He could live and die in this moment where their bodies were one.

Gabe pressed a firm, damp kiss to Max's neck. "I love you, Max. I'm coming back. I promise."

Max closed his eyes for the last time that night as Gabe covered his mouth with his.

THE PACK GATHERED AT the agency to discuss Ben's absence. Ben left Zach in charge of the agency in his stead and Gabe left Zach in charge of Max.

Veronica came to see her son off and cried when she hugged him tight, terrified she'd lose her son. She made Gabe promise to stay in touch every day and demanded Ben keep him safe. Izzie couldn't speak, but the fear and sadness rolled off her in waves. When Gabe hugged her, she broke down in his arms.

Max held his breath, trying to keep all the pieces of his heart together as Gabe and Ben made the rounds, saying goodbye to everyone individually until Ben's arms were around Max. Before Max had figured out what to say, Gabe pulled him close, and Max's lips trembled as they kissed. A large warm hand ran through Max's hair. He breathed in deep, willing himself not to cry. His chest touched Gabe's, and he marveled at the way their bodies fit together, each perfectly sculpted for the other by the goddess herself.

"I'll be back soon," Gabe whispered, leaning their foreheads together. "We know where he is. We'll follow his trail and stop him for good. I'll be home before you know it."

Max didn't know if he believed him, but he had to. They were soulmates, and they'd find their way back to each other. Max closed his eyes and breathed him in, his arms circling Gabe's broad shoulders.

"Okay."

When Gabe pulled back, he was smiling and tears glittered in his lashes. "I love you, Max."

It took everything Max had to step out of Gabe's arms and let him leave. "You, too."

He would love to be angry, to hate Gabe for leaving. But they'd made this decision together, and Max's heart was too broken to hold any anger inside of it.

Gabe left. Max watched until the car disappeared.

He would see Gabe again. Maybe in a matter of weeks, maybe a month at the most. Ben was a good tracker, and he and Gabe would catch up with Stone in no time, especially since they weren't working alone. Gabe would come back triumphant, and he'd finally have closure.

They would be together, and no one would threaten the happiness they'd found.

No one would ever come between them again.

# CHAPTER 4

# IT'S BEEN A YEAR, YOU JERK

A LOT HAPPENED DURING Max's twentieth year.

Stone evaded the agency wolves in Pennsylvania, but Gabe wasn't deterred. "We've got his trail, Max." He sounded confident, excited. "We'll catch him. I know we will. I could be back as soon as the end of the week."

Max's hopes were high and the next time Gabe called, Max's heart leaped. Gabe was coming home. He'd been successful, he—

"He got away." Gabe's voice was drained. "We're still on his trail, but I might be gone a little longer than I thought."

Max tried to smile. "That's okay. Do what you have to. Just stay in touch."

He didn't hear from Gabe for a week after that. Neither did Veronica. No one could reach him.

Rather than sit around and sulk over his absent boyfriend, Max got accepted into the Lycanthrope Academy. It wasn't college, but applicants only needed a high school degree or the equivalent.

The academy was located just off Madison Square Park and was the only school in the city that offered dedicated training for people aspiring to join the LPA. He would need a minimum of three years of training before he became an agent, but Max was eager to work toward it. He wanted to give back to the pack who'd saved his life.

The training was brutal most days. Max had to adhere to a strict diet and a dedicated exercise routine that left him sore and aching at the end of each day since agents had to be fit and ready for anything. The werewolves attending the academy were a mix of pureblooded werewolves and hybrids, so Max felt comfortable among them.

Additionally, the agency had tools he needed to learn to use, like catch poles and tranquilizer guns. When they had lessons involving those tools, the instructors paired him off with a four-legged partner to practice subduing them.

It was wild. Max wished he could tell Gabe and Ben all about it and hear their stories about when they trained in the academy, but there wasn't time. Gabe called when he could but never from the same hotel. Once he called from a hotel in Pittsburgh and a week later from Kentucky. His voice was always tired and worn. When Max touched the pillow beside him, he imagined he was touching Gabe's face, his body.

Despite the distance, they adapted their sex life to the space between them. Still, the empty space where Gabe's bond should have been ached like a loose tooth. They were too far apart to feel the bond between them. Gabe and Ben were hot on Stone's trail but every time they seemed close, he would slip through their fingers.

Gabe didn't know when he was coming home but he always answered with, "Soon."

Just a few weeks after Gabe left, the full moon rose. The sight made Max ache. If Gabe hadn't had to leave, they could have been mates tonight. The pack met up in Central Park and Max showed off his powers beneath the moon's light. He still laughed remembering the glee on Ryan's face when Max levitated him and the shock when Max dropped him. By accident, of course.

Max's list of questions about his connection to the moon only got longer. He wished he could get in touch with Ben's friend on the Council, but when he asked Ben, he said that his friend was on pilgrimage in Italy and couldn't be reached.

Toward the end of August, Max got his first job since leaving college as a host at The Slaughtered Lamb, and he vowed to always be polite to restaurant staff members whenever he ate out. He'd had no idea how difficult and thankless it was until he had people yelling in his face because they'd been waiting fifteen minutes while others who'd waited thirty were patient as could be. Sometimes, Ryan, Zach, Izzie, Kendra, and Veronica showed up for dinner and surprised him.

By September Izzie was making good progress with her speech therapist. She could speak aloud for longer before her voice wore out, but she still relied on the pack bonds for communication. Max wished Gabe was here to see her progress and to support her. Whenever they brought up Gabe, Izzie's mood always soured.

"I'll curse him out when he gets back," she croaked, jaw tight in anger. "That should surprise him."

Max smiled around the ache of pain. "He'll be happy."

Izzie crossed her arms. "He'll wish I never got my voice back by the time I'm done with him."

In October, Gabe went dark on Max. He tried calling Ben, but Ben never answered. Focusing in class was hard. Sleeping was worse because nightmares of Gabe, bloody and broken, made him bolt upright in bed, sweating and shaking.

Zach always seemed to call whenever Max needed it the most, as if their minds were on the same wavelength. He suspected this newfound connection was a benefit of the oath they'd sworn to each other.

Sometimes Max picked up the phone and called Zach first, and Zach listened to Max's fears and doubts without interruption. Max was glad he had Zach. On sleepless nights, Max remembered the prophecy Gabe had told him of once, about a black wolf of vengeance and a monster who clashed, one surviving while the other fell.

He prayed to the goddess Gabe wouldn't be the one who fell but on nights like those, when Gabe was so far away and his fate unknown, it was hard to breathe through the fear.

Max asked Zach, "Did Gabe ever tell you about that prophecy?"

"Once, yeah." Zach's voice was tinny over the phone. "I always thought Gabe survived the encounter 'cause we were together in the future. Now… now, I'm not so sure, Max. But it's Gabe we're talking about. He's strong, and he's got a hell of a good reason to come back. That seer did seem legit, but she was wrong about Gabe and me. So she could be wrong about this, too."

Something in Zach's voice didn't quite convince Max. "But you think she's right about something."

Zach sighed. "The prophecy mentioned the Wargs of the Apocalypse, and we know the Wargs are working with Stone."

Max sighed around a tangle of anxiety in his chest. "What could they have to do with Stone?"

Zach yawned. "I don't know. Their goals are kinda similar. Werewolf supremacy. People that kind of crazy, it's best just not knowing what's going on in their heads."

Max had to agree. "Do you think Stone's gone off to join them or something? What could he be doing out there?"

"Hell if I know. Maybe he's running off to hide with them."

Max shivered at the thought of Gabe, Ben, and the agency wolves running into yet another ambush.

"Max, Gabe could be okay. The prophecy said Stone and Gabe would clash on the night of a super flower lunar eclipse. How about we keep track of the lunar cycles? That way we can know for sure if he'll be safe."

Max checked the lunar cycles online with his heart in his throat. There were no blood moons or eclipses in the near future, but Max's worries weren't soothed when November came and went in radio silence.

For all Max knew, Gabe was dead. He told himself he'd know; he'd feel it in his heart if something terrible happened to Gabe.

But then what the hell did he know?

Zach came up with an idea to keep Max busy toward the end of November. "Why don't you volunteer at the agency on your off days?"

"Are you trying to kill me with work?" Max joked.

"You're going to join at some point. Might as well get some hands-on experience."

Max liked the idea. He already spent weekends studying at the agency, wanting to be close to Ryan, Izzie, and Zach, so he accepted Zach's offer. Max did a number of different jobs around the estate filling in for absences, whether that was by helping Luke in the clinic, doing reception work at the front desk, landscaping around the agency grounds, or cleaning the kennels.

He never worked alone; Izzie, Ryan, and Zach chipped in and helped him when they could. It made Max excited for his future as an agent, and around the estate he proudly wore the badge Ben had gifted him for his birthday. He couldn't wait to be Agent Max Gallagher.

Max wasn't an agent yet, but that didn't mean he wanted to wait to do his part to contribute toward a better society for werewolves, so he created the academy's first werewolf-human alliance club. His goal with starting the club was to create a safe space for werewolf and human trainees to have open conversations about each other's differences in a manner that encouraged education and empathy. The club took off, and Max was delighted when newscasters arrived to do a story on the club and interviewed him.

Before he knew it, Max was being invited onto talk shows. He got so intimidated he tried to back out of the offers, but his mother gave him the encouraging shove he needed. "Max, this will be so important for shifters in the city."

"I know." Max gazed at the email on his laptop screen, still wondering if it was real. "I just... I wish he was here to see this. This is so huge."

"It is." She squeezed his shoulders. "He would be proud of you. Who knows, maybe he can watch it wherever he is."

Max smiled sadly. "I don't think Mars has cable TV."

She laughed. "Do the interview, Max. I'm sure it will mean a lot to Gabe and Ben."

So Max went on live TV, hoping and praying no one noticed the pit stains on his blazer from how badly he was sweating. A few minutes in, he began to relax. He talked more about himself than he had in his life. He talked about how he was raised by a single mom, his abusive stepdad, the Moonborn cult's interest in him, and the LPA and how they'd inspired him to help others.

His throat was hoarse, but he pressed on. "Obviously, I'm not saying all this so people will pity me. I just want people to understand that it's possible for good to come out of terrible circumstances. Trauma changes you, but it doesn't have to define you."

Segments of his interview went viral on social media. It was all a bit overwhelming. After getting home, Max checked his phone and found no response to the messages he'd sent Gabe. Gabe's continued silence dragged him down from the high of his success, and he fell asleep with his phone in his hand.

In late December, Max's phone rang. It was midnight, and an unknown number filled his screen. Max held his breath, his hands shaking and heart pounding. "Hello?"

"Max..." Gabe's voice was almost a growl.

Max's throat thickened; fury made his fingers curl. "You son of a bitch."

Gabe didn't try to excuse himself or even speak. He just listened, panting into Max's ear as Max went off on him for twenty minutes, telling him how scared he was, asking why the fuck Gabe hadn't answered his phone. Where was he? Was he hurt? Was he coming home?

"Montana." Gabe's voice was off. Disjointed. Gruff. It scared the hell out of Max.

Max slumped against his pillows and stared at the ceiling. He swiped open Google Maps on his phone, scrolling until he found Montana. He touched the state with a finger and felt the distance in every crack in his heart. "Why?"

Silence, then he heard shuffling over the speaker.

"Hey, kid."

Max wanted to cry at the sound of Ben's voice. "Hey," he managed, voice gravelly.

Ben sighed, sounding just as defeated as Gabe. "I'm sorry, Max. We've been on foot, following Stone. We were in the wilds for weeks, only just found a town now. Stone's killing historians. It started in Alabama, and we've been following the trail since. Specifically, he's killing historians who made a living documenting werewolf lore. We don't know why, but he's targeting them. We think he's heading for the Canadian border."

Max didn't understand. He didn't care. "Come home."

Ben sighed, the sound tinny. "We're close, Max. We're real close and if we pull back, more folks are gonna die."

Max closed his eyes tight.

"Max." Gabe's voice was like an animal's.

"Come home," Max said, and his throat was raw. "Please, Gabe. Just come home."

"Max," Gabe said, as if Max's name were a lifeline keeping him from sinking into the depths of feral madness. "Max. Max. Max."

Christmas was lonely that year. New Year's was the worst.

In January Max received a postcard, but Gabe had mentioned he was sending one months ago. The postcard was from Minneapolis. In it, Gabe had written only that he missed Max and thought of him every night, and that Max was in his dreams... especially the naughty ones.

If Max weren't so worried, he might have laughed.

He crumpled it up and thought about throwing it away. Instead, he put it under his pillow and kept it there. He'd promised Gabe he would wait. Gabe had promised he would come back, and Gabe Reyes kept his promises.

So Max waited. He waited through six more months of silence. Six months of worried tears, sleepless nights, fury, and numb emptiness.

And now it was July thirty-first, and it was his twenty-first birthday. He stood in the card aisle of some drug store—because his mother was traditional and wanted to give everyone thank-you cards after his party—glowering at all the lovey-dovey romance cards.

He looked twice but couldn't quite find the card that said, *It's been a year, you jerk, and I miss you so much I wanna tear my heart out of my chest and stomp on it. Screw you. Screw this. Screw love.* He wondered if he could get it custom made.

He purchased a box of cards and left the store, dragging his sneakers through the rain. He passed the little bagel shop where he and Gabe had liked to grab breakfast if they were too lazy to cook. Max hadn't gone there in months, and he'd tried to avoid walking past it, but it was no use trying to hide from the memories of their time together when they'd made this whole neighborhood their stomping ground.

He wandered Central Park. It smelled like wet leaves, dirt, and elm trees. He walked past the little trail they'd liked to take through the park at night, knowing if he just followed the trail, he'd pass the places they'd used to sit and make out and see the duck pond where they'd spent many moonlit nights sitting on the shore. His chest tightened and Max moved on.

His phone buzzed and Max's heart climbed into his throat, beating wildly. He tried to squash the hope down, but there was a bitter taste in his mouth nonetheless when he saw Ryan's name on the screen, texting to wish him a happy birthday. He shouldn't still be disappointed.

He just had to cling to what little hope still burned bright inside him, cradle that spark against the icy winds of doubt that tried to extinguish it.

Max had promised to wait, and he kept his promises, too.

MAX'S BACK ACHED AS he lugged a bin full of dirty dishes up the stairs and behind the bar. The Slaughtered Lamb was usually quiet on a Monday but not tonight; hungry shifters crammed into tables, devouring juicy cuts of meat and guzzling beers like they were water. Max unloaded clean plates, wiping them off with a rag.

Glancing around the bar, he noticed a few dirty tables in need of a wipe down. Thankfully, one of the other busboys swept past to clean them, so Max busied himself with shelving clean cups and stacking plates.

"You're on fire tonight, Max!" the bartender exclaimed as Max emptied the bin in seconds, lunging for a second bin full of dirty dishes.

"Thanks!" Max shot him a quick smile and made another trip downstairs, carrying the dishes to the prep room and loading them into the dishwasher. Doing dishes and cleaning tables wasn't the most glamorous of jobs, but on busy nights like tonight, he would leave with a hefty lump of tip money in his pocket.

Max hoped to work his way up to waiting tables in the future as he'd heard the money was much better. The idea of talking to strangers made him cringe but it would be great to make more money. For now, however, he enjoyed the repetition of cleaning tables: just clean, load the dishwasher, unload, and repeat.

He set the dishwasher running and checked the time. His shift ended in fifteen minutes. Assuming the next busboy wasn't late, he could jump on a train and arrive at his birthday party in no time. He'd been so busy this evening he'd worked through lunch, so he'd eaten late, but he still had room in his stomach for cake. He always had room for cake.

Max jumped the stairs two by two and grabbed a rag as he darted around the bar, wiping down a new table. He could practically see the hostess chomping at the bit as she waited by the door, eager to lighten the growing list. He cleaned the table until it shone, then turned around and jolted when he realized the hostess was right behind him.

He motioned to the clean table. "All yours."

"Max, wait up!" She followed him behind the bar as he grabbed clean plates.

"What is it?" he asked.

"There's someone at the door asking for you."

"Really? I'll be over in a sec." That made no sense. Who could be asking for him? Max walked out around the bar, plates balanced in his hands.

"Lobito!"

All the air went out of the room and Max's heart stopped. That voice cut right through the noise of the crowds and the clatter of cutlery. His heart began to race, and he felt it then, the telltale pulse like a secondary heartbeat. The pack bonds were stronger than they'd been in a year.

Max couldn't hear, not the buzzing of the crowds, the clink of ice in the glasses, or the scrape of silverware. Just the pounding of his heart and the echo of another beat, full of the same nervous excitement that paralyzed Max. He turned around.

Gabriel Reyes stood before him for the first time in a year. For a moment, Max almost didn't believe it was him. His ebony hair was longer, tumbling down past his shoulders, his fair skin a deep brown thanks to a tan on his arms and face, and a beard had grown wild and bushy on his jaw.

As those hopeful amber eyes found Max's and the tremble in that megawatt smile turned up the ends of Gabe's mustache, Max's heart wanted to break in two.

He was back. Gabe had returned.

And Max was overwhelmed as the noise of the crowds came surging back, deafening him. What did he do? What did he say? He'd had no warning, nothing but dead silence for months and now Gabe was right *here*.

Beneath the odor of stale sweat and unwashed male, Gabe still smelled just like he had before he'd left, spring flowers and elm trees and mate and *mine*. He was smiling like he hadn't just up and left for so long, and he looked so different yet the same, and he was *here*! He'd come back, just like he'd promised.

Something constricted Max's throat and it wasn't joyful. Gabe was back, and he didn't know where this left them. Had he been successful? Had he killed Stone and put his demons to rest? If not, then how long was he staying this time? For a month, a week? A day?

Max wasn't ready. He didn't want answers. He didn't want to know how long they'd be separated again.

So he did the only thing one could do when reunited with the love of their life suddenly after a year—he dropped the load of dishes in his arms and was gone before they shattered, slamming the door to the basement behind him.

# CHAPTER 5

# STRANGERS

THE FLIGHT FROM EDMONTON, Canada, to New York took a century. Ben watched movies in the seat beside him. Gabe tried watching a movie and occasionally looked out the window but clouds obscured the view.

He wanted to see New York sprawled below the clouds. It had been a year, but it felt like a thousand since he'd seen the city he was born and raised in. He couldn't wait to smell the salty waves of Fire Island.

He missed Ryan and his snarky comments; they could have used his sense of humor. He missed Izzie. He hoped her voice was recovering. He even missed Zach, though they hadn't parted on the best of terms. He missed his mother. She hadn't wanted him to go at all.

He missed New York. He missed the hustle and the bustle of the streets, missed sleeping in his bed and waking up bundled in the familiarity of his den. When he'd gone to bed hungry, he'd dreamed of bagels stuffed with cream cheese and lox and had damn near woken up crying in disappointment.

But more than anything, more than anyone, he missed Maxwell Gallagher. If he never saw New York City again, it wouldn't matter. He'd leave it all behind in a heartbeat and never look back just so long as Max was by his side. A whine rose in the back of his throat, and he closed his eyes tight at the painful twisting in his guts.

Would Max want to see him? Would he be angry? For sure, and Gabe wouldn't blame him in the slightest. But would Max forgive him? He had to. Gabe had made good on his promise and come home to him. He'd hold Max in his arms, breathe in his scent, and that void in his chest would disappear once they were reunited.

Unless Max had gotten tired of waiting for him. Unless he'd found someone else and turned his back on their bond. Someone who was a better mate than Gabe. Someone who wouldn't choose revenge over their relationship.

Something pierced his leg. He gasped and looked down to see his claws had punctured his jeans to the skin.

No. Max would never do that. They were fated to be together. Gabe had never chosen revenge over Max. Everything he'd done and would ever do was for him. But had he made that clear? He knew he'd been a shitty mate-to-be, but surely Max knew Gabe loved him. Didn't he?

Oh Goddess. What if he'd been away too long? What if he'd made Max doubt his feelings? What if—

His vision warped and everything was so much wider, so much closer. A hand fell upon his knee. His heart lurched into his throat when he found Ben seemingly inches from his face. He said something, but Gabe couldn't hear him over the blood pounding in his ears. A thousand different smells came at him and he almost gagged.

Humans were so damn smelly, releasing so many different odors all at the same time. Thousands of different heartbeats slammed his ears, and he jumped as the pilot's voice blasted over the intercom. Noisy. It was too noisy. There were too many smells. The woman in the seat in front of him reeked of some pungent perfume that made his nose itch.

His fangs jabbed his lower lip. Escape. He had to escape. Had to get away from all the smells, all the noises. He couldn't tell which heartbeat was his anymore, all of them thundering in his ears. Like a hare on the run. Like prey.

Prey. They were prey. All of them.

"Gabe, calm down." Ben's gruff voice hissed in his ear. Gabe whined, torn between *Prey, must hunt* and *Ben, must obey*. Gabe flew from his seat, Ben's hand at the scruff of his neck. Faces loomed at him as he passed, gawking at him. He bared his teeth, then found himself being thrown ahead to a door. "Get in there."

Gabe stumbled into a tiny, cramped bathroom. The smells of urine and shit overpowered the scent of sweaty flesh and foul perfumes. Ben pushed Gabe's back against the door and large warm hands grasped his face. "Your name is Gabriel Reyes. You're not a wolf; you're a man. You're going home to Max. He's your mate. You've got a mother, Veronica. She smells a hell of a lot nicer than those people out there. You have friends: Ryan, he's a real wiseass but he's got a good heart; Zach, he's freakishly tall and he's got the soul of a forty-something-year-old; your sister, Isabella, sweet as can be, makes the best tres leches cakes you've ever tasted. Think of them and get a hold of yourself."

Memories swept over him like floodwater pouring over a dam.

*"You're going to be a big brother, mi sol!" His mother had tears in her eyes. His father's arms were big and strong around him.*

*She was so small in Gabe's arms, her face pink and wrinkled. He brought his nose to the downy fuzz on her head and breathed in. His baby sister had the best smell in the whole world—up until she pooped her diaper.*

*Strange symbols covered every inch of the wall, scratched into the wood by overgrown claws. With his long nails and mouth full of fangs, the gaunt man was more wolf than human, his stringy hair clinging to the skeletal outlines of his face. "This is where they bring little hybrid boys no one wants anymore." The knife gleamed and cut his skin as easily as if it were paper. He screamed and screamed but no one came for him.*

*His father clutched a mossy boulder, his body submerged up to his shoulders by the swollen river. "Get him," he croaked. "Don't let him hurt anyone else." Gabe screamed for him as the river pulled him under.*

*"I got you, Lobito." The young man shivered in his arms, clinging to his shoulders as if Gabe were a lifeline keeping him afloat.*

"Gabe." *Max whispered his name with reverie.*

When Gabe opened his eyes, they were laced with tears. He choked, covering his face in his hands. "What's happening to me?"

Ben leaned their foreheads together, his hands steady and strong on Gabe's trembling shoulders. "Keep your head on, kid. We're almost home."

THEY TOUCHED DOWN IN NYC in the late evening. Gabe practically snatched Ben's phone out of his hand and tried to call Max, but he wouldn't pick up. Gabe checked the time and his heart thundered when he realized Max would be getting off work soon.

"Gabe." There was something apprehensive in Ben's voice. "You sure you wanna surprise him like this?"

"His phone's never on when he's at work." Gabe's skin prickled. He didn't like the way Ben was looking at him. "What?"

"We've been silent for months. No contact, nothing."

"So?" Gabe squirmed, wishing they could go faster.

"Nothing." Ben looked away and out the window. "Just don't expect everything to be the same as it was."

His jaw tightened. Max would be thrilled to see him. Gabe could hardly wait to have Max in his arms. He needed to hear his voice, breathe in his scent. Unless—

He rounded on Ben, fangs bared. "You think he's found another mate. Is that it?"

Ben raised both hands to soothe him. "Is that what I said, Gabe? Or is that what you're thinking?"

Gabe growled and fought the urge to punch the window. If Max had moved on... Well, he was so worked up right now he thought he'd kill the poor fool lucky enough to win Max's heart. "Wouldn't blame him. I've been a crummy mate-to-be."

The driver stopped at Ben's first. Ben squeezed Gabe's shoulder. "We did our best, Gabe."

Gabe exhaled his bitterness. "Yeah. Thanks for coming, Ben. I mean it. I don't know how I'd have managed without you there."

Ben grinned. "You wouldn't have." He slammed the cab door.

"Where to, sir?" The driver watched Gabe over the back of his seat.

Gabe forced himself to breathe. He didn't know Max's schedule for certain, but if he had to guess, Max would still be working. "The Slaughtered Lamb on Greenwich Street."

He hadn't showered and he would have liked to shave the animal off his face, but he had to see Max. The cobblestone streets made the ride bumpy, rocking Gabe side to side. He recognized the street, recalling many a drunken night out with Ryan and Zach. The Lamb came into view, UK flags flying in the breeze. Gabe's heart jumped into his throat. He was closer to Max than he'd been in a whole year.

Would Max be happy to see him? Would he be angry?

The car hadn't slowed completely before Gabe jumped out, pulling his backpack after him. His legs were like jelly as he jogged toward the pub with its iconic sign swaying in the warm summer wind: a werewolf, snarling face upturned to the full moon.

He was breathless, not from exertion but from excitement, as he stumbled inside. The smell of roast pork might have made his stomach rumble if it weren't doing somersaults. The hostess was wide-eyed, and he figured his sudden entrance had startled her.

"Maxwell Gallagher. Is he here?"

He almost burst with excitement when she replied, "He is. I can find him for you. Think I saw him a minute ago..." She wandered into the crowd.

Gabe stood on his toes, peering above everyone. The pub was a melting pot of smells from roast pork and beef, to the various scents of other werewolves, and the tangy aroma of limes, lemons, and oranges. But through it all, he caught a whiff of something familiar tangoing with all the other smells: the sweet, spicy aroma of cinnamon and chilis.

A lump rose to Gabe's throat and his inner wolf howled out, *Mate. Mine. Love. Life.*

The crowds parted and there he was, striding from behind the bar. He had a smile that made sunlight dim by comparison and a dash of freckles on his cheeks and cute upturned nose.

His red hair was longer than Gabe remembered, wavy and flopping sweetly over his forehead. He wanted to cry, to call out, but the words were stuck in his throat. He clutched the host stand, urging himself forward on trembling legs and blinking back the tears from his eyes.

*I missed you. So much. Every day, every night. Some nights I wanted to give up and call it all off just so I could come home. You have no idea, Max, the hold you have over me. Some days I didn't know if I'd ever come back but I had to keep trying. I had to see you again. Max, Max—*

"Lobito!"

Max froze. His eyes widened, pink lips parted. Gabe blinked hard as Max turned slowly toward him. His mouth fell open, his eyes as wide as dinner plates. The dishes tumbled from his arms and Max ran—away from him.

The restaurant turned deathly quiet. Max threw himself through a door behind the bar. The chatter returned and some people clapped as the staff rushed to sweep up the dishes. All Gabe's joy had vanished. His insides were cold, and he stood blinking stupidly as he tried to register what had happened and why.

Max wasn't happy to see him. Dread twisted up his insides and he sought the exit, squeezing past people as he stumbled out into the street. He sucked in a breath and realized he was shaking.

*Calm down.* He had to stay calm. Of course Max was surprised to see him. He'd barged into his workplace after months of total silence between them. He had no way of knowing what must have gone on in Max's head during their time apart.

*Does he still love me?*

The thought robbed him of the air he desperately needed.

No. Max was his mate, and Gabe was his. They'd never exchanged mating bites but that didn't mean a thing, not to either of them. The goddess had chosen them to complete each other; they were meant to be together and not one, two, or three years apart could change that.

He would find a way to make this right.

MAX STAYED A FEW minutes past his shift to help clean up the shattered plates. Fortunately, he didn't drop plates very often, so his boss didn't make a big deal out of it. He still couldn't wrap his head around how hard his flight reaction had kicked his butt. Max's hands trembled as he swept.

Gabe had kept his promise and come back. He was standing just outside the front door, the string of his bond twanging like a secondary heartbeat in Max's chest. Max hadn't felt that connection to him in months.

How much was still the same between them? Max's stomach twisted itself into the shape of a pretzel. His hands trembled as he clocked out, waving farewell to everyone and mumbling goodbye. He clasped the knob and found himself short of breath.

Wetting his lips, he shouldered open the door and his breath caught as his gaze wandered right to those amber eyes. Max froze like prey, torn between the howl of his inner wolf, crying out in joy at the reunion of two destined mates, and the sudden urge to run.

Because he'd suddenly realized he wasn't happy to see Gabe. Who knew when he'd take off next? The gall of him just turning up out of the blue after a year of on-and-off communication and while Max was *working*. Maybe, just maybe, Max was fucking sick of Gabe doing things to his heart that no one had any right to do.

Things weren't the same. He knew it, because he was paralyzed with doubt when once he'd have thrown himself into Gabe's arms, bundled himself up in his warmth, and filled his lungs with the smell of safety and home.

Would they ever get back to the way they were before?

"Max." Gabe's low voice made Max's chest tighten. He'd almost forgotten the sound of his voice, soft and warm with a faint Spanish lilt. The shadow of a smile turned up the corner of Gabe's mustache, his eyes fixated on Max like he was the only person in the world that mattered. "Hey."

"Hi." Max cleared his throat, trying to find his voice.

Gabe's eyes softened. Max hadn't realized there'd been such a pinch to his brow until now. Whatever had happened out there, wherever "there" was, it must have been hard. The winds changed, carrying Gabe's scent to him, and Max ached for him, wanted to throw himself into his arms and feel the scratch of his beard as they kissed.

As if Gabe hadn't dropped out of contact with hardly a warning, as if all the nights Max had stayed awake waiting for him to call had never happened. Anger warred with his longing, strangling it.

Times like these, Max wished he was all wolf and that Gabe was, too. Wolves were simple creatures, always happy to see each other no matter how far apart they'd strayed. Being human was too damn complicated.

"Happy birthday."

Heat ran up the back of Max's neck. He almost smiled before he reminded himself he was supposed to be pissed. Gabe had remembered, and that brought him unexpected joy. He succeeded in not smiling but Gabe must have scented his momentary flash of joy, Gabe's tentative smile flourishing undeterred.

"I was hoping we'd be back in time. I didn't get you a present. There weren't exactly any stores out in the Canadian wilderness."

Really? Of all his priorities, getting Max a present made the list? Max remained silent. If he spoke, he worried he'd say something stupid like, *You're the best present I could ask for*. He had to preserve some of his dignity.

"Max, I—"

"Did you find him?" Was the hunt over? Was Gabe here to stay, or would he take off again?

Gabe wet his lips, eyes wide.

"Is it over?"

Gabe hung his head. "No," he said, and the word punched Max in the chest.

Max struggled to breathe through the lump in his throat. "How long?"

Gabe blinked, confusion knotting his brow.

"How long are you staying?"

Gabe looked like Max had struck him. "Max—"

Max couldn't hear it. Anger was all he had, and if he let Gabe talk him out of his anger, then he would crumble. Max's phone rang, and he jumped out of his skin. "Oh crap!" Max lunged for his phone and checked his messages. His mother was asking if his shift was done. "I gotta go. My mom made dinner reservations."

Gabe nodded, uncharacteristically meek and uncertain as he looked at the floor. "Oh. Right. I'd come but I'd probably kill everyone with my stink. I'll see you at home."

"Yeah. Sure."

Max cringed. They'd never used to be this awkward. Max ran to the curb and hailed a cab. He climbed in and before he could regret leaving Gabe outside the restaurant, he was speeding away. Max slumped in his seat. He hadn't seen Gabe in months, but he was ditching him to go to a party? But they'd planned this party for weeks. He couldn't not show up. He growled as guilt gnawed at him. His phone buzzed.

Max's heart jumped, realizing he had messages from an unknown number for the first time in months. They were from hours ago.

**Gabe: On a plane now. Coming home. Miss you so much.**

Max's throat thickened.

**Gabe: Taking off in a few minutes. I'll text when we're in NYC.**

**Gabe: Just got in!! I'll meet you at work. Can't wait to see you.**

Max's lips trembled and he gave in, laughing, crying, or somewhere in between. He probably sounded crazy to the driver, but he didn't care.

Gabe was back. For however long it lasted, Gabe had come home to him. Max didn't know if he was ready to forgive him, but despite the hurricane of doubts swirling inside him, he found respite as he dried his eyes, smiling until his face hurt.

Because damn it, this thing between them was hard—but being without Gabriel Reyes?

That would be even harder.

# CHAPTER 6
# TO BE LOVED

Max arrived at The Woolen Wolf and could barely suppress his smug smirk when the bouncer sniffed at him and checked his ID before stepping aside. The door opened wide for him, beckoning Max to step right in and commence a night of debauchery.

Finally! His days of being under twenty-one were over at last. He grinned as he crossed the threshold, eyes widening as he took in the place. Partially shifted werewolves packed the bar, their claws wrapped around glasses of frothy beer. Shelves of various liquors touched the ceiling.

He waved at the host. "Hi! I'm looking for Kendra Gallagher. She booked a table."

The host led him past the bar as two werewolves engaged in a fighting match, claws flashing and fur flying. Toward the back of the restaurant was a large table where the pack awaited him.

Max smiled at Ryan, already red-faced from drink, chestnut hair overtly tousled and big dorky glasses askew on his nose; Zach, the beads in his braids clinking when he laughed at Ryan's jokes; Kendra sitting across from them nursing some wine; and Izzie looking especially radiant in a black and red dress, tossing back a shot with Ryan.

Ben sat beside Izzie, glowering into his whiskey. Usually, Ben sported a bald head and a neat brown beard flecked with silver, but his time in the wilds of wherever they'd been for months had left him with shoulder-length hair on his head. Max almost didn't recognize him.

Ryan's face split into a grin. "There's our boy!" He leaped up and bounded to meet Max.

"Happy birthday!" the pack cried.

Max smiled at his mother as she rushed to pull him into a hug. "I can't believe it, twenty-one!" she squealed, and Max wanted to sink into the floor as she pinched his cheeks.

"Our baby boy's all grown up!" Max stumbled as Ryan hurled himself into Max's arms and into a full-body hug. He reeked of alcohol. "Happy birthday, man! You're finally twenty-one!" Ryan beamed. "What do you wanna drink first? Their beers are awesome. They've got so many!"

Zach put his elbow on Ryan's head. "Don't drink too much, Max. Hybrids don't have a tolerance to alcohol like pure-blooded werewolves do. Don't kill yourself. Happy birthday, by the way."

Max met Zach's hand in a fist bump. "Thanks. Wow." He took a moment to survey the table that was decorated with balloons and stacked with plates just waiting to be loaded with delicious food. Enormous windows beyond the table provided a view of the street that was flooded with rain lashing at the buildings. "Looks like I just missed a storm."

"No way!" Ryan stumbled to the window and crashed into the glass. "So friggin' cool!"

Zach tugged on Ryan's sleeve. "Don't even think about going out in that."

"Max!" The tropical aroma of Izzie's perfume blanketed him as she welcomed him into her arms. "Happy birthday, love!"

Max gave her a squeeze. "Thanks."

Izzie gave him a searching look. "Tell me my idiot brother came to see you."

Max's smile faltered. "He did," he assured her, trying to keep his tone casual.

She squeezed his shoulder. "I know. I want to kick his ass as much as you do. But I bet he was happy to see you."

Max nodded. "He was."

Izzie took him by the shoulders, looked him square in the eyes, and said, "Were you happy to see him?"

Max had no idea and found himself overwhelmed. "I don't know."

"Good!" she declared, fire blazing in her eyes. Max blinked, surprised. That wasn't what he'd been expecting. "Don't forgive him! Be mad at him. Make him realize leaving you was the biggest mistake he ever made! Do not go easy on him, Maxwell Gallagher. Do you understand?"

Max nodded frantically. "Yeah, yeah, of course."

"And until you forgive him, I won't either." She raised both hands, backing down. "I know, I know. Your happiness is important. If you choose to forgive him, I will one hundred percent support your choice." The fire in her eyes returned, and she tossed her hair back angrily. "But I will remind him of this mistake for the rest of my life. That idiot!" With a growl, she crossed her arms and glared into her cocktail as if it had spit at her.

Ben whistled. "Remind me to always stay on your good side, Izzie."

"Don't even get me started with you! You just encouraged my brother's self-sacrificing idiocy."

Max didn't want to think about Gabe right now, so he browsed the extensive selection of liquors. Honestly, he couldn't tell whiskey from vodka. "Wow. That's a lot." He'd had a sip of wine on occasion but never enough to decide whether he preferred white or red.

Across the table, Ryan grinned at him. "Need a hand? I got you covered. You're gonna love this." He passed a bottle wrapped in a bow across the table to Max. It was peanut butter whiskey.

"Gabe likes this," Max recalled.

"Yeah, have a sip and you'll understand why. Just be careful. It's sweet, but it'll knock an alcohol virgin like you on your ass. Figured you like sweet things."

"Thanks." Max put the bottle in his bag.

"Don't thank me, just get drunk! Come on, you can only do it once as a werewolf! Well, you're a hybrid, you lucky bastard. You can get as drunk as you want, whenever you want... Ugh."

"I don't know what to pick..."

Ryan tugged the menu over and began rattling off all the drinks he liked... which was most of their cocktails. Zach met his gaze and shrugged his shoulders.

Kendra settled in beside Max. "I ordered buffet style. There should be something for everyone."

"Hey, Max!" Ryan shouted, making Zach jump. "Take a sip of my cocktail. If you like it, it's on me!"

Max took a cautious sip. The fruity aftertaste disguised the alcohol. "Hell yeah, get me one!" Ryan waved a server over. Max would have drunk Ryan's cocktail if he hadn't snatched it back.

Across the table, Ben met Max's gaze. Max found himself at a loss for words.

"Here's looking at you, kid." Ben's stern features softened as he showed his teeth in a warm smile and took a drink, the ice clinking against the glass.

It was good to hear the rumble of his voice again and see that soft smile that contrasted with the hard lines of his face. "Thanks."

Ben's silver eyes lingered on him. Max recalled the last time he'd seen those eyes. They'd been hard and frustrated. Max hadn't exactly been happy that Ben hadn't bothered to fight for Max to accompany them. He'd only said, "Stone wants you, kid. You come with us, we're throwing you directly into danger. You're staying, and that's final."

Smiling was difficult.

Ben's mouth twitched. "Still mad at me?"

"No," Max replied too quickly. He sighed. Ben had only been looking out for him, but he was part of the pack, not something to be guarded and protected.

Ben frowned into his whiskey. "I don't blame you. I did try and stop Gabe, but you know how he is. Stubborn as a mule. Letting Gabe go out there was a mistake. He didn't... cope very well with being away from you. He can tell you."

Max hadn't noticed anything off with Gabe, at least not in person, but Gabe's rasping voice during their last call still made him shiver.

"What happened out there?" Max asked. "Where were you guys? Why didn't you stay in touch?"

Ben downed the last of his whiskey, face twisting. "We couldn't. We stayed on the roads as long as we could. Then once we hit Montana, Stone started venturing into the wilderness and we had to follow the trail. We tracked Stone through Montana and over the Canadian border through the Big Drift. He was looking for something, we just weren't sure what. We ran outta food, had to shift and hunt deer, rabbits, anything we could find. Gabe took to the shift too much, relied too hard on his wolf to track Stone, and without a connection to you..."

Max's gut lurched. "Is he okay?" His mind flew to Gabe, all alone in the apartment, worried Max hated him after months apart.

"He needed you, Max. You're his anchor, you know that? You're what keeps him grounded. Human."

Max's chest tightened. "And what about Stone? Gabe says you didn't find him. What happened?"

Ben shook his head, face pinching in bitterness. "We lost him. A damn avalanche cut him off from us. Wherever he was going, whatever he was planning... who the hell knows? We sent out a warning to the Canadian authorities to be on the lookout for him."

"And Gabe was fine just letting him go?"

"We had to. I thought I'd lose Gabe completely to his wolf if we stayed away any longer."

An icy shard of dread pierced Max's heart at the thought. He could have lost him, and it would have been John Stone's fault. Max wished he'd fought harder to keep Gabe from leaving.

"But you did all right, didn't you?"

Ben frowned into his beer. "I missed my pack, but I managed all right. But then, I've always had control over my wolf. After what Stone did to him, to his family, Gabe's struggled to control his wolf. Remember how you struggled with control after what the asshole put you through?"

Max nodded, a lump in his stomach. He meant Richard Moray, Max's stepfather.

"You learned control again, but it was hard. Gabe—" Ben paused, running a hand tiredly over his bushy beard. "Gabe has a pack. He's close to all of us, but it isn't always enough. It's not that he struggles to form the bonds he needs to keep him human. It's more that he struggles to control his inner animal. His wolf controls him."

Max's heart thumped faster. Gabe had mentioned something like that once, about his struggles with control. Max had thought at the time that he was just saying that to make Max feel better until he'd seen the way Gabe looked after waking up from his night terrors: claws sharp, eyes burning yellow, fangs glistening.

"It has a mind of its own and when he's at his lowest, it takes over. Have you ever seen him like that?"

Max nodded slowly, mouth dry. "And that... that happened while you were gone?"

Ben tucked his chin toward his chest. "Close to it. Too close. It happened a lot after his dad died. He'd have episodes where he lost himself briefly to his wolf. We could always bring him back but... sometimes I feel like all it would take is another loss to push him over the edge. That's why you had to stay, Max. Because if anything happened to you, I don't think he would be able to recover. I think he'd be lost for good."

Max balled his hands into fists, hating the very thought.

"Max, I know it was hard not knowing what was going on, but try and talk to Gabe, okay? He needs to know you don't hate him."

"Of course I don't." Max sighed. "I'll try, Ben."

Ben's face brightened. He clapped Max on the shoulder. "It will be good for Gabe to be back among the pack. And it's damn good to see you again, Little Red." Ben's hand fell heavy and warm on his head.

Max couldn't fight back the smile. He'd missed Ben.

"How long—" Max began, but the food arrived and Max loaded up his plate with gooey mac and cheese, Brussel sprouts, and some salad. As he looked around at the pack, laughing and enjoying each other's company, a piece of him that had been missing for months had finally come back.

MAX'S HEAD THROBBED WHEN he opened bleary eyes, and his throat was so dry he thought the only reason he'd woken at all was in an attempt to save himself from dying of dehydration. "Fuck..."

Why had he let Ryan convince him that sixth beer was a good idea? Not that he'd needed convincing after the third. Ryan could have suggested they rob a bank, and Max would have been down for it. His throat was sore, and he remembered laughing and yelling over the din of the bar... just not about what.

"Morning, Sleeping Beauty." Izzie stood over him armed with aspirin and a tall glass of water. Makeup free, she wore sweats and a gray tank top, her long hair tied loosely back with a scrunchie. She grinned, her eyes twinkling. "Ah, I remember the first time I woke up with a hangover. You know, I think werewolves hate us hybrids so much because we can actually get drunk without developing that pesky tolerance after one drink."

Max gritted his teeth as a dull ache lanced through his skull. He sat up and accepted the water and the aspirin. "Thanks."

He crumpled back against the sofa and realized he didn't recognize it. It was a cranberry red and matched the drapes on the windows. "Is this your place?" He craned his neck to look around the back of the sofa and out the window, regretting it as blinding sunlight scorched his retinas and made his head throb.

"Yup. That's right, you've never actually come over before."

Max had been to Veronica's home, and he knew the layout of Gabe's apartment by heart.

"You don't remember coming over, do you?" Izzie bobbed her brows, a positively delighted smile on her face.

"I don't remember much of anything after the sixth beer." His stomach gurgled in remembrance.

"You got all dramatic and didn't want to go home to see Gabriel. Ryan and Zach were ready to offer you a room, but you chose me. Because even drunk, you have good taste in friends." Izzie winked and skipped into the kitchen. "Hungry?"

Max shuddered at the thought of food. "No. Ugh. Why didn't anyone stop me?"

Izzie opened the fridge and grabbed a carton of eggs. "Ben and Kendra tried. I think Ben was too amused, and Kendra wanted you to learn that just because you can have that sixth beer, doesn't mean you should."

Max massaged his temples. "Traitors."

"Call out of class today. Give yourself a break."

Max shook his head and winced. "No. I got myself into this. My grades aren't suffering because of my poor life choices."

She gasped. "Responsibility!" She shrugged. "Can't relate." She bashed an egg against the bowl.

Max's bladder was fit to burst. "Bathroom?"

"Right over there." Izzie pointed to a door just off the entry hallway.

Once he'd emptied his bladder, Max dragged his feet back to the couch and found his sweatshirt discarded on the floor. He rifled through the pockets and found his phone. He groaned when he saw the battery was in the red and cursed at the time. He would have just enough time to run home, grab whatever he needed for class, and jump on a train. He hoped the aspirin kicked in.

"Where am I?" He looked out the window but couldn't see any discernible landmarks.

"Inwood," Izzie said. "The subway's over on Isham Street."

Max checked the location on Google Maps and was relieved to find the station wasn't far. A text notification popped up. It was from Gabe, one of many. Max's heart clenched. Gabe had blown up his phone with messages Max hadn't answered.

**Gabe: All good?**

**Gabe: Coming home soon?**

**Gabe: I'll wait up for you.**

The last message was from one in the morning. Max gnashed his teeth, trying to force away the guilt. Gabe sure hadn't minded making *him* worry. Instead of responding, he turned off his phone, finding the idea of texting with Gabe to be overwhelming. "I don't hear from you in months. Now you're blowing up my phone?" Max muttered and shoved his phone back in his pocket.

"I messaged him." Izzie stirred the eggs in a pan on the stove. "He knows you're with me."

"Thanks." Max sighed.

"Be angry at him, Max. But not too angry." Izzie smiled gently at him. "He still cares for you."

"I don't know how to let it go." Being angry was easier than acknowledging the way his heart sank when he thought that Gabe might take off and leave again. Gabe could have come home anytime he wanted to. Like when Max had begged him. Instead, he'd chosen to continue the hunt and drive them further apart. Max didn't want excuses or apologies.

He wanted the year John Stone had stolen from them.

Max left Izzie's apartment and jogged to the subway. He rode the train to Park Avenue and ran the short distance to the apartment. The streets were quiet, the skies golden from the sunrise. Max took the elevator, walked to the apartment, and turned the key in the lock. The door creaked when Max walked in. It was dark except for the natural sunlight that pooled on the dark wood. The scent of coffee tickled Max's nose.

In the kitchen, Gabe stood with his back to Max. Gabe turned, eyes widening. "Hey."

Max scratched the back of his neck. "Hi."

Gabe cleared his throat. "You eat anything at Izzie's? I made an egg, cheese, rice thing. It should be edible." He motioned to a cheesy substance in the frying pan.

Max's stomach was still queasy from all the beers. "I'm good."

Gabe bobbed his head, using a spatula to transfer the eggy concoction to a plate. "Okay." He smelled of freshly laundered clothes, shampoo, and soap. His long hair had been tied back into a bun and Max noticed Gabe had shaved his beard into a dashing, neat scruff. His cheeks appeared hollow in the light and there were shadows under his eyes, bringing a gaunt, haunted look to his face that hadn't been there before.

A spasm of fear roiled through Max's stomach. He hardly recognized Gabe. He'd lost weight and muscle, and a T-shirt that had once fit tight across his chest was baggy on him.

Fury made Max's hands curl into fists. He wasn't sure if he would snarl in rage or cry. He wanted to throw himself into Gabe's arms, feed him all the tres leches cakes in the world, and never let him out of Max's sight again. Another part of him wanted to turn away and tell Gabe to go back into the wilderness where he belonged.

Gabe attempted a smile but it didn't reach his amber eyes. Max wasn't sure how he looked to Gabe, but his scent was surely betraying every conflicting emotion. "Have fun last night?" Gabe asked.

"Stop it."

Gabe's fragile smile slipped from his face.

"Stop pretending like everything's normal. You know it isn't."

Gabe slumped, his chin to his chest. "Sorry." His voice was so soft, defeated.

Max swallowed hard, trying to ignore the stab of guilt that pierced him.

"One phone call. A text. Email. Anything. Five words, one word. Just to tell me you were fucking *alive*. How hard would that have been?"

Gabe wet his lips. "We went off the grid."

"Hey, Max. I'm going off the radar. Don't worry, I'll get back to you as soon as I can." Max raised his arms and dropped them at his sides. "It isn't hard."

Gabe nodded, eyes on the floor. "I would have. Phones died."

"Then you could have just come *home*." Max's voice broke. "But no. Revenge was more important to you than me having to survive months of dread. Of not knowing. Of praying you were still alive." Max blinked hard, trying to hold on to his anger before it turned into something soft and weak.

Gabe's throat bobbed heavily when he swallowed. He met Max's gaze, his eyes damp and glimmering. "I'm sorry."

That choked whisper ripped the floor out from under Max's feet. "What does 'sorry' matter when you might leave again?"

Gabe flinched. "Max—"

"I'm right, aren't I? Stone's still out there." Max forced himself to hold on to the anger and hurt before it could flee. His sneakers slapped over the floorboards, and he closed the distance until only the kitchen counter divided them. His stomach turned over when he realized how close they stood now, close enough for Max to reach out and pull Gabe against him, feel his warmth, smell him—

Max said through gritted teeth, "How long will you be sorry for? Until it's time for you to take off again at the first sighting of him? Just save it."

Gabe pushed off from the counter as Max tried to stalk past the kitchen and came to stand right in front of him. He froze, inches from Gabe's chest. The scent of him hit Max with such potency, it made him woozy.

"You told me to go," Gabe growled. "I would have stayed, Max. I was ready to, and you told me to go."

Max's hands shook at the reminder. "Was it worth it? Pulling us apart. Nearly losing your mind." Gabe's eyes widened. "Yeah. Ben told me about that. When were you going to? If I'd known that the only other alternative to you dying was you losing your fucking mind, I'd never have let you leave."

Gabe looked away, lip curling to reveal a fang. Max shivered with dread, seeing Gabe so animalistic, as if the line between man and beast were blurring before his eyes. "I didn't know I would be gone so long! How bad it would get without you there."

"Neither did I," Max said, voice thick.

Gabe's breath quickened, a rumble building in his chest. "We were close, Max. So fucking close, so many times. I could smell him. Dirt and grime and wet fur. I would come so close to finally tearing him apart. Snapping his bones. Tasting his blood."

Gabe flicked his tongue over his fangs. Max shivered. "And then we'd find them. Bits and pieces of them. The historians he was killing. Their families crying." Gabe's jaw clenched, eyes widening in fury. "Like he was mocking us!" He slammed his fist down on the counter. Max jumped, his heart in his throat. Gabe's voice deepened to a snarl, and black fur rippled over his arms and face. His eyes flashed.

"Gabe," Max began, his voice small. "You're shifting."

Gabe sucked in a gasp as if he'd been doused in icy water. He raised a hand and touched the tip of his fang. "Fuck," he whispered, his voice shaken. Gabe's eyes dimmed to their normal hue. His fangs shortened. He deflated before Max's eyes and slumped, one hand over his face. His claws pricked at his skin, and Max reached out and pulled his hand away.

"The choices I made had nothing to do with your worth to me, Max." Gabe sounded exhausted in body and soul. "And if I've ever made you doubt how important you are to me, then I'm so sorry."

Max's hands shook as he touched the angular shape of Gabe's jaw, prickly with dark fur. "I wanted to go with you," Max reminded him, throat thickening in anger and something else he wouldn't admit to. "I should have done more. I should have gone." If he'd just fought harder, if he hadn't believed so strongly that he'd only be a burden to Gabe...

Gabe turned his head, his fang scraping Max's skin as his lips brushed the palm of Max's hand. All the breath caught in his throat, and the secret parts of himself he'd locked away behind his hurt and anger were suddenly ablaze. "Next time," Gabe whispered. "If there's a next time—"

Max ached to believe him. He tugged his hand away. "No. There won't be a next time, Gabe. You can't leave again. You can't."

Gabe slumped, his face almost buried in Max's shoulder. His claws dragged across the undersides of Max's wrists, raising gooseflesh. After so many months fantasizing, craving Gabe's touch, the tickle of Gabe's claws on his wrist short-circuited Max's thoughts. He ached for Gabe's hands on him, grabbing his hips, weaving through his hair, his skin hot and bare against Max's body.

"If I had to, I would do it all again. I would go as far away as I had to. For as long as I had to. I will not let John Stone take away anyone else I love, Max."

Max stepped away from him, unable to take another word. "I know how important this is to you. But I can't do this again. I can't share you with vengeance. I can't take any more fear. I can't stand not knowing." Max thought he would shatter into pieces. He was so afraid he'd have to watch Gabe die and that he wouldn't be able to stop him. "This is so fucking hard."

Gabe sank onto a barstool, his face in his hands.

Seeing him so close to breaking down made Max's eyes burn.

"I hurt you, and that's not something I ever wanted to do." Gabe sounded like he was drowning but he pulled himself from the depths and met Max's eyes. "Max, there's no one else for me but you." Gabe's eyes flashed yellow, the wild eyes of an animal.

His teeth were sharp, but he carried on, pushing through the growl in his voice. "I know it's hard right now. I don't know what's going to happen. I don't know if I'll leave again. I don't know if I'll survive. All I do know, Max, more than anything, is that I love you, and I want a future with you.

I want a life with you where we don't have to hold our breaths or fear for our lives."

Gabe's eyes widened, his lower lip trembling as he pulled back, suddenly unsure of himself. The wildness in him faded and he seemed to shrink before Max. "Is that still what you want? A future? With me?"

Max couldn't speak, overwhelmed by the tears on Gabe's face, the devastation in his eyes. Max was still so angry, so hurt. He was sick of worrying that he was going to lose Gabe, sick of wondering how long they had before they were torn apart again.

But damn, he'd forgotten how it felt to be loved by Gabe Reyes. To be someone's entire heart and soul, to have a home for his scarred and world-weary heart.

Max laughed, choked and broken.

"What?" Gabe's eyes darted over his face, wide and frantic.

Max couldn't find the words.

There was no one else for him. Of all the souls in this big, wide world, there would never be anyone for him but Gabe Reyes. Flawed as he was, jagged edges and cracked pieces, Max had made his choice long ago. He'd chosen the good, the bad—all of it.

After a year apart, a terrible year full of uncertainty, loneliness, and fear, Gabe had come back to him.

Maybe he wouldn't stay. Maybe he would leave again and be gone for who knew how long next time. But Gabe had honored their vows to each other, their promise for a future. That promise was cracked, but Gabe had come home to nurture it.

And now he was giving Max the opportunity to choose Gabe back or let their bond fade for good, knowing that no matter what choice he made, Gabe would continue to fight for them.

And Max would, too.

Gabe's breath hitched as Max framed his face, relishing the feel of him between his hands, the sharp lines of jaw and nose and chin. The tremor in his upper lip, the nervous dart of amber eyes, and the incredulous sweep of his brow. Max leaned in, breathing in the scent of him—spring flowers, elm trees, and warm, sun-soaked soil.

So much had changed and yet the fundamental truth never would. The bond that had lain dormant blossomed between them.

Gabe was Max's mate, for better or for worse. Max would have all of him or nothing at all.

A shrill alarm shattered the space between their lips.

"Crap! My classes!" Max lurched away from Gabe and lunged for his phone. His instructor was calling. "I'm so dead!" He'd completely forgotten.

Max tore into the bedroom and grabbed his backpack. Gabe was waiting at the door, holding it open for him. Max hesitated, unsure if they ought to leave things like this.

"Uh, hey... There's this thing tonight at the Plaza Hotel. The mayor is honoring the agency's work in defeating the Moonborn cult." Max's face warmed. "And me, I guess."

"You?" Gabe blinked, wide-eyed.

"Yeah. So, while you were gone, there was this whole... thing." Max squirmed, heating with embarrassment. "I started a werewolf-human alliance club at school, and it got a lot of attention from the media. So I'm getting some kind of award."

Gabe's mouth slipped open. "No way! Max, that's amazing!"

"Anyway, everyone's going to be there, so I'm sure they'd like to see you."

"I'll be there!" Gabe blurted, and Max's heart warmed from his enthusiasm.

"Okay. Bring a suit. You'll need it."

# CHAPTER 7

# WELCOME HOME

As HE NEARED THE end of his shift, it dawned on Max that he and Gabe still had so much they needed to talk about, and it was weighing heavily on Max's heart.

A part of him was still angry, but he knew that beneath that anger was a whole year of hurt. Being apart from Gabe had hurt, and the shroud of fear from nights spent awake asking what if was only just beginning to lift.

"So, talk to him," his mother said through the phone. Max leaned on the bathroom door and ignored the knock from the other side. The bar had two bathrooms and while he hated to be unprofessional and get on his phone at work, he really needed some free therapy. Hence, his mother. "The only way you two are going to get past this is if you talk it out. I know society says men aren't supposed to talk about their feelings but—"

"Fuck that?"

"Exactly."

Max sighed, leaning his head against the sticker-covered door. There was nonsensical graffiti scrawled on the ceiling, probably left by drunks.

"Communication is important in a relationship, Max. For a whole year, you two didn't have that. Now he's back, and if you want to be with him, you need to tell him why you're angry. Tell him what hurt so badly about his departure. I don't know. But don't skip out on the event and go hide in your room."

"I'm definitely going." Even if he hated big social events, he wanted to celebrate the destruction of John Stone's cult, even if the man himself was still out there somewhere. It filled him with pride that the agency and his pack were being celebrated with such a fancy ceremony. "Uh… could you just tell me where I can find a suit?"

After work, Max sought out a clothing store just before it closed and rented a suit. There were many styles and colors to choose from, and Max settled on a pale gray suit with a cornflower blue dress shirt and a black tie. Gabe always liked blue on Max, had said it complemented his red hair.

A train ride later and Max found himself outside the Plaza Hotel. Even though the hotel was an iconic venue, Max had never actually been inside. The doormen rushed to swing open the doors as if he were royalty, and Max's face burned.

He stopped by the concierge desk and they directed him to the Grand Ballroom where the ceremony would take place. Max stared in wonder as the sleek lobby opened up to the Palm Court, named for the four palm trees that flanked the columned entrance.

"Fancy, huh?" Ben stood behind Max, his beard neatly groomed and his bald head nice and shiny. On his arm was a blonde woman with curly hair. She wore an elegant lavender gown that accented her cleavage and pearls around her slender neck. At her side were two young men that shared her blonde hair and Ben's silver eyes. Max smiled, realizing he was meeting Ben's family.

"Hey, Ben. Introduce me."

Ben motioned to the woman beside him. "Heather Brown and my sons, Jackson and Colin."

"Hey!" Jackson waved. His twin looked bored.

Heather shook Max's hand. "So pleased to meet you! Ben tells me you're going to work for the LPA someday."

Max nodded. "That's the dream."

Ben clapped Max's shoulder. "Come on, let's see if we can find the ballroom."

Max followed, remembering Heather was Ben's ex-mate. Ben had mentioned he spent time with his boys on the weekends. Despite their separation, Ben and Heather chatted and smiled at each other like old friends.

"Here we are," Ben said, stopping in the entrance to the ballroom.

"It's beautiful!" Heather exclaimed. Max peered around them and gaped, stunned by the high ceilings with glittering chandeliers, a huge packed dance floor flanked by tables and columns, and a jazz band playing a soulful tune that had people on the dance floor waltzing together.

"There he is, my man Max!" Ryan exclaimed, armed with two glasses of champagne. He came running toward Max and nearly collided with an oncoming server until Zach wrenched him back with a roll of his eyes.

Zach said, with an overexaggerated air of long-suffering, "Let's *try* to get through the evening without you breaking something, Ry."

Ryan gulped his champagne, splashing some down his shirt. "You ever been anywhere so fucking fancy in your life?"

Max laughed. "No way. This is the fanciest my life's going to get. It's all downhill from here."

Heather took hold of her sons' shoulders. "Boys, how about we find a table?" She led them away.

Ben turned to Ryan and motioned to the drink in his hand. "Where'd you get that?"

Ryan led them to a table overflowing with champagne glasses. Ben took a sip and hummed, smacking his lips. "Good vintage."

"Like you know what that means." Ryan snorted. Ben smiled around the rim of his glass and cast his eyes to the ceiling speckled with chandelier light.

Max took a glass for himself and watched the couples dance. He spotted Izzie in the arms of her latest boyfriend of the past four months, the two of them dancing away and stepping on each other's feet. "Is Gabe here?"

Zach glanced around. "Should be..."

Ryan checked his messages. "Said he's stuck on the train thirty minutes ago. Someone save the man a glass of the good stuff." Ryan gasped. "Holy shit, this song is my shit!" He ran onto the dance floor and proceeded to embarrass himself. Ben rolled his eyes and Zach laughed, the sound rich and warm.

The scent of spring flowers and cherry trees caressed Max's nose. Gabe stepped from the crowd dressed in black with a burgundy suit jacket. He wore a little bow tie, and *fuck*.

Why did Max suddenly have a thing for bow ties?

Or burgundy?

Or the way Gabe wore his hair long and tied back, sporting a neatly trimmed beard and mustache?

Max's mouth dried at the very sight of him. Before he could compose himself, Gabe stood before him and his sweet scent enveloped Max.

Gabe's mouth curled into a shy smile and he slid his hands deep into his pockets. "Hey, Max."

Max swallowed, the sound loud in his ears. "Hey."

There was a long, breathless pause.

Zach cleared his throat. "Think I'm gonna go dance with Ry. See if I can out-embarrass him." He took a big step away then darted onto the dance floor.

Gabe drew in a breath, his chest expanding and testing the buttons on his dress shirt. "You look stunning."

Laughing, Max struggled to find breath as Gabe's eyes wandered from Max's shoulders to his toes. "Really? I feel so out of place. Like, where am I?"

"No, no. Luxury suits you perfectly." Max looked up and regretted it as he ran right into Gabe's amber eyes glittering in shades of orange and green like an emerald caught in the light of a flame. Sweat broke out on Max's neck, and desire made his balls tighten.

Max thought he'd still be angry, that the hurt would come at him like a punch to his chest and cave him in. But things had eased since their talk in the kitchen. He'd gotten most of the anger out of his system, said everything he wanted to say.

Well, maybe not everything. Now that some of the anger he'd hidden behind had diminished, something altogether different had risen to the surface, burning hot in the pit of his stomach.

Gabe cleared his throat. "Ben and the others get here okay?"

"Yeah. Yeah, Ryan and Zach are... doing that." They were turning heads as they danced wildly and recklessly to the band's rendition of "Uptown Funk."

"Is Ryan seriously doing the chicken dance?" Gabe snorted.

Embarrassingly enough, yes, he was.

Max looked around and spotted Ben easily as the chandelier gleamed on his bald head. "Looks like the borough president of Brooklyn and the mayor of New York are talking to Ben. Wait, wait, is Izzie getting an autograph from that actress in *Phantom*?"

Gabe whistled. "Nice crowd."

Max slumped in a daze. "It's so wild, all these people here to celebrate the LPA's work."

Gabe squeezed his shoulder. "I think we deserve to be celebrated. Even if Stone is still out there..." Darkness touched Gabe's voice, and Max's heart sank at the reminder.

*Please, no. Not again. I can't be without you again.*

"Max..." A hand settled on his cheek. Max struggled for words as he looked up into Gabe's eyes, fraught and full of so many different emotions. "I know you're still angry at me, but—"

"I'm not." Max's voice cracked, and he wanted to run as his eyes burned. He'd wanted to be strong. "I spent a whole year being angry at you. I can't do it anymore."

Gabe raised his arms toward Max but then dropped them at his sides. Max was grateful, even if a part of him desired nothing more than for Gabe to put his arms around all his broken pieces and hold him together.

"If there's a sighting, if he kills again... will you leave?"

He couldn't bear it, not again. If Gabe left and was gone again for so long, if anything happened to him—

The crowd cheered, making Max jump. Gabe closed his mouth and grimaced, whatever he'd been about to say drowned out by the noise. A guest musician took the stage, and Max thought he recognized her from some popular band.

She introduced herself but Max stopped listening, stopped caring about anything else in the room except Gabe. Gabe parted his lips but before he could speak, a violinist began to play, and the musician invited couples to come and waltz.

Gabe sighed and then smiled, bright and blinding. "If you can't beat 'em, join 'em." He extended an arm to Max. "Dance with me."

He blinked, taken aback. "I can't." His legs were paralyzed at the very thought. Holy shit, he hadn't danced since prom. He didn't even know if he remembered how.

Gabe grinned. "Neither can I." Max looked from his extended hand to Gabe's smiling face. The smile disappeared and Gabe said, "Please, Max."

Max's hand trembled as he reached out, taking Gabe's arm. There was so little of him he hadn't given to Gabe. If Gabe left again, he would take every piece of Max with him, and Max wouldn't be whole without him.

Zach and Ryan cheered by the champagne table. Gabe snorted and ducked his head while Max's face warmed. Ben led Heather on his arm, and she laughed as he pulled her close to dance. Izzie wolf-whistled, her eyes dancing with delight. But everyone in the room ceased to exist as Gabe turned Max toward him, one hand going to Max's waist. Max laughed when he clasped Gabe's waist as well.

Gabe swallowed. "Uh... who's leading?"

"You asked. You are."

"Oh. Okay."

Rolling his eyes, Max put his hand on Gabe's shoulder and took Gabe's free hand in his. He was remembering bits and pieces of his prom. He'd practiced so hard to impress the popular jock who'd asked him.

"I'll move first." He put one foot forward and stepped on Gabe's toes. Gabe jumped and moved his foot back. They took one stumbling step, then another, exchanging awkward smiles and apologetic laughs as toes were trodden on.

Max found himself taking the lead and Gabe followed, settling into a rhythm as the music swelled to the first chorus of the song. Gabe smiled, chandelier light twinkling in his hair. "Where'd you learn to dance?"

"Senior high. Prom." Max groaned at the memory. "The hottest guy in school asked me, so I practiced and practiced. He bailed."

Gabe's face fell. "Why?"

Max shrugged. "He wasn't ready to be seen with another guy. It was fine. I danced with this sweet girl who got ditched, too."

Gabe hummed and took the lead, swaying Max in a circle. Their chests touched, and Max hadn't realized he'd been keeping himself at a distance until Gabe had suddenly closed it. Chests and torsos and hips aligned just right, and Max swallowed hard when he looked up into Gabe's eyes.

"It's not 'fine,' Max." Gabe put his arms around Max's shoulders. Gabe moved them in a slow circle, and Max followed him, every part of him but his feet utterly frozen. "Max, I want to promise you that I'll stay. That I'll never leave again. But I don't know if I can keep that promise."

Max frantically blinked away the wetness in his eyes. He'd known this was a possibility, and he appreciated Gabe not trying to sugarcoat his intentions or make false promises.

"I don't know how long I'll be able to stay before there's another sighting." Gabe touched his cheek to Max's, his stubble scratchy and ticklish against Max's skin. "But can you trust that I'll come back for you? No matter how far apart, no matter how long. I'll always come back for you. Can you trust in that, Max?"

Max swallowed hard, grateful Gabe couldn't see the wetness on his face.

"Max, please say something."

But Max didn't want to. He was done with talking. He grabbed hold of his face, pulled him down, and kissed Gabe Reyes. Fireworks erupted in Max's stomach. It felt like a first kiss until Gabe angled his head and slotted their lips together in a way that was so familiar, it made Max's heart ache.

A strangled sound issued from Gabe's throat, and he clutched at Max like he thought Max would disappear in his arms. Max curled his fingers in Gabe's shirt, touching muscle and bone.

He couldn't believe Gabe was here and not some figment of his imagination, his body warm and hard, the desperate touch of his mouth, the cheeky glide of his tongue.

Drawing back, Gabe caught Max's lower lip between his teeth. Gabe's breath came in hot pants against his mouth, his cheek burned from the scratch of Gabe's stubble, and Max wanted him with a desperation so intense, he could scarcely breathe.

The song ended and the crowd cheered. Gabe asked, breath hot on Max's mouth, "How long until the awards?"

"An hour."

"Good. Plenty of time." Gabe took Max's hand and tugged invitingly.

Curious, Max followed him from the dance floor. Ryan and Zach whistled shrilly at them, and Max's face burned. "Where are we going?" he asked as Gabe led them from the ballroom, not really caring about much else except that Gabe was here, his palm warm and damp in Max's hand.

"Somewhere I can kiss you the way I want to without getting the cops called for indecent exposure." Gabe's voice was low and breathless, and Max's dick gave a twitch against his trousers. He tugged Max close to kiss his cheek, then pulled away to lean on the receptionist's desk. "Hey. I'd like to check in."

Max gaped. "Gabe—"

"Do you have a reservation?"

"Nope." Gabe was giving her his most charming smile. "I know it's last minute, but we won't be staying very long, just the night. Do you have anything available?"

The receptionist checked her tablet. "I have a suite—"

"Perfect, we'll take it."

Max smacked his shoulder. "It would be cheaper to just go to our apartment, like, fifteen minutes away."

Gabe squeezed his hand. "Come on, tonight's special."

Max stood by the elevators while Gabe and the concierge finalized things. Yes, tonight was special. He and Gabe were together again, and if Gabe wanted to be impulsive in his excitement, Max would humor him gladly.

They rode the elevator up to their floor. The minute the doors closed, Gabe had Max's back against the wall, their lips sealed together. The floors sped by all too quickly for Max's liking. The elevator dinged open on their floor, and Gabe moved out of Max's reach and left him grasping empty air.

"I hope that wasn't your best," Max said, grinning as he jogged after Gabe through the long, carpeted halls.

"Oh, you'll see my best," Gabe assured him, feet thumping as he hurried ahead. He almost ran right past their room. He swiped the keycard and held the door for Max.

He gasped in astonishment. "Holy crap!" The room was stunning with high ceilings, a big sitting area with plush, luxurious chairs, and a huge king-sized bed with silky white sheets and gold accents on the gorgeous headboard. Even the bathroom was stunning, with the most inviting bath-tub Max had ever seen.

When he came out of the bathroom, Gabe had opened the curtains to show off the Central Park view. The moon was out, a gorgeous crescent in the sky.

The bed creaked as Gabe dropped down onto the sheets with a groan. Chuckling, Max lay back beside Gabe and gazed up at the high white ceiling.

Gabe stood, kicking off his shoes. He turned away from Max and opened the cuffs of his shirt, fabric rustling as he loosened his bow tie. Max's cock twitched at the sight of Gabe's ass hugged so perfectly by his trousers.

"So," Max said, the blood humming in his veins. "That kiss you were talking about... was it all talk, or—"

Gabe turned around, brows arched. "Oh no. I just plan on taking my time is all." Gabe ran his eyes up and down Max's form. His breath caught, and a rush of desire swept through his stomach.

Max didn't know if he could wait, his cock already stirring to life against the front of his trousers. Fuck, it had been one very long year without Gabe Reyes. Gabe let his jacket slide from his shoulders in a ripple of expensive silk. It piled on the floor behind Gabe's ankles.

"Keep the bow tie on," Max requested, his voice raspy.

Gabe grinned, baring his fangs. "Whatever you want."

Max crawled down toward the edge of the bed so his feet touched the floor and lay back on his elbows, swallowing hard as Gabe came to stand between his open thighs. Gabe's eyes darkened as he stood over him. Craving him close, Max raised his leg and propped his calf on Gabe's hip, twining his leg around Gabe's waist so his ankle rubbed the small of his back.

"You look so good, Max." Gabe gripped Max's ankle and raised his leg high. He gave the shoelaces a tug and eased the shoe from his foot. "Like a pretty little lamb I want to gobble up."

Max snorted.

Glowering, Gabe said, "Okay, wise guy, you try coming up with sexy pickup lines when you haven't had sex in a year."

He removed Max's other shoe and let it thump onto the carpet. Gabe stepped closer to the end of the bed so his pelvis was touching the backs of Max's thighs. Having him there, so close to where Max was aching for him, made Max sigh and wrap his legs around Gabe's waist. He arched his hips, grinning when he rubbed his ass against the erection straining Gabe's trousers.

The breath hitched in Gabe's throat, and his eyes flashed briefly to a wolfish yellow glow. Gabe jumped and raised a hand to his mouth, tracing the curve of a fang.

"Shit..." Gabe whispered, a growly undercurrent to his voice. "Sorry."

Max wasn't afraid of him, even if Gabe's wolf was so close to the surface and craving the time they'd lost. Gabe took one step back, but Max tightened his legs around Gabe's waist. "It's okay," Max whispered, squeezing the sheets and praying Gabe wouldn't make him wait too long. "Don't worry about it. You won't lose control."

Gabe's nostrils flared, his eyes widening. "I don't know that I won't if I… get too worked up."

Max sat up to take hold of Gabe's hands. He pulled and Gabe's knees hit the mattress as Gabe folded. Their chests and stomachs touched, and Max groaned as their hips pressed together. It took everything he had not to rut his aching dick against Gabe's waist, but he held back. He framed Gabe's face in his hands.

"You won't. I'm here. We're together." Max closed his eyes, basking in the bond that burned so bright between them, the harmony between their wolves, content and happy. Max ran his fingers through Gabe's hair, freeing long, wavy locks from his ponytail to tumble to Gabe's shoulders. Gabe shifted his hips and a spasm of want and need went through Max.

"Gabe, whatever you need to do—take your time or don't—I need you to do *something*." Just having Gabe in his arms was making Max so hard he could barely stand it. Gabe rolled his hips, his lip between his teeth and eyes closed tight. Max arched off the bed, breathless with need. "Yeah. Fuck. More. Just like that."

Gabe did it again, and Max's eyes rolled back. He fumbled with the buttons on Gabe's shirt while he occupied his mouth with Gabe's. Gabe sat up and loosened his bow tie enough to flail out of his shirt and chuck it somewhere. Max pulled him back down, crushing their lips together.

Reaching between them, Max tore at his belt buckle and yanked down the zipper. Gabe tugged on Max's pants, and he raised his hips and wriggled out of them. Max fumbled with the buttons on his shirt. "Help me."

Gabe made as if to rip Max's shirt open.

"No!" Max said, much louder than he'd meant. Gabe froze. "Sorry, just—this was really expensive and it's a rental."

"Got it." Gabe grunted, his mouth hot against Max's neck as he worked Max's shirt open. Bucking his hips, Max drove his hard cock against the bulge in Gabe's trousers, and he retaliated with a bite against Max's bare collarbone, grinding his hips into Max's erection.

Panting and aching for more, Max was mindless from wanting, thinking if Gabe didn't fuck him soon, he'd flip Gabe on his back and ride his cock for all he had.

His claws dug into Gabe's shoulder as Gabe kissed his way down Max's chest, stopping to flick his nipples with the tip of his tongue. Max bucked his hips, urging Gabe for more.

Growling in response, Gabe grabbed Max's ass. "Let me savor you, Max. Fuck, do you have any idea how badly I've wanted this? How many nights I fantasized about the things I'd do to you if you were there?"

"Show me," Max said.

Gabe yanked down Max's underwear and he swore he heard Gabe growl when Max's cock slapped heavily against his abdomen. He squirmed out of his underwear and toward the head of the bed, giving Gabe room to sprawl between his legs. Gabe kissed and sucked a trail of hickeys down Max's abs, and Max stopped breathing as his hot breath blazed over his cock, making it twitch and his balls tighten. Gabe took him in his hand and a jolt raised Max's hips from the mattress.

When Gabe swallowed him down to the root, Max shouted at the ceiling and slapped his fist down on the mattress. The hot, wet suction of Gabe's lips had him bucking off the bed. Gabe drew back to suck on Max's cockhead, giving him enough room to fuck into his mouth.

Fuck, he'd forgotten how good Gabe looked when he sucked Max off, ruby red lips stretched wide around him, his eyes dark and mischievous as he let Max use his mouth.

"Fuck... Yes. Oh my Goddess, yes." Max moaned at the ceiling, curling his fingers in Gabe's hair and squeezing. He groaned his disappointment when Gabe pulled off and grinned, his lips flushed and slick.

"I missed this," Gabe said, pressing a kiss to Max's stomach. He reached beneath Max and squeezed handfuls of his ass. "I missed the way you moaned when I sucked you off."

Gabe wrapped his mouth around Max's cock again, sucking the swollen head and licking up precum. "Missed your cock. That perfect ass of yours." He gave one of Max's cheeks a slap for emphasis, grinning when Max whimpered his approval.

Gabe bowed his head toward the back of Max's thighs. "Your pretty pink hole."

The slick, wet heat of Gabe's tongue lapped at his entrance and Max bit his lip to stifle his cry of gratification.

Max grabbed at the sheets and squeezed, drawing his knees up toward his chest as Gabe licked from his hole to his balls. "Fuck. Gabe. More. I need more."

Gabe had the gall to pout at him from between Max's thighs. "You didn't miss anything about me, Lobito? I'm hurt."

Max knew he was joking, but his heart ached. "Of course I did. I—oh!" Gabe sucked Max's left testicle into his mouth, rubbing the other with his thumb. "That's it. Like that." Gabe tongued his hole, breaching the tight ring of muscle and licking into Max. He fisted Gabe's hair, reduced to whimpers as Gabe swallowed his cock back down. "Yes! Yes, Gabe. So good."

Gabe growled around him, and Max's balls tightened. Gabe's eyes flashed as he pulled off Max and knelt back. The front of Gabe's trousers was so tight, Max thought his cock would rip a hole right through it. Gabe rummaged in his pocket and pulled out a packet of lube, grinning at Max's astonishment. "I had hopes." Max reached for Gabe's belt, but Gabe batted his hands away. "You want to reward me? Tell me what you missed most about me."

Max's face burned. Gabe ripped open the packet and rubbed lube all over his fingers, then circled Max's hole, making Max's breath hitch when his finger slipped inside him and curled to peg Max's prostate. He threw back his head, raising his hips to ride every curl of Gabe's finger. "This," he croaked. "I missed this."

"Be more specific."

"Missed... missed the way your fingers feel inside me. The way you"—Max groaned as Gabe's knuckle grazed his prostate—"kiss me. Touch me." Fuck, he couldn't think. "I just missed you. Okay? So fucking much." Gabe covered Max's mouth with his, kissing so deeply and tenderly Max thought his heart wasn't big enough to hold the weight of how much he loved Gabe.

"I missed you, too." Gabe's voice, barely a whisper, wavered. He claimed Max's mouth again. Their tongues tangled, licking and rubbing. Max wrapped his thighs around Gabe's waist and rubbed his dick against Gabe's hard abs. He nipped the shell of Max's ear, his breath hot and wet against Max's skin. "Fuck, I love you, Max. I missed you. I missed you." He punctuated each word with a kiss to Max's neck. Then Gabe covered Max's lips with his, but Max broke the kiss with a gasp as Gabe drove two more fingers into him.

"Gabe." Max panted, tipping his head back to bite Gabe's chin. "Please. I need you now. I need you to fuck me and knot me and tie me to you. Now."

Max fumbled between them and found Gabe's belt. It clicked when he opened it. Gabe's pants only made it as far down as the back of his knees, underwear joining the tangle of clothes until Gabe squirmed out of them. Eyes locked on Max's, Gabe curled his fingers around himself and stroked, getting himself nice and slick. Gabe's lip curled, revealing the tip of a sharp fang.

Biting his lip, Gabe looked down and watched, and Max swallowed, realizing Gabe wanted to see the exact moment he entered Max's body. His breath hitched as Gabe's cockhead breached him. Gabe wiped his hands on the sheets and grabbed Max's hips. A groan rumbled from Max's throat, his head tipped back toward the ceiling as Gabe filled him.

"Oh, fuck..." Max gasped, biting his lip to contain himself.

Max raised his hips, and Gabe's pelvis slapped his buttocks. Their groans of satisfaction mingled. For a moment, they stayed just like that, joined and panting as their eyes met.

Closing his eyes, Max reveled in their union, the fullness inside him an undeniable truth that they were really here, together. Max opened his arms and Gabe fell down on him, catching himself on his elbows. Max held him tight, Gabe's breath hitting his neck in hot bursts. Their lips met in a tangle of tongues and muffled moans, each sloppy kiss punctuated by the hard slap of skin on skin.

Gabe drove Max crazy, ramming him so fast Max thought he'd come then and there, only for Gabe to slow down and draw out almost completely before thrusting home. The alternating rhythm kept Max on the edge, raising his hips to chase his release.

"Fuck, Max." Gabe grunted. "You're so tight around me. So fucking perfect." Gabe moaned his praises and their bodies came together. Max reached down and worked his cock, trying to match his strokes to the pump of Gabe's hips. He whimpered, jacking himself fast until he was close. So, so close.

Gabe was almost there, his knot a growing pressure inside Max that filled him so perfectly, Max was reduced to whimpers. Max jacked his cock in his fist until he'd spilled every last drop across his stomach.

Utterly spent, Max slumped into the blankets and let Gabe take his pleasure as he grabbed onto Max's hips and squeezed hard enough to bruise. A powerful shudder ran through Gabe, and he threw back his head with a snarl that showed his fangs. Max's name was a breathless whisper on Gabe's lips, spoken with the reverence of a man who'd found his salvation. The warm, wet tide of his release swept through Max.

Gabe crumpled into Max's arms, kissing his neck, his cheek, his lips. Tangling his fingers in the damp roots of Gabe's hair, Max held him close to lick into his mouth and suck on his lower lip. Gabe moaned and rocked his hips, and Max arched off the mattress as Gabe's knot tugged at his puffy rim.

"Fuck," Gabe whispered. "I feel like a god when I'm inside you, Max."

Max nestled into his shoulder and closed his eyes. They lay tangled together in only their skin, their bodies joined without an inch of space to divide them.

Max tipped his head back, parting his lips as Gabe leaned in with a sigh, and their lips fit together like matching puzzle pieces.

"There really isn't anything you want to say?" Gabe murmured, running his hand through the red curls on Max's chest.

Max's brain was tingling from that amazing orgasm, and it took him a moment to recall the context of Gabe's question.

"Back in the ballroom, from before." Gabe chuckled and nibbled Max's earlobe. Max squirmed, giggling at the ticklish sensation.

"Yes," Max said, running his fingers through Gabe's hair. Gabe propped his chin on Max's chest, eyes wide and attentive. "Next time, if there is a next time... I'm coming with you."

Gabe's eyes widened.

"I know we said I shouldn't. I know why. But your future is my future. If you leave again, then so will I. We'll face him together, and we won't come home until it's done for good this time. Okay?"

Gabe wanted to object. He could see it in his eyes—the fear, the terror that he'd have to watch Max confront the man who'd torn apart his family. But Gabe exhaled and his eyes cleared. He squeezed Max's hand tight. "Okay, mi amor. Okay. Anything else?"

"Yeah, actually." Max smiled. "I love you. So much. And welcome home."

Eyes twinkling, Gabe pressed a kiss to Max's lips. "Love you, too."

Gabe's phone rang. Sometime during their lovemaking, it had landed on the bed. Gabe reached back, brows knit in a quizzical scowl. His eyes popped open. "Oh shit. I forgot about the ceremony." Max clapped a hand over his mouth. They'd ditched everyone. "Hey, Ry."

"Please tell me you two are done."

Gabe grinned. "Oh yeah."

"Dude, come on…" Ryan sounded pained. "The mayor's gonna give a speech in about twenty minutes. Ben's gonna talk too and get the agency's award."

Gabe looked down at where their bodies were joined. "Yeah, that should give us enough time to—"

"No, stop! I'm not listening!" Ryan hung up and Gabe crumpled into Max's chest, wheezing.

Max's face burned but he laughed anyway. "You're horrible."

Gabe kissed Max's smiling lips. "I missed making your face turn that cute pink color."

Max put his arms around Gabe's shoulders and closed his eyes, thinking he'd missed everything about Gabe and that he'd be damned before he ever let him go again.

# CHAPTER 8

# WOLF POINT

"Good, you're back—eww!" Ryan recoiled from Gabe and Max, pinching his nose. "Well, I guess you guys are on good footing again! Congrats! Ugh, my nose!"

Gabe smirked and ignored Max's elbow in his ribs. They'd arrived just in time to catch the end of the mayor's speech. Microphone in hand, the mayor said, "Please welcome Benjamin Stroud of the Lycanthrope Protection Agency!"

The crowd cheered and Gabe whistled. He looked around but didn't see Ben. "Where is he?"

Izzie frowned. "He was by the buffet a moment ago."

Gabe expected Ben to take the stage any time now, but the clapping went on several more seconds and Ben didn't make his appearance. He gently untangled himself from Max. "Be right back." Max nodded, muttering his own speech off his cue cards.

Something wasn't right. Ben hated making big speeches and posturing, but he'd been so excited for tonight, for the agency to get the recognition it deserved. He wouldn't miss this.

He froze as he neared the buffet table. A pang of misery went through Gabe, but it wasn't his emotions. He was sensing Ben's. "Viejo? Where are you?"

Ben, rigid and still, had his back to Gabe. Heather had her arm on his shoulder. Gabe came around beside them and whatever words he'd been planning died in his throat.

Ben was crying, one hand over his mouth, his face red and eyes wet as he stared down at his phone screen.

Gabe didn't know what to do. He'd never seen Ben so upset in all the years he'd known him. "Hey. What happened? What's wrong?"

Heather whispered, "Someone killed Greg."

Ben's hand balled into a fist. He swung, knocking a tray full of shrimp cocktail onto the floor with a strangled roar of anguish. He was gone before most people had turned their heads to investigate the crash.

Gabe followed Ben's trail. Ben had always been there for him; it would be wrong not to do the same for him. If Ben pushed him away, then so be it. Ben had run out the doors toward the park, so Gabe followed his scent through the trees and along a gravel path.

Ben sat on a bench, slumped over with his face in his hands. He said nothing and didn't move at the sound of Gabe's footsteps. Slowly, Gabe took a seat beside him. He was quiet for a moment, staring into his lap.

"I'm so sorry, Ben. He seemed like a good guy."

"The best." Ben spoke around a sob. "Something—some fucking creature got to him in Canada. Killed him while he was visiting extended family."

"Stone." The words left his lips in a growl.

"We don't know that."

"Greg was a historian! That's why Stone was going to Canada. He knew Greg would be there. Ben, it makes sense."

"How would he know Greg was there?"

Gabe's throat clicked dryly. That was a concerning question indeed. How would Stone have information on a councilman's whereabouts?

Ben rubbed his eyes. "This isn't just some random murder. Anyone who kills a councilmember makes them a target for the Council!"

"And who else is crazy enough to risk that kind of wrath other than Stone?"

Ben sighed. He turned away, hunching over. "I can't talk about this. Not now."

Gabe nodded, feeling numb. "Okay. I get it. But I'm here, okay? The whole pack is. When you're ready." Ben said nothing, and it was clear he was done talking, so Gabe turned and walked away.

Izzie, Ryan, Zach, and Max were all standing behind him, their faces full of worry. Gabe suggested they clear out and give Ben his space, but none of them felt like celebrating. Gabe and Max returned to the hotel only briefly to thank the mayor, then walked home.

Later that night, Max held Gabe tight as they burrowed under the blankets.

"Whatever happens," Max whispered, his gentle hands stroking up and down Gabe's back. "We go together."

Gabe held him close and nestled his face into Max's hair. "Yes, Max."

After tonight, he didn't know what the future held. He wished he could go back to hours ago when they'd lain together in that quiet hotel room. They'd only just regained what they'd lost, and Gabe feared it was all going to be snatched away from him.

IN THE MORNING, BEN called. "Hey."

Gabe's heart clenched at the sound of Ben's voice, hollow and blank. "Hey, Viejo."

If Gabe had expected Ben to talk about his feelings, he was mistaken. "The Council's gathering to give Greg a proper burial. They've invited me, but I want you and Max to come, too."

Gabe glanced at Max flipping pancakes in the kitchen. "Us? Why?"

"Alpha Hanson wants to know why Stone murdered his councilman. I told him Stone was picking off historians, and he wants any and all information we have on him."

Gabe's stomach churned. "When's the funeral?"

"This Friday."

Gabe checked the date. "So three days from now." At least it wasn't a last-minute flight.

"Gabe, see if you can convince Max to come. I know it'll be hard considering the cult targeted him the most, but what he knows could be invaluable."

"What's wrong?" Max asked as Gabe hung up, passing him a serving of pancakes.

Gabe took the offered plate. "We've been invited to meet the Council."

Max's eyes widened, and then he frowned. "We?"

"Yeah. They want everything we've got on Stone. Would you be okay talking to them about your experience with the cult?"

Max's knife slipped as he cut into his pancake. Brows pinched, Max stared down at his pancakes as if they'd committed a crime. Gabe touched his cheek. "I'll be right there with you, mi amor."

Max turned his head, kissing Gabe's palm. He smiled, and though it didn't touch his eyes, it was a valiant attempt. "Sure. If it helps."

Gabe leaned over and stole a bite of Max's pancakes.

THAT FRIDAY, BEN, GABE, and Max boarded an early flight from New York to Montana, where the Council had their headquarters.

As they drove from the airport to the town, Ben pointed out the window at a sign along the road. "See that? We're driving through pack territory. Just beyond those trees is the Rock Springs Pack."

Max sighed in awe. "Wow..." Gabe chuckled at Max's wide-eyed wonder. "And they just live in the wild as wolves?"

"Some live off the land. Others have whole towns to call their own. Wolf Point is on pack ground. They share space with two packs, one that calls the town home, and the other that lives in the wilderness. The town is the headquarters for the Council."

"This is so cool! A whole town just for werewolves!"

They drove another hour and arrived in Wolf Point, a town surrounded by dense forest. The town was modest and built along a long stretch of road. The biggest building was the schoolhouse with the clock tower standing tall amidst the fog. Gabe couldn't imagine the population was much more than a hundred.

They passed a gas station and a general store, a bar and a grocery store along the main road, and then Ben took a right and parked in a motel lot. They would only spend a day in the town of Wolf Point but Ben made sure to check them into a nice room. The motel was rustic, made of lumber with a thatched roof, and the rooms were small but clean.

Gabe settled into bed and Max joined him. The quiet of the woods buzzed in Gabe's ears and as he breathed in, Max breathed out against his shoulder. Max threw a leg across his hips, an arm around his chest, and they napped like that for a time, tangled up together with Max's hand in his.

Ben knocked on their door in the afternoon and told them it was time to head out. They returned to the rental car and drove along a dirt road in the woods, where Ben stopped the car and got out. Gabe stepped out too, pebbles and leaves crunching under his boots. A crow cawed deep within the woods, and the wind whispered through the trees in response.

Ben grabbed Gabe's shoulder. "Hey." Ben glanced at Gabe and then away. "You know I didn't mean to be a hard-ass back when you tried to talk to me about... you know."

Gabe threw his arms around Ben and squeezed tight. "I know."

Ben tensed, then patted Gabe on the back and held him for a few seconds longer. They parted with wet eyes and an awkward clearing of throats. Blinking hard, Ben puffed out his chest. "This way, folks." Ben led them from the road and they walked a path crawling with weeds. Distant howls and yips echoed farther within the trees, and the wind carried the smell of fur matted with soil and leaves.

"Are those... graves?" Max gulped.

Gabe followed his stare deeper into the trees where moss-covered graves loomed. "Looks like it."

Ben said, "This forest serves as the cemetery for councilmembers and their families. These graves hold some of the most powerful and revered werewolves of our history, going back to Yngvar, the first alpha of the Council."

"The Council goes as far back as the Vikings?" Max asked.

Ben ran a hand through his beard. "Well, not the Council as we know it today but there's evidence werewolves and humans were working together even back then. Werewolf and human chieftains would host meetings to discuss problems between their people. I guess that's where the Council got their inspiration from. Tons of councilmembers can trace their heritage to chieftains who raided their way over to what would eventually become America."

He touched the bark of an ancient tree, the roots nearly overtaking the grave at the base of the trunk. "Folk say that the spirits of such powerful wolves make the trees grow tall and thrive."

"I don't get it," Max said, sounding frustrated. "If the Council is so strong, why didn't they help with Stone?"

Ben grimaced, shrugging his shoulders. "They did at first, but he's evaded them at every turn, made a total laughingstock out of them, to be honest. They exist to preserve the peace between werewolves and humans. Werewolves killing humans? Humans killing werewolves? That goes straight to the Council. Werewolves killing each other, killing hybrids?"

Ben raised his hands in the air in a humorous blasé gesture. "Not something they wanna talk about. Guess they figure it makes werewolves look bad, and they'd rather not bring it up."

Gabe rolled his eyes and took Max's hand to keep him from tripping over the uneven ground. "At least until Stone targets one of their own, right?"

Between the trees, wolves filtered in and out of sight. They walked in single file and moved as a unit, each stepping in time with the others. At the front of the line, a white wolf with one eye moved with a purpose and strength.

"That's Alpha Hanson," Ben explained. "Next to him would be his mate, June." He chuckled. "Is that Connor? Damn, the boy's gotten bigger."

Beside the pack leaders trotted a pup trying to keep pace with his parents even as he tripped over his own long legs.

"What are you boys waiting for?" Ben peeled off his shirt. "Let's go join 'em."

They undressed and shifted, falling into rank among the other wolves. The wolves turned their heads and scented the air but didn't slow their pace. At the back of the line, drums beat to the rhythm of each paw step. Four humanoid shifters carried a stretcher bearing the body of the deceased councilman. Gabe recognized Greg at once by his bald head and clean-shaven face lined with the marks of a life well lived, looking as peaceful as if he were sleeping.

Hanson and June suddenly split apart, leaping on top of a fallen tree overlooking a freshly dug grave. Towering over the pack was a statue carved from a tree of the She-Wolf nursing the twins Romulus and Remus. The wolves split up, gathering around the open grave but leaving enough space so that the body could be brought before it. Ben sat between Max and Gabe. The older wolf's body shuddered, and he whined. Gabe and Max pressed close so their flanks touched his.

As the moon rose over the treetops and stars covered the sky, Greg Harris's body was laid to rest and covered with soil. Alpha Hanson tipped his head back and howled to the night sky, and Gabe's fur bristled as the other wolves echoed him. A deep, throaty howl spilled from Ben's throat as the wolf turned his face to the moon. Max's warbling song filled Gabe's ears and made it impossible to resist joining the song of the pack.

When his eyes opened, Alpha Hanson was human. He swept his one-eyed gaze over his pack. "We bade Greg Harris farewell as wolves. Now we'll say our goodbyes as humans. I invite all of you to come to my home just up the road. We'll eat, drink, and remember all the ways his life has colored our world."

The wolves went their separate ways into the trees, shifting to their human forms. Alpha Hanson extended a hand and helped June from the tree, her blonde hair swaying around her naked shoulders. She was heavily pregnant, and a second quiet heartbeat emanated from within her.

Gabe followed Ben and Max back to where they'd left their clothes and they dressed in silence and returned to the truck. Just up the road was Alpha Hanson's cabin, nestled between the trees. It was a two-story countryside lodge with a deck on the second level.

Stepping inside, the house smelled of freshly cooked venison roast and various seasoned vegetables. June had also prepared apple pie for dessert. Various members of the Council had brought their own food, and the dining room looked like a banquet with all the dishes laid out.

Max headed for the bathroom and Gabe grabbed a plate to begin loading up on food. There came a sniff from nearby accompanied by a low growl. Gabe whirled around and found himself under the glare of a werewolf, the strong scent of lunar flowers marking him a pureblood. His appetite threatened to fade as he realized there were others staring and turning up their noses. Spooning mashed potatoes onto Max's plate, Gabe kept his eyes fixated on the table.

He hadn't realized he was surrounded by so many pure-blooded werewolves. He'd had no reason to notice or care, yet these assholes couldn't spare him the same courtesy. Really, *these* people were members of the Council? They should be more open-minded.

Gabe piled a couple plates with a little of everything and sought out Max, who was sitting in the living room before the empty hearth and looking uncomfortable to be surrounded by so many strangers all asking him questions. Gabe held out a plate and settled in beside him as he growled a warning and chased off Max's admirers.

Max sighed. "If one more person asks me about my red fur..."

"People been giving you a hard time?" If anyone bothered Max, Gabe was dragging him out of there.

"No. I mean people have been staring at me but they haven't been rude."

Gabe growled. *Great.* "Where's Ben?"

"Talking with Hanson, I think." Max dug in, cramming his mouth full of thinly sliced venison and creamy mashed potatoes.

Gabe didn't recognize any of the werewolves scattered around the house. He'd only been a little kid when his father had brought him and his mother to Montana for a work trip. Gabe and his mother had gone hiking and fishing while his dad worked, and then they'd been invited over for dinner at Alpha Hanson and June's house. The alpha pair were the only ones Gabe remembered.

"It's been a long time since I was here," Gabe admitted around a mouthful of venison. "Last time I was in this home, my dad was still around and Izzie hadn't been born yet."

Max's face pinched. "Yeah? It must feel weird."

Gabe hummed. It hadn't, not until he realized there was a memory lurking in the back of his brain. He remembered being in this room, sitting on his mother's lap until his father came up to him with a plate of food. He blinked, throat tight all of a sudden.

"Gabriel? Gabriel Reyes?"

A tall, slender man leaned in the archway, a glass of wine dangling between thin fingers. He surveyed Gabe with a raised brow, teeth bared in an intrigued half smile beneath a neat goatee. He smelled sweetly of lunar flowers, marking him as a pure-blood werewolf. He dressed immaculately in a pressed dress shirt and ironed pants, his dark hair parted neatly to one side.

Gabe's skin prickled, a growl wanting to burst from his chest. Something about that smile and wandering gaze, burrowing like parasites under his skin, rubbed his wolf the wrong way. Perhaps he was just unsettled. He was far from his territory and among strangers mourning a man who'd been murdered.

"Yeah. How do you know my name?" Gabe forced a smile, resisting the urge to scratch.

A little laugh spilled from those ever-smiling lips. "I'm so sorry. You probably don't remember me. I'm Councilman McCready. Aaron Mc-Cready. I'm Alpha Hanson's beta—that's his second-in-command, if you're unfamiliar with the council hierarchy. I knew your father back when he served the Council. You're the spitting image." His eyes darted to Max, arched brow furrowing. He flashed his teeth with a curious tug of his lips. "You're rather hard not to notice. Both of you. After all, there aren't any hybrids on the Council—excluding your late father, of course."

Gabe swallowed a growl. The way McCready kept showing his teeth made the hair on the back of his neck bristle. Especially when he did so with his eyes on Max.

"Speaking of your family, how's your mother? It's been years since we last met." He raised the glass to his lips and drank.

"She's good, thanks."

McCready smiled, teeth stained crimson from the red wine. Narrow eyes lingered on Gabe as he took another sip. "Good, good. You look like her. The same eyes, even your nose."

"So I'm told." Gabe tried to smile but it was hard when his skin wanted to crawl off his body.

"Excuse me if I'm rude, Mr. Gallagher, but I couldn't help noticing your unusual wolf form during the funeral. I have never met a shifter in possession of a red wolf. It's highly unusual."

Gabe's jaw tightened. How did McCready know Max's name? Perhaps Ben had mentioned him.

Max had the good grace to laugh. "I know. I've already had quite a few admirers."

"Of course. You must be a sensation wherever you go."

Max's ears reddened. He was uncomfortable, too.

"I hope you both have been treated decently." McCready tapped a sharp nail against the thin glass. "Some would say hybrids have no right to be here tonight, that they have no place in council affairs at all."

Gabe looked into those dark eyes and couldn't read them. They sparkled but they were as vacant as a corpse's. His smile persisted, as if he were constantly laughing at some joke only he could hear. It made Gabe's stomach squirm. "What do you think, Councilman McCready?"

McCready took a sip of wine. He swiped his tongue over his red lips. "I think everyone has their uses in the betterment of our kind, Mr. Reyes. Even hybrids. Your father, especially, taught me never to underestimate the tenacity of hybrids."

Gabe smiled, but it was hard to hold. *You needed someone to teach you hybrids were worthy of respect? Asshole.* But that was the world hybrids lived in, he supposed. "He worked hard all his life to prove that our blood didn't make us any less strong or deserving of respect."

McCready raised his glass. "That he did, Mr. Reyes. It's a shame his work was never finished."

Bitterness formed a lump in his throat. Max took his hand and squeezed tight.

Alpha Hanson addressed the room, "There are urgent matters that we must discuss regarding the circumstances of Greg's passing. But as tonight is a night for remembrance, we'll do so tomorrow at town hall. I'm sure you've noticed our guests, Benjamin Stroud, Maxwell Gallagher, and Gabriel Reyes. They are here to provide us with any information they can regarding Greg's passing. Treat them with respect. Tonight, they are pack."

His single eye wandered to Gabe's and sent a ripple of anticipation down his spine. He and Max had been invited for a reason, and Gabe could only guess it had to do with the LPA's knowledge of John Stone. They must suspect he had some involvement in Greg Harris's murder. Stomach fluttering in excitement, Gabe squeezed Max's hand and stood.

"How interesting. I can't recall the last time hybrids sat in on one of our meetings." McCready hummed, breath misting his wine glass. Something in his tone sullied his posh manners and gave the word "hybrid" an ugly inflection. "This is a memorable evening indeed."

"Nice talking to you, Mr. McCready," Gabe said and silently added, *Hope it's the last time we'll talk.*

"Of course. It was nice meeting you, Max. I'll see you both tomorrow."

"Yeah. Same!" Max had the good grace to smile but it quickly fell away when he turned his back. Gabe glanced back and curled his lip as McCready's narrow eyes followed them from the sitting room.

"'Even hybrids!'" Gabe snorted. "Please. You think he's any happier we're here than these other closed-minded dicks?"

"I don't know how he knew my name," Max whispered, brows knit in confusion. "That really creeped me out for some reason." Gabe slipped an arm around Max's broad shoulders.

"Maybe Ben talked to him." Gabe led him to the door where they found Ben pulling on his shoes.

"Ready to go?" Ben asked. "I wanna say good night to the Alphas first."

Right on cue, Alpha Hanson and June came to see them. June gave Ben a warm, lasting hug. "It was so good to see you, Ben."

"It's been a while," Ben agreed. "This is Gabe and his mate, Max. You're familiar with Gabe. Max will be joining the LPA once he graduates from the academy."

Alpha Hanson dipped his head. "It's a pleasure to meet you, Max. Ben's spoken highly of you."

Max flushed around the ears and tilted his head back to show his throat in deference. Gabe chuckled.

Ben slapped Max on the back. "Lighten up, Little Red. Hanson's not that kinda alpha." He turned to June. "I had no idea you were expecting another pup."

June's face glowed in excitement. "Yes, a little girl. Only two more months to go." She rubbed her stomach in anticipation.

Ben clasped Hanson's hand. "Congratulations, man."

Hanson laughed, the sound as rich and warm as melted butter. "Connor's very excited, aren't you, cub?"

Connor hid behind his mom's legs, face pinched as he tugged on the hem of her skirt. "Mom. I'm tired." June stroked his hair in response and he buried his face in her leg.

"Hey, Con. It's been a long time! You're a big guy now!" Ben put his hands on his knees and knelt at Connor's level. The boy opened big blue eyes, blinking at Ben from under a shaggy mop of fair blond hair. He smiled shyly.

Max smiled. "Thanks for letting us into your home. Your mom and dad make an awesome venison roast."

"Yeah, it's good," Connor agreed.

"It's a delight to see you again, Gabriel." Hanson shook Gabe's hand, his grip firm and warm, causing Gabe's hand to tingle pleasantly when he pulled away. "My, the last time I saw you, you were Connor's size."

Gabe laughed even as something in his chest tightened. So much had been different then. He looked Hanson in the eye. "We're gonna do all we can to help catch Stone."

Hanson's lips thinned. "Yes. He will regret messing with my pack." The anger in his voice ignited Gabe's blood. "We'll see you tomorrow. Good night."

They followed the dirt road from the house through the woods. Max trailed behind, admiring the fireflies glowing green in the darkness. Gabe glanced at Ben and murmured, "Did you talk to McCready, Ben?"

Ben made a face. "That guy? Hell no. Reminds me more of a snake than a wolf."

Gabe's skin prickled. "Maybe Hanson did then."

"Why?" Ben's cigarette flared between his teeth.

"He knew Max's name even before we'd introduced ourselves."

Ben rolled his shoulders. "How's that strange? I've mentioned Max before to Hanson. Maybe he let it slip to McCready? He is Hanson's beta, after all."

Gabe couldn't answer. It shouldn't be strange, not really. If it were anyone else, it might not have stuck in his mind. But something about Aaron McCready made his fur stand on end.

# CHAPTER 9

# THE COUNCIL

Seven o'clock sunlight spilled through the curtains, golden, bright, and prying beneath Max's shuttered eyes, which were crusted with sleep.

Peering over Gabe's bare shoulder, he squinted at the window that had a view of the pine forest across the road. The quiet hummed in his ears until a few crows cawed, and Max sighed, his body warm beneath the blankets. He nestled against Gabe's back, breathing in the smell of his hair and clean skin.

He hadn't realized Gabe was awake and was pleasantly surprised when he leaned his back against Max's chest. Max dropped an arm across Gabe's stomach, smiling as warm fingers squeezed his hand. When Gabe rolled onto his back, Max crawled on top of him and nuzzled into his neck.

"Morning, mi amor." Gabe's voice was gravelly with sleep.

"Morning." Their lips met, slow and chaste, until Gabe slipped his tongue past Max's lips, sliding theirs together in slow, lazy strokes. Their lips were chapped and Gabe's breath was sour, but Max's blood simmered with every gentle press.

"Sleep well?" Gabe asked, his lips tickling Max's.

"Kinda. I was worried about the meeting."

Gabe frowned. "Why?"

Max shrugged. "I don't know. Just wondering what will happen, I guess. That would be something if they all decided to go after Stone."

Gabe's eyes lit up. "Last night, I got the feeling things will be different. Hanson is pissed. Maybe Greg's murder is the kick in the pants the Council has needed to get their act together and hunt down Stone."

Max hoped so. When they were ready to get up, they took a shower together. Max closed his eyes, enjoying the warm steam and the even warmer press of Gabe's body slick and wet behind him. Large hands gently detangled Max's hair, rubbing in shampoo.

He tipped his head back to keep the soap out of his eyes and smiled as warm, wet lips covered his. Max turned around to face him and glided a cloth across Gabe's chest, enjoying the way his pectorals tightened under his touch.

When he drifted down past Gabe's hips, Gabe hardened at his touch. Max gave his erection a squeeze but resumed soaping Gabe's chest.

"We can't," Max said, laughing when Gabe growled his disappointment. "The whole Council will know."

"Let them."

But Gabe settled with a firm pinch to Max's buttock and left it at that. When they stepped out of the shower clad in fluffy towels, there came a knock at the door. Ben's voice called, "Gabe, Max, we should head out. The meeting's in thirty minutes."

Max didn't get the chance to bemoan missing breakfast since Ben had brought a box of donuts for them to snack on in the car as they drove from the motel to town hall.

Max crammed a maple bacon donut in his mouth, then wiped away the glaze on his lips. His stomach twisted at the sight of city hall, an underwhelming building smaller than the schoolhouse a few streets down, though it did boast a domed ceiling.

The golden sunlight from earlier had been choked out by fog and dense gray clouds, and the air was thick with moisture as Max stepped out, exhaling to calm his rapidly beating heart. A distant rumble of thunder warned of a coming storm on the horizon as they climbed the steps to the double oak doors. Judging by the flood of different scents, many of the Council were already here.

Gabe squeezed Max's hand and offered a sweet smile. "Relax."

Max nodded, not understanding why he was so nervous.

Their shoes squeaked on polished wood floors. On the wall hung numerous paintings with plaques declaring the names of each subject.

Ben pointed at the paintings and rumbled, "These are all notable councilmembers. That right there's Kirsten Blackwood. She spent her whole life dedicated to empowering female shifters, trying to make sure they were treated as equals.

"Thing is, once we began to live among society, female shifters were treated differently than their male counterparts. Back in the wild, females were always considered equal to males when it came to hunting and raising a family."

Max spotted an empty patch of wall. "Looks like one of the paintings is missing."

Gabe's hand tightened around Max's. He growled. "My father's."

Ben clicked his tongue in irritation. "Seriously?"

Gabe dropped Max's hand and marched to the wall, slack-jawed and eyes blazing. "It's bad enough he was killed for being a hybrid, but his own councilmembers won't respect him, either?" Gabe scowled. "This fuckin' town..."

Max's stomach churned. He was even less eager to be in a room with pure-blooded werewolves now.

"Gabe, we can brood about this later. Let's go." Ben shouldered past to the meeting room. Gabe followed, jaw tightly clenched. Inside the meeting room, a representative from each state filled every stand.

As far as Max could tell, only one seat was empty, and he guessed it was Greg Harris's. Hanson took his seat in the center beside June and a lull fell over the room. Gabe, Ben, and Max packed into an empty bench.

Max's skin prickled as faint sniffing filled the air. Some heads turned, and narrowed eyes wandered over him. Gabe's hand settled on his knee and squeezed reassuringly.

Alpha Hanson's voice carried clearly through the room. "Greg Harris's murder cannot go unpunished. An attack against one of us is an attack against our pack. We must propose a course of action to ensure this reprehensible act is punished to the fullest extent. John Stone was sighted in Canada shortly before Greg's murder, and Gabe and Ben tell me Stone was taking the lives of well-known historians across the country, though we have yet to learn why."

Gabe's hand tightened around Max's.

Hanson carried on, his voice brittle with contempt. "For years, John Stone and his cult have terrorized the hybrids in our communities all across the country and now not even pure-blooded wolves are safe from his barbarity."

Frantic whispers spread through the room.

"It cannot stand!" barked a representative from Alaska.

A representative from New Jersey slammed her hand on the table. "He must be stopped! My friend lost her hybrid son to that monster!"

Gabe muttered, "And notice how all it takes is one pureblood's death for everyone to get up in arms. Fucking ridiculous."

Ben clasped Gabe's shoulder.

"Why has he targeted one of our own?" a councilwoman from Texas asked. "Greg wasn't even a hybrid!"

Hanson's growl reverberated through the room and the voices of the Council echoed in the sudden silence that fell. "I can't pretend to know his ways, so I brought in three others who are familiar with Stone. Gabriel Reyes, Benjamin Stroud, Maxwell Gallagher of the LPA, please rise."

Max did so, his legs wobbly as every eye in the chamber landed on him.

A councilman from Nebraska sniffed at the air and growled. "You've brought hybrids into this space, Alpha Hanson? They don't belong here. They're half human!"

"Humans are the oppressors! These hybrids can't understand our struggles!"

A flash of anger went through Max. The hate in those words made him feel small and helpless—as if Richard were looming over his shoulder, fangs bared. He found himself drowning as voices surged around him.

"Take that back!"

"They're shifters, as much as we are!"

"Get them outta here! This space is reserved for pure-blooded wolves!"

Gabe bared his razor-sharp teeth in outrage. "My father served on this council for years! I have every right to be here!"

"Quiet!" Hanson's roar cut through the squabbling crowd. His calm returned, going from a roaring flame to a simmer. "These shifters from the LPA single-handedly destroyed Stone's grip on the state of New York. Meanwhile, Stone evaded our detection for years, disappearing just as we'd closed in on him.

"The time's come for us to stand together, whether hybrid or pureblood. John Stone didn't murder Greg Harris without reason. As you all know, Greg was versed in lore going back thousands of years. It's possible Stone targeted him for the knowledge he possessed. Ben, your people are familiar with Stone and his ways. What do you think?"

Ben cleared his throat, scratching at his beard. "Max's stepfather was a member of the cult. Max, would you like to tell them?"

Max swallowed, his throat dry and his heart pounding as the weight of every eye in the room landed on him.

"You don't have to, but it would be helpful, Max," Gabe murmured, squeezing his hand.

Max didn't want to revisit his experiences from a year and a half ago, but if it could aid in the Council's hunt for Stone and stop anyone else from being hurt, he'd be a fool to stay quiet. He relinquished Gabe's hand, knees trembling.

For a moment, his brain was full of static. His dry tongue ran futilely across his chapped lips. He squeezed his hands into fists—he had to say something.

"Um..." He wanted to hit himself.

"Breathe," Gabe whispered.

Max sucked in a breath and just barely heard Gabe exhale. Max echoed him and his mind cleared as he found a starting point. "My wolf is red. Somehow, that made me special in Stone's eyes."

Shit. He'd lost his train of thought. Max tried to gather himself, blinking hard as his eyes darted around the room and settled on Hanson, who was watching him respectfully. Beside the Alpha, McCready leaned forward in his seat, fingertips touching in a triangle. Max's skin itched as those narrow eyes x-rayed him.

"Stone seemed to think that being a red wolf made me important. That it gave me some connection to the She-Wolf, or—"

Nebraska snarled, "Bullshit! Why should the goddess favor a fucking hybrid of all things?"

"That's blasphemy!" another cried.

"The She-Wolf doesn't favor mutts!"

Gabe lurched to his feet. "Call him a mutt one more time, asshole!"

Fury brought Max's claws out, piercing his knuckles. "It's true! He tried to kill me, wanted to rip out my soul and claim it for himself! He wants to be a god! I can't make this shit up!"

"Alpha Hanson, you expect us to believe the goddess would bless some mutt? That's an insult to the She-Wolf!"

Hanson boomed, "We're not here to argue about religion! Councilman Borelli, if you interrupt one more time, you will be dismissed from this meeting. Is that understood?"

Borelli threw back his chair, and it crashed to the ground. "Spare me. I can't sit here and listen to such fucking disrespect! Any wolf in this room who wants to call themselves a pure-blooded son or daughter of the She-Wolf, walk out with me!"

Borelli stomped out and a handful of others followed. The doors slammed. Max's heart hammered against his chest. McCready had the biggest shit-eating grin on his face, his eyes dancing with glee as if this were all nothing but a game show to him. Max wished he could share the councilman's amusement, but he was too pissed off and shaken up.

Hanson huffed. "Good. Maybe now we can finally get through this meeting. Please continue, Max."

Max exhaled, trying to anchor himself. "Stone captured me, tried to harvest my soul. He kept going on about how only he deserved it, how he wanted to be a god and overthrow the She-Wolf. He wanted to use my soul to open the way to the She-Wolf's realm. I escaped. I... awoke something within me. Strange powers I didn't know I had."

"Fascinating," McCready spoke for the first time. "These powers, describe them."

Max's head spun. He still didn't know how to describe his abilities. "I don't know. I could... control gravity and water? Heal my own wounds."

McCready's mouth went slack with what seemed like awe. "If that's true, then it's no wonder Stone wanted you. How could he not?"

"Yes, it's all very interesting." Alpha Hanson sounded more worried than impressed. "This meeting is adjourned. We'll resume shortly once I've had a word with our lore masters. This insight into Stone's mindset is... worrying. Dismissed."

Many left their seats and ventured outside. A handful of others remained, gathering around Hanson. McCready was among the ones who left, shooting a curious stare at Max as he passed.

Ben grunted as he rolled his neck and shoulders. "Let's go wait outside."

Max split off from Ben and Gabe, wandering out into the humid day. The fresh air chased away the odor of old wood and dust so prevalent in the meeting room.

A chuckle came from behind him as McCready descended the stairs, tossing a lighter up and down in his hand. An unlit cigarette dangled between his teeth. Sunlight didn't suit him, Max thought. McCready looked more like a vampire than a werewolf with his thin features and pallid skin.

"Your face!" He laughed, doubling over. "You have no idea just how unique you are, do you, Maxwell Gallagher?"

Max sighed. "I'm not anyone special."

"Modesty. How cute!" He slapped his knee. A smile splitting his ratlike face in two, he lit up his cigarette. He cocked the lighter, a second cigarette held out in offering.

"No, thanks."

McCready shrugged and took a drag. Max tried not to cough. Cigarettes were so bitter smelling. "Really. The monstrous John Stone wants you as part of his great plan. 'I'm not anyone special,' he says!" He sighed, shoulders heaving with mirth.

"You're not insulted?"

"Insulted? With powers like yours, we werewolves could decide our own place among society. It's our right to rule this world as we once ruled the wilds. Think about it, Max. We're werewolves. Why do we let the humans, the weaker ones, dictate how we behave in society?"

He scoffed, expelling a cloud of smoke into the air. "You know, in the old days, we were wild and living among nature. Untouched, pure. It would be something to return to the ways of our ancestors, wouldn't it?"

Max was too used to the comforts that came with living in society. His wolf loved a good run in the woods, but he couldn't imagine how he'd cope in the wilds long term. "I don't know. I like the way things are."

McCready curled his lip, the first real sign of displeasure Max had seen from him. "That's because we messed with the natural order of things the moment we decided to live among humans. The territories managed by the Council are a good start to returning to the old ways, but we could always do more if we weren't so fixated on not pissing off our human overlords."

"Really? Like what?"

McCready shrugged. "Imagine a world with mountains instead of buildings, clean air and wide-open fields instead of pollution and garbage."

"That does sound nice," Max admitted. He loved New York City, but the smells curdled his insides, and he swore there were probably more rats than people, growing fat on bloated trash bags. "I didn't know you felt so strongly about the environment. That's really great."

McCready chuckled, as if something Max said were funny. Max just wished he could figure out what.

"Max?" Gabe's eyes narrowed at the sight of McCready.

McCready stamped out his cigarette. "Don't worry, I wasn't corrupting the mind of our young friend here." He clapped Gabe on the shoulder and gave it a firm squeeze before he walked off.

Gabe growled as the doors closed behind him. "What did he say to you?"

"Nothing, really." Max took his hand and squeezed.

"He doesn't like our kind, Max. You should be careful around him."

Max walked with Gabe back to the meeting room where the Council had assembled again, filling every seat except the ones vacated by the bigots who'd walked out.

Hanson took his seat and silence fell. "We have concluded that Greg Harris, like the other historians, was killed for his knowledge of the history of Romulus and Remus. It's an ancient story dating back to Roman times, and it's one all of these historians were well versed in. Based on what we know of Stone's aspiration to godhood, it bears disturbing similarities with the story of the twins and the She-Wolf. We will now hear the words of our lore master George."

A wrinkled and bearded man, hunched in his seat, stood and raised his withered voice. "There has only been one other who sought the power of the She-Wolf's soul in all our history: Remus the Betrayer. Legends tell of the twins Romulus and Remus, humans who received the gift of shapeshifting when they nursed from the She-Wolf.

"And so much more! There have been numerous translations of accounts claiming both twins possessed powers of the moon! Powers they used to make Rome into what it is now, and they had wolves at their backs to conquer their enemies."

Hanson cleared his throat. "Such accounts are unproven. Please, avoid unnecessary detail. We're pressed for time."

Max's attention, flagging until now, peaked when the old historian mentioned "powers of the moon." He wondered if their powers had been similar to his.

"The betrayer Remus was full of greed," George exclaimed, making some people jump in their seats. "He craved the power of the goddess's soul in the hopes that by slaying her, he would have the power to crush all of Rome's enemies.

"To achieve this end, he had his druids craft the moonblade, a powerful artifact forged for the sole purpose of killing a god. With a howl from Remus, the moon glowed red and fell toward Earth. A portal to the She-Wolf's realm split the fabric of our world!"

There were numerous chuckles from the councilmembers. Hanson sighed. "Again. Please cut to the chase."

George sighed and continued, his formerly boisterous tone subdued and rushed. "The brothers fought, Remus was defeated, and thanks to Romulus, the She-Wolf's soul was saved. Now it seems John Stone wants this moonblade for a disturbingly similar purpose." He plopped back down into his seat, looking put out.

Max cleared his throat. "John Stone used a druid artifact he'd stolen from the Council to siphon hybrid souls. He tried it on me and it was destroyed. How can that same blade be a threat?"

George shook his head. "That blade, while powerful in its own right, was meant to cleanse the souls of normal wolves, not to harvest them. The *moonblade* was crafted to siphon souls like the goddess's herself. The magic in the blade would preserve the power of the soul, even if the body perished."

Ben's face was pinched in confusion. "You're trying to tell me Stone wants to use this blade to... what, exactly? Kill the She-Wolf, absorb her powers? Then what? Armageddon?"

Hanson said, "John Stone must be stopped. As you and Gabe are familiar with his methods, I'd like you and whoever else you choose to be the ones to stop him. Do you have any objections to this?"

Max clasped Gabe's hand. This was what he'd been hoping for.

"Not at all," Ben growled.

Gabe grinned. "We're on it, Alpha Hanson."

"Then that concludes this meeting. Everything from here on will be between Ben, his pack, and myself."

# Chapter 10

# The Hunt Begins

Later that evening, only four hours before their flight back to NYC, Ben drove them to Hanson's house. June made them a delicious beef stew and Max ate more than he should have.

Connor kept his eyes turned down to his plate and once he was done eating, he hid behind his mother for the rest of dinner. Max smiled just watching him. He was so adorable!

After dinner, June put Connor to bed and Hanson offered them dessert and drinks. Max couldn't resist grabbing a slice of cherry pie while Gabe asked for a whiskey.

Hanson led them to the living room. Excitement and nerves had Max clutching his dessert plate tightly. Gabe sat between Max and Ben, bouncing his knee up and down. Smiling, Max touched his leg to get him to stop.

Ben tapped his fingers against his knees and cleared his throat. "So, we've gotta find this moonblade before Stone does. Any suggestions?"

Hanson touched his fingertips together, a frown tugging at his brow. "Historians believe the blade was sealed in Romulus's tomb. However, the tomb's location has been kept secret for years."

Max's eyes widened. "So how do we find it?"

Hanson folded his leg and reached for his cigar case. He lit one and took a few puffs on it as he thought. "If anyone could tell you... hmm. It would probably be the Moon Brothers, an ancient order of monks. Greg was one of them. He'd go away on pilgrimages in the summers. Supposedly, no one outside the Brotherhood is allowed in or out of the monastery. You would have to ask them directly if they could help you find the blade's location."

Ben grunted. "He mentioned them before, but I got the impression he wasn't allowed to say much. Who are they?"

Hanson took a sip of his decaf. "They're gatekeepers of our ancient history. They are quite secretive."

Ben scowled. "So, how do we find them if they're so secretive?"

"Their order is outside Rome in a monastery within the Apennine Mountains. I've been. It's a lovely hike but quite a drive from the city. If Greg didn't know the blade's location, the monks would certainly be in the know. And if Greg relayed that to Stone, I imagine Stone is already on his way to uncover their knowledge. You'll have to find the monks quickly and warn them. I'd send word ahead if I could, but they're completely closed off to the outside world."

Gabe sighed. "So, go to Rome, find these monks, find the tomb, and destroy the moonblade. Sounds easy."

Ben nodded. "We'll leave right away, Alpha Hanson."

"You and how many others?"

"Gabe, Max, and maybe one more. We'll move quicker if there aren't too many of us, and attract less attention."

Hanson paused, his coffee inches from his lips. "You can't be thinking of taking Max with you."

Max's stomach churned. "Of course I'm going. They're my pack. I want to help."

Hanson set his coffee down. "Ben, I can't allow this."

Gabe snapped, "It's not your decision—Alpha," he added more quietly. He'd splashed whiskey across the floor. "Sorry." He jumped up and went to the kitchen, combing a hand through his hair.

Hanson shook his head in disbelief. "Stone seems to think he could use Max's wolf to enter the She-Wolf's realm. I don't know if that's true or not, but for the safety of this world, we need to believe he knows what he's talking about. Max cannot accompany you."

The fork trembled in Max's hand. "If Gabe is going, then I need to go with him, Alpha Hanson. We're mates."

Hanson scrutinized him. "I don't see any bites."

Max squirmed. "We will be. But last time we were separated, it was hard on both of us."

"Gabe almost went feral, Alpha Hanson," Ben added.

Hanson's brow furrowed over his single eye. "Then it's his responsibility to prepare himself and his wolf properly for the separation. You know this, Ben," he growled with the air of admonishing a foolish child. "And furthermore, if this is such a big concern, then perhaps Gabe should stay behind with Max."

Max bunched his fingers in the fabric of his jeans. Would Gabe even consider staying behind?

"It's not that simple," Ben growled, running a hand through his shaggy beard. "You know what Stone did to his father."

Gabe reappeared, clutching a paper towel.

Hanson rotated his chair toward him. "Gabriel, I understand that Stone has wronged your family, but if being parted from Max is so unbearable, then would you consider staying behind with him?"

An unreadable expression gripped Gabe's face. His eyes darted to Max but he said nothing. Max's chest tightened and for one selfish moment, all he wanted was to ask Gabe to let Stone go and stay here with him. And as Gabe looked his way, the sorrow on his face told Max all he needed to know. He squeezed his fists and blinked down at the floor.

Hanson exhaled in the quiet. "Let me make one thing very clear. To all of you. If Max leaves this country, then you will be putting this world in grave danger. If none of you can take Stone's threat seriously, then I will consider your irresponsible actions a crime against the Council, and I will take action to ensure Max does not fall into Stone's hands. Max and anyone else I deem to be in danger from Stone by association will move in with me and my guards at my Vermont home. He will be safer there than anywhere else in the country."

"But I can't," Max said, horrified by the idea of his life being put on hold. "I have school, a job, I—"

Hanson gave him a look that silenced Max. "I understand that, and we will work together to come up with an arrangement that suits us. But I will not allow you to go about your everyday life with this threat hanging over you, over all werewolf kind. Understood?"

Max swallowed at the underlying threat in Hanson's voice. He wanted to argue. Hadn't he told himself he would fight? Hadn't he promised himself that next time he'd be stronger, that he'd fight to stay by Gabe's side?

"Understood." The armchair creaked as Ben took to his feet. "We have a flight to catch. Thanks for your hospitality, Alpha Hanson. I'll let you know when we're on our way to Rome."

Max clenched his fists. Anger flared inside him, anger at Ben, anger at Gabe for making Max feel like a second priority again.

They returned to the car, already filled up with their luggage, and drove straight to the airport. Max sat in the back seat by himself, blinking as the view beyond the window became a blur. He couldn't do this. He couldn't just let Gabe leave again. How could Gabe still agree to go, knowing what had happened last time?

When they arrived at the airport, they went through security and found a place to sit while they waited to board. Ben slumped with his head back against the chair, his mouth slipping open as he wrestled with sleep. Max buried his nose in his phone and texted his mom to tell her they were coming back. Gabe sat a seat over from him, head tilted back and eyes closed, but it was like an ocean had come between them.

Gabe stood and when he met Max's gaze, he hung his head. "Bathroom," Gabe muttered without glancing back. He slipped into the crowd.

Ben snorted beside Max, jolting awake. He rubbed a heavy fist across his eyes. He caught Max staring and his bushy silver brows furrowed. "Don't look at me like that, kid. What do you want me to say?"

"You know what happened the last time, Ben. Why did you just let Hanson—" Max quickly cut himself off, guilt stabbing at him.

"What? Walk all over me, is that it?" Ben growled.

"I didn't... I just... I don't care about what happens to me. I never have, not when it comes to the pack."

Ben sighed, scrubbing a hand across his weathered face. "This is bigger than you, Max. If you don't care what happens to you, then do you give a damn what happens to the world? What will happen to all of us if Stone can actually become a fucking god? Shit. That still sounds fucking crazy. If he thinks your soul can get him into the She-Wolf's realm, then Hanson's right: you can't be anywhere near him."

Max didn't reply, anger robbing him of words. Ben was right. He knew it, and he hated it. He stood and sought out the bathroom. He shoved open the door and found Gabe at the sink washing his hands. Gabe turned to face him, but he couldn't meet his gaze.

"Max, I'm sorry."

He took in a deep breath, blinking away the sting.

"Max, talk to me. Please."

He balled his fists. "You know what happened the last time you went."

"I'll be more careful this time!" Gabe paced, combing a hand through his hair. "I have to go, Max. I have to do this."

"No, you don't!" His voice bounced off the tiles. "No one is making you do this. You can't just take off again!"

Gabe's lips thinned. "You said if this was something I had to do—"

"I didn't know it would be like this! That I'd be saying goodbye to you not once, but fucking twice." Max's throat closed up. He clasped the sink for support. "I wanted to help you; I thought we were in this together. But we're not." He swallowed, blinking hard. Gabe said nothing, sneakers squeaking on the tile as he paced.

"Stone has to be stopped."

"And I'm supposed to keep the bed warm while you're gone." Tears pricked his eyes, and Max struggled to hold on to his anger. "I can't do this,

Gabe. I can't keep sitting awake at night, wondering when you're coming back, if you're even alive."

"You think this is an easy choice?"

"It sure seemed like it." Max didn't recognize his voice. He'd never sounded so ugly before.

"I nearly lost my mind out there without you!"

"Then stay here!"

"He murdered my father, Max!" The fight went out of Max as tears gleamed in Gabe's eyes. "I can't spend our future together waiting for him to come and take you away from me, too! You heard Hanson! You were *there*. He said you'll be in danger if you come with us, and he's right."

"What about you?" Max said, his throat tight and aching. "What if you lose yourself again?"

"I'll be careful, Max. I'll..." Gabe tangled his fingers in his hair, pacing wildly over the tile. "Fuck! I don't know what the hell to do!"

Heart cracking in his chest, Max closed the distance between them and grasped Gabe's trembling hands in his. He didn't know what to say or do. If Stone thought he could use Max in any way to achieve his insane plan, then Max knew it would be selfish and borderline dangerous to go with Gabe. And asking Gabe to stay wasn't an option after the trauma Stone had caused him.

Max had thought this time things would be different. Things were supposed to be different. They'd promised to do this together, and it was a promise neither of them could keep. Max tried to speak, and only a choked gasp spilled out. He tugged Gabe into his arms and held him tight, and they wept together in the bathroom.

Once they boarded the flight, Max took his seat by the window. Gabe settled in beside him but Max didn't look at him. The plane sped across the tarmac, and outside the window he could see when they left the ground behind and soared among the clouds. Yellow lights from buildings far below twinkled like stars in the night.

Fingers brushed his on the armrest and Max thought about pulling away.

How much time did they have left? Hours? A day?

He slipped his fingers through Gabe's and held on tight. Max wished they'd never arrive in New York. He wished he and Gabe could stay adrift among the clouds forever.

THEY LANDED IN NEW York at the crack of dawn on Sunday. Gabe and Max had just arrived home when Ben texted and asked everyone to meet him at his apartment in Dumbo later that evening.

The agency wolves piled into Ben's apartment and joined Ben at the table. Ben sat at the head of the table, looking as if he'd bitten down on a lemon while he growled out the details of their meeting with the Council. The pack listened without interruption, munching on an all-meat pizza Ben ordered for the meeting.

"I don't get it," Zach said, wiping his greasy hands on a napkin. "Stone murdered a councilman, so why doesn't the Council band together and go after Stone? That doesn't make sense."

Ben sighed. "I know. In my father's day, the murder of a packmate would have inspired the Council to take up arms. They aren't the pack I once knew. Hanson called me before we left, and I got the impression he doesn't trust his own packmates. The Moonborn cult is gone, but he believes too many on the Council are entrenched in Moonborn ideology. And based on the greeting Gabe and Max received, I'm inclined to believe him. He trusts only us to get this moonblade. Worse still, there were wolves among the Council who knew exactly where Greg was going when he went to Canada."

Gabe's pizza sat heavy in his stomach. "Someone in the Council was communicating with Stone. Someone wanted Stone to find Greg."

Ben's jaw tightened. "Right. I just don't know who. But when I do..."

Max slumped. "This is a fucking mess."

Gabe said, "He thinks his own people might, what? Deliver the blade to Stone?"

Ben made a face, his brows casting shadows over his eyes. "I ain't in a rush to find out."

Zach's brows were pulled low over his eyes, his lips thin. "Let me get this straight. Stone wants to kill the She-Wolf, become a god, and take over the world. Man... where'd he get this idea from, villains from Saturday morning cartoons?"

Ryan snorted. "I love how everyone's breezing over the moonblade. Never mind that it's a legendary artifact of immense power. Nothing interesting or awesome about that."

"I'm just saying," Zach said, "This isn't very original, is it?"

Izzie's glare could have set the table ablaze as she set her sights on Gabe. "And you're leaving. Again."

Gabe gnashed his jaw. "Later."

Izzie switched to fiery Spanish. "Will there be a later, Gabriel? You just got back, and you're running off into danger again. What about Max? What about Mother?"

"Leave Max out of this! Ma would understand. That's more than I can say for you!" Gabe sniped back in Spanish.

The table rattled as Izzie slammed her fist down. She bared razor fangs. "You weren't there! She prayed every night for you to come home safely. She already lost Father. She doesn't want to lose her idiot son, too!"

Her words cut right through Gabe and his retort died in his throat.

"Squabble on your own time!" Ben barked. "Least, I assume that's what you're both doing."

"You're being selfish, Gabriel," Izzie snapped.

Outrage set his blood boiling. "At least I'm trying to avenge Dad's death!"

"I said enough!" Ben roared.

Izzie slumped in her seat, seething.

Gabe growled. She didn't understand. Couldn't understand, he reminded himself, exhaling and allowing his claws to turn to dull nails. Their father hadn't died because of her.

"Same as last time, Zach will lead in my stead," Ben announced. "Gabe and I will go. I need one more person to come with us."

"Say no more!" Ryan jumped up. "Come on, Ben, you can't expect me to miss out on all the action, adventure, diving into certain death to retrieve a blade from one of the most legendary stories of our kind? This is gonna be awesome!"

Ben massaged his temples. "You're already giving me a headache, Ry. But fine. You can come. You know the history well. We could use your insights."

"I'll stay. Someone needs to comfort our mother," Izzie said, ice in her tone.

Gabe bristled at her passive aggression. "Something you want to say?"

Izzie's eyes blazed. "Why do you keep on doing this? You're not going to be the one consoling Mother when she hears that you've been killed or—"

"Izzie," Ben stated. "You know how important this is to him."

Izzie looked as if she'd been slapped. "You can't just—Ben, please. Gabe just got back. Let someone else go for him!"

"Izzie. I've made my decision."

"Screw this!" Izzie knocked her chair back as she hurtled to her feet. "Fine. Go ahead and split my family apart again, Ben." She turned on her heel and stomped out, slamming the apartment door behind her and rattling the pictures on the wall. Ryan whistled.

"She has a point," Max muttered.

Gabe wished he hadn't heard that.

"Then it's decided," Ben rumbled, his voice like thunder on the horizon, ushering in a coming storm. "Gabe, Ryan, we'll leave on the first flight to Rome tomorrow. Head home, pack your things."

Gabe's stomach twisted. He looked toward Max, only to see him sliding out of his seat and making for the door. Their time was running out. He had no right to ask Max to forgive him or not to be angry with him, but he didn't want them to part like this.

"Both of you, wait."

Gabe turned toward Ben, his throat dry as he tried to swallow at the intensity in Ben's silver eyes.

"This isn't some camping trip into the wilderness. I don't know how long we'll be gone, how far from civilization we'll have to stray to find the moonblade. Being out among nature can be good for our inner wolves, but for long stretches of time, it can wear on our humanity. The pull of your inner wolf will be harder and harder to ignore the longer we're in the wild. Bring something with you that evokes a strong emotion in you. It will be an anchor to your humanity. Choose carefully. I don't want to lose either of you."

"Right," Ryan said. "I'll bring my teddy bear."

"Ry," Ben growled.

"I got it, Ben. I'll be careful."

His skin prickled as Ben's heavy eyes stared right at him. He nodded his understanding.

Gabe took the elevator down and found Izzie waiting in the lobby.

She exhaled, her arms wrapped around her chest. When she finally spoke, it was in Spanish, meant only for Gabe's ears. "He's already been gone for longer than either of us knew him. Father."

Gabe's chest tightened. "He shouldn't be. He should be here with us."

"But he's not." She turned to him, eyes wide and imploring, and she was a little girl again, scared for her no-good, troublemaking big brother. "He never will be, and killing Stone won't bring him back. I miss him, and I wish he were here every single day! Do you see me risking my life, leaving behind the ones who love me, for revenge?"

Gabe's claws dug into his palm. "That's because—look, this is bigger than just me and revenge now! Weren't you listening to anything Ben said?"

Izzie looked him straight in the eyes and said slowly, "If this isn't about revenge, Gabriel, then let someone else kill Stone."

Gabe growled, his nostrils flaring. He couldn't lie, not to himself or to his sister. He had to be the one to put his fangs into Stone's neck. He had to know that the son of a bitch was dead before he could ever rest easy. Raking his hand through his hair, he winced as his claws cut across his scalp.

"Fine! It is about revenge. It's always been about revenge, Izzie. And you know why? No, you fucking don't. Because you don't have to wake up every day realizing that you're the reason Ma cried herself to sleep, that the reason our family is broken is because Dad died trying to save *you*."

The hard lines in Izzie's face softened, and she blinked hard, her tears threatening to rip Gabe apart at the seams. "It wasn't your fault."

Gabe sucked in a breath that cut like a dagger in his lungs. "Save it. I don't believe it. I never have."

"Gabe, don't ruin this." Her voice went low and soft. "Don't throw away what you have with Max. Don't let Stone destroy that, too."

Gabe's anger faded, and he blinked hard, uncomfortably bare without it. "Max is why I've got to stop him. Because if I let him, Stone will take him from me." He sucked in a gasp and his stomach churned. "I won't let him." His throat closed up but he forced out the words, squeezing his fists.

"All my life, I've been living in fear. Waiting for him to come and hurt the ones I love. You, Ma, and now Max... And I don't know if I'll be strong enough to stop him. I'll spend the rest of our lives together holding my breath, and I can't do that. I'm so sick of being afraid, Izzie."

A tear slipped down Izzie's cheek and she pushed it away, her painted lips trembling. "I hate this," she whispered, venom in her voice.

Gabe put his arm around her shoulders. "I do, too."

CHAPTER 11

# EMPTY WITHOUT YOU

G ABE'S MOTHER DROVE THEM to the airport.

The drive was quiet. Izzie slept in the front seat, and Veronica made idle conversation with Kendra. Max smiled good-naturedly, but the bags under his eyes spoke volumes.

Gabe stifled a yawn, frustrated that he hadn't been able to sleep more than an hour. His mind had raced all night, trying to fill him with doubts. He wanted to tell his mother to stop the car and turn around.

But he'd made his decision—Stone had to be stopped. The man was tenacious and as long as he drew breath, Max would never be safe. The divide that had come between them over the last year had only just begun to mend.

Would things be the same between them when he returned? Would Max wait for him, no matter how long he was gone this time? Could Gabe even ask him to?

Veronica urged them on ahead while she parked the car. Gabe stepped out and stood before JFK. His chest tightened, and his knees were wobbly.

"Okay?" Max offered a tired smile.

Gabe didn't know how to answer. He took Max's hand and held on tight, trying not to think about how soon he'd have to let go.

Ben was waiting for them just inside the terminal. Bags were heavy under his eyes too and his chin drooped to his chest. Gabe gave his leg a light kick and he jolted awake.

"Ass," Ben muttered. "You're buying me a coffee for that. Hey, V."

Veronica smiled. It was strained and guilt punched Gabe in the chest.

"You know I didn't want him to come either."

Veronica dipped her head, blinking hard. "I know you'll look out for him."

Gabe snorted. "Mom, I'm twenty-eight. If anything, I'll be watching out for Ben."

Ben checked the time. "Zach and Ry just texted me. They're parking."

Gabe exhaled, squeezing Max's hand tighter. Max squeezed back wordlessly. Gabe wished he could say something, anything, but his mind was blank.

Max looked around the airport, taking a few small steps away from the pack. Gabe followed. Max said, "There's something exciting about airports. I always wonder where the people around me are going, why they're leaving, what their stories are."

Gabe hummed. He couldn't say he'd ever wondered such things. "I'm always too worried about getting through security." Security for werewolves had a few extra steps compared to humans.

Werewolves had to trim their claws prior to flights as a safety precaution, and in the old days, many were required to be medicated due to the misconception that like dogs, shifters would panic uncontrollably during flights, which simply wasn't true for everyone.

A little Xanax certainly didn't hurt before a flight, though, just to mellow out all the noises and scents that overwhelmed werewolves.

Max gazed up at the enormous windows that let the dull gray sunlight stream in. "I always wanted to go to Nevada, Japan, Canada…"

"Where in Nevada?"

"Las Vegas, maybe?"

Gabe chuckled. "Do some gambling?"

"No. I always wanted to see the lights of the Strip."

Longing tightened Gabe's chest. "I wanna take you to Mexico if I—when I'm back." The uptick in Max's heartbeat told him he hadn't missed the moment Gabe's doubts slipped through.

Max's Adam's apple rose and fell heavily as he swallowed. "Your father was from Mexico, right?"

"We used to go on family trips to Mexico every year when I was a pup. I could take you to all my favorite places he took me." He'd love for Max to see the city his father grew up in. Even if his father could never meet Max, just walking the same streets he'd walked with his father, arm in arm with Max, would be healing.

Max's grip tightened on his hand. "So when you come back, let's take a trip there."

Gabe just nodded. *If I—*

Max gripped his arms tight, his orange eyes burning like twin flames. "You have to be careful. Got it?"

He nodded, throat tight.

"You can't rely on your wolf too much. No excess shifting. Stay human as much as you can. Ben told me that you almost lost your head out there the last time. Not again. You can't do that to yourself again." Max's voice was firm but it wavered, and his lips were set in a tight line.

Gabe gripped Max's hands. They were cold and trembling. "Okay, Max. I promise."

"Morning, guys." Ryan walked up to them, backpack slung over one shoulder. Zach towered behind him and waved. His smile was heavy, and Ryan looked worn out as well. Gabe figured he wasn't the only one who would be missing someone.

Ben said, "In case neither of you know, we need to keep a low profile once we touch down in Rome. No shifting in public. No showing your fangs or claws. Be prepared to show your IDs often. Many places won't serve wolves."

Gabe rolled his eyes. "That's so stupid."

Ben grimaced. "It is what it is. I'm serious, both of you. Hunters make a living hunting down wolves there, and no one stops them."

Ryan's eyes went wide. "What about pack territories?"

"Humans police those places."

Gabe gaped. "Seriously?"

"We won't be in America anymore, Toto."

"Was that a joke?" Ryan snorted.

"No," Ben said. "Werewolves are tolerated there, but the ones that act out are fair game for hunters. Keep that in mind. Come on, we better get in line," Ben stated, lugging his backpack across his shoulder.

Gabe dragged his feet after Ben as they approached the line for security. Ben turned to Veronica and pulled her into a tight hug. He murmured something to her and when they separated she had tears in her eyes.

"Zach, you got this." Ben tugged Zach in for a slap on the back.

"I'll do my best." Zach sighed as they parted, sweeping a few braids behind his shoulder like he did when he was nervous. "Just be careful out there, Ben." Gabe's stomach did a flip when Zach turned toward him, his expression unreadable.

As he reached out a hand, Gabe saw Zach's eyes widen. He must not have expected Gabe to say anything to him. Gabe had been heartbroken when Zach endangered Izzie and Max, but Zach had done what Gabe couldn't and been there for Max the year he was gone. Zach clasped Gabe's hand and Gabe tugged him in for a hug.

"Thanks," Gabe said roughly, blinking hard as emotion burned his eyes. "Thank you, my friend. For looking out for him."

"Of course." Zach's eyes were glistening as they parted. Gabe gripped his shoulder, wishing he'd spent more time with Zach before he had to leave. "I'll look out for him, Gabe. I promise. But you gotta come back."

"I will," Gabe said.

"Good." Zach shoved him in the chest and took a few large steps back, thumbing at the corners of his eyes. Ryan squeezed his shoulder and Zach pulled him into a hug, crushing Ryan's head to his chest. Gabe couldn't tell if the salty scent of tears was Zach's or Ryan's or both.

Izzie's smile was apologetic as she hugged him, whispering against his ear, "Dad would be proud."

Then Gabe's chest tightened as he opened his arms, ushering Veronica in close. A sob quivered his mother's shoulders. "Be careful, mi sol," she whispered, her voice choked with tears. "Please. Please, be careful. Promise me."

"I will." Tears leaked from the corners of his eyes and he held her close, taking comfort in the scent of her hair and perfume. He prayed he never forgot it, not this time.

"And you have everything you need? To remind you of your humanity?"

"I do." He had printed pictures of her, Izzie, and Max in his pocket, as well as a bracelet Izzie had given him, and a blouse his mother loaned him that had her scent on it.

Next Kendra hugged him tight and then held him at arm's length to look him in the eyes. "I swear to the She-Wolf, Gabriel Reyes, if you break my son's heart, I will go to Rome and drag you back by the scruff of your neck."

Gabe kissed her cheek. "I'm coming back." Beyond her shoulder, Max watched, his expression guarded and unreadable. Gabe's arms fell to his sides and he trembled as he approached Max.

Max squared his shoulders, fists tight at his sides. If it weren't for the tears glistening in his honey orange eyes, Gabe would have believed Max didn't, or at least didn't want to, care that he was leaving.

Max was like granite in his arms as Gabe pulled his head to his chest. In the pocket of his jeans, he had a picture of the two of them, closer to him than any other memento he carried.

"I promise, Lobito. I promise I will come back for you." He wouldn't leave Max. They both knew the pain of being left, and he wouldn't inflict those same wounds upon him. He'd return. He had to. "No matter how long it takes. So wait for me."

Max's fists clenched in the fabric of Gabe's shirt. His body shuddered as his arms fumbled around Gabe's back, a sob puffing hot and warm through Gabe's shirt. Gabe kissed his hair. "But if I take too long and you get tired of waiting, I get it. I'm not unreasonable; I'm not gonna ask you to put your life on hold for me forever."

Max held on tight. "I chose you." The surety in Max's voice told Gabe there was no arguing, no trying to persuade him otherwise. "Go and do what you have to do. I'll be here when you get back."

Gabe tilted Max's chin up and managed a smile even though he wanted to break down as the tears dampened Max's face. He touched his lips to Max's, closing his eyes tight as Max leaned into his chest.

"Gabe." Ben's voice was low, apologetic. Gabe turned out of Max's kiss and found Ben waiting in line with Ryan. "It's time to go."

Max's hands fell to his sides and Gabe shivered without his warmth. He touched their foreheads together, blinking through his tears so he could memorize every freckle, burn the image of Max's face into his mind. "I love you, mi amor."

Max sighed shakily and touched his lips to Gabe's once more. It barely lasted a second, but it shook Gabe to his core. "You, too."

Gabe had to leave. If he stayed a second longer, he'd break and never leave Max's side. He took one step back then another. His wolf whined deep in his chest, a pitiful sound that left his throat raw. Max wiped his eyes as his mother put her arm around his shoulders.

Gabe forced himself to look away, to turn his back and suffocate the howl that wanted to spill from deep inside him as every step took him farther from Max. He didn't let himself look back, not at Izzie as she consoled his mother, not at Zach, probably crying like a big baby with Max, not at Kendra, who'd kill him herself if he didn't come back.

But he would. Because Max Gallagher was too good to leave behind and if Max didn't understand that, Gabe would just have to make him.

"ALL RIGHT, VIEJO, WHAT'S our first move?" Gabe asked as he dropped into his seat by the window with Ryan in the aisle seat and Ben sandwiched between them.

Ben pushed his backpack beneath the seat. "I booked a hotel for us. We'll spend the night in Rome. Then we'll rent a car and drive to the monastery."

Gabe exhaled, relieved to know they weren't landing somewhere strange and new without a plan.

"Ah, man. Only a night?" Ryan sighed. "I'd love to see the whole city. You realize how historical Rome is to shifters."

"I know, Ryan." Ben yawned.

"I mean, seriously. Werewolves and humans worked together to build the Roman Empire into what it was! When Rome fell, the wolves were slaughtered to near extinction. Nowadays, the Italian government tolerates shifters at best. Don't even get me started on the fact that the twins were the first humans to be changed into werewolves—well, that we know of."

"Okay, I won't." Gabe swiped through his phone, half in and half out of the conversation. "I thought the wolves from the hunting grounds came to Earth and changed everyone. Isn't that why werewolves hate hybrids? 'Cause humans 'messed with our bloodline' or something?"

"Yeah, but it was the She-Wolf spreading lycanthropy to the twins that encouraged humans and werewolves to finally begin assimilating. People looked up to Romulus and Remus. They were heroes to the people back then. It got people thinking, hey, maybe these werewolves ain't so bad. The She-Wolf wanted werewolves and the non-paranormal to live together, so these idiots that say, 'Oh, hybrids tainted our connection to the goddess' are totally missing the point."

"Oh. Right." Honestly, Gabe wasn't much of a historian. "Sure you wouldn't rather be on the Council, Ry?"

Ryan chuckled. "My dad had me pegged as the next lore master. Too bad for the Council the LPA's a lot more exciting."

Gabe texted Max, telling him they were awaiting takeoff. His chest clenched as he hit send. He couldn't get those tear-filled eyes out of his mind and he clung on to the memory of those arms around him, the touch of his lips. He wanted to carry the memory of Max with him. He didn't want to forget.

Ryan grew unusually quiet, his eyes downcast and a frown heavy on his face.

*I wonder what memento he brought. What's his tether to his humanity?*

Gabe hadn't realized how much he'd been depending on Ryan's cheery disposition and resigned himself to a dour flight.

The pilot announced they'd be taking off in fifteen minutes. Gabe's phone buzzed.

**Max: Call me when you land. I love you.**

His throat tightened.

**Gabe: I will. Miss you already. Love you, too.**

Gabe turned on his phone's airplane mode and slumped in his seat.

Sighing, Ben glanced away. "Geesh. You haven't even left the States yet."

Gabe grimaced. He knew he was pathetic.

"Savor it," Ben said, surprising him. "Savor it all. The heartbreak, the pining. It means you got something worth coming home to. Something good waiting for you at the end of all this. Hold on to that, Gabe. Use it to keep you grounded, to drive you. Both of you."

Ryan looked over, his face flushed. "What do you mean?"

Ben shrugged. "We all know who you're missing."

Ryan looked away, his ears red. "I don't miss anyone. I'm excited. Rome's an important city to shifters. I wanna drink in as much history as I can."

Ben snorted. "We're on business, not checking out the local museums."

Ryan put his hands behind his head. "And this is why Zach should have come along. He'd have wanted to see the museums..."

Gabe chuckled, pulling his earbuds out of his pocket and popping them in. He turned on the playlist he'd made for himself and Max—from James Bay to Imagine Dragons—and let the music spirit him away from his woes as the plane carried them among the clouds.

GABE OPENED HIS EYES to a wall of clouds beyond the oval window.

The plane's wing carved through the mist like a blade. Outside, the skies were darkening and Gabe checked the time. He'd slept almost seven hours, catching up on all the sleep he'd missed last night.

Beside him, Ben snored with his head back against the seat. Ryan, plugged into earbuds, was staring intently at his screen, watching a movie that Gabe didn't recognize.

It was a little over an eight-hour flight to Rome. The clouds parted, revealing the ocean below. Miles away from Max, the loneliness came rushing over him. He closed his eyes tight.

*I'm coming back.*

The plane began its descent from the clouds and landed with ease on the tarmac. Once they'd stopped, Ryan nudged Ben awake. Ben grumbled and grabbed his bag, stifling a yawn.

Even though Ben had warned him, Gabe was still taken aback when drivers asked to see identification. Just a glimpse of the IDs declaring them lycanthropes had drivers rolling up the window and driving off. Gabe gnashed his jaw when a third driver refused to let them in his car.

After their fifth attempt, they found a driver who didn't sneer at their identification cards. He still shot them suspicious looks in the mirror, like he thought they'd start tearing up his car like untrained puppies.

Their driver took them to a hotel around the corner from the Colosseum. It was easy to forget his worries as Gabe admired the ancient amphitheater of towering stone. A web of wires twisted through the air, stretching from rusted old utility poles.

Palm trees on either side of the hotel door, a sight Gabe hadn't expected, waved their leaves in the mild humid breeze. Just down the street from the hotel was a park with lush greenery and towering trees of a type Gabe hadn't seen before with long skinny trunks and a fluffy head of leaves.

The hotel receptionist offered them a room with two bedrooms and a sleeper sofa. Ben offered to take the sofa while Gabe and Ryan each took a bedroom. They ordered room service just before the restaurant shut down for the night. Ben had the pasta with mussels, Gabe dug into his rigatoni Bolognese, and Ryan devoured a personal pizza.

Gabe realized to his dismay that in all the commotion, he'd never had time to text Max. Ryan and Ben took turns brushing their teeth while Gabe took his phone into his bedroom, collapsing on a plush, comfy bed. He groaned as all the aches melted away and he relaxed into the mattress.

It was almost eleven o'clock in Rome but Gabe was still on New York time and wasn't ready to sleep. Knowing Max, he was studying for class tomorrow. His heart pounded as he called Max, and eagerly awaited the sound of Max's voice. Their farewell at the airport felt like it had happened a week ago.

"Hey!" Max's voice brought a much-needed smile to Gabe's face. "How's Rome?"

"It's okay. If we weren't on a mission, I'd love to explore. But we'll be heading into the mountains early tomorrow. What are you up to?"

"I did some studying. Watched some TV to take my mind off things. I just finished making dinner."

"Yeah? What'd you make?"

"Frozen dumplings and veggies. I almost fixed you a bowl," Max admitted, laughing sadly.

"Wish I was with you," Gabe said. The bed felt far too empty, too cold.

"Me too." Max sighed. "It's not the same. The apartment feels too empty without you."

Gabe wanted to apologize but what good would it do?

"Where are you?" Max asked.

"In some hotel I can't pronounce. I can see the Colosseum from here. Has Hanson come to take you to his super-secret hideaway?"

"Not yet." Max's voice was heavy. "He called me this afternoon to talk. I'll have to drop out of school but I could attend virtually. I have to take time off from my job." He groaned. "I worked so hard to get that. They'll probably fire me. But I know what's at stake if we don't do this, even though it sucks."

Gabe pouted. "I'm sorry, mi amor." He looked out the window and over the rooftops to where the Colosseum towered over the streets. He took a picture and sent it to Max. "Sent you something."

"Oh. Wow, that's beautiful. Is it a nice hotel?"

"It's all right. The bed's comfy, at least." He wet his lips, considering. If Max wasn't in the mood, he could just say, but Max's voice was doing something to him right now. If he closed his eyes, Max could be right here next to him. "I'd prefer it if you were in bed with me."

He swore he heard Max swallow. "That... that sounds nice." There was an audible crack in Max's voice that made Gabe smile. "I'd like that, too. It's weird, just hearing your voice. Not having you here. I miss you. So much."

Gabe's heart rate shot way up. "You too. Wish you were here next to me. Wish I could hold you, touch you." He closed his eyes and let his hand wander, fingering the clasp of his jeans. He longed for the warmth of Max's body, his hot, gentle mouth against Gabe's skin.

Max cleared his throat. "Yeah. I'd... I'd like that, too."

A smile tugged at Gabe's lips. "Max, is this turning you on?"

Nervous, breathy laughter filled his ear. "Yeah. A little."

Gabe bit his lip to stifle a sigh. His cock twitched against the front of his jeans.

"What about you?"

Gabe squeezed the crotch of his pants and couldn't stifle a grunt. "I'm getting hard for you."

Max hummed, though it sounded more like a moan. "This sucks. I wish I was there. We'd actually be able to do something about it."

"Yeah? If you were here, what would we be doing?"

Max laughed nervously. "I don't know. Uh... sorry."

"That's fine. I just wanna hear your voice."

Max swallowed and for a moment he was quiet. "If I were with you... I'd kiss you. Touch you." He cleared his throat and murmured, "Suck you off."

Gabe grinned. He could just imagine how red Max's face was getting. He might not be the best at dirty talk but Gabe's cock couldn't care less. Just knowing Max was thinking these dirty thoughts about him made him rock hard. He jolted as he wrapped his fingers around himself. He didn't have any lube but he didn't care.

"I love the way you suck my cock, mi amor. You're so good to me." He could just picture Max lying sprawled out between his thighs, fingers wrapped around the base of his dick, flushed lips sucking the head. Whenever their eyes met, it always sent a jolt of desire like an electric current right through him.

Max sighed. "This isn't the same."

"No, it's not. But we're gonna make this work, Max. Close your eyes and touch yourself for me. Please?"

Max's breath hitched. "Okay..." There came the unmistakable snap as a bottle of lube opened. The one they had in their dresser.

Gabe fisted his cock, growling his approval as he pictured Max's hand down his briefs, wrapped tight around his cock. He pumped his shaft, thumbing the head and sighing low as he imagined Max splayed out underneath him, a vista of pink, freckled skin and fiery red hair.

"Goddess, Max. I'm so damn hard for you right now. Wish you were here so I could show you how much you turn me on. The minute I'm home, Max, I swear. Take you right up against the door. Hard, fast." With his hands digging into Max's hips, tugging him down to meet every brutal thrust, Gabe's cock buried to the hilt between Max's round cheeks. "Would you like that?"

"Yes. Fuck. Yes." Max's voice broke, his voice shaky and breathless.

"Are you touching yourself for me?" Gabe knew he was, his acute senses picking up every slick tug of Max's fist. He was working himself faster.

"Y-yeah." Max gulped. Were his cheeks flushed? Was he biting his lip?

"What's the first thing you wanna do to me when you see me again?"

"Want to suck your cock." Max panted, stifling a moan. "I miss the way you taste."

Gabe snapped his hips off the bed, pushing faster into his hand. "Love it when you suck me off. So hot and wet around me. Your lips turn that nice ruby color when you blow me. It's beautiful. Come on, tell me more. Don't hold back on me."

"Want you to... to finger me."

Gabe practically swooned. "Do it to yourself. Imagine I'm there with you."

"Yeah... okay... wait. Gotta put you on speaker."

Gabe snorted with laughter. "Hurry."

A moan fell from Max's lips. "Fuck."

"Are you fingering yourself for me?"

"Yeah. Feels so good." Max's voice shook, his breath quickening.

Gabe gave his balls a tug, then worked his cock in a long, slow pull that had him seeing stars. "Touch your cock. Stroke it nice and fast." Gabe strained his ears and the slick, wet sounds as Max worked his cock got his toes curling. "So good, Max. Play with that tight hole."

Those lewd sounds got faster as Max panted hard, his voice breaking as he worked himself into a frenzy of pleasure. Gabe ached with how badly he wished he could be in the same room as him, working Max open with his fingers, pegging his prostate the way Max liked.

Max panted. "Want you inside me. Want you to give me your knot, fill me up with your cock."

Gabe could see him, his cock in his fist, thighs open wide, supple lower lip between his teeth. He worked his cock faster, already slick with precum. "Can't wait to come home to you. I never wanna be away from you again. I wanna make love to you, bite you, and make you mine."

"Yes." Max gasped, his voice shuddery and desperate. "Please. Knot me. Bite me. Wanna be yours."

He wanted to be buried to the root in Max's hole, those walls tight and hot around him, stretching to accommodate his knot as they mated. Locked together, Max would clamp down around his knot as he came and send Gabe over the brink. He'd ride out every hot pulse of his release, bite down on that sweet spot between Max's neck and shoulder, and claim him once and for all.

Gabe squeezed the sheets as he worked himself closer and closer, every breath short and sharp. "Gonna come, Max. Come deep inside your tight ass."

"So close! Fuck me just like that. Gabe. Gabe! Oh, *fuck*!" Max's voice flowed freely and Gabe wished he could see him tangled up in the sheets, face gripped by desperation as he came thick and wet all across his chest.

Gabe's hips jerked, back arching, and for one beautiful moment, he was suspended in a haze of total bliss—then he was coming, bucking like a wild stallion, clamping down on his lower lip to stifle his howl. He had just enough sense to clamp his hand over the head of his cock before he shot off, possibly staining the sheets and leaving one nasty surprise for the cleaning person.

He collapsed, utterly boneless, Max's name a whisper on his lips as he sank into the sheets, tingling everywhere. His eyes struggled to stay open. He wondered if it was possible to pass out from coming so hard.

"Still there?" Max asked. His voice was raw, breathless.

"Fuck," Gabe answered.

Max burst out laughing. "Imaginary Max is that good, huh?" He sounded smug.

"Oh yes. Even better in person." Gabe reached blindly for a tissue, wishing he'd thought to use one as he cleaned up the mess in his fist. "Maybe some distance isn't bad for us after all."

"Maybe not."

"I'm serious. I want us to mate."

"I know." The longing in Max's voice made tears prick at his eyes. "Me too."

"Wait for me?"

Max laughed. "You're always worth the wait. In the meantime, this phone sex thing isn't so bad. We should do it more often."

Gabe tossed the tissue in the wastebasket, kicked off his jeans, and tugged off his shirt, burrowing beneath the blankets.

"Gabe?"

Gabe had fallen silent. "Just... wondering how much more time we have to talk like this."

"Don't think about that. My class doesn't start until nine. Call me in the morning. Love you."

Gabe tried to smile, tried not to imagine that they were on borrowed time. "You too. Good night."

The call ended and Gabe was left alone in silence. He reached over with a sigh and turned off the lamp, plunging the room into darkness.

# CHAPTER 12

# BROTHERS OF THE MOON

GABE TRIED TO IGNORE Ryan's smug look as he dragged himself out into the living room. "Ben went to get the car for our little road trip?"

"Yup. Got you some coffee from the café downstairs." He handed Gabe a cup of coffee in a take-away cup. "So, did you and Max have a nice chat?" Ryan asked, smirking across the counter at him.

It was hard to keep things secret and personal among werewolves, where the littlest uptick in a heartbeat betrayed so much, much less when they could hear when someone was going to town in the next room.

Gabe remembered having sound sensitivities as a child, made even worse by the fact that he could hear so much more than the average human. Over time, he'd learned to drown out most sounds unless he wanted to hear them.

Still, his neck warmed. "Yeah, actually." The sexual nature of their phone call had been thrilling, but it was even better to hear Max's voice again. Crap. He was supposed to call him. He really wasn't good at long distance.

"How is he?" Ryan asked, his expression genuine.

"Okay, I think."

"That's nice," Ryan murmured. "It's good you've got someone waiting for you."

It was time to embarrass him a little. "Hey, you do, too."

Something slipped in Ryan's smug smile, revealing something vulnerable as he suddenly averted his gaze. "Eh. My mom will probably forget I exist by the time I come back. I called her last night. She told me to pick up a souvenir for her mom. Her mom's been dead for three years." He laughed but it was a strained, uncomfortable sound.

Gabe wanted to hit himself. Ryan's mother suffered from a rare neurological condition that only werewolves could get. She had episodes of forgetfulness and forgot everyone, even her own family.

"Ry, I didn't mean— Look, she's forgotten before, but she always remembers. You're pretty hard to forget." He felt like a jerk for missing Max. At least Max wouldn't forget him.

Ryan hummed, carrying his coffee to the table.

"I meant Zach. You guys been in touch?"

Ryan's ears reddened. "Yeah, we live streamed a football game together." He snorted as he met Gabe's gaze. "You think he's gonna magically decide he's in love with me just 'cause I'm an ocean away?"

Gabe sat at the table with him. "Hey, absence makes the heart grow fonder."

"I'm gonna step on your foot."

"Or you could just, you know, tell him." Gabe cringed as Ryan kicked him under the table. "Who knows? He might be ready to date again."

Ryan scoffed. "Hey, Zach, I know you were in love with Gabe for years. How about some sloppy seconds with a side of rebound?"

Gabe slurped his coffee. "He's moved on. You blind, man? Things are so awkward between us now."

Ryan said nothing and Gabe didn't push the subject. He supposed there was a reason Ryan was holding back. But seriously, Zach and Ryan had known each other even before Gabe entered the picture. He couldn't think of two people better suited for each other.

Ryan's phone buzzed on the counter. He even had a selfie of himself and Zach as his home screen. "Ben's downstairs with the car. Come on, Love Guru. Let's get a move on."

Gabe sighed, wondering what the day held in store for them. He hoped these Moon Brothers were easy to track down. They slung on their backpacks and departed the quiet of the hotel room.

Outside, the streets were packed with tourists babbling in all sorts of languages as they made for the Colosseum. Ben was parked right outside and grimaced at them from the driver's window. He wished they could bask in the warm Italian sunshine and soak in the beauty of the city, but Ben motioned wildly for them to pile in.

Gabe threw his bag in the trunk and dropped into the back seat away from Ryan. Sitting in the back reminded him of going on a trip with his family. "Where to, driver?"

Ben took a gulp of coffee. "Hell if I know how to pronounce the name. It's a nature reserve." Ben readied the GPS. "It's only an hour and a half from the city."

As they drove down the street, passing the towering Colosseum, Ryan asked if he could play some music.

"Sure, just none of that Eminem shit," Ben replied.

"I made a playlist just for our Rome adventures," Ryan explained, connecting his phone to the Bluetooth speakers. Andrea Bocelli's "Con te partiro" played.

Ben hummed agreeably.

They stopped in traffic outside the Pantheon where tourists clogged the streets trying to get parking. Outside the ancient stone structure was the remains of a She-Wolf statue, the head shattered and the body defaced by graffiti Gabe was happy he couldn't read. The statue had been sectioned off with police tape. "The hell happened there?"

Ryan glowered. "Activists want werewolves to be able to worship in the cities instead of out in the wild, so they put up that statue. The humans got all pissed and knocked it down. The protests made the news."

Ben made a disgruntled sound from the front seat. "Sure seems like humans are eager to forget the role werewolves had in the Roman Empire."

Anger thrummed in Gabe's veins. What had once been a city dominated by wolves was overrun by humans. Maybe, just maybe, he could understand what Max had told him about Aaron McCready's ideology of werewolves living free from human influence.

"There'll be plenty of history at the monastery, I bet," Ryan said, sounding cheered by the thought. As the streets became a blur, Ryan sang along in fluent Italian. Gabe's mouth fell open.

"You can speak Italian?" Ben snapped.

"Yeah, of course. My family's Italian on my mother's side! And Irish on my dad's side," Ryan said, as if stunned they didn't know.

"With a name like Kelly, who'd have guessed," Ben groused.

"It's Irish!"

"It's stupid." Gabe stifled a laugh at Ben's surly bitterness. "So why'd you let me fumble my way through conversations?"

Ryan bit his cheek to keep from grinning. "It was pretty funny watching you butcher everything."

Ben shook his head, a begrudging smile on his face. "Asshole."

Gabe found himself humming along. He couldn't understand a word, but the song's grandiose longing made something in his chest tighten. He pulled out his phone and texted Max.

**Gabe: Leaving Rome now. Hopefully we'll find these weird monks. I hope they have answers. I wanna come home.**

"Gabe, put the phone away and look around!" Ryan exclaimed, pressing his nose up against the window.

Gabe dropped his phone onto the seat. The city, now a blend of modern skyscrapers and ancient Roman architecture, gradually fell away behind them, replaced by stone pines with thin trunks and bushy leaves, and rolling hills brown from the sun beneath a deep blue sky.

He could only imagine how good the grass would smell, ticklish under his paws. Even in the throes of his heartsickness, he could still appreciate the beauty of the Italian countryside. His phone buzzed.

**Max: That would be great! Be careful.**

Gabe took a few pictures of the countryside and sent them to Max. Once he saw how nice it looked, maybe he'd worry less.

They traveled beneath the shadows of the mountain range, the peaks lush with trees and golden grass. Ben drove for some time between the trees before he came upon a parking spot within the woods. Hikers departed their vehicles and ventured along the trails sprawling through the woods. Ryan stopped an Italian hiker and asked in perfect Italian for directions to the monastery.

"So, it's called the Monastery of the Moon. It's at the very top of the mountain. He said it's about a day's climb and the monastery's locked, so no one goes up there. Know what that means? We can shift!"

Ben sighed. "Just be careful with the shifting. We could still be caught. Besides, not a good idea to spend too much time as a wolf far from home."

Ryan rolled his eyes. "Whatever, Dad. We're still among pack, and it can't be good for us to keep our wolves suppressed, either."

When Ben continued to glower, Ryan said, "I'm shifting. You guys can be all slow and walk."

They followed a quiet trail from the parking lot, their shoes crunching over gravel and sending up little clouds of dirt. Birds called out to one another from across the woods.

They passed a sign Ryan stopped to read. "'No trespassing, road closed to monastery. Stay out.' Stop me, bitches." He walked around the fence and opened both arms as if to say, *Gonna stop me, punks?*

Gabe snorted and jumped the fence like a badass, making Ryan guffaw at him when he tripped. Ben looked both ways and followed. Gabe breathed in the smell of trees and leaves unspoiled by the fumes and pollution of the city. It set his heart racing, made him want to run and hunt. Not even

Central Park had air this pure. It called to him as a wolf to relish each second of Mother Nature's beauty.

"Great out here, isn't it?" He nudged Ben, who was sniffing deeply at the air.

"Yeah. Hard to deny. Still, we— Hey!"

Ryan threw off his clothes and ran buck naked into the woods. "Wa-hoo!"

Ben gnashed his teeth and pinched the bridge of his nose. "For the love of..."

Gabe couldn't resist. He pulled off his shirt and unbuckled his belt, kicking off his jeans. He could already feel the change coming over him, hair growing thick and fast across his body, that primal urge to run and hunt as powerful as a mating call.

Ben sighed. "You too, huh?"

Gabe pushed his clothes into his backpack and threw it at Ben. "Come on, Ben! Let's find these monks!" His hands became clawed paws, his body changing as he ran, and the wind flowed through his fur.

The smells of the forest swept over him like water from a dam—warm grass, the green smell of leaves, rich soil. The wind whispered through the trees, twigs snapped, and bushes rustled within the woods.

He ran, the soil warm beneath his paws, pursuing the smell of *Ryan, pack, brother, friend*! He allowed Ryan to pounce on him, pawing and nipping, their playful barks echoing into the woods. Ryan ran and Gabe pursued, paws churning up dirt, the sun warm and heavy on his back. The wind carried the smells of prey, birds and squirrels and other woodland animals. Hunger hadn't begun to gnaw at him yet, but he wanted to hunt—crunch bones, taste blood, chase and give chase.

Ryan suddenly stopped, scenting the air. Gabe sniffed and smelled others. Urine, fresh and old, marked the trees. Tufts of fur clung to brambles, and paws had left marks in the soil and on the trunks of trees. Ryan scented one of the trees and growled. Gabe sniffed tracks, huffing at the soil, listening to the worms as they churned beneath the surface.

"Maybe the Moon Brothers," Ben panted, out of breath from trying to keep up with Ryan and Gabe. "Take it easy. This is their territory. They need to know we're not a threat. Let's follow their trail, see if it leads us to the monastery."

THE SUN DISAPPEARED BEYOND the rugged mountain peaks. The heat of the day simmered down to a cool and refreshing breeze. Gabe had spent most of the day as a wolf and now hunted small animals for dinner. Ben declared they stop and rest; he was tired of carrying the backpacks. They sat down on a rocky outcrop at the top of a winding trail. Gabe and Ryan devoured the squirrels and Ben shifted briefly to enjoy the prey as well. After they ate, Gabe coaxed his reluctant wolf to shift and once he was human again, he got dressed.

Ryan buckled his jeans, craning his neck to stare toward the peak of the mountain. "I don't know, guys. I sure can't see a monastery."

Though there had only been trees for miles, the smell of the Brothers hung in the air like a mist. They had an unusual scent that made Gabe want to sneeze, sweet and smoky like incense.

Gabe asked, "Would you even know what a monastery looks like?"

Ben tugged on his cargo pants. "Look, we just keep following the scents. No more shifting tonight. Make sure to anchor your humanity later."

"It's gonna be harder traversing this place as a human," Gabe grouched, but he didn't refuse. His wolf was so drawn to this forest, he'd like nothing more than to roam the woods as a wolf for hours more. Gabe pushed himself up and continued on, shouldering his backpack.

Darkness pressed in and his eyes adjusted easily, yet the tall, sinewy silhouettes of the trees still played tricks on his mind. He had to scent the air several times just to remind himself there were no predators nearby.

"Shit!" Ryan gasped.

Gabe and Ben whirled around and Gabe's claws came out. "What? See something?"

Ryan sighed his relief. "No, something touched my foot, but it was my other foot. Ugh. Thank fuck."

Gabe growled, urging himself to relax. This wasn't Central Park. Anything could be out here—including Stone. A growl rumbled in his chest. He could be tracking them, and they would be none the wiser since the monks' incense blocked out too much. He could be trailing them, silent as a shadow, waiting to strike. Twigs snapped and the underbrush rustled. Gabe whirled around, his eyes darting among the trees.

*It was an animal,* he told himself. *This forest is home to more than wolves.*

The incense in the air made him growl. It was stronger than ever. Either they were getting close, or—

Yellow eyes flickered within the trees like flares of torchlight. Shadows moved deep within the woods. A howl echoed through the night, calling the pack to arms. Gabe's hair stood on end. "Ben, what do we do?"

The silhouettes of wolves closed in from both sides, fangs gleaming in the darkness and growls and barks echoing in the trees.

"Stay calm," Ben murmured, his eyes scanning the area. "They aren't hostile yet. They're sniffing us out. We're in their territory. Be respectful, both of you." Raising his voice, Ben called, "We don't mean any harm!"

The wolves closed in, and Gabe fought the urge to run like a frightened deer as his instincts warred between fight and flight. The wolves pressed in, snarling and sniffing the air.

"They're gonna kill us," Ryan whispered.

"Relax. Now," Ben said out of the side of his mouth, completely frozen as the wolves circled them, sniffing and panting.

Ryan's fear was overpowering. Gabe clenched his jaw to keep from growling, wanting nothing more than to shield his packmate from harm.

"They'll kill us. We'll never get to go home. We'll never see Zach again, or Max, or—"

"Ryan, enough. They're not growling. They're curious," Ben said through gritted teeth. "Let them scent us."

Ryan began to pant, his voice growing harsher by the minute. Fur grew on his arms and face, and his fingernails sharpened to claws. Gabe grabbed hold of his shoulder. "Ryan, stay calm."

As one of the wolves came closer, it bared its teeth. Ryan panicked. He snapped, lashing out with a clawed hand at the wolf closest to him.

"Ryan!" Ben snarled, but it was too late. Growls rumbled like thunder around them, fur bristling and fangs gleaming.

Ryan yelped as Ben seized him by the back of the neck and hurled him into the trees behind them. "Run!" Ben roared and Gabe didn't need telling twice. He tore ahead, racing past Ryan as the wolves howled and others answered the call. The hunt was on, and Gabe and his pack were prey.

"The hell were you thinking, idiot?" Ben shouted, his voice worn and ragged as he caught up to them.

"I panicked, okay?" Ryan snapped, leaping over a fallen tree. "If we die out here, no one'll find our bodies!"

Ben swerved around a tree. "They were scenting us! They weren't gonna kill us!"

Gabe threw himself toward a rock face, claws scrabbling as he heaved himself up onto an outcrop. He lunged, seizing Ryan's hand and pulling him up, then helped Ben find his feet. Lights burned in the night. The uneven forest floor sloped into stone steps. "We're near the monastery!"

"Should we even go? They'll be waiting for us!" Ryan looked from Ben to Gabe, wide-eyed and regretful.

The thundering of approaching paws grew louder, eyes gleaming from the darkness of the hill behind them. Ben shoved them ahead. "Go!"

Gabe latched onto his arm. "No!"

"Tell the guys at the monastery who I am! Mention I knew Greg. I'll hold these guys off and— Behind you!"

Gabe followed Ben's stare and his heart dropped as yellow eyes winked at them from the darkness. Claws scraped over stones, snapping twigs like bones. Stone steps chiseled into the mountainside ascended to another rocky outcrop where a pack of ten wolves stood barring the way forward.

Ben latched onto Gabe's shoulder. "No one move a muscle," he said through gritted teeth.

Gabe suppressed the growl rising to his lips as foreign smells overwhelmed him. His wolf growled inside his head. His claws wanted to come out so he could fight and defend his pack if these strange wolves so much as looked at Ryan or Ben wrong. The wolves were many, but they were gaunt and graying around their snouts. Still, age was no indicator of strength. They were outnumbered and should these wolves choose to do so, they could easily overwhelm them.

Ben stepped forward, coming between the wolves and his pack. "Are you the Moon Brothers? I'm Ben Stroud, a friend of Greg Harris."

One of the wolves, old and white, stepped forward and leaped from the outcrop as gracefully as if he were gliding. The wolves up top snapped and snarled in warning, but the old white wolf pressed on. He circled Ben, sniffing him over, then did the same to Ryan and Gabe. Ryan turned away so his back was against Ben's, not taking his eyes off him.

The white wolf transformed into an old man, deeply tanned and covered in sunspots. He had a long white beard braided down to his navel and equally long hair descending down his back. He hardly had any fat on his body and appeared so frail, a breeze might carry him away.

"Any friend of Greg's is welcome," he said, his voice so quiet it was just above a whisper. "He spoke highly of you, Ben Stroud."

Gabe's shoulders slumped, his claws dulling.

"I am Brother Andre. Come, you must be tired. The monastery isn't far."

Ben clapped Gabe and Ryan on the shoulders. "Relax, kids. We found 'em."

And best of all, they'd arrived ahead of Stone. Gabe only hoped they'd know where to find Romulus's tomb. His spirits light, Gabe followed the Brotherhood as the wolves bounded away up the mountain where the distant torchlights of the monastery burned bright beneath a crescent moon.

CHAPTER 13

# THE APPRENTICE

ANDRE LED THE WAY up the worn stone steps to the monastery at the top of the mountain. Tall stone walls surrounded the monastery, an ancient building that looked like it had been carved from the wood and stone of the surrounding hills.

Statues of howling wolves were posed on either side of the gateway and within the monastery grounds was a vast garden where lunar flowers grew white beneath the moon. In the center of the courtyard, a statue of the She-Wolf nursed the twins.

Lanterns illuminated the garden and the monks of the Brotherhood, who were sitting cross-legged beneath the moonlight. One of them appeared to hover inches off the ground, his hair flowing around him as if in zero gravity. It reminded Gabe of how Max had described his powers.

"Is that, uh, normal?" Ryan asked, eyeing the monk nervously.

"You're witnessing one of our own in direct communion with the goddess," Andre whispered. "It's a delicate process that can take years of meditation."

"Oh, really? That's cool—*achoo!*" Ryan covered his mouth as a monk passed by carrying a smoking incense stick.

The levitating monk collapsed onto his ass and shot Ryan a scathing look. Ryan shuffled behind Ben, who rolled his eyes.

Within the walls of the monastery grounds, with only open sky for miles and surrounded by trees and rugged hills, it was easy to feel as if he'd entered another realm. Sudden homesickness hit him, and he wished he could call Max just to remind himself he hadn't left this world entirely.

Inside the monastery itself, lunar flower incense clouded the air. The incense obscured all other aromas. While Gabe usually liked the sweet fragrance, it was so overpowering it made his head ache.

In the center of the room, a pool of water reflected the moon through a glass dome in the tiled roof. They passed many rooms full of monks deep in their meditation before statues of the She-Wolf.

Gabe hadn't seen anywhere the monks might eat by the time Andre led them to a vast library in the southern wing of the monastery. Gabe breathed in, grateful for the musk of old paper and leather amidst the incense. Shelves stuffed full to bursting with books and scrolls touched the ceiling. Gabe had never seen so many books.

"Come, sit." Andre motioned to some squat stools by a circular window in a quiet corner of the library. Once they were seated, Andre hit a leather-wrapped mallet against a metal bowl. The bowl vibrated and produced a deep tone that reverberated through the room.

"I apologize for our hostility," Andre said. "Before he left for Canada, Greg warned us that someone would come seeking out the tomb's location. For all we knew, it could have been you. How is Greg? We haven't heard from him since he left. I worry for him."

Ben bowed his head. "I'm sorry, Andre, but Greg's no longer with us. He was killed."

Andre's complexion paled. "Killed?"

"By John Stone."

Andre's face whitened in recognition. "Il Mostro. The name we have given him in Italy."

"The Monster," Ryan translated grimly.

"How has this come to pass. Why?" Andre pressed.

Ben said, "We've come here seeking the moonblade, and so has Stone. Stone wants the blade for similar reasons to the story of Romulus and Remus."

Andre gave his long beard a tug, his bushy brows furrowed. "Goddess. How dreadful. Then Greg's suspicions were all correct."

Ben sighed. "What did he tell you?"

"He told us someone was killing historians and believed he might be a target for his knowledge of our order. He warned us to be on our guard."

The doors opened and in walked a monk wearing a robe that obscured his face. He carried a tray. At the sight of them, he stopped dead.

"This is one of our new apprentices," Andre explained. "Would you all like lunar flower tea?"

Gabe accepted a warm stone mug with a single lunar flower petal adrift within the clear liquid. Ben and Ryan took their drinks, and the apprentice bowed and departed toward the back of the room, stopping to browse the tomes.

"Did Greg tell you what had him so paranoid?" Ben asked.

"He warned me that history was doomed to repeat itself. He believed someone would come for the blade's location. And now he's dead, and here you are."

"If Stone targeted Greg, it was for a reason. He had information about your pack."

Gabe's skin prickled. How exactly had Stone realized Greg was a member of the Brothers? Who had told him? Greg traveled each summer, so it was common knowledge among the Council where he went and who he was meeting. Gabe's skin crawled to even think someone on the Council might have had a hand in murdering their own.

Ben said, "He could come for you at any time now. We're here to offer protection."

"And we'd gladly accept, but that won't be necessary." At ease, Andre sipped his tea. "One of our sisters, Kassandra, carries the key to the tomb with her."

"Then we need to speak to her. She's in danger!"

"I already did. The moment we received Greg's warning, Kassandra fled and took the key with her. She knows the danger the blade could represent in the wrong hands. But I wouldn't try to find her. It isn't safe."

"What do you mean?"

"The place she fled to... cannot be reached by conventional means."

Ben growled. "Be specific, Andre."

Andre set down his teacup. "She took the key a few miles outside of Bologna and into the ruins of a town long wiped off the map. A town once called Paradiso."

The back of his neck prickled like he was being watched and Gabe turned in time to see the apprentice look away quickly, his hood flapping around his face. Gabe wished he'd leave; he was being nosy.

Ryan wrinkled his brow. "Why there?"

"The town is the site of an Imprint."

Ryan's jaw dropped. "No way!"

Gabe was in the dark. "A what?"

Andre explained, "A magical explosion dating back to the days of the druid hunts. In much the same way radiation warps and changes the land, this Imprint has altered the world around it. Time is... shattered there. You'll see it for yourself if you go, but that won't be necessary. Kassandra fled through one of the many portals there in an effort to protect the blade. This was weeks ago. We haven't seen her since."

Gabe's head hurt. Portals? Time? What weird sci-fi movie had he landed in? "So, what do we do? Just let her go?"

Andre bowed his head. "Only our monks can enter the portals, using old relics we call pathmakers. The magic secreting from the Imprint reacts to the relics, allowing us to time travel. Kassandra has the key, and the key is safer with her than anywhere else."

So that was it then. Gabe exhaled through clenched teeth. "With respect, Brother Andre. If it were that simple, we wouldn't have come all this way."

Ben's hand settled at the small of his back. "You're sure she's safe? The blade, too?"

"I'm confident of it. Attempting to bring her back would be a poor decision. Thank you for coming to warn us, but you've done your duty. You can return home. Feel free to stay the night. The mountain is treacherous in the dark."

"Thanks for the offer. We'll stay out of the way," Ben assured him.

There came a clatter from behind them. The apprentice had dropped his tray and a handful of tomes.

"Would you show our guests to their rooms?"

The apprentice bowed wordlessly.

Ben stood. "Thanks, Andre."

"Of course. Anything I can do to help. Greg was a dear friend, and his love for our ancient history rivaled our own."

They left Andre alone and followed the hooded apprentice through the halls. The quiet rang in Gabe's ears. Beside him, Ryan's stomach growled. He asked, "Hey, you guys got any food around here?"

The apprentice leading them stayed silent, but a passing woman in a robe said, "Oh, we don't believe in hunger or thirst. The moonlight sustains us." She bowed and walked away.

Ryan squirmed. "That's... fucking weird."

The apprentice led them to an empty room and bowed, then walked away. Inside were three futons, a dresser, and a wall-length mirror. A circular window revealed the dense forest beyond, cloaked in shadow. Ryan looked reluctant to enter. "Why is this room empty? Did someone starve to death in here?"

Ben sighed. "Quit scaring yourself and get some sleep."

Gabe turned to Ben. "We're not really gonna leave, are we?"

Ben rolled his shoulders, eyes heavy with exhaustion. "If the blade is safe, then there's not much we can do. Andre's right. Bringing it back into our realm would be dangerous. This is a good thing. We can go home."

"But Stone's still out there." They couldn't go home empty-handed.

"Yes, he is, and we don't know where. We can't be away as long as the last time." Ben's stare rubbed Gabe the wrong way.

"I'm *fine*, Ben. We can't just go home."

Ben stifled a yawn. "Look, it's been a long day. Let's get some sleep and decide what we're doing in the morning."

Gabe didn't argue, though he wanted to. He undressed, changing into his sweats and a T-shirt Max had bought him with a wolf on it. Ben extinguished the candle, plunging the room into darkness except for the silver moonlight spilling in through the window.

Gabe curled up on his futon and sighed as every aching muscle relaxed.

"Viejo, you don't think someone on the Council played a part in Greg's murder, do you?"

Ben rolled onto his back. The foreboding look in his eyes betrayed his unease. "That's what I'm worried about."

"Why did Stone target Greg specifically? How did he even know about Greg and his connection to the Brotherhood?"

"Gabe, enough. Go to sleep."

He was probably just being paranoid. He burrowed beneath the blankets and turned on his phone. There was no signal in these mountains. Had Max been trying to reach him? Guilt gnawed at him.

**Gabe: Found the Brothers. They're a weird bunch. They know where the blade is, seem to think it's safe. I don't know, Lobito. I wanna come home to you, but Stone's still out there. Can't help feeling that leaving would be a big mistake. Miss you. You'd like it here.**

He hit send anyway, knowing the message wouldn't go through until they were back in civilization. He turned off his phone to preserve the battery, wrapped his arms around himself, and closed his eyes, imagining it was Max's arms around him. He could just make out the smell of Max on his T-shirt beneath the smothering aroma of incense that permeated every room.

"Ryan," Ben said. "Stop mumbling."

"Sorry, but hunger and thirst are not something you 'believe' in… It's like science, medicine, for fuck's sake! I bet these guys don't believe in vaccines or washing your hands after you shit, too!"

"Go to sleep!" both Ben and Gabe snapped.

It was easier said than done. Ben snored while Gabe tossed and turned, listening to every creak of the floorboards beyond their room, the chirping of the crickets and the hum of cicadas buzzing in his ears. He'd never realized what a city boy he was until he'd been out in the countryside and the silence kept him awake. He kept expecting something to break the silence, but he just wasn't sure what.

His eyes grew heavy, and he was asleep before he even realized it.

GABE'S EYES OPENED, ADJUSTING to the darkness of the bedroom. Silence rang in his ears and he couldn't figure out why he'd woken. Ben snored nearby, and Ryan coughed. The moonlight cast shadows of the trees against the ceiling. Gabe rolled over onto his side, hoping he'd go back to sleep.

Something moved in the mirror. Gabe stared into his own reflection—and at the hooded figure standing over Ryan's futon. A pale hand clasped a dagger, suspended over Ryan's exposed throat. It was Andre's apprentice. Horror left Gabe momentarily paralyzed.

*Am I dreaming?* was Gabe's first thought, and then the adrenaline kicked in.

The sheets flew off him and he shot across the room. He collided with the hooded figure, his claws digging into a bony wrist. "Wake up!" Gabe forced out the words through the horror clogging his throat. The pale hand dropped the dagger and caught it in his other, swiping at Gabe's stomach.

Lurching out of reach, he tripped over Ben as he woke with a snarl. Gabe crashed onto his back as the hooded figure charged Ben. Ryan lunged, throwing himself across the apprentice's back. The pair toppled to the ground in a tangle of arms and legs. Ryan's back hit the floor. The apprentice towered over him, dagger gleaming in the moonlight.

Ben lunged, his clothes straining as he transformed between man and beast. A clawed hand seized the apprentice by the throat and hurled him up against the wall. The hood tumbled down, revealing the gaunt, pale face of John Stone.

Claws flashed, tearing across Ben's face. Snarling, his blood spattered the ground, and he doubled over as Stone plowed a foot into his stomach. Stone bared yellowed teeth in a hideous smile and laughter crawled from his throat, wet and slimy like worms. As if he weren't surrounded three to one, as if this were all just a joke.

"Well, now. This makes things interesting," he growled as Ryan, Ben, and Gabe closed in on him, his back against the window. "Much more interesting than if I'd just cut your throats. How about a game then, a bit of a race? You get the key first, and you win! If I get the key, I'll let you say goodbye to your little redhead before I carve out his soul."

Gabe's jaw tightened, his fangs puncturing his lower lip. Stinging pain cut into his palms, and blood dripped hot between his fingers. "You won't get the chance!" He charged, flying at Stone.

The man's grin only widened even as the window cracked and shattered, even as the wind swept Gabe's hair back and they fell, the world a blur. Gabe fastened his claws into Stone's back and lunged for his throat.

The collision with the ground knocked them apart. Gabe tumbled, cradling his head in his hands, and collided with a tree trunk, gasping for air. His whole body ached and stung, his skin shredded from where he'd tumbled over rocks. He tried to stand but the world spun around him. He smelled sickly sweet incense and whipped around, clutching the tree for support. Stone's claws had churned up the earth and kept him from sliding over a steep hill.

Lurching to his hands and knees, Stone's greasy hair hung in a stringy curtain around his sunken face. His hands changed to black claws and his mouth to a hideous snarl. Gabe dropped to all fours as a wolf, his clothes falling away from him in tatters. The aroma of Stone's blood spurred him into a frenzy. He wanted to taste it, hot and coppery, and hear the crunch of bones between his teeth.

"You're not so fearsome to me," Stone growled, his face covered in black fur. "You still look like a frightened little boy." His snarling mouth turned to a long snout. He lunged, fangs gleaming. Gabe pounced, tasting fur and flesh and blood as they collided. Teeth clamped into the meat of his shoulder, piercing flesh. The pain had Gabe whipping around and biting back just as hard.

Stone howled and pulled out of Gabe's reach, leaving him with a scrap of fur in his teeth. The black wolf's lips pulled back from his fangs, his snout wrinkled in fury as he paced, his yellow eyes sizing Gabe up. Gabe circled, not daring to blink, waiting for Stone's next move. He became aware that his back was to the cliff and pressed forward, drawing closer to Stone and away from the drop.

Stone tensed and pushed off from the ground, strings of spit flying from his glistening fangs. They collided, tumbling over, and Stone's jaw locked around Gabe's scruff.

Ben hurtled into the fray, crashing into Stone. Stone's back legs slipped over the edge and before he could regain his footing, Ryan kicked him off the ledge. Tumbling down the hill, Stone rolled for what seemed an eternity until he crashed to a stop at the bottom, covered in dirt and leaves.

Gabe shifted, wiping away the blood dribbling from a cut above his eye. He didn't blink as he tried to make out if Stone was still moving. Far below, Stone heaved himself to his feet, holding one paw close to his chest. With a snarl, his yellow eyes blazing, he ran away into the forest.

When Gabe looked back, Ben and Ryan had shifted. "We gotta follow him. He's gonna go straight for the key."

"Damn straight." Ben panted, finding his feet. "We'll ask Andre for directions. Pack your things. We're leaving now."

Ryan growled, catching his breath. "Hey, it's not that trying to stop a madman from taking over the world isn't fun, 'cause it is, but next time we're in Italy, how about we stick to the tourist traps?"

Gabe blinked blood out of his eye. "Sounds good to me."

ANDRE'S FACE TURNED WHITE. "*That* was Stone? My deepest apologies! You must believe me. I had no idea! I thought he was just a pilgrim. We get so many of them in the summer. I should have been more wary. I'm so sorry."

"That's all right, Andre," Ben said. "It's not the first time Stone's conned someone, believe me. If I have my way, it'll be the last. My pack and I need to get to the desert before Stone does. Any suggestions?"

"Y-Yes, of course." Andre looked faint. "I truly am terribly sorry about all this. To reach the Imprint, you'll have to drive to Bologna. You'll know when you're close to the Imprint. The government has put up warnings everywhere and the roads leading to the Imprint are closed off. You'll have to go to Bologna and walk the rest of the way."

Ben shouldered his pack. "We'll kill Stone before he can get his claws on the key."

"Please, protect Kassandra."

Gabe nodded. "We will."

Ryan sighed. "You sure you guys wouldn't rather go on a walking tour? See the Colosseum?"

Ben clapped him on the back. "Chin up. We've got the car. We'll be there before you know it."

"Wait. Before you leave, you will need a pathmaker, one of the relics I told you of before." Andre had one of his monks fetch the relic.

"Brother Andre," the man panted, running over to them. He carried a wooden box inscribed with Celtic symbols. "One of the pathmakers was stolen."

Andre's nostrils flared. He yanked the box from the monk's shaking hands and shoved it at Ben. "There's no time to waste. Stone has the other pathmaker. He will be able to follow Kassandra through the portals."

Ben opened the box. Gabe peered over his shoulder. Inside was what looked like an ordinary stick with symbols carved into the wood. "What do I do with it?" Ben asked.

Andre said, "Nothing. Raise it to the sky, and the Imprint will react to it. When the portal opens, you must think strongly of your goal. If your motivation is strong enough, the portal will take you to Kassandra."

Ben grimaced. "That's not vague at all."

Andre bowed. "I'm sorry. I wish I could be more helpful. Find Kassandra. Make sure she and the key are safe."

Ben shoved the box in his bag. "We will."

THE SUN ROSE AND set during the hike to the base of the mountain. Bleary-eyed and exhausted, they stumbled to the parking space at the foot of the mountain. Gabe caught a whiff of Stone's scent. "Damn it!" He ran ahead and spotted the empty space where their car had been.

Ben snarled, "Well, shit. Now what?"

The parking lot was empty, the woods deathly quiet. Ben marched to the road beyond the trees. There were no cars in any direction. "It's the middle of the night." Ben sighed. "Probably not gonna be any cars coming up or down this road until midday."

Gabe's heart sank. They couldn't afford to sit around waiting. "We've gotta follow him. We'll move faster as wolves."

Ben squinted his eyes. "Gabe, no. It'll take days to reach the Imprint on foot. You can't spend that long as a wolf. It'll—"

Gabe crammed his shirt in his bag. "I'll alternate! We can't sit around. If Stone gets to the key before us—"

*I'll let you say goodbye to your little redhead before I carve out his soul.*

Stone's words lit a fire in his blood. If Stone got to the key, Max's life was in his hands. Gabe stripped naked and shifted, and all the worrisome thoughts flew from his head. He stopped worrying that he'd fail, and Stone's voice turned to mist in his mind.

Nothing else mattered—only the hunt. He took off, the soil warm and dry beneath his paws as he headed in the direction of the desert.

"Fine! At least carry your own shit," Ben called, tossing Gabe's pack at his paws. Gabe grabbed a strap in his teeth and lugged the bag along even as it slowed him down. Still, he was faster than Ben and Ryan as he loped ahead, grass tickling his underbelly and snagging in his fur.

The moon rose to its apex and then descended toward the mountains. Gabe and the others stopped to rest, and when Gabe opened his eyes, the sun had risen on a new day. They set off through the trees.

The heat of the day soaked into Gabe's fur and he was panting, his paws burning from the hot soil. Ben and Ryan shifted to keep pace with Gabe. After half a day of walking, Ben shifted back and handed out water.

"Gabe. Have some water."

Panting, Gabe nudged the water bottle. Ben glowered at him. "I mean Gabe the man."

Gabe growled. Shifting back and forth would sap his energy. Ben scowled and tossed some water in his face.

Gabe shifted, wiping the water out of his eyes. "Hey!"

Ben shoved the bottle at him.

Gabe drank, guilt gnawing at him. "I'm faster as a wolf. We'll cut our travel time if we stay shifted."

"At what cost?" Ben snapped. He looked Gabe square in the eyes. "Don't do this to me, you understand? Don't make me tell Max that you went feral after I promised him I'd look out for you."

His words made Gabe jolt.

Max.

Goddess, he missed Max. He couldn't remember the last time he'd heard Max's voice. He reached for his backpack and pulled out his phone. He had three missed calls and two messages, all from Max. He could have hit himself.

He paced toward the road to get better reception and dialed Max's number but it went to voice mail. Before he could leave a message, his phone rang.

"Gabe?" Max's voice was like warm sunshine on a cold day.

Gabe swallowed the lump in his throat. "Yeah. Hey. It's me. Sorry, are you in class?"

"No, I had my last day of in-person classes yesterday. I'm in Hanson's car right now. We're heading to Stowe. Hey, guys, say hi to Gabe!"

A chorus of voices made Gabe grin. "Hey. I missed you guys."

Max's quiet laugh, breathy and relieved, made him smile. "I was worried. I couldn't get in touch with you."

"I know. Sorry. I wrote to you. We found the monastery, and—" For a short while, they sat and talked, and the world beyond Max's voice ceased to exist.

*I know, Ben. Don't think for a minute that I don't. Once, this was about revenge, but my life is so much bigger than that. And it's because of him. Everything I do now, I do for Max. For our future.*

*If I fail, then Max will die. So if I have to push myself past the boundaries of man and beast, I'll do it.*

"That Imprint thing sounds dangerous."

"It is, probably," Gabe admitted. "I won't be able to get in touch for a while. But I promise the minute I can, I'll call you. Okay?"

"Be careful. Please? If anything happens to you, I'll be really disappoint-ed."

Gabe snorted. "Not heartbroken, devastated, crushed?"

"Yes. All of it." He was close to tears, Gabe could hear it in the way his voice thickened. He squeezed the phone tight, closing his eyes and wishing he could pull Max into his arms.

"Please, don't do anything stupid. Okay?"

Gabe smiled but it was heavy. "Okay."

But he would. He had to.

Or else one day he might never hear Max's voice again.

They said goodbye. The sun loomed high in the sky and cast long shad-ows. Gabe knelt and called upon the shift. It came over him slowly. His wolf was sluggish and tired, but it would still be faster than on foot.

He stumbled on his paws but his weary bones came to life. All that mattered was protecting his mate. For Max, he'd hunt Stone to the darkest corners of the Earth.

# CHAPTER 14

# A GILDED CAGE

It wasn't long after Gabe left when Max received a summons from the Alpha of the Council. Max was invited to his home in Vermont, though he used the word "invited" loosely. The contents of the email made it plain that Max had no say in the matter, no matter how politely Hanson phrased things.

Max wasn't surprised. Hanson had made it clear he would do whatever he had to in order to ensure Stone didn't get his hands on Max.

And so Hanson invited Max and his and Gabe's immediate family, as well as Zach, to his home. Zach got in touch with Ben's mother to come and watch the agency in his absence. Gabe's family had a history with Stone, and Hanson worried anyone in league with Stone would use them as leverage to get to Max.

Max had one last day of in-person classes after Gabe left. Hanson had made it clear he could continue his education but only from home.

"I'm basically a prisoner," Max grumbled, climbing into the sleek interior of the van Hanson hired to drive them to Vermont. The driver wore sunglasses and a suit and looked about as friendly as a shark.

"Yeah, but in a fancy house," Izzie argued, buckling in.

His mother sat in the second row beside Izzie. "Just try and think of this as a vacation, Max." She didn't sound happy about abandoning her job. "Did you pack lots to read? Try and keep yourself busy."

Veronica stretched out beside Max. "The circumstances aren't ideal but I can think of worse than being stuck in a big beautiful home in the Vermont wilderness."

"Yeah, it'll be like a vacation. Besides, someone's gotta babysit you," Zach teased. Max fought back the urge to bite him.

"I don't need babysitting, thanks."

Zach chuckled.

"Actually, you do," Izzie chimed in unhelpfully. "You cut yourself chopping vegetables for dinner, remember?"

Zach's eyes widened. "What? Are you hurt?" He leaned over and tried to check Max for injuries.

"Get off, I'm fine!" Max said, laughing and brushing away his prying hands.

"Max, I know this sucks," Zach said. "But this is bigger than us."

Max sighed. "I know. Lives are at stake. Maybe even the world. Is it too much to hope Stone got heatstroke and died, made things easy on us? It's good Hanson is taking precautions. I just... I hate this. You know?"

Zach squeezed his shoulder. "It won't be forever. Gabe and the others will fix this. We'll see them again soon. Ryan, too." His smile quivered. An ache panged through Max's chest, and he wondered if the blood oath had connected him and Zach more deeply than he'd thought.

Despite his misgivings, the route to Hanson's home was serene. City skyscrapers became lush rolling mountains. Max tried to call Gabe during the drive and sighed when he didn't answer. Gabe hadn't been able to answer his last two calls or his texts, but Max knew he was busy.

To his relief, Gabe finally called him, and while they chatted, Max's worries lifted. He was on Stone's trail, and Max had no doubt Gabe, Ben, and Ryan would be successful in tracking him down.

Fortunately, the long drive kept him distracted. They passed state lines and drove through the town of Stowe. They stopped only occasionally to use the bathroom at a gas station. Max went inside the gas station to buy snacks with Zach. "Do you think we can trust him?"

Zach grabbed a bag of chips from the shelf. "Hanson?"

Max approached a freezer full of cold drinks. "I don't *think* he's a bad guy. He's nice. Has a nice family. But I don't know. So many of his pack bought into Stone's pure-blood supremacy. They were downright hostile toward me and Gabe and sure, Hanson shut them down. But who is to say he doesn't support Moonborn ideology? Is he really keeping me safe, or does he have some ulterior motive?"

Zach grabbed a can of soda and handed Max some water. "You can't think that, Max. You'll make yourself sick worrying about it. Look at it this way—he's the Alpha of the Council. He's got a huge pack at his back. No one would dare fuck with them."

Max worried his lower lip. "But Stone felt cocky enough to kill their historians. If Stone thinks he can become a god, why should he care about the Council?"

Zach frowned and didn't seem to have an answer.

They took their items to the cash register. "I'm glad Gabe called. I hope he'll stay safe."

Zach smiled thoughtfully. "If he were here, he'd probably say something like... 'Don't be afraid, Lobito. I'll kick his ass if he looks at you wrong. Never fear!' All the while looking stupidly heroic."

Max surprised himself by barking a laugh at Zach's imitation of Gabe's Spanish lilt. "Yeah. And doing that posturing thing he does. You know, where he—"

"Sweeps his hair back and sticks out his chest?"

Max's mouth fell open. "Yes!" he said way too loudly.

Zach chuckled. "Do you think he knows it makes him look like a douche?"

"Hey! I think it's charming when he gets all dashing and heroic."

"Of course you do," Zach scoffed. "You're sleeping with him."

Max winced but Zach grinned playfully. To think Max would be joking about Gabe with his ex. It was... really nice, actually. "You'll find your dashing heroic idiot, too."

Zach hummed dismissively. "I don't know. I think I'm more into geeks."

Max grinned. "Like Ryan?"

Zach choked. "What? No! I just meant... Ryan isn't the only geek I know. I know lots! Tons!"

Max scoffed. "Okay. Sure."

"Shut up."

Snorting with laughter, Max shoved Zach on his way out of the store.

MAX FOUND IT HARD not to smile as his mother, Veronica, and Izzie exclaimed their delight as they pulled up outside an enormous mountainside retreat surrounded by sprawling woodlands. The security guard opened the gate for them. One by one, they exited the vehicle.

"This place is bigger than a whole city block!" Zach exclaimed.

"It's beautiful," Kendra whispered.

"Welcome, everyone!" Hanson and June came out to meet them, the latter carrying little Connor.

"I almost expected lumberjacks to greet us," Max said. It was hard not to be at ease in this fortified sanctuary. There were bodyguards at the door, patrolling the yard, and stationed up on the elevated deck that wrapped around the upper floor of the house.

"No, no, just us, I'm afraid." Hanson helped carry Kendra's bags up the stairs. "How was the drive? Is anyone hungry? June and I hunted a deer this afternoon. The chef is cooking it now."

Izzie whispered, "Chef? Whoa, these people are fancy."

The whole house smelled of lumber and pinecones and appealed to Max's wolf very much. The foyer opened to an enormous great room with tall bay windows that let in so much light it was like being outdoors, and there was an eight-seater dining room just off the huge kitchen. Max smiled at the sight of the fireplace that fit into an accent wall of gray stone.

There were plush sofas wrapped around a huge television, bookcases that touched the ceiling, and silky deerskin rugs on the floor. One rug even looked like bear fur. It was so soft that Max wanted to shift into a wolf, roll around in it, and settle in for a long, peaceful nap.

"Your home is gorgeous," Veronica said.

"Thank you," June replied, smiling warmly. "Connor, say thank you." He hid his face in his mom's neck, earning laughs from the pack.

"Were you expecting a dungeon?" Hanson asked, winking his one eye.

Max's face warmed. "N-no. Not really... Okay, maybe a little."

Hanson barked a laugh and clapped Max's shoulder. "Don't worry. You're not a prisoner here. You can attend virtual classes and go into town as long as you take an armed guard with you."

Max sighed. "Grocery shopping won't be awkward at all."

"Don't you worry about that. My staff here takes care of the cooking and housekeeping. You all just make yourselves at home. The guest rooms are on the second floor."

June motioned for them to follow her. She showed them to their rooms. There were two rooms with twin beds and one with a double. Max and Zach took their luggage into a twin bedroom while the rest of the pack wandered around. Zach looked out the window into the backyard. "Damn. Is that a hot tub?"

Max looked outside with him. "More like a hot spring."

Zach whistled. "This place makes my parents look poor. And they aren't."

Hanson and June led them on a tour of the house. Max was in awe of their accommodations, but that awe turned to unease when Hanson led them to the basement, which was just as big and sprawling as the rest of the house.

Hanson kept his tone cheery as he said, "In the event of an emergency, there is a secret tunnel concealed right... here." He ran his hand over a bookshelf and pulled on the gold statue of a howling wolf. The shelf rumbled along the wall, revealing a dark, winding passage.

Izzie gulped. "Cute. Spooky hidden tunnels are so in right now."

"Of course, I don't think we'll have to use it. I'm sure your friends will get to Stone in time. But in the event that doesn't happen—"

"They will stop Stone," Max said, sharper than he'd meant to. He cleared his throat and bowed his head. "Alpha Hanson," he added more respectfully. "Gabe and the others will stop Stone. I know they will. And they'll come home safely."

Hanson smiled. "Of course. We're talking worst-case scenario here. In fact, I bet you we'll be hearing from them very soon."

Max remained by the tunnel door as the bookshelf slid back into place. He closed his eyes tight and took a deep breath.

He believed in Ben and Ryan. In Gabe.

They would come home. They had to.

# CHAPTER 15
# I'M SORRY

*HE'S CLOSE.*

He ran, paws churning up the earth. The howls of other wolves filled the woods around him. Their voices were full of fury and bloodlust.

*Can taste him. Smell him.*

The sickly sweet incense made him wrinkle his nose.

*Prey. My prey!*

He salivated, craving blood.

*Must hunt. Must kill. Prey. Prey!*

Another scent tangled suddenly with the incense. It was cinnamon and chili. It was *mate* and *mine*, *love* and *life*.

Max. A joyful howl spilled from his throat.

A coppery taste hit the back of his throat. His stomach lurched. His paws turned to clawed hands as he covered his nose and mouth, his eyes watering as his throat prickled relentlessly.

*No. No! What happened to him?*

The ground squelched, wet underneath him. He pulled his hand away in disgust and found his palm slick, dyed red with the blood that watered the soil. He wanted to scream, to cry out for Max, but his voice was gone.

"Gabe! Gabe?"

Max's voice echoed through the trees, but Gabe's response died in his throat. There was no sweetness in his voice. It was wrong, somehow... sinister. It turned his skin cold and made him want to hide.

Yellow eyes burned in the darkness. An achingly familiar red wolf slunk from the trees. Tears pricked Gabe's eyes and he couldn't speak as those yellow eyes left him paralyzed with fright. Those weren't Max's eyes looking back at him, but the eyes of a predator.

The thing wearing Max's skin tipped its head back and howled, a guttural, awful howl. The stars burned, the moon grew bigger—no, it came *closer*, burning red as if in fury. When Gabe looked back, Stone stood where Max had been, the blood-soaked moonblade clenched in his bony fingers.

Despair brought him to his knees. He was too late. He'd failed. Max was gone because of him.

A scream tore from his throat, turned to a growl, then a howl. Gabe ceased to exist as fur sprouted from his body and his hands turned to clawed paws. The grief, the pain, the despair—it all vanished.

*Hunt. Kill.*

A flash of red fur, gleaming fangs.

*Prey. You are prey.*

Fur in his mouth. Bones crunching. Flesh ripping between his jaws, tearing—

*"Gabe!"*

Blood filled his mouth.

*Oh no. Please, no. I killed him. I killed Max. I could have saved him, I could have—*

"Gabe, talk to me. What's wrong?"

A hand fell, warm and heavy on his shoulder. The touch radiated warmth and comfort. He opened his eyes, blurry with tears, and there was dampness on his cheeks.

"Gabe, you're biting yourself. Let go, okay? Easy now."

Gabe's jaw was painfully tight. His arm ached and throbbed, and he realized the pain was what had woken him. He jolted back, gasping as his jaws relinquished his own arm. His fangs had punctured the flesh and left bloody holes and deep indentations in his skin. He gnashed his teeth, fighting back the pitiful pained sounds pulling at the back of his throat.

"Shit, that looks bad! Gabe, you okay?" Ryan asked, kneeling beside him with some bandages.

Gabe's stomach lurched, and he veered away from them as he gagged. Nothing came up. There was no food in his stomach to get rid of. They hadn't eaten yesterday and the hunger had forced them to stay in wolf form. The wolf in them was capable of going several days without food, while their human forms were crippled by hunger pains.

He realized his hands were clawed, dirt clumped beneath his razor nails. He shivered, suddenly cold despite the mild morning air.

"Did you have a dream, too?" Ben asked.

"Wait, you had one?"

Ryan's hands shook as he wrapped a bandage around Gabe's arm. "It was... man."

"Why, what happened?"

Ryan wet his chapped lips. "I don't wanna talk about it."

"It was a nightmare, Ryan," Ben said.

"No. It was more than that. It showed me what happens if we fail," Gabe murmured, stomach clenching. He regretted speaking right away. If that was a vision, then what did that mean for Max? Was he safe right now? He lunged for his bag, fingers trembling as he called Max. "Pick up. Pick up. Come on." The call went to voice mail. "Fuck!"

It had been two weeks since he'd last seen Max. On the occasion they stopped in towns for a proper meal and rest, he'd been able to charge his phone and talk to Max, but that had been a week ago. Last he'd heard, Max was settling in at Hanson's home but he knew little more than that. For a week now, they'd been stuck in the wilds with no towns in sight. Gabe kept his phone off to preserve battery and even with a portable solar bank charger, the battery was running low. Not that it mattered out in the wilderness with hardly any reception.

They moved as fast as they could on foot, but often had to stop to rest and hunt, which only lengthened their journey. They'd move so much faster if they could get a damn car. Every driver they'd stopped had demanded to see their identification, turning them away when they realized Gabe and his pack were wolves. A week ago, they'd come across Ben's rental in the woods, drained of gas. Stone's scent led them into the wilds, and they'd been pursuing him since.

They'd passed the city of Bologna yesterday. Gabe had longed to get in touch with Max but Ben had been adamant they keep moving since Stone was ahead of them. They were gaining on Stone, and heading straight for the Imprint. Just yesterday evening, they'd walked around barriers in the road, and ignored signs warning travelers away from the Imprint.

"Gabe, it's no good. There's no reception out here," Ben said. "Look, we need to stay calm."

"Ben's right. This is the Imprint's work." Ryan sighed, combing a shaky hand through his hair. "The closer we get to it, the more we're exposed to its magical BS. So it's showing us visions."

"Fuck. So all this shit we're seeing could actually happen?" Gabe asked, his voice pinched. Beside him, Ben's shoulders tensed. Gabe wondered what he had seen in his dream.

"Or not!" Ryan added. "It's showing us possibilities. The stuff we're seeing could come to pass or not. The future's hella fluid. Nothing's set in stone—no pun intended."

Gabe growled, "Then how about it shows us a possibility where I'm with Max."

"Well, visions induced by a powerful magical presence will react off our strongest emotion. Fear is *pretty* strong, so—"

"Guys," Ben rumbled. "We need to keep moving. Ryan, you know about Imprints. Is it dangerous to get too close?"

Ryan scratched his chin. His boyish face was sprouting a thick beard from the weeks they'd spent wandering the wilderness. "Some Imprints are. I read about one in Ireland that... dissolved anyone that got too close.

This one, though... Hmm. Hard to say, but the monks didn't seem to think it was dangerous. So far, it's just giving us bad dreams. Any headaches, nose bleeding? No? Then we're fine. Probably. For now, anyway."

"Just what I love, a bunch of ifs, maybes, and probabilities." Ben shouldered his pack. He grimaced and clutched at his stomach. Gabe's inner wolf whined, uncomfortable at the sight of his friend's weakness. "Listen. I know it's hard out here. We're all hungry. But we can't keep shifting like we have been. We're just gonna have to deal with it until we're out of the desert. Clear? Then let's keep moving."

The skeletal remains of cars lingered in the road, some abandoned, others charred and in pieces. It seemed the Imprint's presence messed with vehicles. Even planes seemed to steer clear of this section of sky. As they cleared the rise they were walking up, Gabe quickly realized what happened to aircraft that came too close to the Imprint.

Ryan's mouth fell open. "Holy crap!" He ran up to get a look at the crater in the earth, the force that made it leaving the road cracked and shattered in places. The twisted black remains of a helicopter lay within the crater, its rotor blades tangled up in a pile of trees.

"The Imprint causes so much damage. Damn druids and their magic," Ben grumbled. "Maybe it's good they were hunted to extinction." He turned his back and pressed on.

"Can you blame 'em for hating humans?" Ryan wiped sweat from his brow, blinking hard. "Druids were even more despised than werewolves."

"For good reason," Ben said. "They tried to take over the world."

Ryan shook his head. "Not all of them. Just Atticus's people. He was the King of the Druids. He became power hungry and convinced his followers magic made them superior to wolves and humans. Thanks to what an asshole he was, even the good druids were burned at the stake. Can you imagine how different the world would be if druids and their magic still existed? I mean it still does exist—there are some pretty cool spell books lying around—but still!"

Perhaps the forests would be better protected from pollution and deforestation, but Gabe wasn't sure how magic would have been integrated into society. Druids would have always been feared and loathed by religious groups for their association with witchcraft.

The world was complicated enough without throwing magic into the mix.

THE IMPRINT WAS FARTHER than it looked. Gabe had hoped to reach it before the end of the day, but began to accept defeat as the sun sank lower in the sky. Gabe walked fast during the day, needing the adrenaline to numb the ache of hunger. He wished he could shift, since the heat made his mouth dry and his head throb. Ryan nearly passed out, and they had to stop and take a break.

They came across the corpses of birds decaying in the heat as they got closer to the Imprint.

"Looks like they fell outta the damn sky," Ben murmured.

They shifted to wolves long enough to consume the carrion. Not his best meal by any means, but Gabe would take it. Finally, the hunger pains faded and they traveled on with higher spirits.

The sun disappeared beyond the brown hills and Gabe sighed his relief. His skin was burnt and peeling in places since the trees offered no shade. They were barren and warped, their bark a sickly white. The heat of the day turned cool and pleasant as they made camp among the dead trees using their backpacks as pillows, the ground hard beneath them.

The stars burned bright up above, twinkling against a blanket of indigo sky. He wished New York had stars like these.

He wished Max was here to see them with him.

Knowing it was hopeless, he pulled out his phone but the screen flickered on and off as he tried to type out one of many messages he'd composed over the past several days out in the desert. He couldn't send any of them.

**Gabe: I had a dream where we failed. I failed. I'm restless. I know I've got to find Stone, but all I want is to come home and make sure you're all right. I can't. I won't come home until I know I've done everything I can to make sure you're safe. I love you. I miss you.**

He hit send in vain, knowing it wouldn't go through. The phone told him off like he knew it would. Hurling it into the dirt, he rolled over, facing away from it. He exhaled around the lump in his throat, blinking hard. Max was an ocean away, worrying about him, trying to call or message, wondering what had become of him, why he wouldn't answer.

"I'm sorry," he said to no one and nothing.

How long would it be before he could see Max again, hold him in his arms, kiss the freckle above his lips?

How was his mother? Worried sick, most likely. Izzie was probably still mad at him. He hoped Zach was looking after his family in Gabe's absence.

The joy of being one with the wilds had faded, and he and his wolf longed for the familiarity of pack, den, and territory. He closed his eyes tight, trying to remember when they'd said goodbye, when he'd held Max in his arms. The memory slipped through his fingers like water. He couldn't remember the words they'd spoken as they said goodbye.

He reached blindly for his phone and swiped through his pictures until he found one Izzie had sent him of Max's twentieth birthday. Gabe remembered that day bittersweetly. It was the day when they'd finally accepted their feelings for each other, but it was also the day he'd nearly lost Max when he went off on his own to confront Stone and Richard.

There he was, freckled and red-haired, smiling brightly enough to rival the sun. Gabe hardly recognized the man with his arms around Max. The man was neatly groomed, smiling just as brightly, his nose nestled against the nape of Max's neck. He couldn't remember the last time he'd been so happy, so carefree.

A notification flashed. His battery was on its last legs. Not that it mattered. Out here, phones were useless.

Gabe composed a message, erasing and starting again more times than he could count as the battery dwindled to one percent. He wished he'd done better. He wished he'd stayed, even if he knew staying with Max would only have ended badly for both of them. But still. He wished he'd never left Max's side.

**Gabe: I'm sorry. Goodbye.**

He hit send. The screen flickered to black. It never came back on.

THE PACK ROSE WITH the sun and carried on, pursuing the silhouettes of broken buildings on the horizon. Ryan suddenly stopped, a strange expression on his face, a mixture of confusion and panic.

"What?" Gabe asked.

"My phone's really hot!" He fumbled for his back pocket and yelped, tossing his phone onto the ground and wringing his hands. Ryan's phone smoked, the screen flickering wildly before it exploded in a shower of glass and metal and plastic. "Aw, man! That thing was expensive!"

Ben whipped out his own phone and tossed it into the dirt. "Must be the Imprint messing with them. Leave 'em. They're useless out here, dangerous if they're just gonna explode like that."

Gabe reached for his phone. It was warm to the touch and smelled faintly of burning metal.

*I'll call you, Max. The minute I can.*

He chucked it onto the ground and heard it explode just as they descended the hill, walking along the cracked road into the dilapidated village of Paradiso. Plant life burst from between the cracks in the road, sprawling thick and green across the asphalt.

Ryan admired the greenery and remarked, "This place looks like a bad zombie apocalypse movie."

Gabe couldn't deny the comparison. Plant life devoured what buildings were still standing. The narrowed roads were cracked and uneven, consumed in ivy and sprawling roots. The buildings had to go back thousands of years at least and must have been charming once.

Ozone permeated the air, magic hanging thick around him like a storm cloud.

A burst of laughter tickled his ears. He froze, holding his breath, trying to make it out. He wanted to ask if someone else had heard it but figured he'd look crazy until he heard the uptick in Ryan's heart.

"You heard it, too?" Gabe asked, relieved.

"Yeah, I—"

Horses whinnied, and voices carried through the deserted streets. Gabe walked into Ben, who'd frozen, wide eyes darting around as the dead streets came suddenly to life with people. Spectral horses pulled carriages and carried riders through the streets. A chill shuddered through Gabe as a woman, ghostly and glowing blue like a projection, walked right through him as she chatted in Italian to the woman next to her.

"What the ever-loving fuck?" Ben whispered, sweat glistening on his brow. Every hair in his bushy beard looked like it was on end.

A child ran right through Gabe's legs, screaming as he ran with his friends. They flickered in and out and vanished.

Ryan pushed himself flush against the wall as an old man hobbled past clutching his cane. "I-it's the Imprint. Andre wasn't kidding; time is messed up here. Holy shit. I've never seen anything like this!"

Ben shivered. "Come on. They're harmless. We gotta keep going. We're close now." He still stumbled out of the way of a woman holding a baby to her breast. "Ignore them. We can't slow down. Stone could be here."

Gabe balled his hands into fists and pressed ahead, trying not to cringe as he walked through ethereal bodies going about their lives without knowing that they'd been dead for thousands of years.

They passed through what had once been a piazza with a shattered fountain in the middle of the square. Apparitions flickered in and out of time, people sitting on the shattered stone of the fountain's edge, children running through debris flooding the streets, and couples arm in arm.

"Why?" Gabe murmured, falling into step beside Ryan. "These people look peaceful. Why would the druids target them?"

Ryan sighed. "Their king Atticus was hell-bent on domination of humans and wolves. He and his followers believed their magic made them superior to everyone."

Gabe coughed. The air was thick with dust. His jaw slackened as they rounded the corner into the next street. The buildings had been leveled to nothing but piles of rubble. Going any farther was impossible against the mountain of debris flooding the streets. Ryan gasped. "Holy shit. That's it!"

On the horizon several miles from the village, a great crackling dome of electricity and gray clouds darkened the skies. Everything in its path had been blown apart, uprooting trees and crumbling buildings.

"Holy shit. The druids did that?" Gabe asked.

"Well, not intentionally. It's not, like, some spell or something." Ryan squinted at the horizon, mouth slack in astonishment. "It's a side effect of all the magic they unleashed when they destroyed this place. From what I've read, when you use magic, you have to draw on the elements around you. The earth gives and druids take, that sort of thing. If you take too much, it has consequences for the environment."

A woman screamed something in Italian. Gabe whirled around and found only an empty street behind him.

Ryan's face was white. "She said, 'Run, it's the druids.'"

A scream pierced his ear, and he jumped. Ben cringed, his eyes widening. When he turned around, the spectral villagers were running, leaping from their carriages, grabbing their children as they ran. Roots exploded from the ground, ensnaring people as they tried to flee, squeezing them to death like a snake strangled its prey. The roots had long since withered, but they were still tangled around skeletal remains.

Gabe said, "I had no idea the druids made it as far as Italy."

The villagers ran, casting spectral light that glowed on Ryan's face. "They almost brought Europe to its knees, man. They tried to dominate America, too, till the werewolves sided with the humans and burned 'em at the stake."

"Goddamn, druids were assholes," Ben growled, recoiling as a spectral root flailed above the soil like a snake.

Gabe didn't want to watch anymore, but the screams followed him as he turned his back. "We gotta find a way around this rubble." The Imprint beckoned them from the wilds beyond the village.

They went south and passed what had once been a church, the bell tower crumbled. Apparitions flickered and screams echoed as people ran, seeking shelter in the church.

New apparitions burst in and out of sight, men and women clad in flowing robes, armed with staves and floating spell books, ghostly incantations spilling from their lips. Men and women fell, disappearing as they hit the ground where their shattered skeletons lay.

Ryan tried to read one of the spell books floating by a mage's hand. "Interesting! It sounds like they were speaking Gaelic. My gran taught me some Gaelic. These Celtic symbols are ancient!" Gabe took a glimpse at the strange symbols scrawled upon the pages.

"Guys, this way is clear!" Ben motioned for them to follow him down a narrow road that snaked away from the ruined village and toward the hills.

The wind picked up and the clouds darkened as they drew closer to the Imprint, leaving the village behind them. Apparitions of druids marched to meet them, fading in and out of existence, sometimes bursting directly in front of Gabe's face and giving his heart a jolt. What had seemed a light mist at first quickly became a dense gray fog crackling and glowing blue around them.

"Stay together!" Ben called. "Don't get lost in this!"

Gabe pressed close to Ryan's side, the other man trembling violently beside him. The fog smelled of an oncoming storm, ozone and crackling electricity. And something else. Incense, so faint the wind might carry it away in seconds.

"It's Stone! I've got his scent!" Gabe called. He took off running into the swirling fog.

An explosion of blue light blinded him momentarily. Silhouetted against that searing light was—

"Stone!" Gabe bared his fangs and charged, pelting past Ben and Ryan toward Stone's figure just before the light faded, consuming Stone in the dark mist. Within the mist, that light crackled again like a burst of lightning on the horizon.

A clawed hand lunged for him and in a blur of black fur, Stone hurled himself from the mist at Gabe. His back struck the ground, and clawed hands curled around his throat. Gabe slammed his foot into Stone's hip, bowling him off. Scrambling to stand, Gabe panted. Blood trickled hot and wet down his skin where Stone's claws had nicked him.

Stone's thin face split into a grin. "You're here. Good. It'll be so satisfying to make you watch as I rip the key out of the monk's cold, dead fingers."

Behind Stone, the light sputtered and crackled. Voices cried out from within the blinding light, which was expanding by the second into an archway. Stone looked over his shoulder, eyes wide and glowing with lights. He whirled around and leaped into the portal. The portal closed right as Gabe neared it.

"The pathmaker," Ben said, already rifling through his bag. "We need to use it now!" He withdrew the ancient relic from the box. He thrust it to the sky and waited.

The clouds rumbled with thunder, and a bolt of lightning cracked across the sky and struck the tip of the pathmaker. Ryan shouted, grabbing Gabe when he lurched toward Ben, but Ben didn't appear to have been electrocuted. Ben's eyes were wide, face bloodless in shock.

The runes on the pathmaker lit up and pulsed, and before their eyes, a portal burst into existence.

"H-holy shit," Ryan whispered.

Gabe reached out a hand and his fingers sank into the portal as easily as water. "We need to follow him."

Ryan looked from Gabe to the portal. "All of us? It's a frigging portal! Who knows where it'll send us?"

Gabe growled, suddenly doubtful. But there was no time for doubt. "Then I'll go. I'll find the monk and bring her back before Stone does."

Ben lunged for his arm. "Gabe, you can't go alone!"

"Ryan's right. We don't know shit about portals! We can't all jump in! If I—" Fear threatened to crumble his resolve. He thought of Max, the blood dripping from his chest, possessed by Stone. "If I fail, then someone's gotta be here to stop Stone when he reappears."

Ben swallowed, throat bobbing. "Remember what Andre said. Think of your goal."

Gabe took in a breath. He thought of Max, he thought of Kassandra and the key, he thought of Stone. He charged into the light and—

# CHAPTER 16

# TEAR HIS FLESH

THE SENSATION WAS LIKE missing a step going down the stairs. The pit of Gabe's stomach lurched and for a moment, he was suspended in a place where neither sight nor sound existed. Then, Gabe tumbled, coughing as he choked on dust and dirt.

Rubbing soil from his eyes, he looked up. He lay in a dark tangled forest, the smell of other wolves ripe in the air. The moon suspended, casting light upon the leaf-strewn ground and illuminating the foot and paw prints littering the ground. Howls filled the woods, echoing over the treetops. The wolves weren't howling for the fun of it, nor to summon pack. They were baying for bloodshed.

Arms trembling, Gabe pushed himself up and his eyes adjusted enough to make out the silhouettes of trees. He stumbled over roots and uneven ground. The howls grew louder, rising from the rocky peak of a small mountain. Gabe ascended the trail. He scented cinnamon and chili mixed with blood and terror.

"Max." Icy fear cascaded down his back, raising the hairs all over his body. What in hell's name was Max doing out in these woods? Gabe had to find him.

The ground sloped and Gabe used his claws to cling to the rocky wall to his left to keep from tripping as he climbed. The ashy scent of smoke hit his lungs, and he panicked, thinking there was a forest fire. No firelight lit up the forest below. The scent had to be coming from somewhere above him.

The ground evened out as Gabe reached the bald peak of the mountain. Lungs ready to burst, Gabe slumped and braced himself with his hands on his knees. Sweat stung his eyes and he wiped it away, muscles aching in protest as he pushed on. Torchlight burned his eyes, glowing impossibly bright in the darkness. That explained the scent of smoke.

A huge gathering of werewolves crowded the mountaintop, some in wolf form, others caught between human and animal. Gabe lurched behind a boulder before any of them could see him. Heart pounding, Gabe peered out at them.

The pack had their backs to him and were fixated on whatever interested them toward the edge of the mountain. The more human ones wore all white with a strange symbol stitched into the fabric of their uniform. A wolf howling at the base of a flourishing tree, encircled by the moon.

Shit. Gabe recognized that symbol at once. It had been tattooed on the suicide bombers who'd killed several agents over a year ago. The Wargs of the Apocalypse.

Where was he? He didn't recognize this forest. He didn't even know if he'd wound up in the States when he passed through the portal. All he knew was that Max was here somewhere.

The wolves howled and cleared a path as a robed figure parted the crowd, masked and silent. He was tall, and as demonstrated by the uniform that fit tightly across his chest, clearly male, but Gabe had no idea what he looked like.

What he saw next paralyzed him completely, the fight ripped from him by sheer horror.

The crowd parted for the robed man, revealing an altar.

And Max, bound across the altar's rocky surface with silver chains. John Stone towered over him, smiling cruelly. Gabe lost all thought of self-preservation. All that mattered was getting Max the hell away from these freaks at any cost to his own life. Gabe bolted, claws out and fangs bared. "Get the hell away from him!" No one had any reaction to his roar, not even Max. He lunged for John Stone and tumbled through the man as if Stone were a phantom.

Gabe crashed into the dirt, stunned and horrified. He whirled around and slashed, astonished when his claws went right through Stone's body.

"Max!" He lunged for Max's bound hands. His fingers passed right through them. Max's face was white with fear and he shivered, his eyes fixed on the moon. It was as if he didn't see Gabe at all.

"Max. I'm here, mi amor. Right here. Hey!" Gabe tried to touch his face, his heart sinking as his fingers disappeared into Max's body.

"It's not real," said a cold feminine voice.

A woman stood behind him, her back against a tree. She gazed impassively upon the scene as if it were nothing but an outdoor movie showing. She was robed in the garments of the Brotherhood.

"Kassandra? From the Brotherhood?"

"Who are you?" She arched a brow, narrowing her eyes.

Gabe raised both hands to show his blunt fingernails. "A friend. My name is Gabe Reyes. I came to warn you—"

Gabe jumped as Stone began speaking, addressing the crowd. "Tonight, I take back the powers of a god from this undeserving hybrid!"

The crowd howled and roared.

Gabe's stomach clenched as Max writhed on the altar. "Max, I'm here!" He knelt, trying to take Max's hand. "Why can't I touch him?" His voice broke.

The monk sighed, rubbing her eyes as she came toward him. "You can't. This isn't real, like I said."

"It sure looks real! That's my mate lying like some sacrificial lamb on that altar!"

"Well, it's not."

"Why am I seeing this?" Gabe asked.

Kassandra shrugged. "Portals are... sensitive. The magic is reactive, it shapes itself to whoever enters the portal. So what I see will be different from what you see. I was having a rather nice vision of ancient Rome before you came barging in and interrupted me. What you're seeing has either already come to pass, will come to pass, or can still be prevented."

"What do you mean?" Behind Gabe, Max shivered on the altar, struggling to break free. Gabe turned toward him again.

The monk snapped her fingers next to Gabe's ear. "Pay attention. What you're seeing can still be avoided if it hasn't happened yet."

Gabe's head was spinning. "Wait. You're telling me this is the future?"

Oh fuck. Was there a possibility this horrific scene could come to pass?

Kassandra approached one of the salivating wolves and stuck her finger through its nostril. "The Imprint has shattered time, which results in visions of past, present, or future events."

Gabe still couldn't bring himself to unclench his fists when he watched Max shiver and shake behind him. It was far, far too close to home. "Excuse me for losing my shit, lady. I don't exactly go time traveling every single day."

She scoffed. "I can tell."

"I'm here to warn you. See that man? That's John Stone."

Her eyes went wide. "Il Mostro."

"Yes! He knows you're hiding here. He's after the blade. I came to warn you."

"How am I supposed to trust you?" She touched a satchel at her hip. Gabe supposed the key to the tomb lay within.

"Just let me take the key, destroy it—"

She clutched the satchel to her chest. "Destroy this? Do you have any idea what you're implying? This key is an ancient relic!"

"We're all gonna be ancient relics unless someone stops Stone from getting the moonblade!" Gabe lunged for the satchel.

"Get away! For all I know, you're working with Stone!"

Splitting pain cracked across his jaw. He toppled over, ears ringing. The bitch had slugged him with the satchel, and damn, did that key weigh a ton.

Kassandra took off running. "Go home! I don't need your help or any-one's!"

Gabe rolled onto his back, the stars blurring above his head. He scram-bled to his feet and turned his back on the nightmarish scene. He looked back once at the masked figure. "Whoever you are, you're gonna regret ever messing with my mate."

Gabe stampeded through the trees after Kassandra, the breath clawing from his lungs as he pursued the scent of her incense. "Kassandra!" Kas-sandra's white robe made it easy to follow her through the darkness. There came a snarl behind Gabe. He turned and burning yellow eyes blazed from the shadows.

"Kassandra, watch out!" Gabe roared, throwing himself at Stone as the black wolf materialized from a portal and charged toward her. Gabe col-lided with the black wolf's side and knocked Stone out of the air mid-leap. Jaws snapped at Gabe, and he wrapped his hands around Stone's throat and tried to push him away.

Stone shifted, his face elongated and black with coarse fur. He grinned as behind them a familiar howl echoed over the mountaintop. The fight went out of Gabe. It was the red wolf's warbling howl, but Max's howl had never sounded so *wrong* before.

"Hear that, Gabriel?" Stone grinned, strings of drool dangling from his pointed fangs. "I win. No matter how hard you fight, I win!"

"No!" Gabe snarled, drawing his claws across Stone's face.

Stone yelped and freed himself, blood dripping from where Gabe's claws had cut him.

A heavy claw caught Gabe across the face, then across the head. Gabe crashed facedown into the dirt as Stone charged toward Kassandra.

A blinding flash of light blasted Gabe's eyes as she opened a portal. She had one foot through when Stone's claws wrapped around the strap of her satchel. There was a struggle and then came the telltale buzz of ripping fabric as the satchel tore away from her shoulder. "No!" Kassandra roared.

Stone howled with laughter. "Catch me if you can!" He leaped through the portal.

Gabe charged after him into the light, thinking of Ben and Ryan to guide him through the portal. That horrible, weightless sensation crashed over Gabe, then he tumbled head over heels across warm, dry soil.

Sunlight warmed his face, and he opened his eyes to a pure blue sky. Gabe breathed in deep, smelling sweet dry grass and soil, and struggled to hold back a wave of relief so intense it brought tears to his eyes.

There was still time to prevent what he'd seen. To save Max from such an awful fate.

"Gabe!" Ryan came running and helped Gabe stand.

"Kassandra, I assume," Ben said, offering a hand to the monk.

Kassandra took Ben's hand and stood. "I'm guessing you all came to stop Stone?"

"Yup," Ryan chirped.

Kassandra scowled. "Some job you're doing."

On the horizon miles away, a burst of blue light like a bolt of lightning erupted.

Kassandra whirled toward the light. "It's him. He's materialized. We've got to follow him!"

Stone had the key, but Gabe wouldn't stop hunting him until he could say for certain that such a horrible future would never come to pass.

"Romulus's tomb is in the shadow of Mount Vesuvius. The moon-blade is entombed with his remains," Kassandra said, firelight illuminating her dark brown eyes.

"How far is the tomb?" Ben asked, setting aside the bone of a rabbit that had been picked clean.

"From Rome, about two and a half hours or so by car. From here? I have no clue."

"Nearest city is Bologna. We'll find somewhere in the city to rent a car. If we move fast, we could easily beat Stone there."

"Unless, you know, he rents a car—or hijacks a car, 'cause being in the cult and on the run from the law probably didn't pay much," Ryan said, picking his teeth with a small bone. "You see his beard? That thing's been growing for years. Guy can't even pay a barber to do some basic manscaping." He shrugged thoughtfully. "But I guess overgrown cultist beards are kinda in right now."

"Enough talk. We have to wake early, get the key back." Kassandra rolled over onto her side abruptly.

Gabe shoved his backpack behind his head. The stars winked down at him, the half-moon obscured by clouds. When he closed his eyes, he saw Max's terrified voice and the tears in his eyes.

A shudder wracked his body and he pushed himself up. He reached for his bag and remembered his phone was gone. He had no way of contacting Max. His gut clenched. All he wanted was to hear his voice, to reassure himself that Max was all right. To get that damn image of Max, broken and terrified, out of his mind.

He growled, clawing at the dirt, longing to shift and run. He wanted to tell Ben and Ryan and the monk to go on ahead so he could jump on the first plane back to New York. He had to see Max, had to know he was all right.

His legs twitched restlessly, so Gabe walked away from their makeshift camp to a hill overlooking the Imprint on the horizon. They hadn't gotten far, only passing the ruins of the town. Gabe wished he hadn't lost the printed photos of Max and his family. He ached to see his face, anything to chase away the way he'd looked in that nightmare of the future.

"Doing some stargazing?" Ryan shuffled up behind him and plopped down on the dry grass.

Gabe hummed. "Can't sleep," he confessed.

"Fuck…" Ryan sighed. "What kind of messed-up shit did you see? Did you go to the future? The past? Did you kill baby Hitler?"

"I wish." Gabe shivered, recalling the tears on Max's cheeks, the pulsing runes on the moonblade. "I saw what happens if we fail."

Ryan didn't press him and sat with his knees drawn tight to his chest. "You didn't happen to see what happens if we win, right?"

Gabe sighed. "I don't get it, though. Stone wasn't alone. He was working with the Wargs of the Apocalypse. Stone had someone else with him, a masked man who looked like he was calling the shots for the Wargs. And Max…" Gabe swallowed. His throat thickened just imagining the suffering Max must have endured at the hands of Stone and those terrorists.

"Hey, it's not gonna happen. We're not gonna let them near Max." Ryan's hand fell, firm and reassuring, on his shoulder.

Gabe took in a gulp of air, urging himself to stay calm as his fangs lengthened and his claws pierced the soil. He wanted to shift, forget all the fear and just run back to New York, to Max. "Who was that guy?" he murmured.

"Who?"

"The masked guy I saw with Stone. He and Stone were working together, but it looks like Stone is on his own out here."

"Who knows?" Ryan lay back, his arms behind his head. "Maybe other fanatics know about his plan? Seeing one of their own take such immense power would sure as hell be plenty of reason for the fanatics to crawl outta the woodwork. It would legitimize their BS about how werewolves are worthy of ruling over humans."

Gabe clenched his jaw. Stone could not so much as touch the moonblade. He rolled onto his side and closed his eyes. He had to try and get some sleep so he wasn't a burden to the pack in the morning.

Ryan sighed. "I wonder how Zach and Max are doing."

Gabe said, "Hey, Ry, you're gonna tell Zach eventually. Aren't you?"

Ryan's face colored. He became interested in an oddly shaped leaf. "I don't know. We've got a good thing going between us. Romance might fuck it all up, if he even feels the same way…"

Gabe snorted. "That's so cliché."

"What?" Ryan snapped.

"That romance complicates things. That's not always true for friendships. My mom and dad were friends for years before he worked up the nerve. Turned out she'd liked him all along but she was just too scared to say anything." Gabe nudged Ryan's shoulder. "Sound familiar?"

"I am *not* scared."

"I'm talking about Zach, dummy."

"Yeah, right. It's just obvious Zach doesn't see me that way."

"To whom?"

"Uh, anyone with eyes?"

Gabe shook his head. "Look, life's short. All I wanna do right now is hold my mate and tell him how much I love him. And I can't. Trust me, you don't wanna be in that position."

Ryan fell quiet for a while. Gabe closed his eyes and tried to sleep.

And managed a smile before he drifted off.

THE NEXT DAY, THEY walked with the Imprint at their back. After three days of walking in the heat, they passed beyond the warning signs and the barriers. The distant buildings of Bologna grew closer and closer. Gabe stopped to sleep for the night with his pack within the trees.

Gabe wandered away from the others and sat on a hill with a view of the distant city. Cars sped past on the road below. They would surely arrive in the city by morning. Gabe closed his eyes and curled in on himself.

It felt like he'd been asleep for seconds when someone shook him awake. Ryan's voice hissed, "Gabe, wake up! It's an emergency!"

Gabe groaned, just wanting to sleep a little while longer—

Gunfire cracked and Gabe propelled himself awake. He whirled around to where Ryan stared, ashen faced, toward the trees where he'd left Ben and Kassandra. The wind blew, carrying the smell of gunpowder, silver, and aconitum.

"Hunters?" Gabe whispered. "Shit!" He grabbed his bag and charged down the hill, Ryan tearing after him. Gabe slowed down as they approached, ducking behind a tree.

Kassandra was surrounded by armed humans who were circling her. Gabe's heart dropped. Ben lay sprawled on the ground behind her, clutching his shoulder and panting through gritted teeth.

Fury had Gabe's fangs dropping, his claws piercing his clenched fists.

Ryan whispered, "Hey. Smell that? One of the hunters... he's a werewolf."

Gabe's fury spiked, his eyes locking on a young man whose scent stood out among the hunters. His hair was so blond it was almost white. Cyan eyes regarded Ben dispassionately, as if he were bored.

No doubt about it, he had the scent of a wolf, so diluted with blood and silver it was barely distinguishable. One of their own kind dared to hunt them down. His wolf snapped and snarled, craving blood, itching to run in and fight to defend his pack.

"No," Kassandra whispered. Her face was an ashy color, wide eyes fixed on the blond hunter. "Eddie? Is that you?"

The hunter's narrowed eyes locked onto her, brows furrowing in confusion.

"It's me," Kassandra whispered. "Kassandra."

The hunters gave the blond man curious looks.

The blond hunter lowered his pistol, hands shaking. "K-Kassie? Holy shit. What—"

They were distracted. Gabe had to strike. Now. It happened so suddenly, Gabe couldn't even recall shifting. It came over him, clothes ripping and fur sprouting.

"Gabe, wait!" Ryan hissed.

He tore forward, overgrown nails churning up dirt. The hunters whirled around as Gabe pounced, ripping his claws across a hunter's scarred face. Shifting to his human form as he hit the ground, he seized the gun and ripped it from the hunter's hand. He smashed the pistol across the hunter's face and yanked, bringing the hunter flush against him, the pistol to his head.

"Back off!" Gabe roared. "Step away now, or I'll put a bullet in your friend's head!"

The hunters backed away, guns raised. Kassandra retreated toward the trees. Ben shuffled back, fangs gleaming.

The winds changed, more clearly bringing a scent to Gabe that made him bare his teeth. He locked eyes with the blond hunter, the one who smelled like a wolf. How dare he? How could he willingly hunt down his own kind? How many had died because he'd helped these bastards hunt and kill wolves?

"Gabe!" Ben called, stepping back toward the trees. "We gotta go!"

Gabe's feet refused to move. His body quivered, blood burning with fury as the blond shifter trained his gun on him. A snarl tore from his throat.

*What am I doing? Run! Run!*

But his wolf wanted to fight. *Hunt. Must hunt. Must kill. Tear his flesh, snap his bones.*

The hunter Gabe was using as leverage cried out as Gabe's fangs pierced his neck. The human rationale in him was overpowered as the heartbeats of the hunters and the stink of blood overwhelmed his senses. A roar tore from his throat. The hunter slumped in his arms.

*Shit! Oh shit! What have I done?*

"No! Rafael!"

"Open fire!" one of the hunters cried.

"Hey, over here, you assholes!" Ryan burst from the trees behind the hunters.

Then Gabe was flying, soaring backward as Ben grabbed his arm and tugged him toward the cover of the trees. Adrenaline kicked in and he ran beside Ben, Ryan, and Kassandra, zigzagging between trees.

Bullets exploded the bark, sending shards of splintered wood flying. The roar of traffic grew louder, and they found themselves face to face with the highway. Movement in the trees behind them made Gabe's stomach lurch. His claws came out. They would have to fight.

Ben grabbed Gabe's arm. "Stay calm! We're outnumbered. If we get caught, Stone's got the lead. We're gonna have to run." He turned toward the highway where cars sped by so fast they were blurs.

A tanker truck hurtled past, sending leaves flying. Ben looked both ways and ran, barely making it to the middle of the road. Gabe held his breath, his heart in his throat as Ben hurled himself across the road, tumbling into the grass. "Come on!" Ben roared.

Ryan hesitated. As a car hurtled past, he ran out into the road but then doubled back as an SUV flew by. "Fuck this so much!" Ryan shrieked and he ran, arms flailing over his head as he stopped in the middle of the road, cars zooming past on either side of him.

Kassandra followed, ignoring the cars that honked at her. She made it to the other side. A bullet shattered the ground in front of Gabe and he took a step back, asphalt crunching under his feet.

The hunters came running at him from between the trees. He turned and ran, the wind catching his clothes as a car barreled past him. Two more cars shot past and in the gap after them, Gabe charged, tumbling over in the grass as a truck roared by. Ben and Ryan helped him up, and they followed Kassandra deep into the forest on the other side.

GABE'S REFLECTION STARED BACK at him, baggy-eyed and scruffy-faced. He washed the blood from his body. Little clouds of blood misted the water, and his hands trembled. How could he have lost control like that? He'd only wanted to get the hunters away from Ben and Kassandra. His intention hadn't been to kill.

Then he'd smelled Ben's blood, and the rage had burned him inside out. *Should have killed them. Eaten their hearts, gnawed on their bones.*

He could still taste the blood, hot and coppery in his mouth. Stinging pain ripped him from his thoughts and he realized his fangs had punctured his lower lip. He spat out blood, the sudden rage fading to be replaced by nausea. He left the river and dressed.

"You okay, kid?"

He whirled around and found Ben approaching, bandages twined around his arm where he'd been shot.

Gabe shrugged and pulled on his shirt. "Fine."

Ben removed the bandages. The wound had healed already, though Kassandra had needed to help him remove the bullet before the wound could close. Ben splashed water over his face. "What happened back there isn't 'fine,' Gabe. Don't bullshit me."

"I got pissed off. They had a werewolf among them. I've never heard of such a thing. How could he just hunt his own kind like that?"

"You killed a man, Gabe."

"He would have killed us." Gabe's skin turned cold.

"The shock on your face didn't make you look so sure of yourself."

Gabe's jaw tightened. "I'm *fine,* Ben." He hated the way those silver eyes x-rayed him. He wasn't going feral. He'd promised Max he'd be careful. He couldn't break that promise. "Once we're back in the city, I'll call Max and Izzie. I'll talk to them and I'll be fine."

If Stone hadn't already acquired the moonblade. If Max and Izzie weren't already dead. Who's to say they weren't? Gabe couldn't remember the last time they'd spoken. So much could have happened.

"Hey." Ben's low voice couldn't soothe the frantic pants spilling from Gabe's lips. "Listen to me. We're doing all we can to get to the blade before Stone. Things are working against us right now, but we still have a chance."

"It's not good enough!" Gabe threw Ben's arms off him, sniffing at the air. He couldn't catch Stone's scent. He had to be miles ahead. "We're too slow. We've gotta shift, Ben. We'll track him better, faster."

"Listen to me." Ben turned him around. "Gabe, listen to me!"

The blood pounded in his ears and every sound the forest made was suddenly so much louder—every snap of a twig, the wind tearing through the leaves, the screeching of birds. Smells were all around him, trying to be the first to catch his attention, but none of them was Stone's.

"Gabriel." Ben's face was close, his voice almost lost within the sounds of the forest piling one on top of the other. "Stay with me. Think of Max."

Max was alone. Scared. About to die. Were they still tormenting him, even now?

"I left him there. I left him there with them. He's suffering. How could I just leave him like that?" Guilt tore into him, the forest becoming a blur as tears burned his eyes.

"Gabe? What are you talking about? Max is fine."

"He's not fine!" Gabe had to find him. Now, quickly. Before Stone hurt him. Twigs and rocks stabbed his knees as he collapsed. His jeans ripped, and his claws pierced the soil.

"Gabriel!" Ben's voice cut right through him. Gabe froze. All the sounds cut out, the smells overpowering the air not as sharp as before. His fingers ached, and one of his nails had torn from where his dull fingertips had dug in the ground. He exhaled in a gasp, his chest too tight to manage full breaths.

Unsteady hands squeezed his shoulders. He leaned forward, collapsing against a broad chest. Ben's heart beat fast in his ear and his arms trembled around him, his shaky fingers tangling in Gabe's hair. "Nothing you saw in that fucked-up future has come to pass. If Stone does somehow get the blade before us, then we can still stop him. Max is fine. For now, he's fine."

"I k-keep seeing him crying..." His throat tightened until he could barely speak. He nuzzled into Ben's hard chest, focusing on the steady rhythm of his heart while his own raced out of control.

"I know. We're not gonna let that happen. We're doing everything we can."

It wasn't enough. Gabe couldn't rest, not until he had the blade in his hands. Only then would he believe beyond a doubt that Max was safe at all. But he couldn't argue. He didn't have the strength.

"Come on. Up we go. We need to stay ahead of those hunters."

Gabe stumbled on his feet. He followed Ben away from the river and toward the scents of Kassandra and Ryan. Kassandra sat on a fallen tree, and Ryan paced up and down, flattening the grass beneath his feet.

"Ready? We need to move," Kassandra said, jumping up. "If we follow this road, it will take us to Bologna. But we have to be careful. We're hunted now."

They walked concealed within the trees for the rest of the day. The moon rose and against the periwinkle sky, the bright lights of the city of Bologna winked at them. Gabe's spirits soared as they walked the road into town.

Ben said, "We'll stay in a hotel, then I'll rent a car in the morning."

Ryan yawned enormously. "Not that roughing it with you lot isn't fun, but I'd kill for a comfy bed."

After being out in the wilderness for so long, the smells overwhelmed him: body odor, perfumes, and so many different kinds of food. Heads turned and countless eyes followed them.

It was reasonable for people to stare at Kassandra in her robes, and Ben and Ryan looked like they'd crawled out from under a bush. Gabe's skin crawled and he bared his teeth, scaring away any curious onlookers until Ben nudged him and Gabe realized he was growling.

"Easy," Ben demanded.

Gabe forced his fists to unclench, trying to distract himself from his unease by admiring the charming medieval buildings all made of brick. They passed an elegant brick square with a clock tower.

Kassandra jumped, wide-eyed and looking suddenly small within the crowds. Her cool confidence had faded since leaving the woods. She huddled into herself, her eyes darting around at all the sights.

"What's wrong?" Ryan asked.

She squeezed out of the crowd with a gasp, as if the crowd had robbed her of oxygen, and then she stumbled to a fountain and sat.

Ben said, "Sit tight. I'm gonna find us a hotel."

Ryan ambled over to Kassandra, who was taking deep breaths. "You ever been to a city before, Kassie?"

"Kassandra, not Kassie. I haven't been in a city in years."

"Right. You've been in the monastery. Hey, you got any questions, you can always ask me." Ryan sat beside her.

She looked away, suddenly shy. "Thank you. I think I'll be fine."

Gabe was curious. "You've lived in the monastery your whole life?"

"Yeah, what's that like?" Ryan asked. "I didn't even know women were allowed to join, since it's, you know, the Brotherhood and all. They really ought to change the name. Make it gender neutral or something."

"I've made pilgrimage to the monastery for years now," Kassandra answered, admiring the pennies glimmering in the fountain. "I was born in Venice, but our family emigrated to the States. My brother and I grew up in a small town out in Nevada." Kassandra sighed, tucking her long braid of hair behind her shoulder and smoothing a few braids that were unkempt.

"How did you know that hunter?" Gabe asked.

Kassandra exhaled shakily. "Eddie was my neighbor. We grew up together. He and my brother Vicenzo were close. Hunters burned our home to ash. The same hunters who attacked us. I never understood why Eddie became a hunter, or if he was one all along. Vico's never told me. After the fire, we went our separate ways. He wanted to track down our family's murderers. I wanted to put the past behind me." She swallowed, and there was a grayish tinge to her olive complexion as if remembering made her ill. "So I joined the Brotherhood as an apprentice and after many years, I became a lore master." She jumped as a driver laid on their horn.

The noise of the horn blasted Gabe's ears, and he snarled, covering them. Sounds were amplified, and a thousand different odors demanded his attention. He was closer to his wolf than before, and not in a good way. He could understand why Kassandra looked so uncomfortable.

"The city's not so bad once you get used to it," Ryan assured her. "They have way better food than out in the wild." He motioned toward the many cafés gathered around the square. Gabe's mouth watered as the scents of Italian spices, cheese, tomatoes, and various wines tangoed.

"Speaking of which, let's get some!" Ryan jumped up. "What do you like to eat?"

"I'm okay, actually. My brothers and sisters taught me to survive on moonlight."

Ryan hummed, chewing the inside of his cheek. "How good can moonlight taste, though?"

"By disregarding hunger and thirst, it allows me to focus more clearly on my meditation and I can spend more time communicating with the goddess."

"Okay. Well. I'm gonna go get pizza. Gabe, want some?"

Gabe nodded and Ryan scampered off toward the café, muttering and shaking his head. When he looked back, Kassandra had folded her legs and placed her palms, facing up, on her knees. She turned her face toward the moonlight and closed her eyes. Moments later, she scowled. "I forgot how noisy cities are. I can't concentrate."

"I know someone who can communicate with the moon. Not in the same way you do." Gabe sat on the fountain. "But it's similar."

"Is he a monk?"

Gabe chuckled. "No. He's my mate. He will be, when I... if I... Anyway, he gets these strange powers from the moon."

Kassandra squinted at him. "Powers? How do you mean?"

Gabe wished he hadn't said anything. He'd only wanted to get these melancholy thoughts out of his head. "It's hard to explain. He can... levitate things. Control water. His wounds heal in moonlight. It's unreal."

"This person, is he with you?" Kassandra asked, wide-eyed and interested.

Gabe squirmed under her intent stare. "No. He's back in New York."

"This mate of yours... is he a red wolf?"

Gabe's mouth slipped open. The look in Kassandra's eyes unsettled him. "Why?"

"Is he or isn't he?"

"Yeah. He is. But why does that—"

Excitement lit up her face, bringing color back to her cheeks. "I heard stories like this! Through constant observation of the moon, my brothers and I were granted a vision of a red wolf born with the powers of the moon."

Gabe's stomach churned. "A vision?"

"I must meet this mate of yours! We could learn so much from him."

Gabe frowned, not liking the idea of Max being the monks' encyclopedia of moon magic. "Maybe. I'll talk to him about it when I can."

Ryan returned with pizza just as Ben arrived with news of lodgings for the night. Ben led the way from the square. Kassandra fell behind in the crowds and Gabe stood on his toes and spotted her trapped behind them. He shouldered his way through and she sighed in relief.

"I thought I lost everyone."

Gabe ushered her on ahead. A child ran out in front of him and Gabe stumbled but couldn't stop himself. He toppled to the ground and found himself surrounded by a sea of feet, thundering past him on all sides. He tried to push himself up, but his arms began to tremble. He breathed in and the smells came at him. Body odor. Pungent perfume. Sweat. A thousand different hearts beat, each louder and faster than the other.

*Calm down. It's just a crowd.*

His arms shook as he pushed himself up. Ben and the others were gone. He looked around the sea of people but he couldn't see them. He breathed in, trying to scent them, but these damn humans were too smelly.

*They're gone. Pack. Need pack.*

If he was alone, he was as good as prey. And there were so many eyes on him, all around him, glancing at him, watching him. One wrong move, and they'd hunt him.

*Hunt me? No. No. They're humans. They don't hunt. Stop it!*

Raucous laughter blasted his ears as drunks at a nearby café bellowed at one another. Children screamed. Babies wailed. His heart flew into his throat as a plate shattered, the sound like an explosion. All around him rose a hurricane of sounds as people shouted over one another in so many different languages.

He covered his ears but their hearts went on pounding against his eardrums. Warm blood and sweat scorched his nose. His mouth salivated as he trembled in both fear and elation.

*Prey. Prey. Prey!*

"Sir? Sir? Are you all right?" A man came toward him slowly, reaching out a hand. Teeth flashed, bared in a smile—no, a snarl.

*No! He's not prey! He's old! He's not a threat!*

But the wolf in him reacted before he could stop it. His fangs came out, and a roar tore from his throat. The older man recoiled, eyes huge in fear. He turned and ran and the chase was on! He was *prey*!

The wolf charged, eyes locked on his target as he gave chase. Screams pierced his ears and the humans scattered as he ran on all fours, driven to hunt and chase. The old man stumbled, fell. The wolf's jaws opened wide and for a moment, he could practically taste his plump flesh.

There came a deafening crack. Then he was flying, tumbling over in a heap. Searing pain burned him from the inside out. His fur fell away, his howls became a pained groan as he yanked the silver dart from his shoulder.

"Looky, boys. We got ourselves a feral one." The group of werewolf hunters who'd attacked them last night strode toward Gabe. The man who'd shot Gabe blew on a smoking tranquilizer gun that smelled of hot silver.

"We really oughta kill you here and now, before you take a bite outta some innocent human. It's a good thing your pelt is so nice." The hunter bared his teeth, a few of which were fitted with silver. "Pack him up, boys. He's coming with us."

Gabe's stomach churned but he didn't have the strength to fight. The dart they'd shot him with was tipped with silver, and it was making his whole body feel like it weighed a thousand pounds. The hunter suddenly took aim. "Don't move!"

Gabe's heart sank as Ben, Kassandra, and Ryan lurched to a halt.

The hunter grinned. "Ain't this my lucky day! Four shifter scumbags, all in the same place." Gabe's heart thundered as the hunter lowered his pistol, and he found himself staring up the muzzle. "Start walking. All of you. Or pretty boy here dies. I can do it. Your furs combined will be worth more than his."

The hunters formed a circle around them.

"Ben." Tears pricked Gabe's eyes as guilt ate him from the inside out. "Run. Go!" They had to keep going. Stone had to be stopped.

Ben's lips trembled, and he put his hands up. The hunter kicked his knees and brought Ben down to chain his hands.

"Sons of bitches," Ryan snarled as they brought him down and yanked his hands behind his back. Kassandra was forced to the ground and chained as well.

A foot flew into Gabe's face. His vision turned white and his ears rang.

*I'm so sorry. All of you.*

# CHAPTER 17

# EDDIE

WHEN GABE OPENED HIS eyes, someone had dressed him in torn jeans and a dirty shirt he recognized as his. The metal bars of a large cage enveloped him. His arms were chained with silver cuffs, muting his wolf.

The burn of the silver seared into his wrists and made him gnash his teeth. From the curtained windows and carpeted floor and the constant bumping around, Gabe wanted to guess they were in an RV, but where were they going?

It was still dark outside, so he couldn't have been unconscious for long. Beyond the bars were other cages. Ben sat in one, hunched over with his head on his knee. Ryan was curled up in the cage beside him, Kassandra in the one next to him. Rock music blasted to his left where the hunters had gathered behind a curtain, talking uproariously.

"We're gonna die." Ryan moaned.

"Damn it, for the last time, would you shut up?" growled an unfamiliar voice to Gabe's left. Lifting his head, Gabe spotted a man in the cage beside him. He was tanned and muscular and sported a buzz cut. He wore a leather jacket over a dirty white T-shirt, and ripped dark jeans. "Wish those hunters had just killed me already. Least then I wouldn't have to listen to all the whining," he grumbled.

Gabe gasped as the cuts on his wrists throbbed and stung.

"Vicenzo," Kassandra said, clasping the bars of her cage, "Don't be rude."

Vicenzo's stern face softened when he grinned. "If I weren't so happy to see you, I'd chew you out for telling me what to do."

Ben raised a brow. "Hell of a way to be reunited. How do you two know each other?"

Kassandra growled, "This is my idiot brother, Vicenzo. But you can all call him Vico. He hates that."

Vicenzo scowled at her. "Kassie—"

"Where have you been?" Kassandra snapped.

"Holed up with a pack in some abandoned town in the mountains. I left because I had some dream where you were calling out to me."

Kassandra blanched. "That wasn't a dream. I used our bond to communicate with you across the long distance. Something the monks taught me. I thought for sure I would meet my end trying to keep the key safe. I wanted to... to say goodbye." Her voice wobbled.

Vicenzo's eyes widened. "I knew it. It felt like a dream, but I knew it had to mean something. That's why I left. I wanted to make sure you were safe."

Kassandra scoffed. "You've been gone for years. You left without even saying goodbye. You expect me to think you still care?"

Vicenzo looked wounded. "Of course I do! Just because we were far apart doesn't mean you stopped being family." He offered her a smile that softened his face, one she returned. "Of course, these hunter assholes found me first. The minute I'm outta here, I'm tearing their throats out with my teeth."

"Hey, Eddie!" boomed a voice from beyond the curtain. "Get on it!"

The curtains flew back and the blond hunter, the one who was of their own kind, strode toward them. "Quiet." There was no authority in his voice, which was laced with a southern drawl.

Gabe noticed a silver collar around his neck for the first time. Since there were no burns on his skin, Gabe assumed the collar was lined with something to keep the silver from burning his skin. His stomach churned in understanding. The silver suppressed his wolf. This hunter was nothing more than a slave to these monsters.

Vicenzo bared his teeth, shaking his head. "Fuck you." He spat the words like poison.

The hunter actually flinched, shrinking under the contempt in Vicenzo's eyes, but he didn't bother with a response. Any anger Eddie had evaporated and Gabe hadn't realized how dark and empty his eyes were without that momentary spark. Eddie turned away and dragged his feet toward the curtain, his shoulders slouched. Gabe wondered if he knew how he reeked of guilt and misery. The disgust mixed with pity now. He couldn't imagine hunting his own kind and wondered what had brought "Eddie" onto such a bloody path.

"Know him?" Ben asked.

The muscles in Vicenzo's jaw stood out as they tightened. "We grew up together in Nevada in some dead-end town that got burned off the map by werewolf hunters. Because of him."

Gabe dropped his head onto the metal floor of the cage. He met Ben's gaze and guilt twisted up his insides. They were in here because of him. Because he'd snapped. He closed his eyes tight, trying not to imagine that Stone had beaten them to the moonblade.

He was probably on a plane to America now, going straight for Max.

They'd failed. Gabe had failed, and now Max and the whole world would suffer for it.

"I'm sorry," Gabe croaked, blinking hard against the tears gathering in his eyes.

Ben bowed his head and said nothing, his face twisted in bitterness.

Ryan curled in on himself and stayed that way for so long, Gabe wondered if he'd fallen asleep.

*We lost. It's over.*

The thought brought a lump to his throat. He gnashed his teeth.

*No. No, it can't be over. Not like this. I promised Max. I promised him.*

If he was doomed to die at the hands of these hunters, he would die fighting to get back to Max.

THE HUNTERS PARKED SOMEWHERE and passed by the cages to what Gabe assumed were bedrooms beyond the curtain. They sniggered and kicked the cages as they passed. Ben growled at them and they only laughed in response.

"Eddie? Oi, Edward! Watch your little friends, m'kay?" one of them jeered as he disappeared behind the curtain. They had southern American accents. Gabe wanted to guess they were from Louisiana.

Eddie glowered after them but pulled up a chair and dropped into it. He slouched in the seat and hid behind his phone, uttering only occasional sighs.

Gabe looked out the window. The curtain had slipped open enough to give him a glimpse of the stars, ever-present, twinkling against a blanket of indigo. The moon was bright, almost full. He wondered if Max was looking at the moon, too.

He wondered if Max was still alive.

"So, Eddie, huh?" Ryan sported a wry smile.

Eddie flinched, as if he hadn't expected to be spoken to. He growled a response and left it at that.

"Where are we going?"

Eddie kicked the cage in answer.

"Okay, okay." Ryan laid his chin on his knee. "I get it. I'd be grumpy too if I had your life. Can you at least give me a blanket? The AC's too high."

Eddie rose from his chair and draped a blanket over Ryan's cage.

Gabe tried not to let his surprise soften him to Eddie. He'd helped put others like them in these cages. He'd made the choice to do so. Gabe wouldn't feel sorry for him. But he was a weak link in their captors' chains. Perhaps they could use that against him.

ONCE THE SUN ROSE, the hunters waited around until one of them brought breakfast. The smell of the food made Gabe's stomach roar. The RV set off along the road, and Gabe's desperation peaked. He had to get out of this cage because if he didn't, then Stone would win. If he ever saw Max again, it would be as a corpse straight from his nightmares. Gabe called, "Hey! Where are you taking us? If you're gonna kill us, just get it over with already!"

"Speak for yourself!" Ryan said through clenched teeth.

Gabe scooted onto his back and kicked the bars with everything he had, ignoring the ache in his foot. "You people don't get it! The one you should be hunting is John Stone! Let us go!"

Ben sighed. "Gabe, it's useless."

"I know you hear me! You gotta let us out! The world's gonna fucking end if you don't!"

Laughter answered him from beyond the curtain and the music swelled even louder. Despair turned to fury and he gnashed his teeth so hard, he thought he'd break them. He kicked the bars again.

There had to be a way out. His decades-long hunt for John Stone couldn't end this way. He couldn't let their farewell at the airport become the last time he ever saw Max. He couldn't let the last memory of Izzie and his mom be of their tear-stained faces. A roar of fury tore from his throat and he slumped, panting.

"Fuck!" He collapsed, exhausted and weakening. Tears welled at the corners of his eyes. "We've got to get out. There has to be a way."

The curtain flew open. Eddie shot him a look that might have been menacing if it weren't for the emptiness in his stare. "Y'all shut up back here. Now." His Texan drawl came out in full force when he was mad.

"Listen!" Gabe was seething. "You're a werewolf! You know who John Stone is, don't you? What he does?"

The narrowing of Eddie's eyes might have meant recognition. Or just annoyance.

"He's after the moonblade. You know it? It's the dagger Remus used to try and kill the She-Wolf. I've seen what happens if he gets his hands on it. You've gotta—"

A boot slammed into his cage as Eddie kicked it.

"I said shut it." His voice had no bite to it, as if he were too exhausted to muster the energy for anger. He threw one last weary look at Gabe, then disappeared beyond the curtain.

"Boy, do you sound crazy." Vicenzo snorted.

Kassandra glared at him. "He is not, Vico. Stone is the reason I disappeared. I was trying to keep the key to the tomb from him."

Vicenzo looked from her to Gabe. "Wait. So the stories about Remus trying to kill the She-Wolf..."

Ryan said, "They're not just stories. So you better hope we can get out of these cages."

Vicenzo still looked skeptical, but unease quickly chased away the doubt furrowing his brow.

The day dragged on. The music gave Gabe a throbbing headache. His stomach roared for food, and his mouth was drier than cotton by the time Eddie walked around the cages, tossing in scraps of bread.

"Listen, it's not too late for you, Eddie. You can make up for all the years you spent doing these assholes' bidding. You could be a hero. If John Stone gets that blade back to America, it's over. You could fix every mistake you've made. All you gotta do is—" He flinched when Eddie kicked the cage.

"The hunters have killed hundreds like you," Eddie said, his eyes dead and empty. "You know how many times I've heard a line like that? You think I haven't tried escapin'? That I didn't try freein' others? It's not worth what they'll do to you if you get caught. So save your sales pitch." He disappeared behind the curtain.

Fifteen minutes later, police sirens howled behind them. The hunters started cursing and yelling.

"Hide the beer, quick!"

"I told you to slow down, fucking idiot!"

"Eddie, get back there! Keep 'em quiet!"

Eddie stumbled through the curtain as the RV pulled over. The sirens cut out. Eddie put his hand on his gun which had a silencer on it, his eyes sweeping over the caged wolves. Beyond the curtain, the hunters conversed with the officer.

"They really got you well trained, don't they, Ed?" Vicenzo rumbled, bitterness plain in his voice. "You take a shit when they tell you to as well?"

Ryan's eyes were thoughtful as he stared at Eddie. "Hey. Psst. Can you get something outta my backpack for me?"

Eddie looked at him as if he had five heads.

"It's just a picture of a friend of mine. I haven't spoken to him in a while. I don't wanna be feral when I die. Can you get it for me?"

Ryan's eyes were darkening at the corners. Gabe's stomach twisted. He wasn't the only one losing himself to his wolf.

Eddie glanced at the backpacks dumped in a corner. He shot Ryan a look.

"It's the black one. No, not that one. The one with the rainbow wolf on it. Yeah, that's it."

Eddie rifled through it and zipped it up. He flicked a photograph through the bars.

The darkness in Ryan's eyes faded. Tears glimmered. "Thanks." His voice was a croak. "Thank you, man."

Eddie took a seat, his gun upon his knee. The sunlight, dim and gray as it filtered between oppressive dark clouds, cast little light upon his face. It darkened the shadows beneath his eyes, stole the color from his skin until he looked like a solemn statue. Though he held a gun in his hand, there was nothing about him that commanded power or fear.

"His name's Zach," Ryan whispered, his voice trembling. "He's my best friend, and this is all I've got left of him. I told him... I told him I'd come back, and now I'm just gonna break his heart. I should have told him. I *should have.*"

Eddie dipped his head, his chin to his chest. He closed his eyes and exhaled, all the tightness falling from his shoulders. Gabe hadn't realized how tense he was. He was surprised he didn't tell Ryan to shut up. He just sat there, still as the grave, and listened to Ryan's shuddery sobs as if he were punishing himself. Gabe hoped this hurt him. He hoped that long after they were gone and the world fell into ruin, Eddie was haunted the rest of his life for what he'd done.

AFTER WHAT FELT LIKE hours, the RV suddenly stopped. Eddie and a few others emerged from beyond the curtain.

"Why'd we stop?" Ryan asked, his voice weighted with unease.

"End of the line for you puppies," one of the hunters sneered.

The hunters covered the cages. Gabe could see nothing beyond the tarp thrown over his cage as they were hoisted and carried out. The air was warm and moist with impending rain. Were they out in the country? He wondered how far they were from Rome.

A door creaked. The stink of blood-matted fur and sour urine clotted the air. Another door creaked open and he landed hard, crashing onto his side.

The tarps were thrown off, revealing a basement stacked with empty cages. Claw marks scraped the ground, old blood stains spattered the walls. The hunters stretched, rolling out their shoulders and grumbling.

"Come on, get to it! These pelts need to go to Naples by tomorrow! Let's get the tools ready. We'll start with the girl."

Kassandra huddled into herself in the cage.

Vicenzo's face paled. "No. No, not my sister! Don't you touch her!"

Laughing, the hunters marched out of the basement, except Eddie. He appeared frozen, fists clenched at his sides.

A shudder racked Gabe's body. This was it. He realized that until now, he'd been holding out hope that Eddie would wake up and realize what was at stake, that he would help them. But no one could help them now. They were going to die here.

Stone would get the blade and go after Max, and if Zach and the LPA couldn't stop him, then Stone would bring ruin to the world. Gabe would die so far away from Max, and it wouldn't even be at Stone's hands. He would be tortured until he shifted from the agony, then killed and skinned for his pelt by American hunters.

Ryan's face was ashen. "Ben, what do we do?"

"I don't know!" Ben's voice was trembling as he strained against his chains.

"Eddie." Gabe looked the werewolf hunter in the eyes. "After we're dead, find Stone. He's going to Mount Vesuvius. If he isn't there, then he's in Stowe. Kill him. Promise me you'll kill him."

If they were fated to die here, then maybe this fallen werewolf could be their last hope. Gabe closed his eyes and prayed it would be so. For Max and his family, for the fate of the world.

"Come on, Eddie. If you can send innocents to their deaths, you can send Stone to hell where he belongs! I know you can!"

For a moment, he saw it, the crack in Eddie's stoic armor. He looked so conflicted, so torn. "Can't," he croaked. "There's no escapin' them. I tried. For years, I fuckin' tried. They'll never let me go."

Ben shook his head. "If you let us out, then the Lycanthrope Protection Agency will shelter you."

Eddie snorted, blinking rapidly. "How are you supposed to protect me?"

"We can!" Ben said. "There's a hell of a lot more to the agency than just the three of us. Come with us back to America. We'll keep you safe."

Eddie fisted his hair and paced, lips moving silently as he talked to himself. "Can't. I can't! My uncle will lose it if I let you go. He'll chain me back up. He'll torture me. He'll—"

Vicenzo blinked fast, eyes wet and wide. "Eddie. Please."

Eddie's breath hitched. Gabe swore he saw a flicker of light return to Eddie's dark eyes.

Vicenzo exhaled shakily. "You know, when I saw you again after all these years, I didn't recognize you. Hated your guts, in fact. I thought the Ed I once knew was dead and gone. That he'd become an empty shell. But you're still in there. I see it. Beneath all that silver, there's still a heart in there."

"You don't know that," Eddie whispered. "How could you possibly—"

"Because you're not going to let us die. I know you won't. Because a few days ago when we met again, you had a chance. You didn't take it. Why?"

Eddie took a step back, swallowing hard.

Vicenzo laughed softly. "Don't tell me you've just forgotten what we meant to each other once."

Eddie choked out a pained noise. "Vico, I—I'm not that person anymore. I can never go back to the way things were when we were kids."

"No," Vicenzo rasped, "No, I don't believe that. Maybe things are different, okay, but I still remember what you were like before. You... you loved gardening. Remember? Remember how we'd sit in my mom's garden for hours? Planting things, picking fresh produce."

"Stop," Eddie croaked. He doubled over, gasping. "Stop it. That's not me. The boy you knew died, Vico. He's dead, and he's never coming back!"

"It made you so happy!" Vicenzo blinked frantically, his hard mask cracking before Gabe's eyes. "You were a natural. You wanted to give life back to the earth, 'cause after everything you lost, after all the shit you went through, you still saw the beauty in the world. That's who you are, Ed. You're a fighter. You're a survivor. The boy I loved didn't fucking give up, no matter what life threw at him."

Kassandra sniffled. "You can still be that person again, Eddie. Maybe it won't be the same as before, but you can still try. We'll help you."

Eddie's shoulders shook.

Ben gripped the bars of his cage. "You're reunited with your friends. You've got the biggest shifter agency in the USA willing to take you in and keep you safe. If there was ever a fucking sign from the universe that this is your chance to be free, this is it."

Eddie's shaking subsided, his breaths slowed. Something shifted behind his eyes.

The door banged open. A couple of hunters stormed in. "Quiet in here! Let's start with the girl."

Vicenzo threw himself against the bars. "No! Not my sister, take me instead!"

Kassandra cried out in dismay as the hunters hoisted her cage and carried it toward a steel door.

"Kassandra!" Vicenzo's voice broke as they carried his sister farther away. "Eddie. Please. Do something. You've got to do something!"

Eddie's chest rose and fell faster. The lines around his eyes were more pronounced than before, his jaw tightly clenched. He lurched suddenly in front of the hunters.

The hunters froze. Then, they started laughing. "The hell are you doing, Eddie? Out of the way. Don't tell me you've suddenly grown a conscience."

Eddie blinked hard, his jaw working furiously. "P-put her down. Now."

The hunters exchanged incredulous looks. They set the cage down. One of them cracked his knuckles. Eddie flinched and took a step back. "Don't make me tell the boss you've been getting disobedient on us." He grinned. "You know he won't like that. Might even drag you back down into the basement to teach you a lesson."

Eddie's face went pale. "I... I can't let you hurt them. They were my friends once. I—"

The hunters erupted into laughter. Eddie lunged for the gun at his hip, and their laughter died when Eddie pointed the pistol between them. "Keys. Now."

The hunter sneered. "You little—" His hand flew to the gun at his belt.

Eddie's gun bucked in his grip, the blast muffled by the silencer on his pistol. The hunter crashed to the ground. The second hunter was dead before he had the chance to draw. Eddie's hand shook so badly, he dropped his pistol. "Fuck. Fuck. Fuck." He knelt, knee splashing in blood. He wrestled the keys from the hunter's corpse.

Eddie ran over and unlocked the cage. "Out. Quick!" Eddie barked. Gabe shuffled out and Eddie opened the cuffs on Gabe's wrists, then ran around unlocking the other cages.

"Thank you, Eddie," Gabe croaked.

Vicenzo charged out and went to Kassandra when Eddie unlocked her cage.

Ben bolted for the stairs and looked around to make sure everyone was ready. Gabe nodded as Ben met his gaze, then eased open the door, and they followed him from the basement and into a narrow hallway. They could hear raucous shouting and laughter and the sounds of a TV from upstairs.

Kassandra gasped. She was staring at the snarling head of a wolf mounted on the wall. Gabe shuddered in revulsion. He despised taxidermy as it was, but knowing these wolves had once been human added another level of disgust.

"Don't look," Vicenzo growled, turning her head away. "Old man, we gotta put these guys outta commission. They'll just keep hurting people."

Ben growled his agreement and searched for the stairs to the second level. They passed a living room and Gabe's stomach churned as he peered within. He ventured farther inside, past the sofa, his skin crawling as he walked over the pelt of a white wolf, the head still attached. In a display case above the hearth, wolf fangs were arranged like badges of honor.

"Gabe, come on," Ben whispered. He stood in the foyer before a spiral staircase.

Gabe turned and jolted as he found a stuffed and mounted wolf staring back at him, fangs bared, eyes glossy and dead. He reached out, his hand settling on its soft head. His fangs dropped as fury set his blood boiling. Gabe wished it would come back to life and take revenge on the ones who'd killed it so needlessly.

His claws left scratches on the wooden handrail as they ascended the stairs. He breathed in and smelled the hunters, their sweaty flesh and the stench of death that clung to them a reminder of those they'd killed. Their heartbeats grew louder and louder until he could practically see them clustered behind a door upstairs.

Ben offered him a pistol but Gabe declined. He wanted these hunters to know the fear of the hunt as he tore the flesh from their bones. Eddie raised a foot and kicked in the door. Gabe dropped to all fours and shifted.

The hunters, who were gathered around a sofa, threw down their Xbox controllers and lunged for their weapons. "Eddie," one of them shouted, "what the f—"

"You bastards won't hurt anyone again!" Eddie fired, gun bucking in his hand. Blood burst from between the hunter's eyes.

Gabe tackled one and locked his jaws around his throat, crunching down as blood poured hot across his tongue.

The projector displayed their shadows on the wall as the wolves pounced on the hunters, knocking them to the ground and silencing their screams. The sounds, the smell of blood, it all set the wolf's heart racing. A hunter ran past them for the door, clutching a shoulder that oozed coppery-smelling blood.

*Prey! You are prey!*

The wolf charged, flying over the sofa and snapping at the heels of his prey, bringing him down. The prey thrashed and screamed, baring his white throat. The wolf lunged, fangs piercing soft flesh, blood gushing hot into his mouth. He held the prey fast until it stopped kicking and shuddering.

*"Gabe? It's over. Change back."* The old wolf came close, too close. He'd take away the wolf's prey.

A snarl tore from his throat and he rounded on the old wolf and snapped a warning. Silver eyes narrowed. In an instant the old wolf bared his fangs and uttered a roar. The wolf's snarl died in his throat, his tail curled between his legs. He wanted to roll over and obey, but he couldn't understand why.

*"Your name is Gabriel Reyes! You're not a wolf, you're a man. You have a sister named Isabella, a mother named Veronica. A mate, Max. They're waiting for you to come home, so change back!"*

A red haze fell over his eyes, and everything became a blur.

GABE OPENED HIS EYES and saw the walls of the RV. He lay beneath a blanket. Every muscle ached, and his body was heavy. He struggled to remember how he'd gotten there.

Distant voices outside the RV roused him and he peered out the window. Ben, Vicenzo, Kassandra, and Ryan were gathered outside. Vicenzo paced back and forth, agitation rolling off him in waves.

"All I want to know is why!" Vicenzo snarled, pacing up and down. "Why did you sell out our town to the hunters?"

"I didn't!" Eddie said through gritted teeth. It was the most alive Gabe had seen him. "Joinin' them was never my choice!"

Vicenzo scoffed. "You made your damn choice! You chose to hunt with the bastards who took our parents from us, our friends, our home!"

Gabe descended the steps but kept his distance. He figured these two had a lot of hashing out to do.

Eddie bowed his head and murmured, "I'm sorry, Vicenzo."

Vicenzo laughed bitterly. "Like that makes it any better."

His nostrils flaring, Eddie took a step closer to Vicenzo. "No, it damn well doesn't. But I lost my family that night, too. And the only thing that kept me goin' when the hunters broke me was you. The memory of you, of us, it kept me human."

Vicenzo's hands trembled, his wide eyes blinking fast as he stared Eddie down. "I trusted you, I— Because of you, I lost everything."

"We both did." Eddie's steely eyes were wet with unshed tears. "You're right to hate me. You've waited for this day. We both have." He ripped the gun from his belt and shoved it at Vicenzo.

Vicenzo's face lost all its color.

"So kill me. Put an end to it. It's what I deserve." Eddie's voice broke, his eyes gleamed with tears that wouldn't fall. It was the most human Gabe had seen him.

Vicenzo's hard mask shattered. He looked like a boy, lost and angry, ready to break down. "Fuck you," Vicenzo whispered, voice raw and hoarse. "Like hell you're taking the easy way out. I won't let you!" Throwing the gun into the grass, Vicenzo turned away, his shoulders rising and falling quickly as he warred against his emotions.

Ben looked from Vicenzo to Eddie. He said, "Whatever happened between you two, put it aside 'cause time's running out. Ed, do you wanna die here, or do you wanna redeem yourself and help us stop Stone?"

Eddie's eyes widened. "I... I don't..."

"What do you want?" Ben asked, looking him square in the eye. "You're free now. You have a choice. Tell us."

Eddie's chest rose and fell. He wet his lips, blinking hard. "I... I want to live. I want to help."

"Good. So get that collar off and let's go."

Eddie gave the collar a fruitless tug. "No, sir. With all due respect, I need to keep it on."

Ben frowned. "Can you shift?"

Eddie's eyes widened. "No. I lost my connection to my wolf years ago, and I'm afraid the second this thing comes off, I won't be able to control myself," he admitted, eyeing Ben apprehensively. "B-but I can still be useful!"

Ben waved a hand. "Guess you'll have a chance to prove it, won't you? All right, you lot, let's hit the road. We got us a big bad wolf to catch."

Vicenzo shot Eddie one last scorching look through tear-laced eyelashes. Gabe wondered if he was imagining it, but he thought the fire in Vicenzo's stare no longer burned as brightly. It should be easy to hate Eddie, but it wasn't. His life had never been his own, but perhaps after today, things would change.

C H A P T E R 18

# FIND ME

August neared its end. It had been three weeks since Max had last seen Gabe in person. After Gabe and the others left the monastery, Gabe had stayed in touch when he could but he'd gone silent weeks ago. Max sent message after message and tried calling, but Gabe never wrote back or tried to get in touch with him.

Realistically, Max knew they were in a life-or-death scenario and there wasn't exactly time for phone calls, but that didn't stop his heart from pounding and his stomach churning sickeningly every time he wondered if he'd ever hear Gabe's voice again.

During the day, it was easy to forget his worries. Hanson and June were gracious hosts who provided for their guests' every need. The Alpha took a lot of out-of-state trips, often for several days.

When Hanson wasn't traveling, he spent all day in his office talking on the phone or in meetings on his laptop in the greenhouse. Hanson assured them he had people communicating with airport security, looking for any sign that Stone was back in the country, but Max wasn't reassured, not after how Stone had been able to evade the Council for so long.

Max read by the pool, did his homework in June's serene greenhouse, and sometimes a guard drove them into town for a day trip. Still, no matter how beautiful the scenery or how welcoming their hosts were, there was no

215

hiding what this was: a gilded cage protecting them from a very real threat that could come any day now and shatter the serenity like glass.

In an instant, Max's life could be in danger. The lives of those he loved could be cut short. And since he couldn't contact Gabe, Max had no choice but to wait until that day came.

He stayed awake late most nights, checking his phone every time he was about to drift off. He shivered feverishly as his stomach roiled. Something awful had happened. He just knew it.

Max left a message. "Hey. I know you're probably kicking Stone's ass right now, but if you could just update me, I'd really appreciate it. What happened with the Imprint? Did you find the blade? Anything. I'm really worried."

Understatement of the year. He swallowed hard.

"Please, Gabe. Just let me know somehow that you're safe. Please come back." He couldn't imagine waking up to an empty bed for the rest of his life, never hearing Gabe's voice or holding him in his arms again.

Unable to sleep, Max kicked off his blankets and went downstairs, bypassing the guard hanging out by his door. Down in the kitchen, the light was on. Zach stood at the counter, slathering peanut butter over toast. Max hadn't noticed he'd been absent in the other bed. He smiled and walked past to the fridge, grabbing some orange juice.

"Couldn't sleep, either?" Max asked as he took a glass from the cupboard.

Zach shook his head, frowning. "Felt like something was wrong. Guess I was just being paranoid."

This had been happening more often lately, Zach's sleeplessness coinciding with Max's. It wasn't a coincidence. He could only guess it was the blood oath between them. Max was affected, too. Sometimes when he lay awake at night, he got a nagging urge to talk to Zach, and he would always be awake and willing to talk it out.

"No, you're not paranoid." Max swallowed hard, wiping his eyes stubbornly. "What if the worst has happened?" Max couldn't keep the fear out of his voice. He sucked in a gasp and blinked hard. "If Gabe and the others are hurt, or... or worse..."

Zach's heartbeat escalated in Max's ears. "There's nothing we can do. That's what sucks."

Max closed his eyes and found his bond with Zach. It was stronger than it used to be, like a flower beginning to bud. *"I'm sorry,"* Max thought, sending waves of reassurance through the thread connecting them, and Zach's heart slowed.

Zach sighed. "Did he give you any hints as to what he's up to out there?"

Max thought back to his and Gabe's last conversation. "He mentioned something about an Imprint. Whatever that is."

"Oh!" The understanding in Zach's voice eased Max's fears just a little.

"Why? What is that?"

Zach sliced a banana and layered the slices over his toast. "Ryan was telling me about that when we last spoke, too. He said the Imprint might interfere with our connection."

Max practically sighed his relief. But what if there was another reason Gabe wasn't answering his calls?

"So that's probably the reason why, right?" Max asked.

"Yeah, probably. They'll get back to us as soon as they can, Max."

"What about Ryan or Ben? Have you heard from either of them?"

Zach sighed. "No. Ryan hasn't been answering me either, but he warned that might happen. Look, we can't drive ourselves crazy with this. Wanna watch a movie or something?"

Max didn't, but he couldn't sleep, so he might as well do something other than worry. In the living room, they found a movie they both agreed on and watched, making comments or half-hearted jokes about the poor writing. Laughing made Max's soul lighter, and as the night wore on, his eyes grew heavy and he left Zach snoring on the couch.

He slept but not for long, his alarm waking him up two hours later. Struggling to keep his eyes open, he dragged himself out of bed, threw on some clothes, and had some toast before he sat down at his laptop to attend his classes.

During his lunch break between classes, he tried to call Gabe again but couldn't reach him. Dread formed a lump in Max's stomach, and his appetite diminished. The Imprint must have truly fucked with their connection. He wished he had even a clue about what Gabe might be going through with Ben and Ryan, anything to reassure him that his mate was still coming home to him.

The day dragged into night. Max took a stroll on the deck after dinner. A blanket of stars lit up the night sky, and crickets chirped. He caught Veronica's pleasant vanilla perfume on the breeze and rounded the corner. Izzie leaned on the railing beside her mother, an arm around her shoulders. Izzie spoke softly and soothingly in Spanish. The scent of Veronica's tears made Max's heart sink.

Izzie turned around and tried to smile, but it was a fragile thing.

He touched her shoulder.

"I know," Veronica croaked. "I know he's out there fighting to come home, but... Have you heard anything from him?"

His throat tightened. He wished so badly he could say yes. "Gabe's fine," he told her, even if he doubted it sometimes. "I'd know if something happened to him." He touched his chest, missing the warmth of Gabe's bond.

Veronica sniffed. "I know. I need to have faith in him. But I've already lost a husband. I can't lose my son, not to that monster. Not again. I lost him before, after what Stone did to him. I never thought I'd have my sweet, happy son back. And then he met you, Max, and you brought the sunshine back into his life." She touched his hand.

Max blinked hard. "That's my line. Knowing Gabe... he saved my life." Max made himself stop talking. He worried if he said any more, he'd cry, and he wanted to be strong for her.

"V, there's something I want to ask you."

"Of course." She smiled, intrigue lighting up her eyes.

Max gazed into the star-strewn sky. "Your son is very special to me."

Veronica smiled, her eyes shining.

"You already know that." Max swallowed, his heart racing. "I think I knew he was going to be someone special to me the moment we met. We just... understood each other. Instantly. He showed me that even if I was broken and scarred, I could be strong again. He helped me trust again. He showed me that the world was more than pain and darkness. He brought so much happiness into my life. So when he comes back..."

*If he comes back. Please, please, let him come back. So I can tell him all this in person.*

"When he comes back, because he will, I want us to be mates, and he feels the same way. So... would you accept me into your pack? Your family?"

Veronica's eyes gleamed with tears and she smiled radiantly, a smile so much like Gabe's it almost brought tears to Max's eyes. "You already are part of my family, Maxwell."

She opened her arms and Max fell into them, holding her tight and wrapping himself in her soothing scent. He forgot in that moment that Veronica was human. She'd never taken the bite from her husband, and they'd had a traditional human wedding ceremony in accordance with her wishes. But it didn't make a difference. From the minute they met, V was as much a part of the pack as anyone with the soul of a wolf.

"I was so happy when Gabriel told me he'd found his mate," Veronica admitted, wiping her eyes. "I thought vengeance would rule Gabriel's heart forever after Manuel died. You've brought so much more into his life. I'm so happy he met you, Max."

She left Max alone to stare up at the stars.

He smiled.

*I'll wait for you, Gabe. No matter how long it takes.*

THE DAYS BLURRED ONE into another.

There was still a throbbing Gabe-shaped hole in Max's heart, but life carried on. Max kept checking the lunar cycles online. There would be a full moon in three days, but no blood moons or eclipses. Max told himself that had to mean Gabe was still alive and fighting his way back home.

The guards patrolled day and night. Hanson kept himself busy with calls and traveling on business trips. There hadn't been any sightings of John Stone, but Hanson was insistent that didn't mean he wasn't still a threat. Max didn't give up trying to contact Gabe, even if he knew not to expect an answer.

When Max confided his concerns to Hanson, the Alpha sighed and folded his newspaper over his knee. "I know. It's hard living with so much uncertainty right now. Your life has been turned upside down, your mate is absent, and Stone's whereabouts are unclear."

"I just feel like we should be doing something to help!" Max said, pacing the length of the dining table and back. "I feel so useless. Is there really nothing else we can do other than sit around waiting for Stone to either get caught or come to us?"

Hanson sipped his coffee with frustrating calm. "I understand your frustration, but we can't lose our heads. I admit it is odd that we haven't heard from them in so long. I am growing impatient as well."

Max folded his arms. "And what if the worst comes to pass? What if Ben, Ryan, and Gabe don't come back?"

"What would you have me do, Max? I can't tear apart Rome trying to find them."

"But we have to do something," Max said, voice tight with panic.

"My top priority is your safety. With the Council... the way it is—"

"Entrenched in Moonborn ideology, you mean."

Hanson sighed. "I can't spare wolves to send to Rome to aid in the hunt for the blade or your friends."

Max growled. "What's the point in having a Council to protect werewolf kind if during times like these, we can do so little?"

In the quiet, Max feared he'd overstepped, but he was beyond frustrated.

Hanson took in a slow breath, his expression passive. "I think you're right. The time has passed for waiting around. There is something we can do. Can you bring your friends in?"

Max's stomach tightened. Confused and worried, he jogged around the house gathering his friends and family. They all took seats around the table with Hanson at the head. June was out on errands in town with Connor, so her usual seat was vacant.

Hanson steepled his fingertips, his eye closing in thought. "It has been almost a month since we had any word from Ben and the rest of your friends and family," he addressed them. Beside Max, Izzie blinked fast, her scent souring with fear. Max took her hand and squeezed, and Zach put his hands on both their shoulders. "This silence could be for many reasons."

"Gabriel is alive, Alpha Hanson," Veronica said. Her fists were clenched so tight on the table her knuckles were white. "I know he is."

Hanson nodded carefully. "I'm sure he is, Mrs. Reyes. But it is unsettling that we haven't heard from any of them in such a long time. It is time to prepare for the worst-case scenario."

Bile rose in Max's throat.

Hanson continued. "Max, you and your mother cannot stay here forever. We can't wait for Stone to return to America. We can't wait for Ben and the others to return. It's time to move forward."

Max's breath quickened. "Alpha—"

Hanson narrowed his one eye. "Do not interrupt."

"But..."

His mother took Max's hand. "I know. Please, listen to him, Max. This doesn't mean we're giving up on Gabe, Ben, and Ryan. We just need to play it safe, right, Alpha Hanson?"

"Correct."

"What do you suggest, Alpha?" Kendra asked.

"I'm going to suggest that Kendra and Max relocate. New identities. You can go somewhere no one knows you."

Max couldn't speak. His eyes stung, and his throat ached. Gabe wasn't dead. They hadn't failed. He couldn't accept it. He wouldn't.

Zach cleared his throat. "Gabe would want you to take steps to protect yourself, Max. He'd want you to be safe. Alpha, the LPA can help with this step. Ben's done it before for other shifters. Since you're wary of the Council, Max and Kendra can be put under the protection of the LPA and assigned security somewhere far away."

"You have the power to authorize this?"

Zach nodded. "Ben left me in charge."

Max turned to look Zach in the eyes. "Zach. Don't. Please."

Zach flinched. "Max, this is bigger than you and Gabe now. It's bigger than what any of us want. We're talking about domination over werewolves and humans if Stone gets what he wants. We can't sit around waiting for Gabe, Ben, and Ryan to come back."

Max hated that he couldn't argue. Zach was right, damn it. He couldn't be selfish, not about this. He had to do what Hanson was telling him. Even if it meant leaving Gabe behind. Leaving his life in New York, his friends. The despair tore his heart in two.

His voice calm and trying to be comforting, Hanson said, "If Gabe and his friends return—"

"When," Max said. He had to believe they were fighting to get home.

"When," Hanson corrected. "When Gabe and his friends return, you will be the first to know. Veronica, Izzie, we have to consider your safety as well."

Izzie folded her arms. "I'm an agent. I can take care of myself. I don't need people to protect me."

"I understand the agency has trained you well, but I must insist on taking extra precautions. Your family is connected to Max. If Stone cannot find Max, he may try and use your family as leverage to—"

Hanson's phone rang. He sighed. "Just one moment." Yanking the phone from his pocket, he swiped and answered. "Yes, Santiago. What is it?" Max recognized the name of June's bodyguard. "What?" he snapped, voice sharp. He lurched from his seat and paced away from the table. "What do you mean they're gone?" A snarl edged into his voice. With a heated look back at them, Hanson turned and marched from the room.

Max didn't know what to say or do.

"What was that about?" Izzie asked, glancing toward where Hanson had disappeared.

Max just shrugged. He couldn't find it in him to care.

Hanson didn't come back. After a while his bodyguard shuffled into the room. "The Alpha concludes this meeting. You can all go."

Kendra stood. "Is everything okay?"

The guard looked uncomfortable. "Everyone's to stay inside for the rest of the evening."

"Why?" Zach asked, eyes narrowing.

"Because he said so, that's why. I don't know all the details. Just do as he says. Stay inside, lock the doors." He marched out of the kitchen.

Unease was churning in Max's stomach. He left the table without a word and went out into the living room. The bodyguards around the house were in motion, stationing themselves at the windows, bustling around upstairs. Max's heart thudded. What the hell had happened?

His mother pulled him into a hug Max couldn't quite return. Izzie touched his shoulder as she passed, a worried look on her face.

Unsettled, Max went up into his room and once Zach was inside, locked the door. Dropping onto his bed, he sighed. "What the hell is happening now?"

Zach shook his head. "I'm almost glad I don't know." He drew the curtains, concealing the dark woods from sight. "It's only seven. Guess we're going to bed early."

Overcome by the day's events, Max lay in bed. The conversation with Hanson played on repeat. The Alpha wanted Max and his mother to relocate. Did that mean going into hiding? Changing their names? Spending the rest of their lives living a lie?

Would Gabe be there with him?

He squeezed his eyes shut. Zach turned off the lights but didn't sleep and Max stayed awake with him. In the dark, Zach was silhouetted on his bed, facing the door. Max's eyes grew heavy, and the rapid beat of his heart slowed.

A NOISE WOKE MAX. The red light of the setting sun bled through the gap in the curtain. It took him seconds to identify what had woken him. A phone. His phone. Heart in his throat, he lunged for the nightstand. He checked the time and realized he'd slept for an hour. An unknown number was calling his phone.

"Oh Goddess..." Max's hands shook so badly, he nearly dropped the phone. Could it be? Was it—

"Max? Everything okay?" Zach asked, setting aside his book.

Unsure if he'd cry or throw up from nerves, Max answered his phone. "G-Gabe?"

For a moment, there was only ragged breathing. Then, "Max? Is that you?"

By the She-Wolf, he knew that voice. He would know that voice no matter how much time passed.

Tears welled in Max's eyes. He covered his mouth so he didn't cry. Gasping, he choked out, "Gabe. Oh Goddess. It's me!"

Gabe laughed, or maybe it was a sob. "Max... I'm so happy to hear your voice. Where are you? Are you hurt?"

Wiping his eyes, Max collapsed onto the bed. "Stowe. Hanson's house. I'm fine. Are you okay? It's been weeks!"

"I know. I know, and I'm so fucking sorry, mi amor. I've been so worried about you. I thought I was too late."

"What happened?" Max asked, more accusingly than he'd meant to. "Why haven't you been able to call?"

Gabe laughed wetly. It was such a beautiful sound. "It's a long story. There were hunters involved. Portals. Exploding phones. We just landed in Burlington."

Max's heart skipped a beat. "You're... you're in the States?" He couldn't stop the huge grin that spread across his face.

Zach sat bolt upright in bed behind Max. "Tell me I heard that right. They're back?"

Max nodded frantically, clutching his phone.

"Yes!" Zach exclaimed, punching the air. Max laughed at him.

"Ben and Ryan and a few new friends are with me. We'll have to drive to Stowe, but we'll be there before you know it. Right now, I need you to get Hanson. We have to assume Stone has the blade and if he does, you and everyone else are in danger. They're coming for you."

Max's heart skipped a beat. "What? Who?"

"The Wargs. Stone. The Imprint showed me a vision where they have you."

"But how would they know where I am?"

"Max, later. Get me on the phone with Hanson, please. I—"

But Gabe never finished because the door behind Max crashed open.

Alpha Hanson stormed into the room flanked by two guards. "Out of bed. Now."

Ignoring Gabe's panicked questions, Max rounded on Hanson. "Alpha Hanson, what's going on?"

"Max? Max!" Gabe's voice became indistinguishable when Hanson smacked the phone out of Max's hand and into the darkness.

"Okay, okay!" Max scrambled out of bed.

Zach lurched to his feet. "Hanson, what the hell?"

To Max's horror, two of Hanson's guards closed in on Zach, forcing him back down to the bed.

Max yanked his arm through the sleeve of his shirt. "Hanson, what are you doing?" Something was wrong.

Hanson grabbed his arm with bruising force. "Walk," he said through gritted teeth, and he hurled Max toward the door. Max collided with the doorframe with a yelp.

"What the hell are you doing?" Zach snarled, trying to shove past the guards. "Don't touch him!"

"Restrain him," Hanson said, voice heavy with regret.

The guards grabbed hold of Zach, holding him back. "Max! Don't go!"

Terror seized Max's heart. "Let go of him! Hanson, what the hell is wrong with you?"

Zach broke free of the guards and charged for Max, reaching out.

Hanson struck, grabbing hold of the back of Zach's neck. He hurled Zach against the wall. Zach's head bounced off it with a crack, and he crumpled to the floor.

"Put him in the panic room. Subdue the others. Avoid excessive use of force unless necessary," Hanson said, smoothing the wrinkles in his shirt.

"Zach!" Max tried to get to him, but the guards restrained him, yanking him from the bedroom. "Hanson! What the fuck is wrong with you?" Max kicked and struggled without success. The guards dragged him down the hall.

Doors banged open. Kendra, Izzie, and Veronica came running.

Max screamed, "Don't! Stay back! They hurt Zach. They'll hurt you, too!"

Fury twisted Izzie's face. "You fucking traitors!" She charged, ignoring her mother's warning shout. The guards at either end of the hall came running. In seconds, they were on Izzie, crushing her to the floor. She snarled and thrashed, half-shifted in her rage.

"Get off my daughter! Let her go!" Veronica ran to help, and a guard seized her under the arms. She snapped her head back and into his nose with a crack.

"Give me my son!" Kendra's panicked voice echoed through the house. Max looked back and met her frightened blue gaze as the guards slammed her against the wall.

"Don't hurt them!" Max shouted. "Please, don't hurt them!"

The front door flew open, and the guards wrestled Max outside toward a car parked in the driveway. Oh fuck. Terror froze Max's insides. He couldn't let them take him to a second location, where who only knew what awaited him.

Whipping his head to the side, he lengthened his fangs and tore into the guard's arm. His howl split the air, and he dropped Max. The second guard tried to get a better grip on him, but Max ripped his claws across her scarred face.

He ran, tearing back toward the house where his friends were.

Something whistled. Pain erupted through his leg and he fell. The burn of silver made him scream, and he yanked the dart free from his leg. On the deck above, a sniper kept his rifle trained on Max. Max flipped him the middle finger and collapsed, dizzy and panting. Big, rough hands gripped him and hurled him over a wide shoulder. The car door opened, and Max tumbled into the back seat. Cuffs snapped around his hands.

The front doors opened and shut. Hanson's blurry shape looked over the back of the passenger seat at him. "I'm sorry, Max. Truly." And to his credit, he did sound like he meant it.

Max was still going to kick his ass when he got out of this situation.

If he survived.

WHEN MAX OPENED HIS eyes again, they were in the middle of the woods. He was slung over a guard's shoulder while Hanson marched ahead, his scent sharp and agitated. The Alpha stopped, examining a tree. Max blinked, his vision clearing. A drawing of a wolf howling under a tree had been carved into the bark.

Max's heart fell into his stomach. Hanson had brought him to the Wargs.

Hanson shouted, "Well? I've brought him! Come on out, you son of a bitch." Rage and fear left his voice unhinged and wild.

With a grunt, the guard rolled Max onto the dirt. He raised his head, his stomach turning over as two figures strode toward him from within the shadows of the woods. Paws squelched in mud. Boots kicked away twigs and stones.

Max recognized the enormous black wolf striding toward him with a jolt of horror but not the human walking tall beside him. No. Not a human. He was a shifter by the scent of him. He wore a wolf mask over his face, a duster, and ripped cargo pants. Beside him, Stone bared his teeth and a growl rumbled from his throat.

Stone was here, and he had the Wargs on his side.

"Oh dear," the masked man tittered. "In trouble, are we, Max?"

Max's breath caught. That voice was familiar somehow, cold and mocking like a cat that had cornered a rat. Where had he heard it before?

"Shut up," Hanson growled. "Fucking traitor. Where are they?"

The masked man cocked his head.

"My mate! My son! Where are they? I swear to the She-Wolf, Aaron, if you've hurt them—"

Max's heart lurched. Aaron. As in Aaron *McCready*?

Well, shit. Things were making more sense.

The masked man laughed. "You really are a weak old fool, aren't you, *Alpha*?" He sneered the word with disgust.

"Please," Hanson rasped. "My son. My mate. I brought you who you wanted. Now give me back my family."

McCready raised a hand, motioning. From the trees, two masked shifters appeared. They dragged two bodies behind them, one big and one small. Max closed his eyes as the smell of blood and death hit his nose. He couldn't bear to look.

Hanson's anguished scream tore into his ears. "No! You promised me, Aaron! You promised you would let them live!"

McCready said, "Your time as Alpha is over. My days of living in your shadow are gone, Hanson! You will not stand in my way any longer."

Gasping, Hanson snarled, "The Council will never accept you as Alpha! You will pay for what you've done!"

McCready barked a laugh. "The Council will have no choice. I will bend them all to my will with the might of the Wargs and the power of a god at my command!"

Hanson's clothes ripped as the shift came over him. Hanson grew taller, muscles straining and ripping apart his clothes. Max couldn't look away, terrified and mesmerized as Hanson transformed into an enormous bipedal wolf the likes of which Max had never seen before. With a roar that shook the forest to its roots, the beast charged toward McCready and Stone. McCready didn't so much as flinch.

Hanson was inches from McCready when wolves spilled from the trees, countless wolves, all of them painted with the symbol of the Wargs. They trampled the bodies of Hanson's family and hurled themselves upon Hanson like a colony of ants swarming a carcass.

Hanson writhed and flailed, grabbing wolves in his huge clawed hands and hurling them into trees, but he was overwhelmed by the sheer number of them. The Alpha took off into the forest, pursued by dozens of wolves.

In the quiet of their abrupt passing, Max's ears rang from the snaps and howls of the wolves. Max tried to crawl away. Silver hadn't weakened him since his powers woke up. Silver chains couldn't hold him, but the silver in his bloodstream was wreaking havoc on his body. He was too sluggish to fight. If he could just get away...

"Come now, Max," McCready purred, and he stepped on Max's back. "Make this easy for us. There's nowhere you can run or hide. After tonight, the Wargs will be so much more. We will remake the world for werewolves. And you are our key to the future all pure-blood werewolves deserve."

Max grunted as McCready pushed him into the dirt. He wouldn't surrender. Not yet. "Let me guess: a future devoid of humans and their influence on our kind? Where Moonborn wolves rule over the masses? That just isn't possible. You'll destroy our kind. Humans will rise up; they'll crush us. We're a minority species."

McCready tossed back his head and laughed. "Humans have no power over shifters. We are the superior species, but we've been taught to fear our own power for centuries. To loathe what we are. Enough is enough."

Fingers closed around the hilt of the dagger in his belt. Max's breath hitched as McCready drew the black blade out. It was a hideous, twisted thing, with runes of the lunar cycle pulsing like a heartbeat from the gnarled blade to the hilt.

Max's mouth dried. "You... you have it."

He'd figured as much. Why else would McCready have made such a bold move unless he knew he'd benefit from it? Despair crawled up Max's throat, but he fought it as hard as he could. All wasn't lost. Gabe had warned him of this. Gabe was on his way. Max just had to live long enough to see him again.

"Burn Hanson's home," McCready said to the few wolves who hadn't pursued Hanson. "I want his guards dead, and any friends of Gallagher's exterminated. No one can interfere with the ritual."

Max's vision went dark when McCready covered his eyes. "Sleep..."

THE MOON LOOMED OVERHEAD as Max came to in a sea of werewolves, thrown like a sack across the shoulder of a hulking brute of a man. Eyes glowed in the dark, and the air was rife with the scent of anticipation. Max's stomach churned as he realized for what.

He was going to his death. Tears blurred his vision, making him blink to clear it. His head weighed a thousand pounds as he lifted it, craning to look behind him. His heart sank.

Thousands of burning torches lit up the forest, carried by a small army of werewolves marching among the trees, following the twists and turns of a winding trail into the mountain above.

Max's stomach churned to see the bulk of McCready's forces. With the power of Max's soul and an army at his disposal, was there anyone who could stand against him? He'd bring ruin upon the world, and Max would help him do it.

Tears of despair pricked Max's eyes. He'd doomed his friends and family. The whole world would fall because of him.

The wolves carried him among the trees and to the peak of the mountain. He thought of running but his entire body felt like one huge boulder. Even if he had the strength, he wouldn't get far at all. They must have weakened him with another dose of silver while he was unconscious. Not even the moonlight could aid him. The moon couldn't reach his soul while his wolf was so drained.

He was helpless and at the mercy of his captors.

The ground evened out and the excited whispers of the werewolves swelled around him. Everyone stopped walking and Max tumbled to the ground. A clawed hand curled in his hair and Max gnashed his teeth to hold back a pained yelp as the brute heaved him to his feet. He forced himself to stand just to ease the screaming pain in his scalp.

"Walk!" the brute snarled.

Max turned around and stumbled, almost falling over. He blinked his watery eyes and what he saw turned his skin cold. The werewolves, teeth bared and eyes blazing, had cleared a path for him.

At the end of the sprawling line of wolves was an altar covered in green moss. On either side of the altar stood Stone and McCready. The sight of the twisted moonblade in Stone's pale, spidery fingers turned his knees to jelly. He stumbled backwards and collided with a wall of werewolves.

*Someone will come. Someone will help me.*

"Move, false god!"

A crack split the air. Biting, burning pain spread across Max's back. A scream tore from his throat and he collapsed onto his knees.

"Death to the false god!" the crowd chanted. A rock struck Max's back. "Get up, maggot!"

Another crack. Mind-numbing pain brought him facedown in the dirt, screaming through clenched teeth as his back burned hot. He wouldn't stand. He would not walk into the waiting arms of death.

*I can't die. I can't. I'm not ready. There's so much I have to do.*

His back was on fire, and the shirt clinging to him was soaked through with blood as the lash flayed his skin open again and again. Tears pricked hot at his eyes, and the roar of the crowd deafened the screams he could no longer fight. He'd never known such pain, not even at Richard's hands. He couldn't take it anymore. He had to stand, he had to walk. Anything to get them to stop hurting him.

*No. Not yet. Stall them. Someone will come for me.*

If he could take Richard's abuse for months, then he could take a few more lashes. But as the next lash cracked across the split skin of his back, he realized he was wrong.

Every time he thought the pain had a limit, the lash sliced open his skin and proved how wrong he was. He pushed himself onto his knees and his mind reeled as a wave of burning, slicing pain gripped him. His back was drenched, burning hot. The back of his jeans was wet with blood.

Max took a step, then another, nearing the altar. McCready shoved him down onto the stone surface, and he gnashed his teeth to keep from screaming as the cold of the altar seeped into his lacerated back.

Stars winked impassively down at him. After he was dead, where would he go? He'd always assumed werewolves returned to the She-Wolf's hunting grounds when they died. Faced with the sudden end to his life, his breath turned to gasps at the uncertainty of it all.

Stone's voice cut through his racing thoughts. "Tonight," he cried, his voice carrying through the forest. "I take back the powers of a god from this undeserving hybrid! This hybrid's death is just the beginning of the cleansing our world so desperately needs. Tomorrow night when the full moon rises, I will invade the She-Wolf's realm and take her soul for myself. A new era will dawn when her blood is spilled! An era deserving of only the strong and the pure. All hail the pure new world! All hail the Wargs of the Apocalypse!"

The roar of the crowd deafened Max, and despair wrapped an icy hand around his heart. No one could stand against such hatred. Who would be strong enough to resist? He tried to be glad he was leaving this world, if only so he wouldn't be alive to watch Stone ruin it.

The twisted blade gleamed as it suspended over his chest.

*No one's coming.*

Max closed his eyes.

*I'm going to die. I'll never see my friends again, or my family.*

Tears scorched his eyes, and his throat tightened.

*Gabe.*

He barely held in the sob that tore at his throat.

*I never got to see you again. I wanted so much for us. To be your mate, to grow old with you. To be a family. If there's an afterlife, I'll wait for you.*

"I love you," he choked out, not caring who heard. Tears spilled from the corners of his eyes. "I love you, Gabe! I love you!"

*So come find me.*

The dagger penetrated his chest, punching the breath from his lungs. He shivered as the cold bite of the blade spread throughout his body.

In the sky above, the moon bled red, staining the forest in crimson.

Max's chest shuddered under the blade's assault, his bones cracking. He screamed as a wolf's snout exploded from the gaping hole in his chest, red with his own life's blood. Max's body twisted and he could only scream as the wolf kicked and clawed itself from the hole in his chest. Around him, wolves howled to the blood red moon. The red wolf stumbled from the altar, eyes a feral yellow and devoid of humanity.

Stone croaked, "Yes. Yes. Come to me, beast." He doubled over, driving the blade into his own chest and blood poured down his skin. Stone's face was pale and bloodless. He was dying.

Then, Max's own wolf ran toward him, seeking a host. The wolf hurled itself upon him, into him. Stone's eyes flickered, and then they burned orange.

The ritual was complete. Shivering, Max stared up into the night sky.

McCready roared. "Burn the town of Stowe! Don't leave a single human alive! The time of humans and their corruption is at an end!"

Wolves howled their victory to the night sky.

Eyes twinkling beneath his mask, McCready glared at Max. "Throw our friend here in a ditch. He's served his purpose."

The stars twinkled in an inky black sky. Bloody moonlight pooled across Max's skin. His eyes closed, and darkness came for him.

# CHAPTER 19

# FERAL

From the airport, Gabe and the pack rented an RV and drove from Burlington toward Stowe. Gabe hadn't been able to reach Max since Hanson suddenly interrupted their call. The worry made Gabe feel nauseous.

"Whoa. What the hell just happened?" Vicenzo asked, looking out the window.

"The moon just turned red!" Ryan said, eyes wide.

Gabe looked out the window. The moon glowed an ominous red over Stowe. The sight made Gabe's heart hammer in his chest. If it was the blood moon from the prophecy, then the hour of his confrontation with Stone loomed closer. He'd know for sure if there was an eclipse.

Gabe had debated over the years whether he would survive the prophesized confrontation or die. If that blood moon truly signified the final hours of Gabe's life, then so be it. Gabe would give up his own life without question if it meant saving Max.

Ben asked, "Have you been able to reach Max?"

"No. I don't understand," Gabe growled. "I thought Hanson would do what he had to in order to keep Max safe. So why would he just take Max away like that?" He'd recognized Hanson's voice, had heard Zach shouting and Max's confused and frightened voice. What the hell had Hanson done?

Ben sat beside Gabe, white-knuckling the wheel. "Something happened. If I had to guess, Stone did something to make him hand Max over."

Where was Max?

Was he hurt? And what had happened to the rest of the pack?

"What if we're too late?" Gabe tugged at his hair, ignoring the sting.

"Keep your head," Vicenzo called from where he sat on a leather sofa. "We're almost there, so don't start moping now."

Kassandra paced, lips thin with worry. "Are we far from Stowe?"

Ben glanced at the GPS. "Almost there." The words were grunted through tightly clenched teeth. He sped up even as he spoke.

Kassandra collapsed into a cramped booth next to Eddie. "I hope we make it in time."

Ryan sniffed out the open window. "Hey, anyone smell smoke?"

A car hurtled past, going well over the speed limit.

The closer they got to Stowe, the more vehicles flew by in the opposite direction. Gabe's heart sank as the stink of smoke got stronger. Clouds of smoke towered over Stowe, and firelight flared. Ben pulled over just as they arrived in town. Bolting from the RV, Gabe stumbled onto the road and jogged toward the town. Soot and smoke stung his eyes.

Behind him, Ben and the others pursued. "Gabe, wait up!" Ben called.

Gabe wouldn't stop. He had to know that Max was still alive, that he wasn't too late. Buildings blazed and the howling of sirens filled the night air as firefighters flooded the roads to combat the fire before it spread to the forest.

Ben caught up to him, breathing hard. "Holy hell. What happened?"

Gabe swallowed, tasting ash in his throat. "The Wargs, this has to be their work."

Ryan panted as he came to a stop behind Ben. "Since when do they have the numbers for this shit? They went from targeting oil companies to *this*?" He shook his head. "Whatever. We gotta find Zach and the others. We'll find Max faster if we work together."

But as distant howls split the air, finding Max proved to be only one of their many problems. Gabe's skin prickled and his fangs dropped. Beyond the barricade of fire trucks, screams erupted, then snapping and snarling.

Gabe bucked Ben's hand off his shoulder and ran, peering around the fire truck.

A pack of wolves surrounded the firefighters and charged, tearing at their throats, ripping their flesh. One of the wolves looked up, snout soaked in blood, yellow eyes gleaming. He turned toward Gabe and uttered a hoarse bark that commanded the pack's attention. They advanced, growls vibrating the earth. Ben and the rest of the pack came to stand shoulder to shoulder with him.

Ben called, "We fight our way through!"

Vicenzo cracked his knuckles, grinning. "Bring it on, freaks!"

"Let's go, dipshits!" Eddie roared, raising his silver pistols.

Ben shifted and charged as a wolf, and his jaws locked around a warg's throat.

Ryan clapped Gabe's shoulder. "Go on ahead! We'll handle this!" He blurred past and lunged, swiping a clawed hand and bowling over one of the enemy wolves.

As the wolves fought, Gabe ran around the blockade of fire trucks. At the corner, shifters smashed the windows of a convenience store, making off with anything of value within. Laughter split the air as werewolves hurled firecrackers into the windows of apartment buildings, laughing louder as screams erupted from inside.

Gabe turned away, stomach churning, and pushed on heading east. He lurched to a halt as a truck hurtled around the corner with wolves crawling all over the hood of the vehicle. The truck collided into a burning building and with a deafening crash, the building flooded the street with bricks. The explosion knocked him off his feet as the truck erupted. He huddled, his face in his hands, ears ringing, as the heat of the flames drew sweat from his pores.

His legs shook as he stood coughing as smoke seeped down his throat.

"Help me! Help!" A woman's screams pierced his ears as she flew around the corner. With one look at his furred arms and sharp claws, she screamed again in fright. She turned away, only to stare into the snarling face of a werewolf. Gabe darted toward her but he wasn't close enough. With a single bite, he tore her throat apart and her screams died in a gurgle as she collapsed. The werewolf sniffed the air, his hackles rising. Blood dotted his fur.

The wolf shifted to a man. "You ain't pack," he growled, "You here to help these pitiful humans or join us?"

Gabe bared his teeth. "Where's your leader? Where's Stone?"

The disheveled man cocked his head, a growl rumbling in his chest. "Stone? That fool? We don't answer to him!"

"Answer me!"

The werewolf's claws lengthened. "No. Don't think I will, hybrid."

Gabe braced himself, ready to pounce. A blur of brown fur descended upon the werewolf. The werewolf choked and thrashed as Zach's jaws closed around his throat, crunching bone. Then Zach shifted, fur falling away.

Gabe's heart soared. "Zach, you're alive!"

Zach spat out blood. "Just barely. Hanson locked us in the panic room, but the guards let us out when the place went up in flames."

"What about Kendra? My mother?"

"Kendra and V are looking for Max! Izzie's helping authorities evacuate people." He gripped Gabe's shoulder. "Come on, the reunion can wait. I know where they've taken Max!" He ran.

Gabe flew after him. "You do?"

"Yeah. One of the terrorists told me before I tore out his throat. They took him to Bear Mountain in Putnam State Forest. We'll find him, Gabe. I'll make sure he's safe, no matter what!"

A pack of wolves came charging after them, abandoning the human corpses they'd been ripping apart. "Go!" Zach shoved him ahead. "Find the covered bridge and keep going!"

Gabe hesitated, torn in two. "Be careful."

Zach grinned. "I always am."

Gabe wished he could stay, but his heart cried out for Max. He turned and ran, following the signs that pointed the way toward Bear Mountain's hiking trails. The town fell away behind him and the howls and screams soon faded. For a while, he worried he was going the wrong way until he spotted the covered bridge suspended over a brook.

Someone screamed within the bridge. "No, stay away!"

Gabe charged and passed beneath the covered bridge. The silhouette of a wolf loomed over a woman, cowering in fear on the floor. She smelled of ash and smoke, the odors masking all other scents. "Hey, leave her alone!" Gabe shouted, bearing his fangs and claws. The wolf whirled toward him. Orange eyes flashed in the darkness, glowing like little flames.

Gabe's throat tightened, and he blinked hard as his eyes misted over. There was no mistaking that red fur, though it was matted with dirt and leaves and stained crimson with minor cuts. No mistaking those big ears and bright soulful eyes, though the eyes were narrowed and the ears flattened back.

"Max?" The words were a choked whisper.

The woman stumbled to her feet and ran away into the woods while Max was distracted. What had Max been doing? It had almost looked like he was going to attack her. No. That couldn't be right. He'd only scared her. Max had probably shifted to escape Stone and run into her, that was all.

Gabe couldn't believe it. Nor could his inner beast. There was no joyful howl deep within his soul, no inner voice crying out to run to his mate and bundle him in his arms. There was no scent of cinnamon and chilis.

*Not mate,* the wolf whined, but Gabe wouldn't hear it.

"Max." Gabe fell to his knees. Max was alive. All those weeks apart, he'd dreamed of the day when they could see each other again, and it had finally come to fruition. It hadn't happened the way Gabe had wanted; there were werewolves on the prowl, tearing things apart to find Max. But they were together, finally, and there wasn't anything they couldn't do.

Only something was still so wrong. His instincts were screaming, *Not mate! Not mate!*

"It's me, mi amor. It's Gabe. You're safe now, and we're gonna get through this."

Slowly, Max's tail began to wag and Gabe couldn't fight the smile that burst across his face as sobs poured freely from his lips. "I missed you. So much. You have no idea."

Max whined, paws shuffling in anticipation.

"We'll never be separated. Not ever. I promise you." Gabe opened his arms. "Let's go home, Lobito. Come on."

Max bounded toward him and Gabe's arms flew around him, savoring his soft fur, waiting for him to shift and hold him in his long freckled arms.

Blinding pain ripped his world apart.

Max's body rumbled with a snarl, and his fangs crunched into Gabe's shoulder. Confusion warred with pain, warred with disbelief. "Max!" He choked, eyes blurring as tears sprang from them. He was paralyzed, torn between the urge to struggle, to fight and free himself, and the confusion telling him that this was his Max, Max who'd never hurt him, and that this couldn't be happening. It didn't make sense.

"Max? What—"

His own blood soaked his shirt, pouring hot down his wounded shoulder.

"Max! Stop, please. *Please*."

Through his tears, he squinted at the wolf atop him, his orange eyes blazing, wild with hate and bloodlust. This wasn't Max. He looked like him, smelled like him—but no. No, he didn't. His scent was off. He didn't smell like Gabe's mate, like cinnamon and chilis and home. He smelled like blood and fury. This was a trick. A look-alike. Had to be.

The Max look-alike hurled Gabe across the floor. He crashed into the wall of the covered bridge, gasping for air. The wolf prowled toward him.

Red moonlight gleamed in orange fur and now that Gabe was closer, he noticed black stripes in the wolf's fur. His lips pulled back from blood-soaked fangs and he laughed, he laughed and changed before Gabe's eyes, fur falling away, eyes going from burning orange to the black-brown of murky water.

As Stone stood before him, Gabe realized his greatest fear had come to pass. Despair made his knees weak and left him paralyzed.

"When's the last time I saw such despair on your face? Not since our time in our special room, I believe." The wood creaked under Stone's bare feet as he came closer, splashing in blood.

Gabe inched back, holding on to the wall to keep himself steady as his vision grayed. His breath grew short and he swallowed hard, trying to hold himself together. "Where's Max? Where is he?"

Stone's bloody lips split into a grin, and laughter croaked from his pale throat.

"Tell me where he is!" Gabe's voice broke and betrayed his desperation.

"Little Red met the Big Bad Wolf and got eaten alive."

Gabe's claws came out when he wrapped them around Stone's neck. As Gabe slammed Stone into the wall, he was still grinning in a way that made Gabe's blood boil. "Don't fucking joke around with me! I know he's alive! Tell me where he is!"

"You know," Stone croaked, his smile straining as Gabe squeezed his throat, drawing beads of blood, "what he told me before I ran him through? 'I love you, Gabe. I love you.' He cried. Just like you're doing now. Crying like a boy. You're still such a little boy." A cold, clawed hand touched Gabe's face, nails cutting into his skin.

"Give him back!" Gabe roared.

Stone laughed. "How possessive of you, Gabriel. Like he's a trinket I stole from you."

Gabe laughed. It was unhinged. "This is a trick," Gabe rasped, even as his throat ached to contradict him. "You're hiding him. Tell me where he is, and I'll kill you quickly."

Stone clasped his wrist, his claws stabbing at Gabe's arm. His feet kicked and flailed as his face turned blue.

"Tell me!" Gabe roared, and it was wild and hysterical.

Sudden pressure made Gabe's ears clog and his knees buckle. The bridge creaked, the ceiling shook, and dust rained down on him. The floorboards snapped under his feet and Gabe fell, one foot plunging through and into the icy waters of the brook.

The bridge was coming down. How? Gabe scrambled to his feet as Stone collapsed, hacking and gasping. Strings of bloody spit dangled from Stone's mouth and he bared crimson teeth in a grin just before the roof of the bridge came crashing in.

Gabe hurtled to the other side and collapsed facedown on the dirt road, coughing as a wave of dust submerged him. His ears rang as silence settled in, then gravel crunched behind him. He turned, blinking away dust as Stone leaped—no, *flew* over the ruins of the bridge, as if carried by beams of moonlight.

Gabe tried to move but his body was suddenly impossible to lift. Gravity crushed him into the ground. As Stone smiled, silhouetted by the moonlight, Gabe realized why. He'd stolen Max's powers along with his soul. Stone plowed his foot into Gabe's stomach. Coughing and retching, he panted as Stone kicked him over onto his back.

Gabe's chest ached. Stone was telling the truth. Max really was— He closed his eyes, unwilling to look into that gaunt face any longer. He searched for Max's bond within him and found nothing but a hole in his heart. His heart, which was in pieces in his chest.

A foot slammed down on his chest and knocked the air from his lungs. "You failed, Gabriel. Like you failed your father. Like you've failed, all these years, to forget about our time together." Thin fingers ran across his cheek, cold as the touch of a corpse. Max's touch had always been so warm, so gentle.

He'd never see Max smile or hear his voice. He'd never wake up to the sight of his face, never sit and talk with him about his day. Never hold him in his arms and kiss him or see the future they'd dreamed of making together.

It was over. It was done. Max was gone. He was *gone.* He was—

His denial crumbled and he no longer wanted to fight even if he could. He screamed his horror, his grief, his fury and despair to the smoke-blackened skies.

Nothing mattered, not this world nor the people in it or what became of it. Why should it? What point was there to living if he was destined to live with half his soul missing? There was no saving a world in which Stone was a god.

Stone was right. He'd failed despite his hardest efforts, despite all he'd sacrificed and left behind. Nothing had made a difference. Whether he surrendered now or died on his own terms, the world would end with the howling of wolves.

He didn't want to be part of a world where Maxwell Gallagher didn't exist.

Spidery fingers caressed his face, smearing the dampness on his cheeks. Breathy laughter rumbled, hot breath that smelled of blood scorching his cheek.

"I tried so hard to break you. To remind you of your place as a hybrid. But you always found reasons to keep on going. Your family. The LPA. Little Red. I hope you understand how satisfying it is for me to finally break you." Cold fingers grasped his lower jaw and squeezed. "So I won't kill you. Not yet. I've waited decades for this, Gabriel. I want to savor it."

The pressure pinning Gabe to the earth disappeared, leaving him too weak to move even a finger. Stone's frigid hand closed around his ankle. The gravel cut Gabe's back, shredding his shirt. The clouds opened, and the moon observed him impassively beneath a dark, starless sky.

Deep in his chest, his wolf pawed and whined. Gabe had surrendered, but the wolf in him hadn't. The wolf still wanted to fight, to kill, to devour. A growl spilled from his throat, and his claws tore at the dirt.

The wolf had been fighting to come to the surface ever since he'd left Max the first time. Gabe had fought his beast, denied and feared him. He thought if he let the wolf out, he would lose himself.

What was the point in fighting anymore? What was left of him to lose? Being human was too painful, too hard. He wanted to forget he ever met Max Gallagher, forget the future they'd dreamed of building together. Forget all of it.

It was time for the human in him to die and the wolf to come out.

As the snarl tore from his throat, as his claws lengthened and he bared his fangs, all thought fled his mind. Ben, Zach, and Ryan turned to ash, their names and faces gone as if in the wind. His mother and father smiled before their faces cracked and shattered, their arms decaying as they held out a baby, his little sister. Her name was... her name was...

He put his arms around a timid red wolf, scarred and broken, and buried his face in his fur. The wolf leaned into his touch, and despite everything, he entrusted Gabe with his fragile heart.

*No. I don't want to forget this. Let me keep this memory of him. Please. Just one.*

He reached out and the red wolf vanished, exploding into dust at his touch. He looked into the orange eyes of a red-haired man, his face full of freckles. His hands held on to Gabe's face as he brought their lips together. Max kissed him and Gabe's world turned upside down.

And he *wanted*, for the first time since his father died. He wanted Max. Sweet Max with a damaged soul that was more open than it had any right to be. Max, who with one eager kiss promised a future of tenderness, passion, and love.

He'd wanted that future, more than anything. He would have died for it, fought for it with every breath he had. Because Maxwell Gallagher had deserved a life where he was loved and wanted, and he'd made Gabe feel worthy of a life beside him, a peaceful life free of bloodshed and vengeance, where it was just the two of them.

And Gabe had failed to give him that. He'd failed both of them.

Gabe opened his arms and drew him close, held on tightly as Max faded to dust in his arms. "I'm so sorry, Max."

He stood alone, surrounded by darkness. His legs vanished, then his hands and his torso. His face was wet, but he couldn't remember who he wept for.

A howl rose at the back of his throat, building until he thought it would tear his throat apart unless he let it loose. His lip bled as his fangs pierced skin. The smell of blood crawled into his nose, made his mouth water even if it was his own. His heart pounded, growing louder and louder.

*"You're weak. Unworthy of commanding us any longer."*

His wolf towered over him, consuming him in its shadow. Enormous jaws rained drool on him, scorching breath whipping his hair back. The sight filled him with despair, knowing he didn't have a chance of fighting back, and with relief, knowing the pain and regret would disappear.

*"You're mine,"* the wolf growled.

*"Yours,"* Gabe agreed. He closed his eyes as the wolf's jaws consumed him.

A howl split the woods. The wolf's jaws snapped around a bony wrist. With a roar, Stone raised a hand and gravity knocked the wolf off his paws. He flew, the wind in his fur as he hurtled backwards, tumbling down a hill. He rolled to a stop, the world spinning around him.

The wolf rose on trembling paws and shook leaves and dirt from his fur. He ran beneath a starless sky from the smell of smoke and flames as the fire consumed the trees, from the shadows of a life that slipped from his memory as easily as the wind through his fur. Unhindered and unbroken, free from all burden and pain.

When the smell of fire and smoke faded and dawn broke through the darkness of the trees, the wolf found a quiet den and curled up. He rested his aching bones, licked his wounds, and laid his head on his paws.

Something hurt. It ached inside him, a dull throb that wouldn't go away. He didn't know why it was there or what was missing deep in his soul.

The ache soon faded, and he forgot it was ever there at all. Soon nothing mattered, only that he was tired. So tired.

The wolf closed his eyes and slept, at peace.

CHAPTER 20

# YOU ARE MY LIFE

*So this is what dying feels like...*

Max's whole body ached, and each breath made his chest feel like it was caving in. Even moving a finger was difficult.

*It kind of blows.*

His life, though unfinished, had been a good one for the most part. His father had run out on the family, but his absence had only tightened the bond between Max and his mother. Richard had come into the picture bringing a whole mess of trouble with the Moonborn cult and Stone. And then... then there was Gabe and the LPA wolves.

Gabe. If there was one reason he wished he could linger just a little while longer in this world, it would be to see Gabe one last time. Only he knew that "just a little while longer" would never be enough.

He hated to leave his mother. He'd promised her to be the man of the family, the only man in her life who hadn't left her or hurt her. Now he was doing both.

He wished he'd been able to join the LPA. He'd wanted to give back to the ones who'd helped him and help others who had been hurt the way he'd been.

His fingers curled, squeezing something soft.

*I don't want to die. I'm not ready.*

His eyes opened to empty white space. Where was this? Purgatory?

246

"Max? Max!"

A bearded face loomed over him. He vaguely recognized those silver eyes and his scent, coffee and beard oil.

*Ben? You died, too?*

"Hey, Kendra. He's waking up."

"Oh, Max!" His mother's tearful face leaned in, her lips soft against his cheek. She smelled like salty tears and perfume.

*Oh, Mom. You, too? We're all dead? At least we can be together.*

"How are you feeling? You gave us such a scare."

*Mom, don't you understand? We're dead, all of us.*

Max's mind flew into confusion. They were dead, right?

"Where is he? Where's my boy? Max, my man! You're all right!" Ryan's scruffy face grinned down at him. "If you can survive, maybe Zach can, too!" Arms flew around him—then something ripped out of Max's arm. He recoiled with a shout, lurching to the other side of the bed and cradling his arm to him.

"Ry, you moron! You ripped out his IV! Get a nurse in here!" Ben shouted.

Max blinked, realizing he wasn't in an empty white space but a hospital room. If the stinging pain in his arm was anything to go by, he was very much alive. Only he couldn't understand how. "Mom," he croaked, his throat dry. "I don't understand. What happened?"

"We found you in the woods beyond Stowe, bleeding out in a ditch. We thought..." Tears sprang to her eyes. "They'd tortured you. Stabbed you."

Max's skin turned cold, recalling the moonblade gleaming as it was suspended over his chest. Stone's grinning face. The lash against his back. He exhaled shakily as the memories faded. "I thought I was dead, too. How did I survive?"

Ben eased him back to the pillow. "In time, kid. I know, it's been a while."

Max smiled despite his confusion, gazing at Ryan and Ben in disbelief. "It's great to see you guys again." His heart lurched. "Is Gabe with you?"

Ben's smile fell away. Ryan blinked hard and looked down at the floor. Max's heart sank. "Where is he?"

"Honey, one thing at a time," Kendra said, rubbing his arm.

Ben sat on the sofa, elbows on his knees. He scrubbed a hand across his bushy beard and sighed. "We were kidnapped by werewolf hunters in Italy while looking for the moonblade. That's why we took so long to get back. We came back as quickly as we could, met up with Zach and your mom in Stowe."

Ryan growled, "Those werewolves burned the town to ashes. There's nothing left. Firefighters are still putting out the fires in the woods."

Before Ben could speak, someone groaned behind Max. Max turned and his mouth fell open. Zach lay in the bed next to his, bandages around his chest. Ryan bounded to him and knelt, taking his hand. "It's okay, Zach. We're here. You're okay."

Max struggled for words, alarmed to see Zach so weak. "What... what happened to him?"

Ben said, "When we found you, you were minutes from death. Zach claimed he could still feel the blood oath between you two. He thought there was still a chance to save you. His life for yours."

Tears burned Max's eyes. "He chose my life?"

Ben nodded, his eyes glistening. "And the blood oath you two swore honored his sacrifice by sparing your life."

Max was speechless, swallowing hard as his throat tightened. Zach would die because of him. "You all just let him?"

"Hell no!" Ryan's voice was thick with grief. "I wasn't there. If I was—"

Max flinched from his anger. "Ry, I'm so sorry."

Ryan shook his head and went to sit next to Max. "I'm happy you're alive, Max, but Zach was—*is*, damn it—my best friend."

Max barely swallowed the sob that pushed past his lips and put his arms around Ryan. He thought Ryan would push him away and knew he'd deserve it, but Ryan clung to him as soft sobs shook his shoulders.

Ben said, his voice calm but wavering with emotion, "He made a promise to you, and to Gabe, and he kept it to the letter. A sacrifice like Zach's fulfills the terms of the oath, but since he's still alive, it looks like the oath recognized the sincerity of his sacrifice…" Ben's tone was thoughtful, hopeful even. "And even rewarded him with life. I've heard of such a thing before, but I couldn't be sure—"

Ryan's head jerked up, red-rimmed eyes wide in disbelief. "So you mean he'll live? You knew he'd live, all this time?"

Ben raised both hands. "I did my homework, Ry. The Council would never have loaned me that tome if I didn't study the terms of the oath front and back. Zach was willing to die to save Max, and that's what spared his life, too. The oath knows when it is being conned. There have been others who'd made such a sacrifice in the hopes of evading death, and they died. It's very clever and specific magic. If Zach tried to sacrifice himself for any reason other than to save Max's own, he would have died then and there. Think I liked keeping him in the dark? It was for his own good."

Ryan dropped his face into Max's shoulder with a shuddery sigh. "You're paying for my therapy once we get home."

"So he'll be all right," Max said, utterly relieved. He patted Ryan on the back and Ryan moved away, his face turned to the side as he wiped his eyes and sniffled.

Ben sat in the chair beside Zach's bed, his silver eyes roaming Zach's ashen face. "The doctors gave him a transfusion of my blood to help him heal but even wolf blood can only do so much. The rest is up to him. But he's a fighter. He'll come back."

Max swallowed, trying to find the courage to ask the question again that threatened to turn his insides to knots. "Where's Gabe?"

A sigh fell from Ben's lips. He blinked, and Max's heart sank when he realized Ben was fighting back tears. He looked down at the tile floor, his shoulders slumping. "Don't know." His voice was rough, raw.

Panic tightened like a fist in Max's chest. "Where is he? Does anyone know?"

Kendra shook her head. "We haven't seen him, Max. Not since we left Stowe."

Max wrestled with the fear constricting his throat. They hadn't seen him. That didn't mean he was dead. "Was there an eclipse after the blood moon?" His heart hammered in his ears.

"No," Ben began.

"Then he's alive. He's probably looking for me."

"Max." Ben's voice broke. He looked away, his hands clasped so tightly in his lap his knuckles were white. "We felt Gabe's bond snap."

Max's heart fell into his stomach.

Ryan squeezed Max's shoulder. "He's not dead. I'm sure of it. But we think he went feral. He kept losing control while we were in Italy. I think your disappearance was the... last straw."

Max didn't care. He swung his legs over the side of the bed and collapsed. He let his mother and Ben help him to his feet. His legs were weak but he felt better than he'd expect for a guy who'd been stabbed in the chest. He touched the spot where the blade had punctured his skin and found there wasn't even a bandage there, just a gnarly scar.

"You had a nasty wound," Ben said. "Zach's sacrifice reversed the damage, but he took the brunt of it in exchange."

Max touched the scar on his chest, then reached down and squeezed Zach's hand. "Thank you, Zach."

"Max, you need to stay in bed," his mother urged. "Izzie and Veronica are out looking for him. They'll call us if they find anything."

"No. I need to find my mate." He'd spent enough time waiting on Gabe to come home to him. If he wouldn't come home, then Max would have to find him and drag him back. "Where are my clothes?"

Kendra sighed, shaking her head. "They're ripped and bloody. I brought you a change."

Max grabbed his clothes and stumbled to the bathroom. Slipping inside, he threw them on, a red flannel shirt and jeans. He breathed in and his stomach lurched. His sense of smell wasn't anywhere near as sharp as before.

Closing his eyes, he tried to sense the pack bonds but found his own heart beating alone. Loneliness washed over him. He'd worked so hard to forge those bonds with his pack, and Stone had ripped those threads apart, severing him from them.

After Richard's abuse, Max had fought his way out of feral fury and reclaimed control of his wolf. It had been a hard, emotional journey. And now that he was finally in control again, confident again, Stone had ripped his wolf from him. His grief turned to fury, and he balled his hands into fists. He was getting his wolf back.

When he emerged, he faced the pack, trying to figure out how to say it. He was sure they'd sensed it. "Stone took my wolf."

Ben sighed. "That's what we feared."

"Shit... that means he got access to your moon magic," Ryan growled.

Max couldn't be worried about that now. Finding Gabe was all that mattered. "I can't track like I used to, so I need someone to come with me."

"I will." Kendra rose.

Max vaguely recalled Stone saying something about the full moon. His stomach turned over. "We're short on time. He's going to open a path to the She-Wolf tonight while the moon is still full. That's when my powers are at their strongest. We've gotta stop him."

Before then, he had to find Gabe. Quickly. Once the sun set, there would be no time to choose between finding Gabe and confronting Stone. Panic threatened to freeze him in place. "How far are we from Stowe?"

"About an hour," Kendra answered. "I'll drive you."

Ben stood. "In the meantime, we'll come up with a plan to deal with Stone and the Wargs. Listen, Max."

Max froze by the door, knowing what he was going to say. "I'll find him. We'll come back together."

"Just be careful, Max. Okay?" Ben's voice shook. "Gabe's humanity has been deteriorating ever since we lost touch with you. If he thought you were dead... he might not be the same."

Max gritted his teeth. "I don't care. He's brought me back from the brink time and again. Like hell I'll ever give up on him."

Max tried to calm himself, even as it seemed his breath was running away from him. "I'll find him." He clenched his fists and closed his eyes tightly. Gabe had promised him that he would come home, and Max wouldn't let him break that promise. "Come on, Mom. Let's go."

MAX DIDN'T RECOGNIZE THE town of Stowe. The buildings still standing were blackened husks, and debris flooded the streets. The roads were closed, and police and firefighters filled the streets, combing through rubble. A barricade at the entrance to town deterred any from entering. With the window rolled down, Max could taste the ash at the back of his throat.

Stowe was a small town, and Stone and McCready's people had left only corpses and ash in their wake. He shuddered at the thought of what they could do to New York if Stone possessed the She-Wolf's soul.

"They won't let us in," Max said, unsure how to proceed.

Kendra frowned, brow furrowing. "While we were looking for you, Zach told us he'd sent Gabe toward Bear Mountain, so he would have walked the same trail we did." She drove them around the ruins of town and along a dirt road toward the mountain trail. "How does it feel, not being a werewolf anymore?"

"Like I'm missing a limb," Max admitted. He hated it.

His mother rubbed his shoulder. "You won't feel that way forever. You could always accept a bite. Perhaps Gabe can give it to you?"

Max liked the idea of being turned by Gabe, but... "It won't be the same. I wouldn't be me." He would be just a normal wolf without red fur or lunar powers. "My fur color and my powers have caused me nothing but trouble, but they're part of who I am. I'm okay with being different, and I don't want to lose that. I'll get my wolf back." He had to keep telling himself that. Stone couldn't succeed.

Kendra stopped before the wreckage of a bridge that formed a dam in the brook. She stepped out of the car and sniffed the air. "I smell him."

Max's spirits soared. "You do?" Damn it, he missed being able to smell Gabe's scent.

"Yes." She sniffed again and her lip curled. "Stone was with him."

Max shuddered just imagining that Stone might have Gabe in his clutches. "Shit. Does he have him?"

Kendra shook her head. "No. The scents are divided. Stone went one way through the brook. His scent's lost." She jumped down below and scented the air. "Gabe's scent goes east."

Max stepped on something. The shredded remains of some clothes lay scattered at his feet. He vaguely recognized the red T-shirt. "This was his." Max picked up a scrap and sniffed. He could only smell dirt. His mate's scent was lost to him, and Max's heart clenched. "I can't smell his scent anymore."

Kendra rubbed his shoulder. "That's okay. Scent matters, but it isn't everything. Gabe will always be your mate, fated for you by the goddess. You don't need a scent to tell you that."

Max blinked hard. "Yeah. I know."

Kendra accepted the scrap of Gabe's shirt and sniffed. "His scent's very strong. Come on!" She bounded ahead and Max followed, trying to keep pace. Even in human form, werewolves were especially fast and Max found himself losing ground to his mother as she hurried ahead, on the hunt.

Max lost track of the time they spent roaming the woods, but his feet were sore and the skies grew dark and overcast, making the red moon easier to see. It wasn't eclipsed. Gabe was still alive, he had to be, but they had only a few precious hours of daylight left to find him.

Kendra galloped over the uneven ground while Max tripped and stumbled. She tried to stop and wait, but Max urged her on ahead. He hated being human, wished for nothing more than to shift and run unhindered as a wolf.

Max feared how much he was slowing her down until he almost walked into her, sniffing around the corpse of a rabbit. She took off, heading farther into the woods. Max inspected the rabbit, which was ripped to pieces and mostly eaten. What remained was stiff with rigor mortis. Gabe had been a wolf for hours, and recalling Ben's concern for Gabe's humanity, this made Max's stomach twist.

Max followed a trail of his mother's clothes, picking them up as he went, and found that she'd shifted to a full wolf and was leading the way, nose to the ground. She stopped outside a den and sniffed around.

Max asked, "Did he sleep here?" There were old paw prints and black fur tufts, and the entrance had been scent marked to ward away visitors. The white wolf whined in response. She sat down as if in wait.

"You think he might still come back?" Max asked, hopeful. A wolf always returned to the den, no matter how far the hunt took him.

The white wolf dipped her head in response and lay down, her head on her paws.

Heart pounding, Max joined her. He caught his breath and closed his eyes tight.

*Please, let me find him. Let me find him and bring him home.*

The quiet of the woods couldn't soothe him as every second he waited for the silence to be broken. Untold minutes ticked by and they sat and waited. It was midday now. Time was fleeing fast. Beside him, Kendra whimpered and looked to him, eyes uncertain.

"Wait," Max said, beseeching her. "Just a few more minutes." His voice shook and betrayed the pain he couldn't hide.

Kendra stood up, dirt and leaves clinging to her fur. Her pointed ears flicked back and forth and she stared intently toward the west.

"What is it?" Max's unsteady hand settled on her back. He didn't dare to hope, but his heart beat faster as birds took flight from the trees. Something was coming. His mother's body vibrated with a low growl and she came to stand in front of Max.

All the breath left Max's body as a black wolf lumbered from between the trees, his head down low, yellow eyes blazing with feral fury. He flattened his ears, his lips pulled back to reveal glistening fangs.

*That's not him. That's not Gabe.*

Max couldn't believe it, but then he saw the scars cleaving through the black wolf's skin. Kendra left Max's side and the wolves circled like yin and yang, their growls thrumming deep in their chests. Max froze, unsure who to run to, terrified that he'd have to watch as the two people he loved most tore each other apart.

"Gabe," his voice came out small, choked. "Gabe, it's me. Max."

The black wolf wouldn't look at him, refusing to turn his back on Kendra as she kept him at bay. Max didn't know what to do. He hadn't wanted to believe Gabe had gone feral, but he couldn't recognize the wolf prowling toward his mother. Max inched closer, leaves rustling under his feet.

His throat was painfully tight but he knelt and opened his arms. "Gabe, you have to remember. We're mates. I'm here, I'm all right. Let's go home, please."

Those wide, furious eyes locked onto him and he got no warning before the wolf charged him. A flash of white fur intercepted him as Kendra slammed into him. The wolves collided. Kendra locked her legs around Gabe's neck, her fangs lunging to take hold of his scruff. The black wolf crushed her beneath him, his fangs ripping at her fur.

Through the panic freezing him in place, Max realized the worst had come to pass and if he didn't act, he'd have to watch as Gabe and his mother killed each other. He lunged for a stone and hurled it. Gabe yelped as the rock caught him across the head. Kendra lay panting, blood matting her white fur. Max had to break them apart.

He picked up another stone and threw it at Gabe but missed. "Hey! Come on! Follow me!"

The black wolf snarled and charged toward him. Max ran but had no hope of getting far as hot breath blazed at his heels and fangs tore at the hem of his pants. The wolf collided with him, and the ground vanished under Max's feet. He flew, tumbling over roots and cutting himself open on jagged stones. He landed, breathless and aching, in a heap on the forest floor. The ground trembled beneath him as the wolf pursued him.

Max struggled to stand, gasping as pain racked his ankle. He collapsed onto his knees, trying to find a grip on a stone or a root. He had to get away. Gabe was going to kill him. Max dragged himself until his back was flush against the rocks behind him. "Gabe. Please." His throat closed up, his eyes burning hot and his vision blurring as the wolf came closer, fangs bared and hungry for his neck.

"Please remember." He racked his mind, searching for something, anything he could say that might make Gabe remember who he was. "You're from New York. You have an apartment on Park. You're with the LPA. Remember Ben, Zach, and Ryan?"

The wolf advanced, growling. Max feared those horrible snarls would be the last thing he ever heard. "You have a sister, Izzie. Veronica, your mother..."

But it wasn't working. There wasn't a shred of recognition in those furious eyes. "Gabe, come on... How could you forget them?" Max's throat ached as he tried to keep his despair at bay. "What happened to you? Did... did you think I died?" Max asked, understanding. "Is that why you're like this? I'm here, Gabe. I'm alive. We're going to go home."

The wolf's snarling died, and it regarded him warily. Had he gotten through? Max choked back a joyful sob. Gabe was still in there somewhere, trapped in the clutches of his inner beast. He could still reach him. "Do you hear me? Gabe—" He reached out, and it was a horrible mistake.

The wolf struck and Max's arm became trapped between his jaws. He gnashed his teeth as blood wept down his arm. He didn't dare move, didn't utter a sound that might spur the wolf on. The wolf's frenzied snarls vibrated down his arm. His own bones creaked beneath its jaws.

Tears burned as they slid down his cheeks and he gasped for air, hoping the wolf would tear out his throat just to make the pain go away. This wasn't Gabe; he would never hurt Max like this. Gabe was gone, and Max didn't know if he'd ever get him back.

But he wouldn't give up on Gabriel Reyes. He had pulled Max from the depths of feral despair time and again. The wolf could have killed him by now—something was holding it back. He had to believe that Gabe was somewhere in there, fighting to come back to him.

The wolf growled louder as Max's hand settled on his furry cheek and he curled his fingers in warm, dense fur.

"Gabe, c-can you hear me?" Max gritted the words out through clenched teeth, his vision blurring as he looked into wild eyes filled with hate. "I came for you. Stone almost killed me, but I fought my way back to you because we were meant to be together. I need you to focus, okay? I need you to fight this for me. I need you to come back."

Max gasped as those jaws released him. Wide, mistrustful yellow eyes gazed into his without blinking. The wolf tried to move away, but Max clung on tight to his fur, pushing himself onto his knees. His hand drifted through dark, bushy fur and settled on the wolf's neck.

He growled weakly in protest, then fell silent. Max leaned in until his face was nestled in the wolf's fur. Putting his arms around the wolf's neck, he held tight, the way Gabe had held him once when he was feral and lost.

"You brought me back. Time and again. You never gave up on me, and I'll never let you go. Don't give up on us. You're my soulmate, Gabriel Reyes. You're my home. I never want to be away from you again. I want to wake up every day and see your face. I want to grow old with you. I want to eat dinner with you. I want to raise a family with you. Find us. Find our bond and come *home*."

For a moment, Max feared it wouldn't work. He was human now, and Gabe was feral. He couldn't feel the bond that once burned so bright between them. It wouldn't work. It wouldn't be enough.

The shift started. Max could feel it beneath his fingers, the rippling of muscle and bone. The feral fury left the wolf's eyes, and they became the color of amber. Huge paws became clawed hands, then soft, trembling fingers curled in the dirt. Black fur rained from scarred, tanned skin like ash.

With a great gasp, Gabe broke free from his shift, his head thrown back like a man breaking the surface of a deep, dark lake. Gabe collapsed limp and gasping into Max's arms.

It didn't matter if Max was human and Gabe was a werewolf. Max might not be able to feel their bond anymore, but Gabe could. Even if Max never became a werewolf again, that wouldn't change their love for each other. Stone and McCready had destroyed so much, but what Gabe and Max had was soul deep, and nothing and no one could ever change that.

Max's heart raced when Gabe lifted his face from Max's shoulder. Their eyes met and he couldn't tear himself away from Gabe's gaze, a lump rising in his throat when he realized how close they were. Gabe blinked and a tear left a track down his cheek, but he didn't speak.

Eyes never leaving Max's, he ran his thumb over Max's cheek as if to make sure he could truly touch him. His heart thumping a joyous rhythm in his chest, Max lifted shaking hands to Gabe's face, touching sun-kissed skin. Lips trembling beneath a full scruffy beard, Gabe framed Max's face in his hands and gazed at him as if he were seeing the sky for the first time.

"Max." Gabe's voice was hoarse and broken as he leaned in, pressing the lightest of kisses to Max's cheek, his brows, his jawline.

Gabe wound his arms around Max's shoulders and pulled him into the sanctuary of his embrace. Max collided with Gabe's chest, enveloped in his warmth. He couldn't speak, he didn't breathe, as if the slightest word or movement might cause him to wake up. A voice inside Max screamed out that this was real, but after the hell they'd walked through to get to each other, he was numb.

When their eyes met, Max could hardly see him through the tears blurring his vision. He came to life, throwing his arms around Gabe's shoulders, and Gabe's lips trembled as he crushed his mouth to Max's. His defenses crumbling, he gave in, leaning into the warmth and power of Gabe's body. Even after a month apart, their bodies fit together so perfectly. They'd been made for this, for each other. Max would believe that until his last breath.

"You came back." Max's voice was a croak, and his shoulders shook as he broke down.

Gabe gathered Max against him, kissing his wet cheeks, his forehead, his lips. "Yeah, Max," he gasped, voice shaking. "Yes. I'm here, mi amor. I'm here, and I will always come back for you."

Max buried his fingers in Gabe's long hair and tugged him in for a kiss. Their mouths collided, noses bumping, and Max shivered as Gabe ran his tongue over Max's lips.

As their lips parted, Max traced his mate's angular jaw beneath his beard, thumbs gliding across his cheekbones. He was real. Real, and here. After all the times they'd said one devastating goodbye after another—Gabe Reyes was in his arms, and Max would never let him go again.

"I just... I can't believe you're here. I waited so long for you." Max closed his eyes tight, trying in vain not to break down.

A warm, steady hand cupped his cheek. "Look at me, Lobito." Max couldn't deny him anything. As tears spilled down his face, Gabe kissed them away. "You are my life, and if I'm ever stupid enough to forget, then leave me to my beast."

Max pulled Gabe's face toward him and claimed his lips. Sighing long and low, Gabe curled his fingers in Max's hair. They held each other for a long time, and then Gabe extended a hand to him and they walked through the woods together.

Kendra was waiting for them. Her wounds had healed, and she smiled, tears in her eyes, and walked with them to the car. She dressed and offered Gabe a blanket but he refused and shifted. Although Max was nervous at first, Gabe's eyes were their normal amber color. The black wolf laid his shaggy head in Max's lap as they drove, and he was unable to wipe the smile off his face as he ran his fingers through Gabe's fur.

Nightfall was near, but Max wasn't afraid anymore. They would never say goodbye again. Whatever came next, he and Gabe would face it together.

# CHAPTER 21

# TOGETHER

WHEN THEY RETURNED TO the hospital, Gabe sat with Max while a nurse treated his bites. Gabe held his hand tightly, trying to apologize without words in front of the nurse. Gabe also had his wounds tended to. Once they were alone in the cafeteria, Gabe's guilt overwhelmed him, and he kissed the bandage on Max's arm. "Max, I... I'm so—"

Max touched his lips to Gabe's, running his hand up and down Gabe's shoulder. "You weren't yourself. I'm just happy you're back."

Kissing Max, having him near... he wanted to pinch himself to make sure he wasn't dreaming. "I'll make it up to you." He reached around, slipping his fingers in Max's back pocket and squeezing. Max's eyes danced with delight, and the dazed little smile Gabe earned made him feel like flying.

Ben and the others came stampeding into the cafeteria. Gabe smiled and waved, blinking back tears at his mother's joyful face. He opened his arms and Izzie beat his mother to him, crushing him to her in a backbreaking hug. She then proceeded to trap him in a headlock and rain punches on his shoulder. "Don't you ever scare us like this again!"

Gasping, Gabe freed himself and stumbled into his mother's embrace. As Veronica pulled him close, Gabe closed his eyes and held her tight, savoring her warmth and comforting scent. "I missed you both," Gabe choked out, struggling to speak around the lump in his throat.

Veronica looked him in the eyes and smiled with trembling lips. "I'm just happy you're all right."

Though Ben's face was worn, he smiled radiantly and threw his arms around Gabe. Ryan started crying like a baby.

"Sorry," Ryan choked out, rubbing his eyes. "First, we thought Max was dead. Then you disappeared, then Zach—"

Gabe's smile fell away, fear tightening into a lump in his stomach. "Zach? What about him?"

Ben motioned for Gabe to follow him as they departed the cafeteria and returned to the hospital room. As they walked, Ben explained. With every word, guilt swelled inside Gabe until he thought it would eat him alive. Max might not have the spirit of a wolf anymore, but he still reached out and clasped Gabe's hand, sensing his distress even though Gabe stayed silent.

Ben left them at the door to the room, and Gabe blinked hard as he laid eyes on Zach, who was lying weak in the bed, bandages around his chest from where he'd stabbed himself. He clasped Zach's hand like he hadn't in over a year and squeezed tight. "Thank you, my friend." He wished he'd never doubted Zach's devotion to Max, to Gabe himself. If Zach fought his way back, Gabe was paying for every round of drinks they shared together for the rest of their lives.

"I'm sorry." Max's voice quavered. "He was trying to save my life. If I could have, I would have told him not to."

Gabe didn't know what to say. His oldest friend or the one he loved? He shuddered at the thought of being in a situation where he had to choose one life over the other. Taking Max's hand from his shoulder, he pressed his lips to Max's fingers and squeezed tight.

There came a knock at the door. "Sorry. Am I disturbin' anythin'?"

"No?" The confusion in Max's voice made Gabe turn his head. He managed a smile as Eddie sidled in, head down and eyes looking anywhere but at them. He was like a scolded dog. Ever since they'd escaped the hunters, he'd been quiet and subservient. Gabe didn't blame him. Gabe would be lying if he said he trusted Ed wholeheartedly, but he'd saved their lives and allowed Gabe to return to his mate, and for that, Gabe would give him the benefit of the doubt.

"No, Eddie. You're fine. Did you need something?"

"Uh, the old man—"

"Don't let Ben hear that."

Eddie winced. "Ben, that's right. He wants to see everyone in the RV."

Gabe sighed, wishing he could stay with Zach. He stood. "Thanks, Ed. Max, this is Eddie. He helped us escape the werewolf hunters." Eddie tipped his hat, then hurried out the door.

"Ben did tell you about the hunters, right?"

Max nodded. "A bit. Was he captured with you guys?"

Gabe got the door for them as they stepped out. "No. He was one of them."

Max turned toward him, wide-eyed. "One of them?"

"I know, but just remember he helped us escape."

"Can we trust him?"

Gabe tugged him close. "Without him, I wouldn't be beside you. I think he wants to change. Besides, it doesn't sound like joining was his first choice."

They left the hospital and walked around to the parking lot where Ben had parked the RV. Inside, Ben and the rest of the pack were waiting. Gabe sat between Veronica and Izzie on the sofa. His mother put her arms around him and said, "Please shave."

"I don't know. Max likes it."

"But you have such a pretty face..." Veronica sighed, fussing with his beard. Gabe grinned and moved out of her reach.

Kassandra sat on one of the old cages eyeing Max with interest. Vicenzo stood away from the others and reclined against the kitchen counter. Ben paced like a caged beast before he turned and faced the pack. "We have an hour and a half before the moon comes out."

Kendra chewed on her nails. "How are we going to face an army of that size? We need more people."

Ben said, "Eddie and I came up with a plan. First, Max, I'd like to know what happened to Alpha Hanson."

"McCready betrayed Hanson. He abducted Hanson's family and used them as leverage against Hanson to get me into his clutches."

Gabe snarled. "I knew I didn't like that son of a bitch!"

Max wet his lips. "He's a monster. He killed Hanson's family."

Ben's face was pale. "Hanson... Is he...?"

Max shook his head. "I don't know. He was chased into the woods."

Ben paced. "This is huge. Stone's had a member of the Council in his pocket for years! This explains why he was able to evade detection for so long, and how he tracked down all those historians. Greg... Motherfucker! This is bad..."

"Hey, can we get back on the subject, y'all?" Eddie cleared his throat. "We need more people to face the Wargs. I can help with that." He flushed as all eyes landed on him.

Vicenzo sneered. "More werewolf hunters? That's the last thing we need right now!"

Ben leaned on the counter, scratching his beard thoughtfully. "Hear him out. Speak up, kid."

Eddie wet his lips. "I contacted them after the attack on Stowe. They just arrived in Vermont an hour ago. They want to meet."

Vicenzo curled his lip. "You're still in touch with werewolf hunters?"

Kassandra rolled her eyes. "Cut it out, Vico!"

Vicenzo flinched. "Kassandra, really? You wanna cooperate with a bunch of hunters? After what they did to our family?"

Ben rounded on Vicenzo. "We ain't got time for this shit, Vicenzo. We need all the help we can get."

"Kassandra, we're leaving," Vicenzo said. "I don't work with werewolf hunters or their pets."

Ryan's eyes widened. "Call me a pet one more time—"

"Enough!" Ben's voice drowned out the rumbling growls. "You wanna leave, Vicenzo, go right ahead. This is bigger than our own petty grudges."

"Petty?" Vicenzo snapped.

Kassandra threw up her arms and grabbed Vicenzo's shoulders and shook him. "Enough, brother!"

Vicenzo's fury evaporated, and he just looked hurt and confused.

Kassandra glanced at Max, then stared her brother down. "Don't you get it, stupid? If we fail, the world as we know it will end. We're pack tonight. We must be."

Vicenzo shook his head in disbelief. "I can't believe you—"

"We don't have time for this!" Gabe jumped as Max's voice erupted. "Stay or go. Stone has to be stopped. Nothing else matters. If you don't want to help, then just leave."

Gabe bit his cheek to keep from grinning. He loved it when Max took charge. It was a rare and sexy side of him he never got tired of seeing.

Vicenzo's jaw tightened, and he bowed his head.

Max faced Eddie. "Edward? Eddie?"

Eddie managed a small smile. "Just Eddie."

"Nice to meet you. How many hunters are there?"

"Twenty, maybe more. They're not like the men I worked for," Eddie said, looking Ben in the eyes. "These men hunt shifters like Stone and those terrorists. They have no love for werewolves, but they know the difference between good, decent people and monsters. Their leader, Angus, is a good guy. He'll help us."

Vicenzo shook his head. "Listen to this shit... There are no good werewolf hunters. We're prey to them. They'll shoot us in the back!"

Ben growled, "Then that's a risk we have to take. We're in no position to refuse help."

Vicenzo lurched toward the door. "I'm not walking into a fucking trap." The door slammed behind him.

Kassandra jumped off the cage and darted after him, mumbling, "Sorry."

Ben patted Eddie's back. "Good planning, kid."

Sensing the time had finally come for action, Gabe rose to his feet. "Let's go meet these hunters. Never thought I'd say that aloud..." Before they left, Gabe wanted to check on Kassandra and Vicenzo. He stepped out into the parking lot and found them easily with all of Vicenzo's shouting and snarling.

"What would our parents say, Kassandra? Their son and daughter, working with the same people who fucking killed them!"

"Are you stupid, Vicenzo? Max is the one from the stories the monks told me. If Stone has his soul, then this world will end!"

"It's a story, Kassandra! What happened to our family was fucking real and I will not dishonor their memories by working with hunters!"

Gabe leaned on a parked car, observing the siblings. Kassandra shook her head, her hair flying around her shoulders. "This isn't about revenge. Not anymore."

Vicenzo's eyes blazed beneath his furrowed brow. "It was never about revenge for you, Kassie. No, you locked yourself away in a monastery for years, hiding in your tomes and your meditation."

"Our parents wouldn't even recognize you. The things you've done, all in the name of revenge... 'the Beast of the Apennines,' that's what people call you!"

Vicenzo's jaw tightened. "At least I'm trying to make the world a safer place."

"You've killed people."

"I've killed hunters, Kassandra! They're not people, they're animals!"

"And you get to decide who lives and who dies? What has happened to you?" Kassandra's voice shook. She turned and stormed past Gabe and into the RV. Turning away, Vicenzo ran a clawed hand across his prickly scalp.

Gabe looked at Vicenzo and saw himself after his father was murdered, angry and vengeful, believing he was judge, jury, and executioner because of the scars he bore from his past. It was no way to live.

Gabe said, "Your sister's got the right idea. Max's powers are something you gotta see to believe, but if Stone's people are willing to burn an entire town for their cause, then it's more than just a story."

Vicenzo deflated with a sigh. "I know," he admitted, and it looked like it pained him.

Gabe wondered if he could reach him, penetrate that armor of anger he hid behind like Ben had reached him when he was lost, angry, and hurt. "When I was a boy, Stone took me from my family. Tortured me." He rolled up his sleeves and showed the scars on his arms. Shock rippled over Vicenzo's face. "My father was killed trying to save me. I believe Stone used me to get at my father and kill him."

Vicenzo's eyes widened. "Sorry. That's... that's awful."

Gabe tugged his sleeve down. "I spent a long time being angry, like you. I hurt people who hurt others the way I'd been hurt. If I'd been older, stronger, I probably would have killed them. But you're better off helping those who've been hurt. No matter how many assholes you kill, there'll always be more. Helping others gives you purpose, it heals you. Violence doesn't. Soon you won't be able to distinguish yourself from the ones you're hunting."

Vicenzo looked away, his jaw working hard. It was angular in shape from how often he'd clenched his teeth in anger over the course of his life. "Spare me the lecture. All right? I *have* helped people. I've given grieving families peace. In my own way."

Gabe nodded, uncertain if he could get Vicenzo to reconsider. He'd been doing this much longer than Gabe had and was set in his ways. "Fine. If you want, though, there's a place in the LPA for someone with a passion for helping others. Our methods are different but effective. We focus on the victims, not their attackers."

Vicenzo squinted at him. "I have my ways, and it works. So skip the sales pitch. I'm not walking back into that RV as long as we're working with hunters."

Gabe fought back a sigh. "If Stone wipes us out tonight, hunters are gonna be the least of your problems."

Vicenzo turned his back. "I'm gonna die one way or the other. It doesn't matter how or when."

Gabe dropped his arms to his sides. There was nothing else he could say or do. Ben would have done a better job. Or perhaps not. Perhaps Vicenzo was beyond help. He tried to tell himself it didn't matter as he turned his back and marched toward the RV. The sun was sinking fast. Time was running out.

MAX WET HIS LIPS, his stomach twisting as his nerves mounted. "So, where are we meeting these hunters?"

Eddie looked out the window, watching the woods hurtle past. "The outskirts of the town of Jericho. Angus thinks the Wargs will target the town soon."

Max's stomach churned. "How do you know these hunters?"

Eddie shuffled his feet. "They worked together with my group from time to time. They never seemed too happy about it, but they did what they had to in order to apprehend ferals and criminal shifters who escaped justice. My group delighted in torturin' any wolf, no matter how innocent." A shiver ran through him.

Max still didn't understand how a werewolf had come to work for hunters. "They didn't like your clan, so won't you be in danger if you go to meet them?"

"Actually, they wanted me to join 'em. I should have. I'd have been treated better, probably." The corners of Eddie's mouth turned down. "Not that my uncle would have let me. He loved remindin' me I was just his huntin' dog."

"Your uncle turned you into a hunter?"

Eddie folded his arms over his chest, closing himself off. Max fell silent, unsure if Eddie would speak further about it.

"Things will be better for you now," Max said, hoping to ease his worries. "Ben won't let you be mistreated."

Eddie looked down at the floor. "If he lets me stay."

"He will. Do you want to stay?"

Eddie's eyes widened, vulnerable and full of fragile hope. In a blink, he was impassive again. "I just wanna help."

Ben pulled over and stopped the RV at the foot of a hiking trail. The door opened and Max followed the pack out into the woods. He shivered, remembering the last time he was in these woods. Gabe's hand fell warm upon his shoulder and soothed his fears.

Izzie scented the air. "Smell that? Hunters."

Max couldn't smell a thing, just the pines and mountain air. He frowned, disliking how cut off he was.

Ben shushed them, holding up an arm to freeze them in place. Shadows moved deep within the trees and Max's breath hitched when he realized they were surrounded by armed men and women. Pistols flashed, and belts covered in rows of silver bullets shone in the moonlight. Max's skin turned to ice.

"Don't move," one of the men growled in a gruff English accent, glaring at them. He was burly and bearded and had an empty eye socket.

"Angus, it's Eddie." Eddie took a tentative step forward.

Angus lowered his pistol. "Good to see you, lad. This your pack, then?"

"I—yeah. For now, anyway."

"These your packmates?" Angus eyed Ben.

"Yeah. Ben Stroud. We're here to stop Stone and his fanatics from tearing apart Vermont."

"Follow me. Keep up." Angus shouldered ahead and his hunters followed him.

Max exhaled. Gabe chuckled and wrapped his arm around his shoulders. "Unnerving, huh? Thought my stomach and bowels changed places."

"Yeah." Being surrounded by trained werewolf killers armed with silver and smelling of aconitum was not an experience he wanted again.

Gabe squeezed him. "Don't worry. I'll protect you."

Max shoved him, his face burning hot. "You're so cheesy."

Angus snapped, "You two want some privacy on your little date? Hurry up."

Max ducked his head, embarrassed, and Gabe grinned and led him onward. Max stumbled and realized the ground was tattooed with paw prints.

Soon Stone would open the portal to the She-Wolf's realm. Once he killed the goddess, he would presumably have the power needed to wipe out any human settlements with ease.

Max's stomach churned. "Stone can't win this."

"He *won't*." Gabe's arm tightened around his shoulder. "I'll be dead in the ground before I let him—"

The thought made Max's legs weak. "Don't." He grabbed Gabe's arm and forced him to stop, to look him in the face. "Don't ever say that. You're not dying, and neither am I."

Angus suddenly stopped moving, and his hunters froze. Angus peered through some binoculars. "I see campsites," Angus said. Max strained his eyes and could make out distant firelight.

"That's them," Max said.

Angus stared. "What are those bastards waiting for?"

Max cast his gaze to the cloudy sky. "For the moon to come out."

Max knew for a fact his powers were strong only in the presence of moonlight. Stone would need to wait until the clouds moved away from the moon. Then all he had to do was howl, and the world as they knew it would bend and break.

Ben said, "We have to strike now before the moon has time to come out."

Angus reached for his gun. "The time's now, ladies and gents. Innocent lives are depending on us. Those beasts have got an army, but I've got the toughest sons of bitches in the USA. If we don't end them in Vermont, they'll spread like a bloody plague. They'll come for you and your families. Are you gonna let that happen?"

The hunters drew their pistols, crossbows, silver baseball bats and whips in defiance.

Ben turned to his pack. "We're ending this now. Stone and his pack cannot leave this town alive." His eyes softened. "It's been an honor, knowing each and every one of you. You're my family. All of you."

Heart in his throat, Max reached out and found Gabe's hand.

Gabe's lips trembled when he smiled. "I'm with you, Max."

Gabe laced their fingers together and Max held on for dear life.

# CHAPTER 22

# ONE WILL FALL

THE HUNTERS AND EDDIE advanced down the hill toward the werewolf encampment. Max and the pack flanked the hunters. They'd all shifted into either full wolf form or a half shift, and Max wished badly he could join them. He didn't know how to use a gun, though one of the hunters had given him a spare silver crowbar that he carried strapped to his hip. A part of Max was terrified he'd be a burden to his pack without the ability to shift.

As if sensing his anxieties, a big black wolf pressed against his side. A bushy tail curled around his waist; a cold nose bumped into his hand. Max touched the top of Gabe's head right between his ears. He touched his mother's white fur when she came up to his left side.

Max wasn't afraid for himself. "Both of you, be careful," Max said, holding them close to his side.

The wolves were waiting for them in the clearing, silhouetted by the dying light of their fires. The hunters raised their crossbows as the wolves bristled, their growls like a rumble of thunder on the horizon. Ben's big silver wolf came to stand in front of the pack, ears flattened back and fangs bared. Max yanked the crowbar from his belt loop.

The wargs parted as the only person on two legs marched toward the hunters. It was McCready, his eyes glinting faintly beneath the slits in the snarling wolf mask. A low chuckle rumbled from his chest.

"I admit, I admire the tenacity of the human race. I will remember you, how your kind fought against impossible odds to escape your doom, how valiantly you failed." Those narrow eyes found Max's. They widened briefly. "Gallagher. My, my. It's hard to be bored around you, isn't it? You're full of surprises."

Gabe snarled, coming to stand shoulder to shoulder with Kendra as they stepped in front of him.

"Hybrids… just the sight of you reminds me of the wretched state of this world. How far our species has fallen." McCready's claws lengthened. "This world was ours once. The She-Wolf set wolves free upon this world to claim it as our own. It should have been ours! Instead, the humans bent us to their will. They corrupted us, turned us from our original purposes. Made us their dogs! The pure and powerful will never suffer at human hands again!"

The furious howling of the wargs split the night.

Gabe snarled, his body vibrating with it. Max touched him between his ears, his hand steady. He wasn't afraid. Gabe was here, they were together at last, and Max was going to fucking stand and fight with his mate or die with him.

"Kill them!" McCready roared. "Cleanse this world of humans, their pets and their filth!"

The wargs charged past the masked man, shaking the earth.

Ben howled and the pack answered his war cry.

"Aim!" Angus roared, and the hunters in the front line dropped to their knees, aiming down their crossbows while the ones behind raised their guns. "Fire!" Angus roared, spit flying from his mouth. The wargs lunged, jaws gaping. Many were blasted out of the air, their bodies twisting as silver burned through the flesh to the bone. As they fell, Ben led the pack in a charge, tackling the ones who'd fallen.

Max charged, Gabe at his side, and swung his crowbar into the skull of a fallen wolf. Bone crunched, the impact traveling up his arm and tingling in his shoulder. Gabe drove his fangs into the throat of a writhing wolf, ripping and spraying blood.

"Keep on hitting them!" Angus bellowed. "Don't give those wounds a chance to close!"

Ben bowled a wolf off her paws and Ryan pounced in a blur of white fur, tearing into her throat. Veronica swung her silver whip at a crowd of approaching wolves, slicing into them. Their flesh sizzled and burned. Izzie and Kendra were there to defend Veronica from any wolves who escaped her aim. Black and white blurs, Izzie and Kendra charged, ripping and tearing and leaving their opponents sundered in the dirt.

Eddie and Angus stood back to back, gunning down wolves who charged at them. Eddie lobbed a silver grenade at a pack of charging wolves. The bomb erupted, ringing in Max's ears, and shards of silver lacerated the wolves and forced them to assume a human form. Blood wept from wounds that wouldn't close as the humanoid shifters screamed in agony.

As a wolf lunged at him, bloody fangs gaping for his arm, Max recoiled. Gabe pounced in a blur of dark fur, jaws crunching into the wolf's shoulder. Max swung with a roar, cracking the crowbar across the wolf's skull, which split as the skin sizzled and smoked.

Moonlight bathed the bloody clearing as the moon made her appearance from behind the cloud bank. Stone. Where was Stone?

Movement atop a distant hill caught Max's eye. McCready ran, a red wolf at his side.

"Gabe, we've got to get to them!"

Gabe snapped his jaws in agreement and charged.

Wargs pursued Gabe and Max, trying to cut them off.

"I got your backs!" Eddie called, chucking a cannister through the air. The cannister landed behind Gabe and Max and spewed clouds of tear gas. Any pursuing wolves who didn't stop in time ran through the cloud and out the other side, pawing at their faces and howling. Eddie chucked a few more cannisters that erupted, obscuring the enemy wolves in clouds of gas. "Go!" Eddie shouted.

With his mate at his side, Max ran for the hilltop in pursuit of Stone and the masked man. His heart thundered, feet slamming the earth.

This was it.

One would rise and one would fall, but Max would be damned if it was him or Gabe who met their end tonight. Not now, not when there was still so much they had to experience together.

Max caught his breath once they'd ascended the hill. He ran his fingers through Gabe's fur and a growl rumbled through his body. The black wolf leaned into Max's side, and he squeezed fistfuls of coarse, dark fur. His heart was in his throat, but Max forced himself to look Gabe in his amber eyes and say, "This is it. You and me. We're finishing this together."

Gabe growled lowly, flashed his amber eyes, and leaned into Max's touch. Holding his breath, Max started forward again.

At the top of the hill in a clearing within the trees, Stone and McCready stood beneath the moonlight. McCready laughed, his shoulders heaving from exertion. "Watch, the both of you! Watch the end of your world and the dawn of another. A world free of the taint of humans and hybrids, where werewolves reign supreme in that world that should have been ours!"

Stone threw back his head and howled. Stone's howl was a hateful sound that raised the hairs on his arms. It was unnatural, evil. Only a monster like Stone was capable of twisting a wolf's beautiful howl into something so dreadful.

The earth trembled. Gravity pushed him back down, weakening his knees until he thought they'd snap if he resisted. Max collapsed, unable to move. Gabe managed to drape his body over Max's, shielding him.

Through watering eyes, Max watched with dread as the moon swelled, growing larger and hurtling closer. The stars burned, streaking across the sky as they fled from Stone's call. Then a lunar eclipse hid the blood moon from view as if the moon herself were hiding her face in horror. The sight turned Max's skin to ice.

With one last hoarse howl from Stone, the pressure forcing Max and Gabe to the ground blew apart the space around them like a nuclear detonation. Max coughed, choking on dirt. Gabe stumbled, shaking his pelt free of debris.

As the dust settled, there was nothing but wide-open space around them. Stone's howl died out, and an explosion of white light blinded Max. Shapes flashed before his eyes, and though he didn't want to look, he did anyway. He had to see for himself, even if he feared his mind couldn't take it.

A pack of spectral wolves strode from within a tear in the universe. It was as if a curtain had been opened, a curtain Max never knew was there, giving a glimpse of a world beyond. Endless green fields, rolling mountains. The hunting grounds.

The spectral wolves threw back their heads and howled and—

And they were singing to Max. Their song reached into his soul where a piece of him lay curled up, alone and forgotten even by himself. Their song made his eyes burn, carved open his chest, and wrapped around his heart.

Why? Why did their song tear him to pieces and make him whole all at once?

One of the wolves looked right at him while the other smaller ones sang. Those eyes bore straight into his soul. They *knew* him, these specters that, for all he knew, could be from the past, present, or future, these wolves who might not even be alive, but Max prayed they were. They had to be. He had to know them. Maybe he already did, he realized, as some forgotten part of Max ached for them, for this pack that were no more than ghosts to him.

"Max," whispered a soft, feminine voice right into his ear.

His breath hitched around a sob.

"I've been waiting for you. I love you. I miss you. Sweet, sweet Max. Come. Find me."

Tears were wet on Max's face. He reached out a hand that passed through the spectral wolf before him. "Who are you?" Max whispered. "Where are you? How can I find you?" He had to know. He had to run, straight through that portal, howl and howl until their song answered his.

He had to go home.

*Home. No. Wait. What? I have a home. I have a pack. I—*

He blinked fast as his eyes burned, trying to seal away the emotion brimming inside him. Max tore his gaze away from the spectral wolves and toward Stone. Stone stood among the ruins of the trees, impassive and untouched, red-and-black striped fur shivering in the wind.

The masked man rose to his feet, his mask cracked and shattered. Aaron McCready bared his teeth in a savage smile. "Watch closely, hybrids," he said, his voice hushed with excitement. "Don't look away. We're shaping history. Here, now." He tossed the sheathed moonblade to Stone.

Stone leaped into the air and caught the dagger in his jaws. Armed with the moonblade, the tool of this world's demise, he shifted to a man and took one step into the portal.

"Gabe, now!" Max roared, and he and Gabe charged. McCready lunged, tackling Gabe into the dirt. Stone whirled toward Max as they collided, their bodies knocking sickeningly together. The moonblade fell in the grass behind them.

Then Max was suspended, flying high into the air. Stone grinned, gravity at his fingertips, and Max struggled, frustrated by how weak he was as a human.

Over Stone's shoulder, McCready and Gabe struggled. McCready's clothes ripped as he shifted to a wolf. McCready charged at Gabe. Shifting back to a man, Gabe seized a stone and bashed it across his skull. Yelping, McCready dropped into the grass.

With a downward swipe of Stone's hand, Max plummeted, and the collision with the ground knocked the breath from his body. Aching, he tried to stand and found himself gasping for air as a clawed fist wrapped around his throat.

Max's vision blackened at the corners. Held high off the ground, Max had a view of Gabe, naked and bloody. Seizing the moonblade, Gabe charged. Stone didn't have time to look before he stumbled forward with a grunt as the blade pierced his back and exited through his chest. Stone's blood stained Max's clothes as he collapsed, desperately sucking in a lungful of air.

Crying out, Stone seized up, then started thrashing, and an ethereal glow spilled from where Gabe had stabbed him. Stone jerked and shuddered as a red wolf materialized from his body, shimmering like a mirage, and galloped toward Max. Max stumbled as the red wolf passed into him.

The smells of the forest crashed over him, blood and fur, pine trees and grass. The bonds Stone had shredded reassembled in his chest. Each thread lit up and hummed, connecting him to Ben, to Zach though faint, to Ryan and Izzie, to Kendra and Veronica. Max could feel his packmates again, and he could have wept from joy.

Then the bond connecting him to Gabe was set ablaze. All of Gabe's primal fury crashed over Max and left him shaking with fear and exhilaration. Max gasped, doubling over from the shock of it as fire burned in his chest. The thread between them had always felt warm like the sun, but never like this.

A big, clawed hand settled on his shoulder, warm and strong, and squeezed tight. The touch was familiar and yet so wrong all at once.

"I got you, Lobito. You're safe." Gabe's voice rumbled deep in his chest, as close to a growl as Max had ever heard it. Fur covered Gabe's arms and face, and his mouth was full of fangs.

Gabe towered over him, his face twisted in anger and covered in dark fur. His eyes were inky black, the pupils a wolfish yellow. He was consumed by his inner wolf, barely human. But it was more than that. Somehow, Gabe had grown to nearly eight feet tall. His body was bursting with muscle.

And his face... Max shuddered. He was looking into the face of a wolf. The thing before him was a bipedal beast, bristling with barely contained rage. He looked like Hanson had, and Max couldn't understand how or why.

Something was wrong. The thing towering over him wasn't the man he knew and loved. Something had awakened within Gabe and changed him, and Max didn't know if he'd ever get him back.

MAX WAS AFRAID. GABE could see it in his eyes. He didn't blame Max; Gabe was afraid of himself, of the thing that had awakened within him. He didn't want to lose himself, but if he held back, he feared they wouldn't leave this hilltop alive.

*I won't lose myself, not again. Not this time,* Gabe promised himself as he faced Stone. And he believed in that promise. Even as fury lengthened his claws and made his lips curl, he sensed a purpose to the anger fueling his resolve. It wasn't mindless or instinctive. His beast was still under his control, tethered to the bond between him and Max. The moment Gabe had opened his heart to him, Max had soothed the darkness inside him and given it a name: love.

It was for this love he would fight. It was for this love he would win, or die trying.

And from that love, from the bond that tied their hearts together, strength flowed into Gabe. He grew taller, towering over the monster who'd once tormented him. The muscles in his arms grew taut. Thick, wiry fur sprouted from his flesh. The growl in his throat felt bigger than thunder. His claws shredded the ground as he hunkered down, ready to pounce.

"Gabe," Max whimpered. "Holy shit. You look different. What the hell is happening?"

Gabe didn't understand it, either. He was shifting by the second, but not to his wolf. He was stuck between man and beast, but he was still in control, and it was because of Max.

Goddess... How in the hell had he ever thought he could do this by himself? When they were together, they were so much stronger than they'd ever be apart.

"What the hell have you become?" Stone snarled, eyes wide in his sunken face. "This... this changes nothing! You'll die here and now, Reyes!"

With a furious roar, Stone began the change, dropping to all fours. The blood stopped flowing from his chest as the flesh knit itself together. Eyes wide, fangs bared, he prowled toward them as his black wolf.

The black wolf of vengeance and the beast of hate circled beneath a bloody lunar eclipse.

The song that howled in Gabe's heart for Max became a roar. His blood burned hot. The fury pounded in him until all he could do was throw back his head and scream his rage to the night sky. He charged toward Stone, shaking the earth as he hurtled toward him on two legs.

Stone's black wolf lunged. Gabe shot out his hand and grabbed Stone by the throat. Snarling, Gabe hurled Stone down the hill as easily as if he were a ragdoll. Stone tumbled to a stop at the edge of a roaring river. Gabe thundered down the hill after him and hit the ground. Gabe braced himself on all fours, shredding grass and churning up soil under his claws.

Stone stood. Water lapped under his paws. Stone flew at him and Gabe raised his claws, ready to counterattack—but the collision never came. Stone was suspended in midair, kicking and thrashing and snarling in fury. Max, his hands outstretched and glowing with red moonlight, held him in place.

As his tormentor writhed, helpless, Gabe realized that after all these years, the tables had turned. The hunter had become the prey. Gabe lunged. His claws flew across Stone's exposed stomach. The strength pumping through Gabe enthralled him. Blood spilled hot and wet across his fingertips, spattering in the grass. Stone howled and collapsed as Max let go, and he writhed in the grass like an overturned roach.

Gabe grinned, relishing the sight of Stone's exposed stomach gleaming with blood. Then Stone shifted to a man, growling through clenched teeth. The split skin of his stomach hadn't completely mended before Gabe tore it open again with a swipe of his claws. Stone's pained howl died in a choked grunt as Gabe wrapped his claws around his pale throat. Snarling,

Stone clawed Gabe's face, ripping apart the skin around Gabe's eye, and blood blinded him.

Stone bared his teeth, choking out laughter. "Another scar to add to the collection, hybrid. You'll carry all my marks with you long after I'm dead! You will never be free of me, boy. I will live inside your head for the rest of your life!"

Gabe smashed his fist into Stone's nose. His laughter became a gurgle as he choked and sputtered. Gabe hit him again and again until he'd turned that leering grin into a bloody mess.

"No," Gabe snarled through a mouthful of fangs and blood. "I'm not yours." He wasn't a boy anymore. He wasn't someone John Stone could torment, not any longer. "I've got your marks, but that's all the hold you'll ever have over me again."

Gabe drove his claws into the warm cavity of Stone's abdomen, and his body spasmed. "Tried to break me, didn't you? You fucking couldn't."

Stone's eyes rolled back. Gabe shook him by the throat, forcing those black eyes back on him. "You tried and tried, and you failed! Know why?"

For everything he'd lost and all he'd endured, he'd found more than John Stone ever could hope to have. "'Cause I had my pack to pick me back up, time and again! You have nothing!"

Gabe wrenched Stone in close, panting in his bloody face. He looked the monster in the eyes, and saw the fear that left them wide. Gabe parted his jaws and showed Stone his fangs, long and sharp. "This is for my father. His name was Manuel Ignacio Reyes. He was more of a fucking wolf than you'll ever be!"

Stone's roar was choked into strangled grunts as Gabe put his fangs into the pale skin of Stone's throat and tore. The taste of his enemy's blood was like a drug, and he wanted more, wanted to rip Stone limb from limb with his teeth until he was nothing but bloody pieces. The world disappeared around him. He fell into darkness, and lost himself to his primal hunger.

When he looked up, his wolf towered over him, powerful and terrible. *Kill him. Rip him. Devour him.*

No. He'd done what he had to do. It was finished.

The wolf bared his fangs. *Kill. Kill!*

He would tear apart every single one of Stone's packmates until not one of them could threaten what was his. His Max. His pack. His family. Control was slipping, fleeing beyond his grasp. His ears rang, his body shuddered from the growl deep in his chest.

"Gabe, stop. Stop, it's over!" Hands fumbled across his back. Warm arms closed around him and held tight. "Gabe. Gabe, that's enough." A soothing hand ran over his fur, though it trembled.

A vision appeared in his mind of two doorways. Blood oozed beneath the cracks in the wood of one doorway, compelling him toward a path of feral madness and an eternal hunt. The other teemed with the sounds of life. The voice beyond was soft and sweet.

A scent called out to him, sweet as cinnamon and chilis. It smelled like mate and mine, and love and life. As the madness crawled from his mind, he became aware he had a choice. To surrender to his feral instincts, or not to. He could give in to the beast and hunt forever, but he didn't want to.

"It's over. I'm safe. We both are. Come back. Please, come back."

*The hunt is over,* he told the wolf. *You can rest now. It's over.*

The wolf fell silent and hid its fangs, lying down with his head on his paws. He closed his eyes and all the tension left his body. The beast was at peace, for now.

Gabe took in deep breaths, and when once he'd smelled only blood, he clung on to the soothing scent of *mate* and *mine*. He grasped the thread tying him to Max and used it to pull him from the depths of his fury. His eyes opened and he found himself looking up into a freckled face with eyes the color of honey.

The quiet of the night only amplified the river's roar. Gabe bolted upright. He raised his hands, expecting to see claws twice his size and nails several inches long. "What do I look like?" he rasped, touching his face. He feared he'd find a snout and pointed fangs. Instead, he had his regular nose and that gross rugged beard.

"Hey, it's okay." Max's voice was gentle as he squeezed Gabe's shoulder. "You're you again. Your normal handsome self. Just a bit bloody."

Gabe exhaled his relief. He had no idea what had come over him but he'd feared he'd never return from the bestial rage he'd lost himself in.

Gentle fingertips caressed his cheek and Gabe couldn't resist leaning into the touch. A sigh fell from Max's trembling lips.

"I thought you weren't coming back for a moment there," Max admitted, blinking hard.

Gabe eased himself up and didn't realize how weak he was until he slumped forward onto Max's shoulder. Strong, warm arms went around his shoulders and Gabe's muscles slackened as he sank into Max's arms. He held on to Max's shoulders and basked in the warmth of his body, searching for the smell he knew and loved beneath the dirt and blood as he nuzzled into his neck.

Their foreheads touched and Gabe lost himself in orange eyes. "How could I not? Everything I've done, everything I'll ever do, it's for you."

Max laughed softly. "I don't know. You looked pretty happy tearing out Stone's throat."

Gabe grinned. "Okay, that was for me, a bit. Mostly for my father, for you." The reality of it sank in, and he clung on to Max, suddenly overcome. Over Max's shoulder, Stone's body turned the river water red with blood. "It's over, Max. It's really... He's gone."

"I know." Max's lips brushed over his bare shoulder, and his arms held Gabe tightly as his body shook with emotion, tears burning hot in his eyes.

Stone had haunted Gabe's dreams since he was a boy. He'd lived each day anticipating the moment their paths would finally cross. He'd gone from a grieving boy, to an angry vigilante, to training with the LPA and helping others, all in the hopes of finding the man who'd torn a hole in his family. And it was all over. The man who'd taken his father from him would never harm another soul, and his dreams of godhood had died with him.

"It's over." Max grasped his arm and helped him stand. "Let's go. We need to find the others."

Gabe stumbled, clutching onto Max for support. Turning them around, Max froze. Gabe found himself staring down the muzzle of a pistol inches from his face and his mouth ran dry.

McCready stood, bloody and clad in the tattered remnants of his pants, and tutted his disappointment. "Look what you've done." He gave Stone's limp, bloody body a distasteful nudge with the tip of his bare foot. "Stone was very useful. It's rare to meet someone whose goals so align with yours. But let's face it, he would have stabbed me in the back at some point. I should thank you for taking care of that eventuality for me."

Gabe put a hand on Max's chest, trying to urge him behind himself, but Max stood firmly at his side. His stomach churned just looking into McCready's face, knowing a member of the Council had been working with Stone all these years. How many secrets had McCready shared with Stone? "You're the reason he was able to hide for so long. You're a traitor to all shifters."

McCready laughed. "You really think that was the extent of my help? That all this was Stone's idea? How generous. Stone was ambitious, yes, but he was a dog. All dogs need a handler. Stone only got as far as he did because I knew Greg Harris and learned of his association with the monks. His fascination with the history of our people proved to be invaluable. Stone, good dog that he was, played fetch for me. I told him when and where Harris would be in Canada. Fast forward about a year and a half later, and Stone delivered the blade right into my hands."

Gabe longed to rip this slimy man limb from limb. "How many innocent people did you betray to Stone?"

"Innocents?" McCready's face twisted in a sneer. "No one who sides with our oppressors is innocent. Not you hybrids, not your father... Now, he was a clever man, for a mongrel. He almost ruined everything."

Max tightened his grip on Gabe's shoulders. He must have sensed the way every muscle in his body went taut.

McCready's lips curled into a sick smile. He came closer, feet splashing in the water overflowing from the river. "What? You really thought it was all just a coincidence? That Stone just happened to pick your filthy family because of your father's presence on the Council? I'll give Manuel Reyes some credit, Gabriel. He figured out my association with the Wargs, and of course, I couldn't allow him to tell anyone on the Council. Stone was all too happy to clean up that particular mess for me. Our goals aligned just perfectly, like we were meant for each other. Whatever will I do without him?"

Gabe's jaw ached, his breath coming in short bursts. *That* was why his family had been targeted. All these years, he'd asked himself why, never quite coming up with a suitable answer. Now he knew, and the fury made him shake. "You're the reason I was abducted. Why my father was killed. It was..." Words failed him.

"Your father loved his family. Every man has his weakness, something he'd give up everything to protect." He turned the pistol on Max, and Gabe's heart roared in his ears. "Love is a weakness. So long as one has something to lose, it's so easy to take that love and turn it into a weapon."

Max spoke, his voice clipped with fury. "It's over. You're finished. Your plan failed and your accomplice is dead. Alpha Hanson's going to know everything you've done. You won't get away with this!"

McCready barked out a laugh, baring teeth stained with blood. "Hanson! What do I have to fear from Hanson? That fool is running around feral in the woods! When I told others of the future your powers could bring us, dozens flocked to join the cause overnight. Don't you see? The peace between humans and werewolves is a fragile thing. All it takes is a push, and both sides will dissolve into a race war that will rip this country apart, ripe for the victors to resurrect it from the ashes of our human oppressors!"

Glee sparkled in McCready's eyes, and he smiled, wild and crazed. "Stowe was just the start. If the Council has the balls to challenge me, I finally have the strength to challenge them, the strength to put humans in their place!"

Gabe laughed. "Yeah? I'd like to see you march your rabid dogs to New York. You'd be laughed out of the city. You've got the numbers to destroy a tiny town full of defenseless humans. Try your luck against NYC. Face it, McCready, you're done for. You'll be opposed by werewolves and our human allies everywhere you go."

McCready sneered. "You're blind, Reyes. This revolution has been a long time coming. For years, we've watched humans bind us to their laws, oppress and shackle us, while the Council rolls over and lets them. This country is full of werewolves hungry for a return to the old ways. They're in hiding, but all they need is a show of strength to find the courage to step into the light and tear this country apart. As Alpha, I will lead them into the light."

McCready pressed the pistol against Max's head. Everything inside Gabe screamed at him to move, but he feared Max would be gunned down right in front of him. McCready waved the gun between Max and Gabe. Gabe's heart sank as McCready took aim right between his eyes.

"McCready," Max began, his arm trembling around Gabe's shoulders. "Don't do this."

"I'm not heartless," McCready assured him, his smile pleasant. "Say your goodbyes."

Something was stuck in Gabe's throat. They'd come so close to having a life together. So close, and in seconds, it would all be torn away from them. He blinked hard as Max became a blur through his tears. "We almost made it, mi amor." Almost wasn't enough, not nearly, but if the alternative was never loving Max Gallagher, then it would have to do.

Max's lips trembled. "This isn't how it was supposed to end."

Gabe squeezed his shoulders, pressing their foreheads together. He breathed Max in by the lungful, throat aching. "I know."

Tears spilled from Max's eyes and he tugged Gabe into his arms. His shoulders trembled as Gabe held him tight. "I love you, Gabriel."

Gabe smiled despite it all, blinking away his tears so he could look Max in the eyes one last time. "I know. I love you, too."

Max's lips tasted of salt as they claimed his.

"You saved my life, Max Gallagher."

Max had never looked more beautiful in the morning light, even as he cried. He captured Gabe's face in his hands and guided their lips together one final time. Gabe tried to ready himself for death, for the finality of it, but as Max kissed him, he accepted that he'd never be ready to say goodbye to him. He curled his fingers in beautiful, soft copper hair, relished the way their chests touched with every shuddery breath, how perfectly their lips fit together. He was grateful that in the final moments of his life, he had someone he loved so much that no amount of time in the world together would ever be enough.

The blast of gunfire tore through the woods.

But neither Max nor Gabe fell. Opening his eyes, Gabe found his own shocked confusion on Max's face.

McCready clutched at his chest and his hand fell away crimson. The gun toppled from his hand and he stumbled forward. He looked over his shoulder and huffed his laughter. "Well played." He grunted, then toppled over into the roaring river. The current carried his body beyond their reach, and Gabe hoped he never laid eyes on Aaron McCready again.

Vicenzo lowered a hunter's silver pistol and grinned at the shock that must have been on their faces. "Ah, that felt good. For such a mastermind, he sure has a fat head, doesn't he?"

Max slumped over, gasping his relief. "Thank you, Vicenzo."

Gabe grinned. "Knew you'd make the right choice."

Vicenzo's face flushed. "No need to lay it on thick. I just wanted to shoot one of these bastards."

Whatever his reasons were, Gabe had never been happier to see anyone. Gabe howled, contacting Ben and the others to let them know they were all right.

"I hope they're all right," Max said, panting as he and Gabe scaled a hill, sunlight blinding them as they reached the top.

Through the light of dawn, they materialized: Ben, battered and bruised but all the more foreboding for it; Izzie and Veronica, their faces lighting up at the sight of him; Kendra, her arms open wide as she ran to embrace Max; Eddie, looking ready to pass out while Ryan chatted his ear off with a triumphant grin, a fist high in the air. Gabe opened his arms and hugged the two most important women in his life. Max threw his arms around his mother and got crushed in a group hug by Ryan.

Kassandra ran to greet Vicenzo, smacking him upside the head until he shoved the moonblade at her. Her mouth fell open. "You got it back! Amazing! Look at this craftsmanship!"

Ryan snorted. "'Oh, cool, check out the deadly weapon we all nearly lost our lives trying to obtain!' I mean, it is kinda cool, but was it worth the trouble? No. Not really."

"I must take this back to the monastery!" Kassandra swooned, tracing the runes on the hilt that each resembled a phase of the moon.

Ben side-eyed her. "Tell me you're gonna destroy it."

"Of course! It's far too dangerous to go back in that tomb."

Ryan frowned. "Maybe one of us should go with you just in case. Wouldn't want any more 'apprentices' trying to steal it."

Kassandra shot him a look. "That was a one-time thing."

Ryan grinned. "Yeah, but you know I'm never letting you live it down, right?"

Max yawned. "Guys, can we get back to the hospital? I'm aching everywhere, and I'm sure Zach's awake by now."

Gabe rubbed Max's shoulder. "Tired? I'll carry you."

Max shook his head. "No, I'm—whoa!" He laughed as Gabe scooped him into his arms and carried him, bridal style, back toward the RV. The others laughed but Max nestled into the crook of his neck. He was asleep in Gabe's arms before they got there.

# CHAPTER 23

# CHILD OF THE MOON

WHEN MAX WOKE, THEY'D arrived at the hospital. Waiting for them, propped up against the cushions and looking surly, was Zach. Relief made Max smile. "How are you feeling?"

"Like I stabbed myself in the heart." Zach grunted, managing a strained smile. "But I'm alive." He jumped as Ryan tackled him in a long, tight embrace, then put his arms around Ryan's shoulders.

"Thank you." Max wished he could find words to explain what it meant to him, knowing Zach had been ready to give his life for him.

Zach met his gaze and smiled warmly. "I'm just glad you're alive... and that I'm alive. I thought I was done for."

Ryan untangled himself from Zach to glare at him. "The one time I go away, you almost kill yourself! I'm never leaving you alone again!"

"It was for Max's sake!" Zach looked wounded.

"I know, but—but—" Ryan looked ready to combust as relief and fury overwhelmed him.

Izzie rolled her eyes. "Boys, just say you missed each other and leave it at that."

Zach sighed. "Ryan, I promise, next time I get any self-sacrificey feelings, I'll call you."

Ryan looked away with a snort. "No. What you did was noble as hell, I just... I thought..."

He tugged Ryan's head to his chest. "But I'm fine now. And we're going home."

Max sighed at the thought. He missed New York more than he could say. Gabe grinned beside him. "First thing I'm doing is ordering a bagel with cream cheese and lox."

Izzie leaned back in her chair. "We'll have to come back under better circumstances."

Ryan chuckled. "Come on, this was my kinda vacation, aside from all the death. How many tourists can say they thwarted an attempt at lycanthrope domination?"

The door opened and Kassandra and Eddie walked in, bringing some snacks for everyone. Eddie tripped over his feet when he caught Vicenzo glowering at him from the sofa. "Uh... anyone want beef jerky? Or—"

Vicenzo snorted. "I don't bite. Give it here."

Eddie handed Vicenzo the jerky like he was sticking his hand in an alligator's mouth. Vicenzo ripped open the bag and chewed, eyeing Eddie. Kassandra sighed and said, "Do I need to remind you, brother, that without Eddie's help, we would have been overwhelmed?"

Vicenzo grunted and chewed his jerky. He swallowed, face twisting as if it tasted bitter. Glancing at Eddie, he cleared his throat. "Well, those hunters didn't shoot us in the ass. So, fine. You did good." Kassandra kicked his shin. Vicenzo cringed. "And thanks. For your help," he said through clenched teeth.

Eddie's face reddened. "No problem. It, uh... It felt good to be helpful to my own kind for a change."

Silence fell as Vicenzo quickly averted his gaze and chewed more jerky. Max thought he could see some color in his cheeks. At least they weren't at each other's throats anymore.

Ben walked in with coffees for everyone. "Ed, gotta hand it to ya, those hunters saved our asses."

Eddie smiled into his coffee. "Thanks. They're good guys."

"What's your next move? Got any plans for the future?"

Eddie looked into his coffee as if searching for answers. "Honestly, I have no idea. I thought I'd live and die with the hunters. Now… I don't know."

Ben had a twinkle in his eyes.

Gabe nudged Max. "Here comes the sales pitch."

"Join the Lycanthrope Protection Agency," Ben offered. "You can make up for all that time you spent hunting your own. Your skills could be useful to us. It'll be good for you."

Eddie blinked rapidly, brows furrowing. "I… Are you sure?"

"Positive. You'd be great."

"Yeah. Yeah! I mean—" Eddie cleared his throat, red-faced. "I'd love to join. Make up for all the stuff I did as a hunter by helpin' others. That good with you, Mr. Stroud?"

Ben shook his hand. "Call me Ben, and yeah. That's good with me."

Vicenzo gazed thoughtfully at Eddie, his face devoid of anger. "Me, too. I wanna join your pack."

Ben looked from Vicenzo to Eddie, bushy brows furrowing. "There ain't gonna be any fighting. Clear? Not on my time. Can I trust you guys to behave?"

Eddie glanced at Vicenzo, wetting his lips. "Yeah, of course. I'm in."

Vicenzo's eyes burned into Eddie, and Max got the impression he wasn't staying for anyone but Eddie, even if he wouldn't admit it. Vicenzo had proved himself trustworthy, but when it came to Eddie, Max wasn't sure where the two of them stood. Vicenzo growled, "If he does, I will."

Max smiled despite his misgivings, realizing this rowdy pack had just gotten bigger.

Early the next day, the pack gathered at the airport. Vicenzo hugged Kassandra tight and wished her farewell in Italian. Max watched from the side, sipping his coffee to avoid passing out from exhaustion as Gabe and the others said farewell and thanked her for her help.

"Max, come on, don't fall asleep!" Gabe, grinning radiantly at the prospect of finally returning home, motioned for Max to follow them.

Stifling a yawn, Max rose and trudged after them. He waved at Kassandra but she wasn't moving toward her gate. "Max! Wait one moment, please." She hurried toward him, her face rife with apprehension.

Max smiled, unsure what she wanted. "Thanks for all your help. We should hang out if we come back to Italy."

She smiled. "That would be nice, but my duties keep me at the monastery. Max, there's something I need to tell you. May I?"

Max glanced at the pack, already submerged in the bustling crowds of the airport. "Sure." He could find them easily by scent, and their flight wasn't for an hour.

Kassandra took in a breath. "Through constant study of the moon, we commune with the goddess herself. We have learned her name, Amaris. And she told us a story of a wolf with the powers of the moon."

Max's heart leaped. If that was true, could there be another like him? "You mean, there's someone else out there with these weird powers?"

Kassandra bit her lip. "Not quite... The story tells of a red wolf pup who is abandoned by his mother and raised by a shifter and a human. The father, the human, leaves when the red wolf is a newborn. The red wolf is raised by his adoptive mother, not knowing who he truly is."

Something dropped in Max's stomach. It had to be a coincidence. Max wasn't the only boy who'd grown up without a dad.

Kassandra went on. "The years go by until one day he awakens his powers. Using these powers, he is able to return home to his pack, to his mother, and they are finally reunited."

"I don't get it." Max's voice broke and he cleared his throat. "What are you trying to tell me?"

Kassandra looked him in the eyes. "There is only one red wolf with the powers of the moon living among us. The story is about you, Max. You are the goddess's long-lost son, a child of the moon."

Max laughed. He laughed hard, even as his stomach churned and that ethereal voice from beyond the portal echoed in his mind.

*"I've been waiting for you."*

"No. Sorry. That doesn't make any sense." He choked and wiped his eyes, smiling even as his heart tried to escape his chest. It *didn't* make any sense. He was just a guy raised by a single mom after his cowardly father ran out on them.

"Max, you know this is true. Only you can open the way to the She-Wolf because she has willed it so."

Max shook his head. "No. No, you're wrong."

"Listen." Kassandra gripped his shoulder. "If you don't believe me, then try and open a portal to the She-Wolf's realm. She will allow you to. She has been waiting for you to return home."

It made sense, he realized with a surge of dread. Stone had wanted his soul so he could open the hunting grounds. Why would Max have such an ability... unless the She-Wolf wanted him to return home?

Max bucked his shoulder, throwing her off. "I'm sorry. I don't know what to tell you. I'm not who you think I am. All right? And—and you know, even if this was true, and it's not, it doesn't matter to me. I don't care about the She-Wolf. I already have a home, and my family is here, with my pack." Kassandra tried to speak but Max said, "I'm not some demigod. I'm just a guy from a broken family. I don't care where these powers come from. I'm not Stone. No one is meant to enter the hunting grounds."

"I'm sorry." Kassandra bowed her head. "I didn't mean to upset you. I only thought you might want an... explanation. A reason as to why you are so different."

Max had. For so long, he'd wanted to know, and now he realized not knowing had been so simple.

"Sorry. I only meant to help." Kassandra took his hands and smiled. "I hope you can someday be at peace with this knowledge. If you have more questions, look to the moon for answers."

With one last smile, she departed, disappearing into the crowds. Max watched her leave, the world around him a blur.

"Max?" He barely heard Gabe. "Everything okay?"

Max took in a breath, grounding himself. He smiled and took Gabe's arm. "Let's go home."

With Gabe's arm around his shoulders, Max walked to their gate.

No. He would not look to the moon for answers. The cosmos, the hunting grounds—the only place in this world that held any value to him was wherever Gabriel Reyes was.

His mother was Kendra Gallagher. His home was New York City. His place was there, with Gabriel Reyes and the LPA pack.

That was all he needed to know.

# Chapter 24

# MOTHER

Max exhaled to release the butterflies fluttering in his stomach. He smoothed his hands over the front of his suit, making sure there wasn't a wrinkle in sight, and adjusted his bow tie. He combed his hands through his hair to force any stubborn locks back in place. His heart pounded, and he blinked hard to keep himself together.

It was happening. On this day, September 29, Max would claim the man he loved as his mate. They'd spent a month planning this ceremony, making sure everything was perfect and that the ceremony coincided on the night of the full moon. After all they'd endured over the years they'd known each other, and even before that, tonight marked a new beginning. They'd never be separated or hurt again. Nothing would come between them.

Wiping his eyes, Max checked the time. The butterflies in his stomach fluttered again. In a little over an hour, they would be blessed by friends and family under the full moon in preparation for their lives together. It had been a long time coming. Stone and his fanatical plots had kept them from fulfilling this promise to each other, but nothing would stop Max from claiming Gabe as his.

Legs a little shaky, he stumbled out into the living room. The sun had gone down over Central Park an hour ago and the streets were dark. Max gazed out over the shadowed park where he and Gabe would gather with the pack.

His lips trembled as he smiled for the thousandth time that day. He couldn't believe it was finally happening. Stone was dead, and Gabe's hunt for vengeance was finally over. McCready was dead, although according to Ben, Alpha Hanson still hadn't been accounted for, which was troubling. There'd been a few sightings of wargs by the occasional hiker, but it sounded like they were in hiding in the woods, leaderless and bereft. Max had his wolf back, his *Gabe* back, and life was fucking good.

He couldn't believe he'd lasted until the next full moon without bursting from anticipation. He'd worried something bad would happen to interrupt this long-awaited day. So much had already tried to come between them.

Before he could begin to worry again, two arms wrapped tight around his chest. Warm breath drifted across the crook of his neck, and pointed fangs nipped at his skin. Max shivered, leaning back into the warmth and strength of his soon-to-be-mate's body. Gabe's wavy locks tickled his skin, and though he was clean-shaven and handsome as could be, his face was still faintly scruffy against Max's neck.

"I thought we weren't supposed to see each other before the ceremony," Max said.

Gabe chuckled, deep and low into Max's neck. "That's just for silly human weddings. Why, feeling superstitious, Lobito?"

"Yes," Max said honestly. "Now a whale will jump out of the lake and ruin the ceremony."

Gabe snorted, nuzzling into his neck. In the window's reflection, a big grin lit up his face. "And let's say something does go wrong? I'm still taking you to my bed tonight."

Max's face warmed. "You don't care about the ritual?"

Gabe shrugged. "It's nice and all, but all that matters to me is that we're mates at the end of the night. I've waited too long, Max, and not just for tonight." He turned Max around to look into his smiling face, his eyes aglow. He nuzzled their foreheads together, then breathed in deep as he pressed his face into Max's neck, scenting him. "I've been waiting for you all my life."

Max swallowed, throat tight, and tangled his fingers in soft black hair. He'd been waiting for someone like Gabe, too. Someone he could trust with his life, someone who wouldn't leave or hurt him, someone he could raise a family with, built on a foundation of kindness, love, and trust so their children would have only the best upbringing. He'd found it all in Gabriel Reyes.

Hand in hand, they left the apartment and walked two blocks to Central Park. The moonlight cast shadows of the leaves on the pavement, and the wind whispered sweetly through the trees and the grass. Gabe led them off the path and let go of his hand. As was customary in mating ceremonies, Max and Gabe were to hunt prey for their respective packs. It was an old custom, but it symbolized their ability to hunt and provide, to show their families they were a good match.

Max carefully removed his suit and folded it over the branches of a tree. He couldn't help glancing at Gabe, admiring the way the moonlight glimmered on his scarred physique and the way the shadows played across his skin.

Gabe shot him a look over his shoulder, eyes alight with hunger as they wandered Max's form. Max shooed him. "Be good." It would be awkward if they already had mating bites before the ceremony.

Gabe growled and looked away, shifting fast into a beautiful black wolf. Max grinned. "I bet I'll catch a rabbit before you."

Gabe barked his disagreement and made Max laugh before he shifted. He bounded to Gabe and licked his snout, pressing their sides close together. They took off into the woods, and though their paths diverged, as always they found their way back to each other, each clutching a rabbit in their jaws. Max shifted back and dressed. "I definitely caught it before you."

"I was a little distracted." Gabe swatted him across the bottom with his suit jacket.

His face warmed up and he buttoned his shirt. "I hope you won't be quite so slow in other areas."

Nestling against Max's back, Gabe nibbled his neck. Able to feel the growl rumbling deep in Gabe's chest as his fangs grazed Max's neck, Max barely suppressed a moan. "Then stop distracting me." He drew a wet stripe up Max's neck with his tongue. As Max laughed and squirmed out of his arms, Gabe pursued him through the woods and back to the lakefront.

The crowd clapped as they emerged from the woods with the rabbits. Kendra's eyes were glistening with emotion. Ryan whistled, thumping Zach on the shoulder. Izzie and Veronica cheered. Ben smiled beneath his bushy beard, Eddie and Vicenzo standing beside him.

Gabe's and Max's path split, and Max knelt before Veronica and offered her the rabbit as Gabe did the same to Kendra. She helped him to his feet and embraced him, and Gabe murmured something to her that made her laugh and wipe her eyes.

Veronica pulled Max into a hug, and he held her tight. "I promise, as long as I live, I'll take care of him."

Veronica kissed his cheek, her eyes dancing with affection. "I never doubted it, Maxwell."

With their families appeased, Gabe and Max met beneath an archway covered in vines and flowers. The high priest stood between them, and Max faced Gabe, blinking stubbornly to keep the tears at bay. He wanted to remember every detail of his face, from the way he smiled, to the adoration in his eyes, to the quiver in his lips as he took Max's hands.

The priest tied their hands together with multicolored ribbons, binding them together, and invited them to take their vows before the goddess.

Max held his lover's gaze, swallowing as his throat constricted with emotion. "I've been waiting all my life for you, Gabriel Reyes. For someone I could entrust my heart to, someone I could share a future with. You saved my life, and I choose you, in this life and in the next. Before the goddess, I promise to love and protect you, to hunt and provide for you, to be the best father I can to our pups. You're my best friend, my soulmate, and the love of my life. Now and forever."

Gabe exhaled, his eyes glistening. "Gonna be hard to top that, but here goes..."

The crowd rumbled with laughter.

"Our lives haven't been easy. We had to go through hell and back, before we met and after, but we've always found our way back to each other. If there's one thing I know above anything else, it's that we were meant to be together. You've given me so much love, Max, and I can't wait to give it all back to our family. I'm going to be the best I can be, for you, for our pack. I promise you, Max Gallagher."

The high priest said, "Repeat after me. Before these witnesses, I, Gabriel Reyes, vow to love you, Maxwell Gallagher, and care for you as long as we both shall live. I take you, with all your faults and your strengths, as I offer myself to you with my faults and my strengths. I will help you when you need help, and will turn to you when I need help. I choose you as the person with whom I will spend my life."

Gabe repeated each word, his eyes never leaving Max's, and when it was Max's turn, he swore his vows to Gabe. They sealed the promise of their love with a kiss and as the ribbons fell away from their hands, Max put his arms around broad shoulders, laughing and crying as Gabe hoisted him into his arms. Wrapping his legs around Gabe's waist, he touched their foreheads together as he gazed down into shining amber eyes.

"I love you," Gabe whispered, lips trembling as he smiled.

"I know," Max said, running his thumb across a scarred cheek, damp with joyful tears. "I love you, too. So much."

Their lips met as the audience erupted into applause.

Max and Gabe joined the pack at a banquet table loaded with dishes such as filet mignon, stew, mushroom barley soup, and other rustic recipes. The rabbits they'd caught had been cooked, and as was customary, Gabe and Max offered each other a bite of the freshly caught prey. Once they'd eaten, the pack tucked in.

Ben reminisced about his mating ceremony to Heather; Ryan made jokes such as, "Lookin' forward to tying that other knot, huh, Gabe?" Zach looked embarrassed by association until he laughed along with him; Izzie teased her brother with stories about their childhood; Eddie smiled shyly and congratulated them; and Vicenzo told them Kassandra had returned safely to the monastery and destroyed the blade.

The band played a folksy tune and invited Gabe and Max to dance to the soaring notes of flutes and violins by the lake. Max's breath hitched, his stomach fluttering as Gabe drew him close and they swayed together beneath the moon. He winced as he trod on Gabe's toes but Gabe only laughed.

The band started up a foot-stomping number and the pack gathered around to dance, clapping hands and stomping feet. Izzie got the crowd going with a duet of "Senorita" with Kendra. At one point, Ryan and Zach sang a number. Max's ears ached, so he went in search of somewhere quiet to sit along the lake. He removed his shoes and rubbed at the soles of his feet, grinning despite the ache.

His mother came up to him and she put her arms around him. "You both look so handsome."

Max squeezed her shoulders. "Thank you." His smile faltered as he recalled Kassandra's story. He took a sip of champagne and vowed not to dampen tonight's joy.

"You and Dad didn't have a mating ceremony, right?"

Kendra smiled. "No. He wanted a traditional wedding. I wanted to honor our customs, make him a part of it, but love is about compromising. You're no longer one person, and sometimes you have to make sacrifices for their happiness, and if they're a good partner, they will do the same. Otherwise, the relationship won't work if it's one-sided. You two have been through so much and never given up on each other. It's so clear to me neither of you will have that problem." Her eyes glimmered with happy tears. "You're very lucky, both of you."

Max swallowed around the lump in his throat. He hoped his mother would someday find a man who could treat her with the same devotion Gabe showed him.

"I was worried, you know," Kendra began, eyeing him with apprehension. "I thought you'd have a guarded heart after Richard disrupted our lives... I worried you wouldn't let someone see the best of you."

"I felt that way for a long time," Max admitted. "But never with Gabe. Loving him isn't hard or hurtful. It was so easy. It scared me a little."

Kendra rubbed his hands. "I'm very proud of you. It takes courage to open your heart to someone, especially after what you went through."

"What *we* went through," Max corrected. "The Gallagher pack is hard to break."

She grinned and squeezed his shoulder. "That's my boy."

Max's breath hitched.

*Am I your son? In bond, yeah, but in blood?*

"What's wrong, hon?"

Max grappled for words, unsure where to even begin. He didn't want to make it sound like he was accusing her of lying to him. "Kassandra, the monk... she told me something. A story about a red wolf, like me. She told me why I have these powers."

Kendra's eyes widened and her scent soured with worry that made Max's heart sink. "Oh. About time we finally got some answers. Well, was it helpful?"

Max wet his lips. "It was... confusing. She told me that I'm—" He hesitated, laughing just admitting this out loud. He sounded crazy. "She told me I'm the goddess's son. The She-Wolf's missing pup from some story. That she'd abandoned me to live with a shifter and a human."

Kendra's expression was unreadable.

Max began to sweat. "I don't believe it. It's crazy, right? You're my mother."

Kendra said nothing as she stared into her lap.

"Aren't you?" Max's voice was barely a whisper, shocked by his mother's silence.

Kendra swept a lock of blonde hair behind her ear. "Yes, Max. Of course." She took his hand, but her lips trembled. "I am your mother. But I didn't give birth to you."

Max couldn't speak, all his relief fading to utter confusion. His stomach ached, like he'd been punched, and a rush of emotion swept over him. She'd lied to him. He swallowed the sour feelings and took a deep breath. He needed to hear her out.

Kendra exhaled shakily, squeezing his limp fingers. "I couldn't have children of my own. I had to give up on that dream of mine. It worked out at the time. Your father had never wanted children anyway. Finding out the woman he loved was a werewolf was a big enough surprise. He couldn't have committed to raising hybrid children."

*That's why he left?* Max realized, and something in his chest ached.

"So I focused on my career, he on his. I decided it was for the best as our lives got progressively busier. Then one night I found you."

Max blinked hard. "You found me?"

"You'd been abandoned on our doorstep in upstate New York. You were this little thing. Your eyes had barely opened. I wasn't even sure if you were a werewolf or just a small dog, not at first. You were whimpering and cold, so I held you close and you shifted in my arms to a baby boy. My baby. I didn't know why you were there or what heartless person had left you, but I fell in love with you the moment I held you in my arms. I believed you were a gift from the goddess herself. Maybe that isn't so far from the truth."

He'd been left. Abandoned. Why? Why hadn't the She-Wolf wanted him? Max didn't know what to say. He was torn between shock and confusion. "Is that why Dad left?"

Kendra stared out over the lake, wringing her hands in her lap. "I'd told him we'd never have children. Then I walked through the door with you.

I wouldn't give you up and to his credit, he tried, Max." He'd left before Max had even turned one. He hadn't tried very hard at all, had he?

Max looked away as his eyes misted, struggling to speak around the guilt.

"Honey?" Her hand settled on his back, rubbing gently. "What is it? I understand if you're upset. I should have told you a long time ago."

Max shook his head. It wasn't that. He wasn't angry, or even surprised anymore. He was just sad. Max's throat clicked as he swallowed. "I ruined your marriage."

"No." Kendra seized his hands and held tight. "No, Max. You saved my life. You are the blessing I'd been waiting for."

Max sniffed hard and rubbed stubbornly at his eyes. His throat ached, and he could hardly speak. "He would have stayed if I hadn't—"

"Listen to me, Max Gallagher." Gentle fingers weaved through his hair. His mother smiled, blinking back her tears. "Our love died the moment we were married. I wouldn't change a thing. I'm so grateful that you're my son."

Max crumpled into her arms, holding on for dear life as years of pent-up feelings surged through him. He hadn't realized until tonight that for all these years, he'd blamed himself for his father's departure, even thought that deep down, his mother hated him for it. He'd worried this conversation would ruin the relationship they'd tried so hard to build after Richard came into their lives. Now, he should have felt closer to her than ever before.

Except... she'd lied. She'd kept such a monumental piece of his past from him, and he only had more questions. About the goddess. About why he'd been left. He might never know.

Suddenly feeling smothered by her embrace, he wriggled out of her arms. He couldn't look at her, but the scent of her guilt and hurt walloped him. "Do you believe Kassandra, then?" Max asked, trying to keep his voice light and casual.

"I always thought you were a gift from the goddess. It would explain those strange powers, why you're so different from other shifters. And the cult's obsession with you."

Max's shoulders slumped. He was at a loss for what to do with this revelation. "I don't know what to do. Kassandra told me I could open a way to her."

"Do you want to find the She-Wolf, Max?"

Max wanted to know those wolves who'd sung to him. He wanted to know—

"Not really." The words were punched out of him by a stab of guilt. How could he even think about leaving behind his mother to go in search of a stranger who'd abandoned him? "My home is here, with you and the pack. Everything I want is right here."

But now he knew that a secret part of him had always been missing. *Come. Find me,* the ethereal voice had whispered.

Max's heart lurched, his mouth ran dry, and he realized he was terrified of what he might find in the realm beyond theirs. Why? Why had she left him? Hadn't she wanted him? Hadn't she loved him? Max closed the door on those thoughts before he could spiral.

Fuck. He was sick of being abandoned. He wouldn't waste his time on anyone who decided he wasn't worth sticking around for because he knew now that wasn't true.

Max was wanted. Max was loved, by so many, and he belonged here with his pack, the people who'd chosen him and never given up on him. He took his mother's hand and they looked out over the lake together. The moon hid her face behind the clouds, and a piece of Max he couldn't ignore howled for her light.

# CHAPTER 25

# MATE

"Where are we going?"

Gabe stifled a grin as they left the ceremony, their hands clasped and the howling of their pack seeing them off. "Somewhere I can finally have you all to myself."

Their shoulders bumped together. "Where might that be?"

He squeezed Max's fingers, excitement simmering in his stomach. "You'll see. It's a long drive, but it'll be worth it."

The last several weeks leading up to their ceremony had been stressful as Gabe had worked tirelessly to get everything done on time, and he couldn't wait for Max to see the fruit of his labors. Max squeaked as Gabe grabbed his hips and set him down on the second seat of his motorbike. His mate smoothed his hands over the leather. "It's been a long time since we rode your bike."

Gabe had to chew his lip to keep from telling Max just how damn ravishing he looked straddling his bike. "I missed this beauty." He swung his leg over the seat and popped a helmet on Max's ginger head. Once both their helmets were on, Gabe started the engine, his heart purring as Max's arms wound tight around his chest.

They left Park Avenue behind and soared among the traffic on the Hudson River highway heading for upstate New York. Within an hour,

305

they had left the city behind and the emerald hills of the country enveloped them.

"Is where you're taking me within the US?" Max asked through the Bluetooth speaker, sounding weary.

Gabe grinned. "Yeah! We're almost there!"

Among the stinging scents of car emissions, Gabe scented sweet grass and the aroma of trees, hay, and horse manure. They sped past vast open fields where silhouettes of cows and horses grazed beneath the moonlight. Gabe drove them off the highway and down a narrow dirt road. Aside from the rumbling of his bike, the night was peaceful and quiet now that they were away from the main road.

They passed a few more farms and quaint country homes before Gabe, heart racing, pulled into a driveway and removed his helmet. Unable to keep from grinning, he swung his leg over the bike and held out a hand to Max. "Welcome home."

Max dropped his helmet, mouth agape. He looked to Gabe in astonishment, a grin bursting across his face. "Gabe. I can't believe it! We got the house!" He threw his arms around Gabe. They'd started house hunting for somewhere quiet and serene to raise a family a few weeks ago. Max had fallen in love with this home, and they'd put in an offer, but Gabe had kept it a secret when they'd become the new owners.

Gabe's hands trembled as he retrieved the key. He offered his hand and welcomed Max over the threshold. As he switched on the lights, Max gasped. On the lower level, a great room welcomed them with an open kitchen and dining area, and a big stone fireplace in the middle of two archways separated the kitchen from the living room. The only furnished room so far was the bedroom. Gabe couldn't wait to make the place their own.

Gabe chuckled at Max's slack-jawed astonishment. "It can be our country getaway, somewhere we can go on the weekends. Or we can make it our primary residence. It's up to you." Where they lived wasn't of importance to Gabe. All he cared about from now until the day they died was that they were together.

Grinning from ear to ear, Max stood on his toes, pushing his mouth against Gabe's. Gabe encircled Max's slim waist and drew him close, his blood simmering as their chests touched on every inhale. Their eyes lingered, and Max stroked the fabric of Gabe's tie, his plump lower lip between his teeth. "I love your apartment and the city, but I like it here, too."

Gabe rubbed his shoulders. "Then we'll have both. After everything, I think we deserve a peaceful getaway."

His mate kissed him, practically vibrating with excitement. Laughing, Max moved away to the living room. He sighed at the sight of the fireplace. "I've always wanted a fireplace. We're keeping it lit year-round."

Gabe snorted. "Okay, but if we get sweaty, I'm making the most of it." He squeezed Max's hand and led him outside to the backyard, flicking on the outdoor lights. Max smiled and gazed up at a blanket of stars in a cloudless sky. Far away, coyotes howled as they began their nightly hunt.

"I was thinking we could put a pool over there, maybe some more seating at the top of the hill," Gabe said. He also wanted to install a firepit outside.

"A pool? That would be awesome."

Gabe accompanied him back inside and led Max around toward the front entryway where a spiral staircase led to the bedrooms. There was another guest room, but Gabe led Max past and to the bedroom. Moonlight pooled on the canopy bed, filtering through translucent curtains swaying from the canopy.

Beyond the windows, there was a view of the shadowed trees and the open fields beyond their driveway. Gabe's heart sang at the thought of shifting and running as a wolf through those trees with Max.

Max wandered to the window with a dreamy sigh and took in the view of the forest and rolling hills. Gabe dropped onto the mattress, groaning as he finally took the weight off his sore feet. He loosened his tie, eyes wandering to Max's silhouette bathed in moonlight.

Bouncing his weight up and down on the mattress, Gabe grinned when he caught his mate's attention. His mouth quirked at the color in Max's cheeks and the way his eyes wandered Gabe's upper body, his Adam's apple rising and falling. Sprawling out, Gabe kicked off his shoes and let them clatter to the floor. He patted the empty side of the bed.

Max ducked his head, hands deep in his pockets as he sidled up to it. Gabe chuckled at his sudden shyness, then grasped Max's wrists and pulled him down. The mattress creaked under their combined weight as Max settled in beside him, his head nestled atop Gabe's chest.

"What did you tell my mother?" Max asked. His hands smoothed over Gabe's chest, playing with his silky tie as he loosened it. He opened Gabe's collar, and Gabe smiled when he caught Max eyeing his exposed throat.

Thinking back, Gabe grinned when he recalled the tears in Kendra's eyes. "Back when I gave her the rabbit? I told her I would always provide for you, that you'd never want for anything. I thanked her for allowing me to be a part of her pack."

"Charmer." Max's lips covered his and Gabe's eyes fluttered closed. He traced the curve of Max's hips beneath his suit jacket, envisioning the shape of him even with his eyes closed.

"I mean it, Lobito," Gabe murmured, lips brushing Max's. His mate's eyes were a warm orange. "This is it. You're it. Stone's gone, McCready, too. It's just us now. We have our whole lives together to do whatever we want."

Max's lips trembled when he smiled. "I hope so."

"I know so." Gabe clasped his hand and brought his slender fingers to his lips. "Nothing's tearing us apart, Max. Anything comes our way, we're facing it together." The backs of his fingers skimmed Max's jaw, thumbing his supple lower lip. "I'm not leaving you. Not ever again."

"I know," Max whispered. "I'd drag you back anyway if you tried."

Gabe chuckled. "What's the first thing you're looking forward to in our lives together?"

Max's lips quirked against Gabe's thumb, parting and dragging across the palm of Gabe's hand. The mattress squeaked. Draping himself across Gabe's body, Max ran one hand up and down Gabe's chest. His warm mouth fluttered over the pulse beating in Gabe's throat.

"Making you mine. Finally." A low growl gave Max's words a seductive edge.

Laughter rumbled from Gabe's lips. Of course. "I know. I kept you waiting."

Max met his gaze, a sweet smile softening the points of his fangs. "You're worth the wait."

A shiver ran down Gabe's spine.

"What about you? What are you looking forward to?" Max murmured, his voice vibrating against Gabe's throat as he mouthed a warm trail down his neck to the collar of his shirt. He popped the button at the top of Gabe's dress shirt. Gabe's breath hitched, his fingers curling in the sheets in anticipation.

"I'd rather show you."

He put his arms around Max's shoulders and rolled them over. Max looked delicious sprawled beneath him, his ginger curls tousled, lips part-ed, and his eyes wide and dark with desire. He straddled Max's waist, hardly knowing where to start as he loosened his tie and Max's chest rose and fell faster. Holding his breath, he ran his hand over Max's ironed shirt to the front of his trousers. A gasp spilled from Max's lips, his hips arching up into Gabe's touch.

Enraptured orange eyes gazed at him in a reverie, and Gabe felt like a god. He'd imagined Max's face so many times beneath the Italian stars, but no fantasy could compare to the flesh-and-blood man beneath him. He could stare at Max forever, his brow puckered in desperation, a plump pink lower lip between his teeth.

He was so lucky this beautiful man was his. Gratitude swelled within his chest and he claimed those sweet, panting lips and tangled his fingers in soft copper hair. He nuzzled his cheek to Max's, tracing the shell of his ear with his mouth. "I'm one lucky guy." He wished he could look Max in the eyes, but he thought he'd cry if he did. Max held him close, his fingers bunching in Gabe's shirt.

"Me, too." Max's voice trembled and Gabe couldn't hold back, covering those supple lips with his. Their tongues slid together, and Gabe fumbled with Max's shirt, popping buttons. Max's Adam's apple bobbed beneath his lips as he moved to his neck, his pulse fluttering under Gabe's mouth. He curled his fingers in Gabe's hair, and his breath came faster when Gabe sniffed the base of his neck.

Parting his lips, Gabe sucked and nipped at that sensitive spot, and a moan slipped from Max's mouth. Tonight on the full moon, Max's scent was even more potent than usual. His fangs longed to come out and bite, claim what was his. But he wouldn't, not yet.

"Patience, mi amor." He wouldn't rush this. He'd waited so long to have Max underneath him. Breathlessly, Max nodded, his eyes dark, watching and waiting. Gabe worked away at Max's buttons one by one, his heart thundering, breath quickening as bit by bit, Max's body revealed itself, his skin milky white and dotted with freckles like a constellation of stars.

Gabe bowed his head, holding his breath so he could hear the way Max's heart raced, almost as fast as his. He splayed his hands on Max's chest, running them over an expanse of smooth, warm skin. Pinching pink nipples between his fingers, Gabe pulled and squeezed. Max panted, arching his chest into the touch. Gabe's cock, hard already, gave a violent twitch. During the full moon, even slight touches in the heat of the moment could be overwhelming.

Gabe kissed from freckle to freckle, parting his lips around a rosy nipple that was hard under his ministrations. He kissed the smooth planes of Max's stomach, licking at his abs and enjoying the way they tightened at his touch. Dipping his tongue into Max's navel, he followed soft curls of ginger hair leading the way beneath his trousers. Gabe clasped Max's belt and opened it with a click.

Max raised his hips, aiding Gabe in pulling his trousers down to his knees. His boxers strained around a heavy cock, the tip already dampening the fabric. Gabe longed to take him in his hands, in his mouth, but he held himself back, rocking onto his heels to drink in Max's flushed face and tousled hair, his lips red from his fervent attention, the freckles that dotted his pale skin, his nipples hard, and chest heaving.

"Fuck, you're beautiful, Max."

Max grinned, eyes widening a little. He laughed, probably from embarrassment. Propping himself up, he opened the buttons of Gabe's shirt. Breath hitching, his skin tingled under Max's warm, eager hands on his bare skin.

Max squeezed Gabe's pectorals and played with his nipples until they hardened like pebbles under Max's attentive hands. He palmed the seat of Gabe's pants, tugging down his trousers and his boxers, and Gabe's cock slapped hard against his abdomen.

"Lube?" Max murmured.

"Dresser," Gabe said with a grunt. He barely refrained from begging him to hurry.

A cap popped and Gabe bit his lip. Arching back with a groan, he pushed his hips into Max's fist, hot, slick, and tight around his cock. He crumpled into Max's neck, raining kisses on his skin in praise. His mate was so good, so attentive, working him with such familiarity, as if Gabe's cock were an extension of Max's own body. He'd never find anyone that knew his body better than Max did.

Gabe wrenched Max's boxers down. He slicked his hand with lube and fisted Max's cock, working him in long, tight strokes, squeezing the knot at the base of Max's slender cock. Max clung to him, panting between moans and shameless whimpers. The sounds he was making... Gabe wouldn't last long.

"Need you inside me." Max gasped. "Now, Gabe."

Gabe needed it, too. He urged Max down to the sheets and Max opened his legs, knees up to his chest. Gabe wanted nothing more than to fulfill some of his dirtiest fantasies here and now, but this wasn't about him. Max was more than that. He would take his damn time, worshipping every inch of Max. Clasping his ankle, Gabe raised it to his lips and kissed it. Laughing softly, Max squirmed as Gabe kissed the sole of his foot. "What are you doing?"

He worked his way up Max's leg over short ginger hairs to the back of his knee. "Making love to you. Every inch." If Max was impatient, he forgave Gabe for it when he stroked Max's cock to every touch of his lips.

Peering through his lashes at Max, Gabe was delighted to see his head fall back, his chest rising and falling fast. Gabe opened his lips against the back of Max's milky thigh, kissing down toward his pelvis. Max gasped, body jolting when Gabe licked from his hole to his balls. His balls were heavy in Gabe's mouth, drawing up when he swirled his tongue in a tight circle beneath them.

"Fuck, Gabe!"

He kissed the base of Max's cock, licking in a long stroke to the crown, which he circled with his tongue before swallowing Max to the root.

Max whimpered and pumped his hips while Gabe bobbed his head up and down, riding every roll of his hips. Grabbing a fistful of Gabe's hair and rocking his hips faster, Max nearly choked Gabe with his cock, and the lewd little sounds spilling shamelessly from his lips ignited Gabe's blood.

Max groaned, breathless and frustrated when Gabe pulled off him, his hips gyrating for friction. Gabe made up for it by lapping at Max's hole, worshipping it, pushing his tongue into the heat of him, and Max's claws scratched at his scalp.

"Gabe... Oh my—*fuuuuck...*" Max whined. "Need you. Now. *Please.*"

Gabe leaned down and kissed those swollen, pleading lips. "I got you, mi amor. Gonna fuck you good. Make you howl for me."

Craving more of Max's sweet voice, Gabe squirted some lube onto his fingers. He pressed between Max's thighs and sank into that tight, familiar heat. Max squeezed his ass around Gabe's fingers, sucking him in. He swirled his fingers, and Max clawed at the sheets, ripping them under his claws. Max growled, his orange eyes flashing like twin bursts of flame.

Seeing Max's inner beast so close to the surface nearly undid him. Gabe withdrew his fingers and replaced them with his cock, pushing in slowly. He held Max's gaze, those orange eyes at half-mast and Max's lip between his teeth. Gabe was almost all the way in save for his knot, which was already quite large.

Knowing it would likely hurt Max a little, he refrained from sheathing himself completely. He held Max's gaze, loving the way he gasped when Gabe drew back as far as he could stand to and entered him again in slow motion.

Max raised his hips, panting, silently asking for more, to be joined with him, and Gabe couldn't deny him anything. Thrusting his hips, Gabe eased himself inside and closed his eyes, euphoric as Max's tightness squeezed around his cock. They were one, one body and one soul.

Gabe crumpled against Max's chest and devoured his lips. As their bodies came together in deep, powerful thrusts, Gabe saw stars. "Fuck, you feel so good, mi amor," he whispered and groaned when Max squeezed around him.

Max panted, guiding Gabe's mouth to his. His mate wound his legs around Gabe's waist, and his claws tore into his back. Gabe couldn't tell if it was his voice filling the room so carelessly or Max's. His scalp stung as sweaty fingers fisted his hair, crushing their swollen lips together. He tasted blood and wasn't sure who'd bitten who.

Moonlight bathed Max's skin, the sweat glimmering on his chest like diamonds. Gabe drew out slowly and Max threw back his head, exposing the long white column of his throat. He mouthed at the thin skin, and Max's moan vibrated beneath Gabe's lips. Squirming and wriggling his hips, Max bit down on his plump pink lower lip so hard Gabe feared he'd make it bleed.

"Don't tie us," Max whispered.

Gabe shivered, unsure if he could stop it as little jolts of lightning built at the base of his spine, curling his toes. "Why not?"

Max leaned up to capture Gabe's lower lip between his teeth. "Because I want to tie you."

A groan rolled from Gabe's throat at the idea of Max leaning over him, filling Gabe with his cock. He'd never been fucked before, not for any specific reason, really. He knew how Max enjoyed being fucked, riding every thrust of Gabe's hips, the way he moaned when Gabe filled him. "Fuck," Gabe whispered, jolting his hips and chasing his impending release.

"Bite me, claim me." Max panted, his cock slapping against Gabe's stomach. "Then I want to claim you. Fuck you. Bite you." Max's face was flushed, but his eyes were dark with desire.

"Fuck, that sounds so good." He'd never bottomed for anyone before, but fuck, he would do anything for Max. He wanted Max inside him. Needed to feel the pleasure and pain of his bite. Gabe was too far gone to avoid knotting Max if he came inside him, but he had to honor his request. He pulled out of Max's slick warmth, hissing his disappointment, and Max's mouth quirked.

Reaching out, he traced the length of Gabe with a finger and, fuck, Gabe had to bite his lip to keep from coming then and there. Max wrapped his fingers around him, one hand at the nape of Gabe's neck to guide him down against Max's chest. "Max. Fuck. Make me come."

Max jerked him fast, kissing Gabe's neck and shoulders, closing his teeth around the shell of his ear. "Put your teeth in me."

His ribs shuddered with each frantic gasp as Max brought him closer to nirvana, his toes curling until he thought his legs would cramp. His fangs lengthened, and a growl built in his throat.

Chanting Max's name in a reverie, he bucked like a stallion, riding Max's fist, and roared when he erupted, fangs sharp and long. Gabe lunged, biting down on the spot between Max's neck and shoulder, and Max clung to him with a shout that was both pained and victorious.

Limbs slack, Gabe rolled off of Max, his mouth quirking into a smile when Max laughed at him. Groaning, he was astonished to feel the tingles of his orgasm in his toes and the soles of his feet, as if his release had surged from the very depths of his body.

The warm dampness of Max's body draped over him, and Gabe cracked open his heavy eyes. Little rivers of blood ran down Max's neck. Gabe traced the bite mark with his fingers, entranced. It was perfect. It was Max's. Tears pricked his eyes, and Max's mouth trembled when he covered Gabe's lips with his.

"Does it hurt?"

Max nodded, baring his teeth in a smile. The moonlight caught in his red waves and bathed his milky skin in silver light. Gabe couldn't look away, thinking Max was as fair and lithe as a fairy from Scottish myth.

"I love it," Max said, his voice thick. "I love you."

Gabe's heart ached. Max was still hard between them, but Gabe was spent, his own release slick on his stomach. Goddess, though, he *needed* Max still. Max glided his fingers between Gabe's thighs, his hand coming away slick with cum, and he ran them over Gabe's entrance. "Yes, Max. Yes."

Pressing inside, Max used his long fingers to work Gabe open and slick him with his own cum. The intrusion burned but everything below the waist was so tender, Gabe arched his hips into it. A shuddery breath escaped him, and Max's chest rose and fell quickly, his heart pounding hard where their chests touched. "Okay?"

Gabe nodded, his blood simmering. Max drew away to grab the lube and coat his fingers, then massaged Gabe's aching prostate, and a shudder racked his body. He didn't think he could come again so soon, but his body was willing to try, ever so blissful and sensitive.

Max sighed, curling his fingers. "You feel so amazing."

Warmth spread through Gabe's cheeks. "Yeah? Nice and tight for you?"

Max moaned his reply and introduced a third finger, burying it in him to his knuckles. He curled them and Gabe's eyes rolled back at the ache that tingled deep in his balls.

"Fuck..." Max said breathlessly, eyes heavy-lidded and glowing. His cock twitched against Gabe's thigh. His balls must be turning blue.

"Max," Gabe rasped, surprised to find his own cock rising to the occasion. One of the benefits of being a werewolf on a full moon, he realized—no refractory period. "Now. I need you to..."

Max nodded, eyes wide and intent. "Yeah, love. Okay. I will." Gabe raised his hips, needy and impatient for his mate to make a mess of him. Max grasped his own cock and Gabe swallowed, admiring the deep red hue and the swollen cockhead, how long and thick it was.

Leaning over him, Max rocked his hips and breached him, opening him up with a sharp burn that had Gabe breathing through his teeth. Max froze above him, his hot breath hitting Gabe's mouth in heavy puffs.

Gabe raised his hips. It hurt but he needed this. He needed to be claimed by Max. He grinned. "Come on. Don't hold back."

Max grasped the backs of Gabe's thighs to steady himself, opening Gabe's legs wide for him. His pelvis pushed hard against him, and Gabe groaned his gratitude as Max closed his eyes.

"Goddess, Gabe. You feel so good." Max drew his hips back, the pressure inside Gabe receding—then filled him up again, igniting sparks up his spine.

Gabe clutched at Max's shoulders, his thighs squeezing Max's waist, and Max rolled his hips faster, sending waves of pleasure arching through Gabe. He ran his fingers through Max's hair, squeezing the roots that were damp with sweat. Leaning his cheek into Gabe's hand, Max smiled, soft and dazed, and Gabe's heart split down the middle.

He grabbed the back of Max's neck and pulled, crushing their lips together, tongues tasting and tangling as they moaned and panted into each other's mouths. The burning sensation gave way to something more, something mind-numbing, overwhelming.

"Max," Gabe gasped, overcome, and raised his hips. "Fuck, you're gonna make me come again."

"So good…" Max drove his hips forward, his pelvis striking the backs of Gabe's buttocks. "You're taking it so good. Just like that. Do that again!"

Gabe raised his hips and met Max's thrust halfway, and the sounds they made were unhinged. It wasn't synchronized or orderly; it was desperate, mindless, messy. Theirs, all theirs, a dance only they knew. Gabe bucked his hips with abandon and sometimes they missed, but sometimes they collided and when they did, it was like a neutron star collision.

The pressure inside Gabe swelled, hard and unyielding, as Max's knot filled him. Gabe clung to Max, crying out wordlessly as with every thrust, Max's knot swelled until he was so full, so thoroughly owned, all Gabe could do was howl as he came.

Max's cock pulsed inside him, and he moaned. "Perfect, you're so perfect." Then Max's fangs were in his neck and white filled his vision. The wet heat of his mate's release spilled inside him, and the burning pain of his bite—it overtook Gabe and he drifted, weightless and throbbing everywhere.

As Max's fangs pierced him, all of Max's emotions flowed into him. The pleasure and jubilation of their joining. His joy, dizzying and all-encompassing because finally, at last, they were one and there was nothing between them.

His love. Goddess, Max's love washed over Gabe and overwhelmed him. Gabe was loved, so very loved, and what a thing it was to be loved so fully by Max. He was going to spend the rest of his life being the best mate in the world. His mate would never regret him, never.

Warm lips, soft in contrast to the sharpness of his fangs, suckled kisses into Gabe's neck. He eased open his eyes and blinked, his vision blurry from sweat or tears, he couldn't tell. Max was beautiful above him with his cheeks flushed pink, skin dewy with sweat, and ginger bangs damp and stuck to his forehead. Turning his head, he kissed Gabe's palm, closing his eyes as if Gabe were the sweetest thing he'd ever tasted.

Licking at the blood flowing from Max's bite, he dropped his heavy arms around Max's shoulders as his mate pushed sweaty hair from Gabe's forehead. There was so much Gabe wanted to say, but in his post-mated bliss, all he could do was nuzzle their foreheads together and capture Max's face in his hands. Their bodies were tied together. They were one in every sense.

"Mate." Gabe breathed in, and his wolf growled his delight.

Max nuzzled into Gabe's neck. "At last." He sighed.

# CHAPTER 26

# WEATHER THE STORM

"SORRY. I THINK I left new scars on your back." Max's face warmed in embarrassment.

Gabe smirked, gliding the washcloth across Max's thighs. He sported a new scar across his eye and down his cheek, which he'd earned during his final fight with Stone. In Max's opinion, it gave Gabe a dangerous and sexy look. "Those are scars I definitely don't mind keeping."

Max would always remember the day Gabe bared his scars to him. Seeing Gabe's scars, he'd realized he wasn't alone, that someone out there understood him.

"I hated my scars for a long time," Max admitted. Gabe took his wrist, his thumb smoothing over the pale marks across Max's arms. "I thought they were a weakness. Then I saw yours."

"And thought, 'Thank the goddess, at least I'm not that sad asshole.'"

"No!" Max slapped his shoulder. Gabe chuckled. "Now I like them."

Gabe smiled, his hand settling on Max's chest. "I like mine, too. They're how we understand each other." Gabe pursed his lips in thought. "I bet Stone never expected that I would connect with someone through the scars he carved into my skin." Gabe smiled. "That they'd be anything other than a source of pain."

"How are you feeling?" Max asked. He realized he hadn't spoken to Gabe about Stone's death.

Gabe pressed a kiss to the corner of his mouth. "Like I could have you again. Now."

Max's heart quickened, a dizzying rush of desire rippling through his stomach. Well, the full moon would still be up for a while. Max kissed Gabe's shoulder, tasting sweat. "Are you feeling better since Stone died?"

"Oh. Yeah. It's like a storm's finally stopped."

Max took his hand and held tight, pleased to hear this. "Your dad would be proud." He regretted speaking as Gabe's brow pinched and a shadow darkened his eyes.

"I wish he could have been at our ceremony." Gabe blinked hard. "I tried not to think about it. That he wasn't there. But..." He ducked his head.

Max sat up before Gabe could withdraw into himself. His hand settled on Gabe's cheek, wiping away a tear, and Gabe's lips trembled when he kissed Max's hand.

"It's okay." Max wished he could be strong but seeing Gabe cry made him cry, too. Maybe it was the mated pheromones.

"He'd have loved you, Max. That's what makes it so hard."

Max pulled him close, drawing Gabe's face to his shoulder as Gabe ran his hands up and down Max's back. Taking a shuddering gulp of air, Gabe drew Max's knuckles to his lips and kissed them firmly. "He's at peace. That's all that matters. I wanna take you to visit his grave tomorrow." Gabe wet his lips. "It's an empty grave. His body was never recovered from the river. But still, I feel close to him when I'm there."

"Sure. We can go in the morning." Max wished he could have met Gabe's father, too. He wished Stone had never taken his father from Gabe. How different would their lives have been if Gabe had never crossed paths with Stone? "I like your father already," Max said. "He raised you. And thanks to his sacrifice, we got to meet."

Gabe nodded, managing a watery smile. "I know. His death set me on the wrong path. But because I was on that wrong path, Ben offered me an alternative. Through the agency, I met you. Life's cruel and beautiful like that."

He hadn't thought about it that way. Gabe touched his lips to Max's and stifled a yawn.

"I wore you out," Max said, laughing as he lay back against the pillows, Gabe's head to his chest.

"You did." Gabe snaked a hand under himself to rub his backside, and Max's face flushed warm with delight. "How's your bite? Does it hurt?"

Max shook his head. The wound was already scarring under the moonlight while Gabe's was still bleeding slightly. "There's something I want to tell you."

Gabe raised his brows, sprawling out on his stomach with his head on his arms. "Of course, mi amor."

Max wet his lips. Gabe had already been so open-minded when he'd told him about his powers. Would he think Max was insane? "Kassandra told me something before we returned to the States. She told me the goddess's name, Amaris, and… and that I'm the She-Wolf's son. My mother confirmed her story."

Gabe continued to gape at him, and Max's face burned. "M-my mother adopted me. She found me abandoned on her doorstep. She didn't know where I came from, who left me. It was the She-Wolf. Amaris. I just don't know why."

Gabe gazed in wide-eyed astonishment. "Are you serious?"

Max wished he hadn't said anything. "I know, I sound crazy."

"No! No, I just… Wow. This explains so much. It makes sense," Gabe said, laughing softly. He looked at Max in awe. "I knew you were special, Max. Feels nice to be right."

"That's not even the weirdest part, though. Back when Stone opened the portal, I heard a voice calling to me. She wants me to find her. To go home."

"So those spectral wolves we saw were your… your family." Gabe swallowed, his throat bobbing. "And what do you want?"

Max blinked hard, clutching Gabe's hand. "I don't know."

Gabe brought Max's fingers to his lips. "Hey. It's okay. It's a big decision. Besides, you don't have to figure it all out tonight. Take your time. Just… I'd understand, you know? You deserve to know your heritage. But if you do decide to leave, don't be gone for too long. And come back for me. Okay?"

Heart clenching at the scent of Gabe's worry, Max kissed his fingers. "Of course."

Max exhaled, feeling relieved Gabe didn't look down on him for admitting his feelings. His mate was right—he didn't need to figure out what to do. Not tonight. If the time ever came when he found the nerve to venture beyond this world, Gabe would be by his side. That alone gave him strength.

"Are things good between you and your mom?"

Max's heart lurched. "Uh… Yeah. Yeah, I…" But the sudden tears in his eyes contradicted him. He'd tried so hard to deny it, but the stab of betrayal came rushing back. "I'm such an asshole," he said, voice choked.

Gabe's brow furrowed. "What? No."

"The She-Wolf abandoned me. My mother could have left me, but she gave me a home. A family. I shouldn't be angry, but I couldn't even look at her after she told me. I hurt her. I could smell it." Frustrated and guilt-ridden, Max closed his eyes tight. "Fuck. I'm such an awful person."

Gabe pressed a warm, damp kiss to Max's forehead, and he stroked his hand up and down Max's back. "It's a hell of a lot to learn, Max. You're allowed to be surprised, hurt, angry. Just not too angry. Not for too long."

Max nestled close, bundling himself in Gabe's warmth.

He closed his eyes and let Gabe's tender kisses lull him to sleep.

EARLY THE NEXT MORNING, Gabe drove Max to a small cemetery nestled among the hills. "He wanted to be buried here," Gabe said. "It's far from the city, but Dad grew up in Millbrook after my grandparents emigrated." Gabe pointed west toward the town a mile away.

"It's beautiful here," Max said, breathing in deep.

Gabe smiled, scenting the air, crisp and cool with the coming autumn, pristine as only country air could be. He snatched Max's hand, his legs unsteady as they followed the winding path to the cemetery. He didn't want to break down. He always did when he visited his dad's grave, but he wanted today to be a good memory, the day his father met the man he loved.

At the foot of an oak tree, Manuel Reyes's grave awaited them. The headstone declared him a beloved father and husband. An understatement, but it would have to do. Gabe exhaled, dismayed when he realized his eyes were wet. Max stopped. "Do you want a minute?"

Gabe shook his head and tugged Max's hand, urging him to follow. Gabe knelt at the foot of the grave, laying a bouquet of fresh flowers in front of the smooth headstone. He gazed at it, his mind suddenly full of his father's smiling face, the comforting scent of his aftershave.

"Hola, Papá." Despite the ache in his throat, he smiled. "It's been a while. I know, I'm a bad son. But I brought someone to meet you."

He squeezed Max's hand and Max squeezed back, holding tight. "This is Max. He's my mate. He's sweet and kind and more than I deserve. He makes me so happy." His arm went around Max's shoulders, his heart full of love and joy as Max nestled into his side. "I'm glad you two can finally meet."

Max smiled. "Thank you for your sacrifice, Mr. Reyes. For letting me meet your son. He's the best thing that's ever happened to me."

Gabe clenched his jaw and looked away, squeezing his eyes shut to hold himself together. When he couldn't fight his tears, he buried his face in Max's shoulder. Max rubbed his back, his arms sturdy and strong around him. Gabe braced himself for a wave of grief and sadness, and there was some, but he was also happy. Happy the two men he loved the most could meet, and grateful for Max's presence in his life.

"Tell me about him," Max said.

Gabe wiped his eyes, sniffing. "He liked hot sauce." Max snorted, his eyes alight. Gabe laughed, too. "No, really! He did. He always carried a bottle around, to restaurants, to people's houses…"

They chatted for a while until the cold began to get to Max. "You can stay. I'll wait by the bike." Max kissed his cheek and rose.

"I'll just be a minute." Gabe squeezed his hand, admiring the way Max's ginger hair contrasted with the pure blue sky. "Thank you, mi amor. Not just for today, for every day."

Max smiled radiantly. "Of course." Gabe watched him leave, his heart full. He turned back to his father's grave and reached out, clasping the cool stone.

"I did it, Pops. John Stone will never hurt anyone again. It's what you wished. I took care of Mamá and Izzie, or I suppose they took care of me. So don't worry about them, or me. You can rest easy. It's been a long time coming, I know."

His phone buzzed in his pocket. It was Ben. Gabe stood, pacing away from the grave. "Hey, Ben. What's up?"

"First off, congrats. That was one hell of a ceremony." Something in Ben's voice was heavy.

"Is something wrong?"

Ben sighed. "I hate to be the one to wreck your newly mated bliss, kid, but this is urgent."

Gabe's stomach churned over. "What's wrong?"

"It's Alpha Hanson. He's been killed."

Gabe couldn't have predicted such an awful turn of events. He sat up, a hand going to his hair as he struggled for words. "Shit. How? Why?" Last he'd heard, Hanson had been chased into the woods by a pack of McCready's wolves.

"The news broke an hour ago. His body was brought before the Council."

Gabe swallowed hard, feeling sick. "Brought by who?"

Ben was quiet. He didn't have to speak. Gabe knew, and the blood turned to ice in his veins.

"McCready's alive."

The autumn chill grew colder by the second, biting.

"Yeah." Ben exhaled with a growl. Gabe could just see him rubbing his temples and grinding his jaw. "With the Alpha dead, McCready's next in line to lead the Council. There will be pushback. An Alpha hasn't been removed from his position like this in decades. There's a chance McCready won't be permitted to assume Hanson's position. But we all know the ace McCready has up his sleeve. I don't know if the Council can stand against the Wargs. If he becomes Alpha... Gabe, we haven't seen the worst of what he could do with that kind of control over shifters."

Gabe had an idea, and he feared for the future between werewolves and humans.

Grabbing hold of his fear before it could run away with him, he forced himself to smile. "Then we'll just have to stop him. It's what we do, Ben. We've dealt with his kind before. Stopping crazy werewolves hell-bent on world domination's our thing now."

Ben scoffed. "Sure is starting to feel like it."

"Max is waiting for me. Gotta go, Ben. Stay safe."

"Yeah, you too, kid."

How much longer would they be able to "stay safe"? The uncertainty made Gabe feel small and defenseless. Pocketing his phone, he gazed down at his father's grave and sighed, smiling tiredly. "Looks like I spoke too soon." He looked to the blue sky and waved. "Till next time, Papá."

He found Max reclining against his motorbike. There was no easy way to tell him why Gabe smelled of worry and uncertainty. He drew Max to his chest. "McCready's alive." Max's wide eyes looked to him, full of the same doubt and fear as Gabe. "But it's okay. I'm in this with you, Lobito. If he comes for us, then we're facing him. Together."

Max put his arms around Gabe and held him tight. "Together."

The future was uncertain, hurtling toward them like a coming storm, but they were pack—family. Let the storm come. He and Max could weather it, together.

# Chapter 27

# Alpha

## Hours ago

Blood coated the back of Aaron McCready's throat. Hanson lay at McCready's feet as a man, broken and bloody. The thrill of the hunt still pounded through McCready. It had taken weeks to track him, but not even an Alpha was safe from McCready and his wargs. How the mighty had fallen...

The wargs who'd survived the encounter with the hunters and the LPA yipped and barked in jubilation, snouts red with blood from the hunt. Their numbers were fewer, but McCready wasn't deterred. In the coming weeks, he anticipated a revolution among werewolves unlike any seen in decades.

Panting, McCready dropped Hanson's ankle and turned, towering over the most respected wolf in the country. Hanson coughed, each breath wet and rattling.

"You... How could you?" Hanson rasped. A bubble of blood burst at the corner of his lips. "I... trusted you."

McCready bristled at the hatred in the man's one good eye. As if Hanson still believed himself superior, even after the flesh had been ripped from his bones. McCready stepped on Hanson's chest, and the man writhed, a spasm of pain going through his broken body.

"I've watched you weaken this council long enough, old man." Excitement thrummed in McCready's veins like a shot of morphine. "This council held werewolves back for years. Your reliance on humans has only weakened us." His claws extended, and he prodded the tips of his nails against the raw skin of Hanson's chest. He could see a sliver of white rib twitching with every pulse of his heart. "I will lead us out of the shadows. I will take back the world that once belonged to us!"

Hanson's single eye narrowed. "You... will lead our species to extinction, McCready. You will doom us."

A shudder racked the Alpha's body as McCready drove his claws through Hanson's chest as easily as if he were sinking them through wet paper.

"Aaron... Please... don't do this." Hanson panted through a mouthful of blood.

McCready laughed and closed his claws around Hanson's pumping heart. The Alpha's back arched, his eye going wide in surprise, his mouth parted in a silent scream. Hanson gazed at him in horror as McCready ripped his heart from his chest, and then that single eye dulled. The scent of Hanson's voided bowels scorched McCready's nose as the great Alpha died in his own shit and blood.

He thought he felt the organ beat once more in his hand, still clinging to life. No. Hanson was dead and gone, and his hold over shifters died with him. McCready lunged, fangs piercing the heart. Swallowing down the last piece, McCready gasped and threw his head back to the dark clouds. Nothing happened.

He'd read the accounts in ancient texts of wolves who'd consumed the heart of an alpha of the council. Something should be happening, and now he feared the stories weren't true. A growl built in his throat. "Come on!" he roared, voice breaking. Desperation clawed at him. His heart pounded hard in his throat. Or was it Hanson's heart, pulsing in his stomach? "I've proved my worth! Now reward me!"

Nothing. He felt the same.

The moon peered from behind the clouds, glowing silver on his skin.

"Come on!" He screamed, and his fury turned to agonizing pain as his leg shattered. He collapsed with a howl, clawing at the dirt as limb by limb, his body broke. It was like every scene from a bad werewolf movie, as if he were an observer outside his own body. His clothes ripped and fell from his body in pieces as his muscles swelled and bones elongated. Cramps racked his legs as the bones grew and his body changed.

His screams turned to snarls and pants as his face elongated and all human thought fled his mind.

No. No, he couldn't forget. He wouldn't lose himself to feral fury. McCready closed his eyes tight and clung on to memories he'd long since buried. Of his mate and his children. His mate's radiant smile and her curly hair. His son's laughter. How warm his newborn daughter felt in his arms.

The smoke in his throat as their home burned. The fear in his son's eyes when McCready pushed his infant daughter into his arms and said, "Take her and run, son. Don't look back." His mate's beautiful brown skin stained with blood. The laughter of the hunters as they pursued his children through the woods. The wet heat of his own blood soaking his clothes as he writhed on the ground, the silver bullets in his flesh rendering him powerless to save his family. The moon gazed impassively down at him.

*Goddess,* he'd thought. *Why? I served you well. I did. Why would you let this happen?*

The clouds hid her face. She turned her back. She abandoned him and his family, the purest of wolves, who'd done nothing but worship her and live their lives in her service. She was no longer a goddess worthy of his respect.

A roar tore from his throat as his fury anchored him to the beast trying to burst from his skin. He tore into the dirt, his head thrown back as he roared at the hidden moon. He slammed the earth with clawed hands, shaking the ground, and found the strength to stand. He towered over Hanson's corpse on two legs, his breath escaping him with harsh snorts and pants. He touched his face and felt a snout and two pointed ears.

No. He was no beast.

His name was... Aaron McCready.

Humans had taken from him, taken from all wolves. They defiled the Earth, dirtied the pure blood of werewolves, and bound wolves to their will.

Never again.

With a roar, he brought his hand down on Hanson's skull, shattering the Alpha's face into pieces beneath his huge fist. His harsh pants and snarls morphed into words no wolf should be capable of speaking.

"I'm the Alpha now," he snarled to the corpse at his feet, his snout splitting in a grin frothy with spit and blood. The age of men would soon be over. McCready threw back his head and let out a roar that shook the trees to their roots, and his wargs howled with him.

A murder of crows took flight from the trees and blackened the skies with their wings.

What's next for the pack? Don't miss the final installment in Gabe and Max's story!

The Lycanthrope Protection Agency #3 – The Moon Always Rises

# THANK YOU!

Thank you for reading! If you enjoyed, please consider leaving a review on your preferred platform of choice. Indie authors like me depend on word of mouth reviews like yours. Additionally, please consider recommending this series if you enjoyed it! Thank you again!

Sign up to my newsletter to receive a free prequel to The Lycanthrope Protection Agency series, Before Moonrise. This novella features forbidden love, friends to lovers, possessive werewolves who adore their mates, and sexy times on a beach, in a barn, and a broom closet just to name a few locations. Additionally, you'll receive bonus content, cover reveals, and news about new releases. What are you waiting for?
Sign up now at www.CJRavenna.com!

# ABOUT CJ

CJ Ravenna loves to tell stories where the ordinary meets the extraordinary. Her books often feature an explosion or two, possessive and protective werewolves who adore their mates, steamy and swoony romance, and of course a happy ending. Connect with me on:

My website: www.cjravenna.com

My Facebook group: Ravenna's Ravens

Instagram: @cjravenna

TikTok: @cjravenna

Goodreads: goodreads.com/cjravenna

Bookbub: bookbub.com/authors/cj-ravenna

# ALSO BY CJ RAVENNA

**The Lycanthrope Protection Agency Series**
Before Moonrise (Jin & Marcus. Newsletter exclusive)
To Hunt A Moonborn Beast (Gabe & Max)
Child Of The Moon (Gabe & Max)
The Moon Aways Rises (Gabe & Max)
The Moon Over The Oak (Zach & Ryan)
Redemption Under The Moon (Ben & Isaac)
Fire and Moonlight (Eddie & Vicenzo)